Dear Tina

The White Rose and The Lady

Richard de Methley

With much love

Richard de M x

1

Published by White Boar Publishing Enterprises 2011

www.whiteboarpublishing.com

© Richard de Methley

Richard de Methley has asserted his right under the Copyright, Designs and Patents Act 1988 to be identified as the author of this book.

A CIP record for this book is available from the British Library.

ISBN 978-0-9557480-2-8

Cover design by Debbie Kelsey and Richard Lyne-Pirkis

Cover photograph of Bodiam castle by Anthony McCallum, WyrdLight.com

Prepared and Printed by

MPG Biddles Ltd, Kings Lynn, Norfolk. PE30 4LS. Tel : 01553.764728

www.mpg-biddles.co.uk

Dedication

This book is dedicated, not least, to Diana L-P with whose loving support I first wrote it, and who typed the original manuscript, Bless her! Since then it has gone through many transformations, been published once, November 2007, and has now been revised and reissued.

But also to Andrea Atkinson without whose persistence, kindness and constant, warm encouragement I would **never** have completed the series, of which this is the second book. She has been such a real Stockport Star in every way!

Another invaluable stalwart has been Simon Carpenter, my 'Admiral Red-Pen'! He has read every single chapter, paragraph by paragraph; checked my Botany, Herbology, Medical skills and Anatomy. He is also a deep water sailor, and his advice on wind and sea was masterly. He has corrected my language and punctuation, suggested fantastic changes to the text where I had got myself in a dreadful muddle…and forced me to re-think and re-work many parts that he thought were simply not good enough! Just terrific!

Finally I could not have written these books without the amazing richness of the Google website: 'Nicky's Seeds'…and of the superb knowledge of Nicola herself, whose website it is and who gave me terrific personal help with streamside plants and wayside flowers, especially with waterside plants around Narbonne in the 12th Century. Her help was just invaluable.

The warmest of thanks also go to my Graphic Artist, Debbie Kelsey, whose support and encouragement has been enormous…who has done all the really clever stuff with both the cover and the actual 'guts' of the book…***and*** to Ed Jones my IT Guru who has organised my website and always been on hand to help when I have found myself floundering in a morass of IT over which I have little grasp…if any! Bless you all.

Richard de Methley. September 2011.

About the Author

Richard de Methley lives in Nailsworth with his ginger cat, Paddypus, and his Baby Clio, called 'Ruth'! He is named after the town of Methley in West Yorkshire where a branch of his family settled at the time of the Norman Conquest, and now follows in the footsteps of his cousin, Violet M. Methley, who was famous between the wars for her children's novels of Dragons, Vampires and the Supernatural.

He is a Medieval and Tudor Specialist of Worcester College, now the University of Worcester, has fought in armour on horse and foot alongside The Knights of Arkley; trained and flown hawks and falcons; is an expert on Castles, especially those in the Welsh Borders, and has been a teacher for forty years, fourteen of those as Head. He is also noted for his workshops on Creative Writing and his History Seminars on the Murder of Thomas Becket, the Hastings Campaign, the Wars of Edward Ist and the Fall of Wales.

He wears a cloak and carries a sword!

Chapter 1...On board the Mary after El Nazir's attack.

S ir Gui de Malwood stood on the *Mary's* shattered forecastle, stunned, as he watched El Nazir's great fighting dromond pull steadily away from them, unable to accept what had happened, and still calling out, "Alicia! *Alicaaa!*" even though he knew she could no longer see or hear him. Beneath him their own ship wallowed sluggishly, heaved-to with her sails reefed up and tied to her topmost spar. Sheets and halliards flying free in the wind, some trailing in the sea, her shattered timbers graunching against each other, as Thomas and his crew fought to turn her bows away from the wind and the shoreward waves, as they punched their way into her battered hull.

And all the while Gui just stood there, oblivious, cursing his men on *the Pride* whom he had charged with her life...and who had so cruelly failed to protect her.

Below him, and all across the blooded deck, his command sat slumped with exhaustion amongst the litter of discarded weapons and the butchered remnants of their enemies. Here a severed arm, there a battered head, hands hacked off and left like discarded gloves, some still clasping weapons, and everywhere the deck was thick with congealing blood, fragments of bone, scattered brains and human faeces, or slimed with the greasy, pink coils from some poor wretch's carcase, like a butcher's fresh filled sausages. And there were arrows sticking up like porcupine quills from almost every surface, all slip-slopping amongst the water, swirled with blood and mucus, that continued to gush in from the great hole smashed in the *Mary's* side.

And, in those few moments Gui knew real, sinking despair; felt as though his heart were being torn from him, his mind ravaged by anger and grief, till all he could do was roar out in impotent rage and pound his mailed fists on the shattered timbers of the *Mary,* face filled with blood, powerless to stop El Nazir from taking Alicia from him

"I will find you! *I will find you!*' he shouted across the sea, his voice echoed by the screaming gulls that swooped and wheeled above him. "My Love! *My Love!*' he cried out in an anguish of despair. "We *will* come for you!" The words torn apart by the wind as the great dromond pulled away from him faster and faster, the beat of the hortator's drum fading as she did so, while he stood in catatonic shock, watching it carry his very heart's life away from him, as he shouted his misery to the seabirds and the open skies. Every thought a shocking jangle that made his heart burn within his breast.

'How can this be happening to me? How can I live without her? Dear God, *what will they do to her?*...and poor Agnes? And where are they going to first? *Where?* Fucking heathen, infidel *bastards!* Rape, murder, destroy...that was all those barbarians understood, and they hated Christians more than any other, torturing them to death for fun! Burning them alive on crosses...and Christian women? It did not bear thinking of. Bastards! *Bastards!* And de Brocas? *Filthy, murdering French swine.* How dared he! How *dared* he murder and attack those I most love. First my parents and now my beautiful Alicia, betrothed to me with God and my King's blessing? Marriage...to de Brocas? Impossible! *A sin against all the laws of Christian men!*

And his heart and spirit groaned at his imagining the Baron touching his Alicia, pawing at her, fondling her, entering her as Nazir had said he would, sullying her with his lust for an heir from her womb. And he cried out again, the pain twisting his bowels til he bent over in agony, his arms wrapped around his belly, his lungs tightening til he could barely breathe, "No*!* No! *Noooo!*"

★

For Sir Richard and Father Matthew, as much as for many of their men, the sight of Alicia and Agnes dragged below the decks of the great galley had been no less shocking...and powerless to stop her leaving, they too had rushed to the sides and shaken their fists and roared out their defiance at El Nazir as his galley had rowed away; oblivious to the sea spouting in through the *Mary's* smashed bulwarks til brought to their senses by Tommy Blackwood's enormous voice.

"*Ho there, My Lords!*" Their huge ship Master shouted, his booming voice breaking in on their thoughts, as he beckoned violently at Gui's commanders. "Sir Richard, de Beaune, *John Fitzurse*, damn your hide man! *Wake up!* If we don't shift ourselves we will be food for the bloody fishes. This fucking tub is sinking! My lads can't do this on their own! *Get those idle bastards bailing!*" he roared, stabbing his fingers furiously at where their men were slumped about the deck. "*Get those buggers moving, My Lords!* Chain of buckets...fucking helmets. *Anything!* Every time we heel to port, the sea's bursting into her. If we don't get rid of this bloody water," he shouted, kicking his feet at it, "we'll lose her! God be Praised the day is calm. If any kind of sea had been running she'd be gone!

And we must lighten her as much as we can, My Lords, and raise that gash further out of the water. Get rid of all these bastard bodies, and anything else you can think of. And will someone catch that fucking horse, *before it's the first to go over board!*"

With that, and the bellowed orders from Gui's commanders, all now roused to urgent action by the Master's fierce demands, everyone seemed to jerk back into life and move at once. Some to bail, some to pump, some to shift and clear the debris from their fight; and in short order, with Gui's massive Master-at-Arms calling them on, his commanders adding their weight to encourage them, the deck was swiftly sorted: smashed bodies tossed overboard, alive or dead; broken timbers and torn rigging following, and box after box of supplies and assorted weaponry dragged up and also thrown over the side til the sea immediately around the *Mary* was covered with bobbing wreckage, discarded stores and bloodied corpses. The barrels of longbow shafts that could not be replaced among the only things saved.

Merlin was caught and tethered, Beau, Sunburst and Gillygate taken from their stall the same, and then the partitions knocked down and also cast into a sea already littered with the smashed and burned remains of the two corsair

7

galleys they had destroyed, along with the broken bodies of their crews and fighting men.

But it was not enough! Though the huge gap torn in her side by El Nazir's artillery was now further above the waterline, the sea still bubbled and spouted into her every time Thomas tried to turn the *Mary* towards the shore, and she was already listing.

"What more can we do, Thomas?" Sir Richard called out. "My lads are all pumping and bailing like fury, but we cannot hold the water back. Much more of this and we'll be in it up to our necks."

"*We must try and fother that bloody hole, Sir Richard!*" he shouted back, and turning to his Mate, "Adam, muster all the crew you can find, and break out the winter canvas…and all the ropes you can find."

"Oakum, Master Thomas?"

"No, Lad! We don't have the time to do a proper job, but if we can just cover that bloody hole, we may be able to make Houat at least, maybe even Nantes itself, it's only fifty miles or so, and once in the river, and out of these waves, we should be fine. Now, yarely, my lads, *Yarely!*"

"What's 'fothering' My Lord?" Fitzurse asked Sir Richard anxiously.

"No idea, Master-at-Arms!" his tall guard commander drawled at him lazily. "Some weird sailoring term I suppose?"

"It's an ages old method of patching holes in desperate circumstances!" Father Matthew answered tersely, coming up beside them both. "Usually you take a big sail, stitch it all over with oakum, the tarred shreds from old ropes, tie a good hawser to each corner and pass the whole thing under the ship until the hole is covered! Only they haven't the time to do all that, so they're going to do the best they can with just a heavy, winter sail."

"God Aid us," Fitzurse burst out, shaking his head. "Like patching a barn door with a handkerchief! They must be bloody mad!"

8

"Better that than drowning, John," L'Eveque drawled at him. "Go now, and give de Beaune a hand, and keep the lads moving. Keep them busy, and their minds occupied, we don't want 'em getting lazy now, do we?

"What about Sir Gui, My Lord?" Fitzurse asked as he turned away. "He needs someone too."

"What indeed about Gui, Father?" Sir Richard asked as his Master-at-Arms barrelled amongst his men, pointing to where his friend was still standing, looking out to sea: "We need him here, Matthew, busy amongst us. I know he is shattered by what's happened. We all are! But brooding will do neither him, nor us, any good. I cannot lead these men the way he does. He needs to snap out of and get '*doing!*'"

"Leave him to me, Richard," the tall Benedictine said in his lilting Spanish voice, patting L'Eveque across his shoulders. "He will come-to shortly. He knows his responsibility, I assure you. The trouble will not be to get him '*doing*'...it will be persuading him to stop! To take time to plan things properly and not leap about like a herring on a griddle!" he added, making Sir Richard laugh. "Meanwhile, do all you can to help Master Thomas, and see if we have any swimmers amongst us? Ask Jean as well. If so, make sure Thomas knows. We're all in this together, and somehow that fother has to be drawn under the *Mary* for it to work...or she'll go down and us with her!" And with that he strode off to join Gui on the shattered forecastle.

★

With the *Mary* heaved-to and her sails brailed up, drifting with the current, everyone worked like fury, either bailing with anything they could find, working the crude leather pumps that the ship carried or struggling with the thick winter canvas the crew had dragged from its stowage beneath the sterncastle. And within the hour they had the bulk of it ready to drag over the side, three of Thomas's crew and three of Gui's command ready to plunge over and attempt to swim under the *Mary's* fat,

9

scarlet bottom, each dragging a light line that would then be used to pull the heavy hawsers, now firmly attached to each corner of the fother, under the ship and up again.

By then, despite everyone's best efforts, the *Mary* was appreciably lower in the water, so it was now or never and with a *splash!* the men chosen were over the damaged port side, with their lines in their hands, and after a moment's bobbing up and down to get their breaths, they dived, and all who could ran across to the other side of the cog to watch for their return.

A minute passed. Then two…then longer!

Until, with a mighty gasp, the first swimmer burst from the surface, holding up his line, then another and another, until four had safely made it. But that was all. Two were lost. Their lines snagged on the barnacles and weeds that clung to the *Mary*'s fat bottom. Too far to go forward… too far to go back, swept away by the currents, never to be seen again, and all were saddened by it.

But then was not the time to mourn, and with the light lines recovered, the heavy hawsers were pulled safely under the *Mary* and up again over her starboard bulwarks, and with half the swimmers drawn up out of the sea and jumping in again on the port side to guide it, the whole fother was pushed over the gashed hull and into the sea. With all those not bailing or pumping hauling steadily on the ropes, helped by those swimmers still starboard side in the water, the huge fother was pulled down and under the *Mary* until it came up as hard against the jagged hole as it could be forced, and with a shout of triumph the crew tightly lashed the heavy ropes down around the starboard rails, and pulled all those overboard safely onto the deck.

It was done!

And not a moment too soon, for already her bilges were overflowing, the water sloshing and swirling over her bottom boards and over their feet. Also seeping in around the rock still embedded in her starboard side, another hour and she would have gone. Even with the fother in place the water still spurted in little jets around the sides, but nothing compared to how it had been, and once the bilges were cleared, Master Thomas reckoned that with constant bailing and pumping they could still save her.

"Bravely done, lads! *Bravely done!*" Thomas roared out, his eyes alight with pleasure, hands on hips. "Wine all round from my own stores, you whoreson idle bastards! Then let's see if we can get this old tub to move herself.

Yarely done, m'boys! *Yarely done!*" And patting the *Mary's* tall mast with an affectionate smile, he swung round and went across to join his crew and check the lashings that held the fother fast.

Chapter 2... Father Matthew puts Gui straight

U p by the shattered forecastle Father Matthew put his arm across Gui's shoulder, and turned him so he could see his face. "Gui...I cannot really know how you feel, but I can imagine it: anger, despair, hatred, revenge? All of those and more probably. And fear. Fear of what may be happening to Alicia, and Agnes. Where they are going now? And how to catch up with them at Grise...and kill de Brocas?"

"Yes, Father. All of those. But mostly rage, at myself, for not doing more. For putting Alicia in such danger, when she begged me not to. For not being with her when she needed me most. *Everything!* And the thought of de Brocas forcing himself on her...marrying her out of hand...is just too terrible even to contemplate. That *bastard* Father! That absolute, double dyed, wicked, fucking *bastard.* And those two French traitors," he added spitting the words out in disgust. "Those *Cousins!*" and he groaned and leaned his head against Matthew's shoulder.

"Gui," he said gently, cradling his hands around Gui's head, "truly he is a bad man, even evil. If there was one man I would pick up a sword against, it would de Brocas. He is everything you say, and more. But, Dear Boy, we cannot know everything before hand. Sometimes, despite all we can do, or plan for, bad things happen. But God can give us strength, Gui; remind us we are not alone, show us the way to get things done. Give us friends to help along the way...and courage to carry things through even when they look impossible. Look around you, Dear Boy," he said, turning the young man in has arms. "See how your courage and that of your men and their commanders have defeated your enemies...and with only a handful of good lives lost, against the hundreds who were slain today, or drowned chained to their oars!"

"But El Nazir has taken Alicia, Father!" Gui replied in anguish, looking down across the *Mary's* broken timbers and blood stained deck, at the battle scars and at the arrows still sticking up everywhere…and at Alicia's mare, trembling and looking for her mistress. "Despite all we could do he still seized her. Soon the Baron will have her, and Agnes Fitzwalter, and we are *weeks* away from Narbonne, more now that the *Mary* has been so badly smashed up…"

"Yes, My Son," the tall priest went on gently, turning him back to face him. "All that is true. But mooning up here feeling sorry for yourself, away from your command that needs you to lead them, is *not* going to get Alicia back! For that you will need every drop of the courage, determination and brains that God and your parents gave you the day you were born. And they gave you plenty, Gui. I was there remember?

"Well, not really, Father. I was too little at the time!" And standing back, he grinned.

"Better my boy. *Better!* Now listen," he went on, shaking Gui firmly as he spoke. "Down there you have a command that respects you. Even people who love you! More on the *Pride*. Though God knows what has happened to her? You want Alicia back, and to bring judgement to de Brocas?"

"*Yes*, Father."

"Then pull yourself together, Gui," he said sharply. "And get down there and lead them! *They need you.* Sir Richard, de Beaune, John Fitzurse, good as they are, are not in command of this expedition. *You are!* And frankly, right now, you are neglecting your duty. You should be down there with them, *My Lord Gui de Malwood*," he said definitively, firmly shaking Gui's shoulders again. "Not up here indulging yourself in self-pity, and tearing yourself apart over something you can do nothing about, at least as long as you are stuck on board this battered, leaking, sinking ship!

I am with you also, Gui, for I owe that to your parents whom I loved greatly. As did many others, including the King's Grace…as I do you and Alicia. As the King does himself, as I explained to you and Alicia after the fire. You don't know what you can achieve until you try…nor who will come out of the woodwork to help you? Look how Allan–i–the–Wood came to us, wholly unexpected, with the remainder of his verderers at Beaulieu. How

13

many others may yet join us on this quest? *The cherries will not fall unless you shake the trees, Gui!* If all you do is sit beneath them and wait, feeling hopeless and sorry for yourself, waiting for them to fall…all that will come down will be empty stones on stalks, rotten fruit and wasps to sting you! *Right?*"

"*Right,* Father!"

"*Good!* There is hope for us all yet. So, Dear Boy, get down there and start shaking those trees! Now, come on, and let us join the others, they have done quite enough without you. What's needed now is plenty of zap and bustle! *Everything forward and trust in the Lord!*" And drawing Gui towards him he kissed his forehead, and blessed him, before turning him to walk back down together and join the others, now gathered below the mast and waiting.

★

"Splendour of God, Gui," Sir Richard L'Eveque lazily drawled later, as they leaned across the torn bulwarks beside the *Mary's* shattered side. "I'd not want to go through all that again in a hurry! That must be one of the swiftest, most dangerous actions that I've ever taken a hand in. Sea fights are definitely *not* my favourite occupation!"

"The lads did well, Richard. Great fighting spirit, great determination…and courage. So did Merlin, bless him, with his hoofs and teeth. Picked one of those bastards up and shook him like a rat." There was a pause then as they both looked across to where the *Pride* appeared to be still struggling. "Richard," he said then quietly, turning to face him, "I owe you and the lads an apology,"

"Apology?" the big man drawled. "From my ever present Lord and Master?"

"Yes, my friend," Gui replied with a sigh. "I should never have left you and the lads, and Thomas of course, to have done all this," he went on, gesturing across the cleared deck, and down at the fothered hole in the *Mary's* side. "All I could think of was Alicia, that *bastard* de Brocas, and my own pain:

14

leaving you and the others to cope! Bad leadership, Richard; won't happen again. Sorry!"

"Gui," his friend said turning to him, his hand on his arm. "You and I have known each other a good few years now. And you have covered for me with Sir Yvo on more than one occasion. Remember," he added, in his lazy, laconic style, "when I was absent from duty? Chasing after the delicious Laura, and your father nearly caught us in the hay barn?"

"Yes, you hid, she ran out, and I took the rap; you rotten bastard!" And both men laughed.

"Well, Gui. This is just like that. You would have done the same for me. And I haven't just watched the very Love of my Life dragged kicking and screaming away across an enemy's deck and been powerless to do anything about it. The point is you are here now!"

"Thank God for Father Matthew!"

"Mmmm, in more ways than one, Dear Boy. Without him we would all be in a far worse case, as otherwise we would be leaving more injured men behind than I care to think of."

"What's the damage?"

"Don't know clearly yet. Ask Fitzurse. He's coming across now.

"John, what's the butcher's bill amongst the men? I haven't had time to check them myself. "

"Eight slain My Lord, and six badly injured," he said, wiping his bloodied armour with a damp rag. "But Father Matthew is with them and says they'll live, and should be able to travel with us. Thomas lost several of his crew as well. Other than that, there are some nasty gashes and not a few bumped heads and bruises, but nothing worse. Considering how many attacked us, we got off lightly"

"Lightly, indeed, John!" Gui exclaimed, thinking about what Father Matthew had said to him earlier.

"Whom have we lost?" Sir Richard asked heavily.

"Robert of Burley and John Ditcher, My Lord," Fitzurse replied, looking at the tall knight. "James Goodchild, Peter Miller, Young Robbie Cooper, Ned Bowyer and...and..."

"Charles Lafitte and Raoul de Cluny," De Beaune chipped in, as he too joined them, cleaning his sword blade as he walked. "Two of mine from Burgundy, leal men, both, Sir Gui. They will be missed."

"Robbie's mother will take it hard too, My Lord," Fitzurse growled softly. "She has none other to care for her now, not since Simmy, died last winter. The Lady Alicia will be sad, too. He was a favourite with her!"

"Don't worry, either of you," Gui replied, his nostrils flaring at the mention of Alicia's name. "Malwood will always look after its own. I will make sure the old lady's alright. And your people, too, Jean. Wages will still be paid. Don't look so amazed, none will be forgotten on this trip. The same for Thomas' crew. Our little Lady would insist on it."

"That's good, My Lord," Fitzurse replied, grinning. "And the lads will have the usual sale of effects, not that any of them had much about them, mind you, but it will all help. What about their bodies?"

"Over the side with the rest, I am afraid, John," Gui answered him, jerking with his thumb. "We can't afford the luxury of a burial, and I don't want the stench of death around us either. I am sorry, but that's the way it has to be."

He turned away then and walked past the damaged side of the ship, towards the forecastle, to look again where the *Pride* was still rolling her fat yellow girth from side to side, his thoughts racing as he pictured Alicia as he had last held her in his arms...last seen her. He sighed. Where was she now? *Sweet Lord!* What were those bastards doing to her? And how *long* before they caught up with her and de Brocas? And he growled deep in his throat, banging his hands on the ship's railings.

"Are you alright, Gui?" L'Eveque asked, coming up beside him, looking out across to the Île de Houat, and the hard line of the mainland beyond.

"No...not really. Just thinking about Alicia. Wondering what in God's name is happening to her. I am so angry, Richard! *So bloody angry!*"

16

"I know, Dear Boy," he drawled. "I know. But we *will* get her back, Gui," he said, putting his long arm across Gui's armoured shoulders. "You *have* to believe that. I do! That filth will not escape these...these murderous assaults. We *will* bring him to Justice, Gui...and his hell-born daughter. We have all sworn it!"

"I know, my friend. I know. But it is very hard to accept her loss to us, and Agnes, too," he added swiftly. "Especially when we had planned things so carefully. Oh...*shit!!*" And he banged the rail with his mailed fist. Then, forcing all thoughts of Alicia aside, he said: "Anyway...what's next, Richard? We cannot afford to lose any more time between here and Narbonne. Nor any more men either!"

"We got off lightly, as I said," his guard commander replied lazily, with a grin. "I thought the boys fought well, the first real fighting that most of them have ever faced. They kept their heads and did what they'd been taught. What they really need Gui, is some heartfelt praise from you. For they fought for you, as much as for themselves, and so far you've said sod all to them!"

"You are *so* right, Richard. I hang my head in shame. First a bollacking from Father Matthew, and now one from you!" He grinned ruefully, "Just not my day! No matter, I will speak to them soonest, and I expect a few flagons of wine, if there are any still unbroken onboard, would not go amiss either...and a handful of extra silver in their pockets when we land? Tommy's boys as well, on both ships. They've earned it."

"That would be a grand gesture, My Lord," his big Master-at-Arms said, just then returning to them. "That'll put a bit of extra heart in 'em! Though they'll lose the money to the first sloe-eyed whore they meet," he said with a grin.

" Or in the first tavern they come to," Sir Richard added, smiling.

"And you will get warm thanks from my Burgundians also, My Lord," de Beaune said, joining them by the rail. "Mercardier always dashed us a little extra after a hard won fight, as you are going to. We will not let you down!"

"I never thought you would, Jean," Gui added, flexing his left shoulder. "Now, away and find that wine, Master Blackwood was talking of earlier, you have more than earned it. And I'll break out the flagons when we reach land, or they all be as soused as herrings and just as bloody useless!"

But before anyone could move there was a great shout suddenly from Fitzurse, who was standing over one of his men, urgently beckoning. "My Lords! Come quickly, and Father Matthew. This lad, Davy Coulter, has found something you ought to see."

Chapter 3... The Baron's message is found.

I n moments they had all stridden swiftly across the *Mary's* tilting deck to join them. "What have you found, Davy?" Sir Richard asked his young soldier quickly.

"Come on, Davy, lad," the huge Master-at-Arms encouraged him, laying a massive hand on the man's shoulders. "Nothing to be afeard of. We all know you lads go through the bodies for coins and such. Things you might sell. That's spoils of war, Davy, that is. Done it myself afore now. That's normal after a battle. Just show Sir Richard what you found. He won't take the box from you."

"W..well, Sir Richard," the young man stammered slightly, shocked to be confronting his Commander. "I was-was going through one of those bastard's pockets, quickly like, Sir Richard, to see if there might be s-something there, specially as his armour was far better quality than any others we'd been throwing over, and-and I-I found this My Lord." And with that, his large grey eyes dark with anxiety in his round face beneath a shock of brown hair, he gingerly opened his hand to reveal a beautifully chased silver box, inlaid with gold and studded with finely cut green stones.

"Emeralds, no less, young Davy Coulter," Sir Richard said, drawing in his breath. "And gold. That is certainly a very fine box, Sergeant," he drawled, lazily, his eyes suddenly grown hard. "But nothing worth calling us all over for, surely? Just spoils of war, man, as you said."

"No, Sir Richard. That's right. But it's not the box that's important, My Lord. It's the message inside it!"

"Message, Fitzurse?" Gui questioned him sharply.

"Yes Sir Gui. Inside the box."

"I-I thought there might be c-coins inside it, My Lord" Davy Coulter broke in, petrified. "But-but there weren't. Just a small piece of rolled up paper. I would have thrown it away, like. But the Sergeant saw me with that," he said, his voice shaking a bit as he pointed to the chased silver box still in Sir Richard's hands. "I-I was showing what I'd got, Lord. To-to my mates like. And to the Master-at-Arms. He glimpsed the-the paper inside, and thought you should see it also. So-so he called you over," he added, his voice trailing away.

"When I saw how lovely that jewelled box was, My Lords," his big Master-at-Arms said calmly, "and then caught sight of the paper inside it, I thought that if anyone kept something written inside so valuable a box, it might be important."

"Well done, Master-at-Arms," Gui said, quietly. "Well spotted."

"Now, lad, show us the message," Father Matthew said softly, holding out his hand. "No-one is angry with you, Davy. But these are difficult times and that message might be very important. You have done well."

"It was the Master-at-Arms who spotted it, Father, not I. I would have thrown it overboard with his body and all the rest of the rubbish. Here it is," and fumbling underneath his surcoat, he handed over a tiny roll of the finest paper. "Can I go now, Father?"

"Yes, Davy. Of course. Go now and join your mates. Sir Richard will see you later I expect, and give you back your box."

And while the trooper ran off, his brow wet with nervous sweat, to be surrounded by his friends, Father Matthew very carefully unrolled the message that Fitzurse had rescued for them.

"Now, what do we have here, I wonder?" And stretching it out, he held it up to the light. "Six words and one bunch of numbers...and all in tiny writing."

"What does it say, Matthew?" Gui asked him sharply.

"Mmm, not easy to read. Still: 'Red. Hoedic. Jules. Lucas. Green. 4/5. Bordeaux.' That's it!" And everyone was silent for a while as they all took in its significance.

"*Sweet Wine of Christ!*" Gui swore at last, letting his breath out in a sudden swoosh. "That's us isn't it? *That's us!* The 'Red' is the Mary, on its way to Bordeaux...which we were. And those two bastards need no recognition..."

"And Hoedic is over there, Lords," Master Thomas boomed at them suddenly, from over their shoulders. "From where those bastards jumped us!" He added, pointing over the Mary's shattered Port quarter. "The island next to the one where the *Pride* is still struggling; and those numbers are the days we could expect to take in getting here! Seems to me those fucking bastards knew all about you from the moment you left Brest...even sooner, from Malwood!"

"Except which boat the girls were on," Sir Richard said, in his usual drawl, smacking his hands together. "Our little trick would have worked beautifully, because those wild buggers attacked the wrong ship. It was only our misfortune that we put those two French bastards with them on the *Pride*. Oh...*shit!*"

"One thing's certain, Lords," Thomas said loudly. "Someone had all this planned. It *was* a trap, Father. As you thought!"

"But how?" Gui asked, astonished.

"Pigeons, Sir Gui, I expect," Father Matthew said suddenly, lowering the message.

"*Pigeons*, Matthew?" He exclaimed, stunned. "*Pigeons?* Are you mad? You eat pigeons not fly 'em about like a kite on a string!"

"No, Gui. The Arabs have been using them for generations to keep themselves informed about troop movements throughout the Holy Land. Most Crusaders are too hide-bound with their own supposed superiority to barbarian infidels to give it thought. But that's what this is," he said, holding it up again. "A message to be carried by a pigeon. Tiny, very fine paper, rolled up and placed in a minute brass cylinder and tied to the pigeon's leg or behind its wing.

21

And a pigeon can fly as fast as a falcon. Same sickle shaped wings, hundreds of miles in a day some of them. Have to be trained though, and expensive! Someone surely wanted you stopped, Gui. And very badly."

"And we all know who that is!" Sir Richard drawled softly. "The *so* good and friendly Lord Baron Sir Roger de Brocas."

"I think, Gui," the tall Benedictine said in his soft Spanish lilt. "That we will need to be extra careful as we journey south from Nantes. If the so good Baron can get at us out here, on the very edge of the Atlantic…he can probably get at us anywhere!"

"Dear God…is there no end to his wicked scheming? He got two of his people into Castle Malwood that we know of. How many others, I wonder? For surely those two fucking, 'Cousins', could not have done this," he said, taking the tiny roll from Father Matthew's hands. "They had neither the brains nor the patient skill!"

"No matter, Dear Boy," Sir Richard said lazily, "forewarned is forearmed. They will not take us by surprise again. That lad of mine, young Davy Coulter, and John Fitzurse, Bless him, deserve a gold coin each for this day's work. That knowledge could yet save us all!"

"Right, my friends," Gui said then, "Back to work. If we don't keep bailing…and pumping, this old tub is going to go down!"

As the others left, Sir Richard watched Gui flex his left arm and massage his shoulder again where the Baron's arrow had been cut out. "How's the wound?"

"Oh, not so bad," Gui said, wincing as he rotated it. "Matthew said it would be stiff. He has some sort of foul ointment to rub in later. Smells like horse shit!"

"Well," Sir Richard laughed, "in my experience the worst a medicine tastes or smells the better it often does you. Stop moaning. A little more of this sunshine and you'll be fine. I thought you moved well today. Not much wrong with you then!"

22

"Where is my Shipmaster," Gui said, still rubbing his shoulder. "Surely now we can get moving? And what in Heaven's name is happening over there?" he added, pointing at the *Pride*, showing little sail and still rolling about near the shallows. "Those bastards will be aground in a moment if they're not careful!"

"Never fear, My Lord," Thomas Blackwood boomed at him, his rolling walk carrying him lightly across the Mary's deck. "Your Shipmaster is right beside you, and Adam and the crew have been busy. Look!" he pointed to where his men were running up the ratlines. "They are breaking out the sail now, and I shall have her under command again in a moment.

But gently, gently. I have no wish to rip anything away, and we are still over half a day's sailing from the river, and the best part of another to Nantes. And as for the *Pride?* She seems to be manoeuvring herself through the channels between the rocks. Robert Christchurch's a good Master. Knows what he is doing. He'll be up to us shortly, you'll see. Then we will know more! Meanwhile keep your lads pumping...*and bailing!*" he shouted over his shoulder as he rolled away to take the tiller. "*Don't want to be fish food before dinner!*"

And laughing, he bent to hurl a whole shattered section of the Mary's sterncastle over the side as if it were mere kindling from the forest, before laying his great hands on the tough tiller bar, to turn her broken head towards her canary consort, now moving at last to join them, and away from the drifting corpses and smashed debris that marked their desperate struggle with EL Nazir's corsairs.

Chapter 4...How the Red and Yellow Cogs set sail for the Loire

Four cables away, on board the *Pride,* less than half a mile, there was a deep feeling of dejection and shame. Although she had not been as badly damaged as the *Mary,* just her forecastle smashed about and a great chunk taken out of her starboard side...as if some great beast had leaped from the deep and torn a huge bite out of her timbers. She had not been holed. There was no water pouring in. And while the men had fought like demons, leaving the deck littered with bodies, great splashes and pools of blood everywhere, as if someone had gone mad with buckets of scarlet paint, nevertheless they had lost the two most precious charges for which they had been especially chosen.

The Lady Alicia de Burley and Mistress Agnes Fitzwalter had been ripped from amongst them, and they had been unable to prevent it. Men they had trusted had proven to be traitors, and they all felt responsible for their loss, not knowing what to say to Sir Gui, nor how he would take the vicious theft from amongst them of someone so special to him, and her close companion.

One moment they had been cheering on their comrades on the *Mary*...the next they had been under attack themselves as the great dromond had swept down upon them, almost from nowhere it seemed: had hurled two great rocks into them, boarded them, seized hold of Alicia and Agnes, cut herself free...and then was gone in a moment!

The men couldn't believe it.

Allan-i-the-Wood couldn't believe it! The Lady Alicia gone...his little Agnes gone too! Poor, lovely lass. What would they do to her? How could he get her back? And, *God's Blood!* What would Sir Gui say to them all?

He looked around him. Many were still stood staring after their attacker, now pulling rapidly away from Sir Gui's command, herself now wallowing, sterncastle battered, forecastle almost demolished and a great rent in her side low-down across the waterline. What it must be like on board her now, the young Under Sherriff could only guess at!

As for themselves, with the *Pride's* Master slain, and the ship herself still not under anyone's command, unless the crew did something soon they would pile up amongst the rocks and all would be lost. Not for him a watery grave!

"*Simon Cooper!*" he turned and roared at the Mate, then standing motionless, looking down at the vast pool of blood around Robert Christchurch's smashed body. "Are you the Master's Mate on board this bloody tub, or just a fucking waste of space?"

The Master's head hanging by its thread of gristle, truly was a gruesome sight, and the two shattered carcases of the men on either side of him so brutally hacked down, blood every where, were not much better. Altogether they were enough to stall any man.

"*Aye,* Sir!" The Mate said sharply, shocked out of his trance.

"Do you want to walk ashore, *damn your eyes?*"

"*No,* Sir!"

"*Then don't just stand there, you idle bastard!*" he roared, jabbing his hand furiously at him. "Get the fucking crew working! *NOW!* Before we pile up on those bloody rocks and become part of the scenery!"

"But...the Master..."

"The Master is *dead,* Simon! *You* are in command of the *Pride* now, until Tommy Blackwood says otherwise. So, jump to it, man. The *Mary's* in a bloody mess and needs us. And right now this tub is wallowing about like a drunken whore at a wedding! *Get your lads working!* Hordle John, *to me!*"

With that, as if thrust with a hot iron, Simon snapped back to life, shouting at his crew, themselves no less laggard, who ran to the sheets and halliards to bring the sail under control; while two of the Lions dragged the Master's body to the rail in a long smear of blood and swiftly tossed it overboard. Then, as the *Pride* continued to drift helplessly towards the shore,

25

driven by the tides and currents, Simon took hold of the great tiller bar, shouting to his men to seize the quants, kept for the very purpose of poling her off any rocks that she might draw close to, until the sails could fill and way be got on her once more.

Meanwhile, on the main deck, the Under Sherriff and Hordle John also got their men moving: dragging the corpses to the side and quickly throwing them over, severed limbs and hands the same, swabbing down the decks with buckets of water drawn up from the sea, and pulling out as many arrows as were worth saving from every surface from which they were sticking up.

The horses too needed caring for after the wild violence of the fight that had sometimes raged around them, especially Caesar, whom Allan tended to with mucking out and fresh hay and water. And Bouncer his great hound, who had snarled, leapt upon and bitten the enemy with his massive teeth, as many as he could get them into, and was now busy sniffing and gurrying over every bit of bone or gristle he could find before someone smacked him off it.

"How are we doing?" He asked the giant swordsman, coming up to him as he finished mucking out his horse. "Oh, fair to middling, Master Allan," he replied, turning to lean back against Caesar's stall. "The lads have cleared the decks. Got rid of the bodies and are now trying to keep out of the way of the crew. After you gave the fucking Mate such a bollacking, they have been up an' down those ratl'ns like squirrels after nuts!" And he laughed

"And about time too! If I hadn't bawled at that stupid bugger, we'd've been on those bloody rocks in no time! Dear God, John. *What a fucking mess!*"

"Yes, Master Allan. Not clever, is it? Gawd alone knows what Sir Gui will say when we get up to him? Sweet Jesus, Fitzurse was right..."

"Right? What about?"

"About those two bastard Frenchmen. They bloody Cousins. He said he didn't wholly trust 'em. But what else could I do? Sir Gui told me to put the girls in their care, and the moment that bloody great galley came at us, that's what I did. Put 'em in the Master's cabin and told those two sods to guard'em with their lives! Those were my orders. Then we were hit by those bloody great rocks, next Lady Alicia was screamin' her head off, with two of your lads hacked down and the Master almost cut in two before her eyes, blood everywhere, and a moment later we was boarded! I dunno' Master Allan, if there were anythin' more we could've done?"

"I saw all that, and came running. But by then there seemed to be hordes of the buggers between us and the girls. No matter how many we killed or shot down, Bouncer going for them tooth and claw, Agnes screaming out, "*To me, Lions! To me!*" and kicking and biting for all she was worth, those two fucking bastards had them both trapped and onto that bloody great galley before we could even get to the stern rail. Then they were gone! Still can't believe it. Hate what happened as I do, that was the swiftest piece of piracy I've ever witnessed! But how can we explain that all to Sir Gui and still keep our heads...I don't know? Anyway, John, what's the butcher's bill?

"You may find this hard to believe, Sir. But, apart from the Master and those two either side of 'im...we haven't lost a man! Lots of cuts and bruises, some of them really nasty that might yet turn sour, and a few bites!" he added with a grin, looking down at Bouncer, frolicking among the men. "But no more lives. And even those badly hacked about might be saved once Father Matthew can get a hold of 'em."

"That's a gift from God if ever I heard of one," Allan-i-the-Wood replied, eyebrows raised. "Given the numbers we slaughtered, I thought we'd been really hammered! Someone up there must love us. Well done the lads...yours and mine! Sorry about Bouncer, he just got a bit carried away!"

"No worries, Sir. The lads love 'im, they'll not take a few bites amiss. And, yes Sir, they did do well! Really well, especially as this is the first time in a proper fight for most of 'em. Different from a dust-up outside the George and Dragon on a Saturday night, that's for certain. But right now they're feeling as fucked-up about Lady Alicia and Mistress Fitzwalter as we are. Taken it real bad. No matter how you look at it we failed in our duty. It will take a lot to cheer 'em up I can tell you."

"Well, we will just have to see what we can do. Sir Gui is as fair a man as I have ever met, and Sir Richard too. It may not be as bad as we are all thinking and he banged him on his shoulder. Then turning to look outboard he growled tersely, "What the hell is that bloody Simon up to? Surely we should be moving properly by now?"

And so they were, but for all his initial hesitancy at the start, Simon was a good Mate. He had been with Master Robert for some years, and knew the *Pride's* ways, and how to handle her in cramped waters, so he had kept the sail well brailed up, enough to give him steerage way, but not enough to allow her to run onto the rocks that were all around them. With a man up in the main chains, by the anchor, with a lead and line to call the depths, and others standing by with the long, thick quant poles to fend her off if necessary, he was confidently feeling his way through the narrow channels around the base of Houat, but only moving slowly, before spreading more sail and turning towards the Mary, now well down by the head.

Even from four cables out, everyone could see she was in serious trouble, her forecastle practically demolished, sterncastle badly damaged, a great gash in her side, and those on board running about throwing things into the sea.

"What are they doing, Simon?" Allan asked urgently, striding across the deck. "And why aren't we sailing faster?"

"Lightening the ship, Master Allan. Trying to get that gurt great hole above the water line. And until we are clear of they rocks, and out of these narrow channels, we can do no more. Then we can let the old *Pride* have a bit more sail and we'll be up to the old *Mary* soonest I assure you. I might have been a bit slow off the mark at the start, Master Under Sherriff, but I know this ship well and I know what I'm doin'. Me and my lads'll not let you down. Trust me!"

"What're they doing now, Simon?" Hordle John called to him moments later as they twisted out of the last channel. "What's that they have on her side?"

"Looks like a fother. Their spare winter sail I expect," Simon called back to him. "Thicker canvas. If they can get that over the side, pulled under her and

28

hauled up tight, they can cover that hole. Stop most of the water coming in. Look! There it goes. Now we'll see. We're clear of the last channel now. Yarely, lads, *yarely!*' he shouted to his crew. "Loose some more sail, and let's get this fucking tub moving."

★

Moments later they all heard a great roar of triumph rush out from the *Mary*, and shortly after saw her crew race up the ratlines, her sail begin to break out and her head gently come round towards the distant coast, and Simon shifted his tiller over to meet her, ordering his crew to spill the wind out of the *Pride's* sails and heave-to, so the *Mary* could meet up with her consort at last.

Releasing the tiller to another senior crew member, Simon ran to the rail, where Allan-i-the-Wood and Hordle John swiftly joined him, both ships settling down less than a half-a-cable's length apart. Neither Master wanting their ships to be too close for fear of doing further damage.

"*Ho there, Simon!*" Thomas Blackwood roared out. "Lost a bit here and there then? Where's Master Robert?"

"*Dead!* Cut down by those two French bastards who took the girls. One moment all was well and we were nearly there, the next moment Robert and the two men beside him were hacked down, we were bombarded out of no-where, and all hell broke lose!"

"That's bad, Simon. He was a good man," Thomas shouted back to him. "So that's why you went out of control?"

"Yes, Master Thomas! The moment Master Robert was cut down he let go of the tiller, the *Pride's* head came up into the wind, and she was in irons."

"What happened then?" Sir Gui called across, cupping his hands so his voice would carry above the crying gulls dipping and wheeling above, as they swooped onto the sudden harvest floating all around them.

"Alicia screamed!" Allan-i-the-Wood shouted his reply. "She saw Master Robert and two of my men hacked down before her eyes, and screamed her head off! But before we could reach her those two French bastards had seized her and Agnes, the galley grappled us athwart the tiller, and hordes of the buggers poured on board."

"The lads fought like demons, Sir Gui," John of Hordle bawled across at his commander. "You would have been proud of them, Sir Richard. They fought like the lions on their chests! And we drove them back right to the stern. Thought we were winning, slaughtered them, bodies everywhere, while all the time they were just withdrawing."

"By then they had what they'd come for, My Lord," Allan-i-the-Wood added. "Jules and Lucas had seized both girls right from the start. And despite doing all they could, shouting, kicking and biting, they were carried across to the other ship like washing bundles. Then they cut themselves free, outed her oars and were off like a fox after a rabbit. We all feel dreadful, My Lord. Shamed by it. But the lads did all they could. Truly. It just wasn't enough!"

"But I blame myself, My Lord," Hordle John shouted again. "As soon as they attacked I did as you had ordered and put the girls in the Master's cabin and told those two buggers to guard her with their lives. *But they were traitors, My Lords!* Tied some green silk on the stern, put on green arm bands, slaughtered the Master and grabbed the girls. If I had kept them with me they would have been safe. I'm so sorry, Sir Gui. Bastards! *Bastards!*"

"Don't feel so bad about it, John, though I admit I cursed you all at the time...but they dished us up too. You can see what damage they did, and we had twice the men on board. You can't be blamed for carrying out my orders. We both trusted the wrong men! Take it off your backs, all of you, and stop beating yourselves up. None of that will help Alicia...nor Agnes. What we've got to do now is get to land. Anywhere if necessary, but Nantes if we can. Master Thomas thinks that's possible as long as we don't go too fast and rip the fother off, the sea doesn't suddenly get up, or the sky fall on our heads!" And there was a general laugh.

"What's the tally, Master Sherriff?" Matthew called to him. "Do you have many injured?"

"Lots of cuts and bruises and several nasty wounds. Even some bites, I'm afraid. Bouncer got a bit carried away. But they'll live till you can get to them. And, with God's Grace, Father-Sir Gui-apart from poor Master Robert and the two men beside him, we didn't lose another man! Good skills and training, and a lot of luck! How about you?"

"Only three altogether! That's excellent. We thought you'd been slaughtered. Much the same, here. We lost eight...and several badly injured. Seems we both got off lightly!"

"So, Master Thomas," Simon Cooper hallooed him. "Where away next? With that fother you'll need to go gently. We should be able to keep close to you all the way."

"With the wind where it is, and how it is, we ought to make the Loire. It's only fifty miles or so, and the sea and currents are with us hereabouts. We'll steer for the Horse Islands and then turn in closer to the coast...but as you say, we must take it slowly. Once we're into the estuary, and out of the sea, we should be safe and able to show a bit more canvas. With God's Will, we might still actually get in to Nantes tonight as long as we don't lose the wind. So Harrow Away, lad. Get your boys on their feet. *And you lot,*" he roared, turning back to his own ship, and the cheerful faces of the men she carried, "*keep bailing!*" And they all laughed.

And as his crew leaped to do his bidding, the giant shipmaster strode back to the *Mary's* great tiller bar, and with the wind steady in her coat-tails from the North West, the sun tilted over the meridian and the sea still a deep shimmering blue, crests foamed with white, the *Mary* finally turned her fat scarlet body towards the shore, her yellow consort close to hand.

Behind them, on that hot July afternoon, the scattered wreckage of their fierce encounter with El Nazir's corsairs wallowed in the long Atlantic rollers as they lazily swelled towards the shore, gently turning it all up and over as the swept towards the land: an arm, a leg, a box of stores; oars and whole pieces of shattered hull…and eyeless corpses, hundreds of them, the empty black holes stark within each white and wrinkled face; and above and all around them the gulls screamed and swooped and gabbled over the human debris left in the *Mary's* wake as she pushed towards the Loire, the *Pride of Beaulieu* by her side.

Chapter 5...Sir Gui arrives at Nantes

B y the time the sun began to sink in an orb of blazing glory towards the far horizon, through a cloudless azure sky, the two great cogs had long passed the Horse Islands and the Cardinals, and turned their fat bellies to draw closer to the shore. With the *Mary* leading, her crew and Gui's command still furiously bailing, both ships sailed slowly down the coast, dipping their shoulders into the long rollers from across the Atlantic, their wakes leaving a torn blue-white track the mewling seabirds still followed.

Behind her The *Pride*, too, dipped and swayed across the edges of that great ocean, the shore a mottled green and brown as she reeled steadily past. Small groups of houses, like squares of white cheese on a coloured plate, their red roof tiles a brilliant splash of life, showed where villages and hamlets lay half hidden amongst the hills. And from time to time small fleets of fishing boats, like darting rainbows, with white and dun coloured sails, bustled around the not too distant shore, nets cast between them or lines hanging over their sides.

The Bay of Biscay, so often wild and turbulent, was more kindly that day. The sea sparkling beneath the Westering sun, the deep troughs shark-blue and green, as the *Mary,* a chuckling bone in her teeth, pushed her shattered bow up the wide estuary of the Loire that would take them safely up to Nantes at last.

Beneath the ruined forecastle, Father Matthew was still busy plying his trade, binding the wounds of those who had come to him for help, rubbing in salves and herbal oils, and stitching and splinting those few who had been more seriously injured, his hands and apron red with blood, his brow furrowed with concentration and concern. Soothing and encouraging he moved amongst the men, especially those now coming to him with torn and blistered hands from the constant bailing and pumping.

Seeing Gui and Richard beckoning him as they left the hustle of the main deck, back to the damaged sterncastle to sit down, he smiled, acknowledging their invitation to join them with a helpless shrug of his shoulders as he gestured around him at the many men he was still tending, too busy just then to talk. And it was a while before he could leave what he was doing and come across with Jean de Beaune to join them.

"How are things, Gui?" he asked calmly, dipping his bloodied hands into a bucket of salt water before drying them on a piece of rough linen at his side. "And how is the fother holding?" he added, pointing to where Thomas Blackwood and Adam were looking at it over the side.

"It's alright, Father, still there, just about. But the lads have to keep at the bailing and pumping, turn and turn about. He's more worried about that rock still in her side," he added as their ship master, moved to examine it. "If that comes lose we'll be in trouble all over again!"

"We're lucky it's not worse! Our boys are now producing blisters for me to salve as well as wounds. Much more and you'll have no fit men left to command."

"Fine Job's Comforter you are, Father," L'Eveque drawled at him, stretched out on a pile of brigandines, arms behind his head, the sun flickering off his blood stained armour and soiled cyclas. "You're just the rain cloud I need on a picnic afternoon! At least we're still afloat!"

"For the time being at least!" de Beaune said, picking his teeth as the *Mary* suddenly lifted and bobbled over the tumbling race that marked where river met the sea, the *Pride* following her, dipping and tilting as she too crossed the bar; the change in water, from deep, rolling swells and chopped waves, to the more gently, ruffled surface of the estuary easing her motion enormously.

At that their Ship Master, like the great bear he was, came booming up beside them. "Well, My Lords? Well? We bloody made it! " And he banged his hands together with a mighty **clap!** "And despite a few mild panics along the way, that fother held too. And with the quieter water at last we can now show some more sail."

"Thomas, I owe you more than I can say," Gui said, grasping the Master's great calloused hand with a huge grin. "Well done, my bully! *Well done!*"

"Thank you, My Lord! I said I'd get you here...and I have done. And, Sir Gui, you owe me nothing. I did it as much for your father, God Bless him, as I did for you."

"All the same, Thomas, I will leave you with plenty to repair both ships. That's the very least I can do. And money for the families of those lads you lost today. How much longer before we reach Nantes?"

"And can the lads stop bailing?" Sir Richard added, sitting up on his elbows.

"It's thirty miles up this river according to my charts, Sir Gui. And if this wind keeps steady, and nothing finally carries away, about two hours, three at most. About sunset, I'd say," he added looking at the sun. "And about the money, My Lord. Thank you!"

"And the lads, Thomas?"

"Right now, Sir Richard," and turning he roared across the deck. "*Avast bailing you idle bastards!* And you can stop the pumps too unless I think she needs it. All right, My Lord?"

"Yes, Master Thomas, and thank you," he drawled with a smile, in his lazy fashion.

"Right, My Lords. Now we're in smooth water at last, I'll chase my men up those ratlin's and get some more canvas on her!" And tipping his head he turned and rolled across the deck, shouting and roaring as he went, his crew galvanised into action as he called their names, his Mate, Adam, taking the Mary's tiller in his own hard hands.

And as the men shook out the reefs that had held her sails back, Gui and his commanders watched as their men threw down their bailers at last,

Some came to the *Mary's* side to watch her sail up the broad expanses of calmer water and gaze at the distant banks on either side, like open arms ready to enfold them, cheerfully exclaiming at every new and unusual sight; while others just fell back and lay slumped and exhausted on the torn deck. The *Pride* too, in all her bold, canary glory sailed close behind them, her broad sail, with its great ram's head, also spread further to catch the wind.

"So!" Gui exclaimed, rubbing his hands together briskly, his chain mail mittens hanging from his wrists. "A few more hours and we'll be on our way at last!"

"Is that wise, Gui? Father Matthew questioned him quietly, gesturing to the men behind him slumped across the deck.

"Those lads are pretty beat-up to me, My Lord," De Beaune added. "And we need 'em fresh. I've campaigned in France, Sir Gui. It's not England!"

"Oh, come on, Jean," Gui sighed. "You're as bad as our good Benedictine here. What's the matter with you all?"

"Oh, just feeling a bit weary, I suppose. Lost two of my best men too!" the swarthy Burgundian sighed ruefully, leaning against a broken stanchion. "But nothing, I suppose, that a jar of warm red, a hot tasty meal and a pretty girl wouldn't cure."

"And a soft bed!" Sir Richard added with a groan. "This has been a real bugger of a day, Gui! We are all worn out and fed-up. Bruised, battered and ashamed. We've lost the girls, most of our stores are bobbing about the Atlantic, and the men are crocked. Look at them," he urged him, gesturing over his shoulder. "They've shot their bolt, Dear Boy!" he exclaimed, picking up a dropped crossbow and shaking it at him with his lazy grin. "And there must be the best part of four hundred miles still to go from here to Narbonne: half the length of England! And you ask what's wrong?"

"Gui...Sir Richard's right," Father Matthew said firmly, standing up. "Especially now we're so nearly there, despite all that the good Baron has tried to do to us," he added bitterly. "I know you want to press on as fast as you can. So do we all. But even if we make Nantes tonight, it will be after sunset. We have neither horses for the men, nor waggons...and we need them, Gui. And we need to replace the stores we threw overboard as well. And, above all we need a good meal and, at the very least, a proper night's rest."

"So do the horses, My Lord," Fitzurse added, as came to stand before him. "They won't come off easy after all this, not Beau and Merlin...Sunburst and the rest. Give us twenty four hours at least, My Lord, get properly sorted and leave the day after tomorrow, first light."

There was a pause then, as they all looked at Gui, and waited, Sir Richard in particular looking at him with a wry smile, remembering what Father Matthew had said earlier about getting him to stop!

Gui looked at their serious faces, his mind already half made up: Matthew, steady, looking at him through half closed eyes; Richard with that quizzical, raised eyebrow of his; Fitzurse concerned, de Beaune resigned...and grimaced. "Oh...very well!" he exclaimed, standing up to look out across the *Mary's* bows as she moved in towards the river at last, the huge estuary now behind her. "I value what you've said, and you are all quite right, of course." And taking a deep breath he said. "So...we'll take *two* days here, not one!"

But look, all of you," he went on as they gasped in pleased surprise. "It's obvious that de Brocas has no intention of letting us get to Narbonne if he can possibly avoid it. So whatever you do once we've landed, keep the men under arms...and under control. Brittany is still a part of the Empire that Henry left to Richard, so we should be quite safe, but de Brocas may have spies everywhere. Anything could happen...just look at today? And don't waste it, for this will be the last stop before Bordeaux."

"It's a shame we can't all sleep on board," Father Matthew said, getting to his feet.

"No, Father!" Sir Richard said, stretching lugubriously. "No! *Absolutely no!* Before we set out for the best part of three weeks filthy, dusty, travelling across half of France, maybe more with waggons in tow, and no doubt sleeping on hard ground, come rain or shine...or in whatever bug-ridden, disgusting flea pit we can find along the way, I want two decent nights between the sheets. You may be used to a stone cell and Spartan living, Matthew, and you can sleep here if you like. *But not me!*"

"Well, some will have to," Gui said tersely. "We brought four waggons loaded with gear when we set out, and while most of that may well be bobbing about the Atlantic just now, the sumpters and their panniers are still with us on the *Pride,* along with Sunburst and Gillygate. And if we leave any of that unguarded... then by morning it will all be gone.

We need stabling for the horses, and they will need to be watched too. Fitzurse, you Jean and our good Under Sherriff, can sort out who goes where amongst the lads. But leave Hordle John in charge on board, it will be good for him, and choose another of your likely lads to be with the horses. Then you and Allan-i-the-Wood must come and join Sir Richard, Father Matthew and me at the sign of the Angel on the north bank of the river, just across from the Île de Nantes."

"How do you know of such a place?" the tall Benedictine asked astonished. "You've never been there before!"

"Goodness me Father," Gui grinned broadly, "a hole in your knowledge at last? I am almost bereft of speech!" and he tilted his head. "Tommy Blackwood, of course. He knows *everything!*" And they all laughed.

"How are we for money, Dear Boy?" L'Eveque drawled. "It will not be cheap to stay at an inn, feed the lads, buy horses, especially good ones, and carts, if we can find 'em. And there is no point in buying a collection of broken-winded, spavined old nags for the job we have in hand either. We'll need good solid mounts…and with a turn of speed in 'em too if possible!"

"That won't be a problem in Nantes," Matthew said, leaning over the side, watching as the *Mary* entered the river proper at last, the wind still creaming her along nicely, no water now spurting from around the fother. "Nor will finding good horses be one either," he added, turning to speak to him. "There is a Benedictine Abbey at Vertou, just outside the city. Don't forget I have the authority of the Holy Father in my scrip!

The Abbot there, Father Hugo Gravier, will give us all the help we need. He'll make sure you're not offered rubbish horses to buy, and will put us all up for a night or two if needed. And there's a castle of sorts. But its gates will be closed by the time we moor-up. And there is no curfew in Nantes because of the port. And because you hold the King's Warrant, we won't have to pay Port dues or local taxes either!"

"That is excellent news! Is there anything you don't know, Matthew?" Gui asked him with a smile.

"Apart from dockside Inns," Sir Richard said laconically, with a quirked eyebrow and his lazy smile.

"Oh, this and that," the tall monk replied, looking at Sir Richard's long sprawled figure with a laugh. "How about you, My Good Lord of Malwood?" And he tilted his head gravely while the others laughed.

"Not much!" Gui yawned, leaning his back against the shattered remains of the stern castle, while he watched the *Mary* pushing upriver. "Old Father Gerome gave up on me years ago. Said I was borne to plague the life out of him, poor old boy. Alicia was the one with all the brains!" And thinking of her, he sighed. "Still, my father taught me to fight, keep account of everything and the importance of planning, and mother taught me to care for people, so I didn't do too badly…which is why we came so well prepared. So money is not a problem, yet. The two strong boxes we brought with us are filled, and if we need more, we can seek out a Templar House as I said.. Sir Yvo made a big deposit in London and I have his mark with me against our needs."

"That little escapade with that bastard, El Nazir, has set us back weeks," Richard said. "Even if we get the horses we want, we'll now have to journey over-land to Bordeaux, and by the time we get there de Brocas will be long gone."

"He's been gone weeks already," Gui replied, "So a few more won't make much difference."

"It's nearly two hundred miles to Bordeaux from Nantes," Matthew broke in. "I know, I did it with your father, years ago: pretty wild countryside, with lots of small villages along the way, very twisted trackways and several small rivers until Bordeaux…we should aim for forty miles a day, say five days."

"We'll bugger the horses at that rate," Sir Richard drawled, stretching his arms out as he spoke. "So why not push 'em a bit more and cut a little more time off the journey. We're going to have to buy more at Bordeaux at that rate anyway. Four days."

"Because your way will bugger the men as well, My Lord!" de Beaune chipped in. "You've not travelled long distances in France before. I have, and as I said, it's not like England, soft and green even in summer. And with all due respect to Father Matthew, I bet when he travelled with Sir Yvo they had no waggons with them? Seven days…even ten!"

"Mmm, you're quite right, Jean. We didn't…just he and me and a sumpter apiece. Well noticed!"

"Thank you, Father. And we are going even further south, My Lord. It will be hard, hot, and very dusty. Horrid for all, and water will be a problem. These lads are all we have, and they have already taken a beating. Of course, Sir Gui…Sir Richard, it's up to you, but allow a week to ten days and I'll guarantee we'll *all* get to Bordeaux in one piece…short of another fracas like this one today. There's no point in pushing everyone so hard that they're worth nothing when we get there."

"That is good advice, Jean," Gui said. "I can see why Mercardier recommended you to me. Then tapping Sir Richard's mailed feet with his toes, as he lay there with his lazy smile he added. "It would be wonderful to get there more quickly, Richard, but we have Beau and your Merlin to think of too, as well as the girls' mares and the men, and I don't want any charger but my own under me when I meet de Brocas!"

With a languid groan his tall guard commander got to his feet at last, and came to stand beside Gui, resting his arms on the *Mary's* scored rails, as they both looked at the distant banks of the Loire, leaving the others to talk amongst themselves.

By chance they had crossed the bar at the height of the tide, and with the wind still in their tails, and Thomas having set more sail as they entered the smooth waters of the great river, as he'd said he would, they might even make Nantes before sunset. He, too, wanted to get to Narbonne as soon as possible, but Merlin was his favourite, huge and strong, good natured but a terrific fighter when called upon, and not to be risked unwisely. He could see him now, ears pricked forward, huffing through his nose, looking for his master, and he turned towards Gui then, and smiled.

"You do know, Gui," he said seriously, with no affectation. "There is no way we can leave anywhere tonight. No matter how much you might want to. We all need a proper rest after this morning…especially the wounded. It's not lack of courage, Gui, nor lack of desire. You know I will follow you anywhere, anytime. Just prudence and a simple question of basic logistics. We have no carts and no horses either. And, as Jean said, these lads are all we've got right now, and we need to take a bit of care with them."

"Yes, Richard. I know that," he said, turning to face his friend, nudging his fist on his shoulder. "I have *never* doubted you: your loyalty, nor your bravery and courage, for all your lazy ways, my friend, they don't fool me. I know how organised you are, how fierce you are in battle! When danger threatens, Richard, there is no man I would rather have to guard my back. And the lads look up to you and trust you, as I do. I just want to get there *so* badly, and I miss her *so* much that I am in danger of becoming reckless! So…you are *all* right. We must rest and get things properly sorted.

Nevertheless we'll still have to treat this whole journey as if we were in enemy territory with a bandit behind every tree or boulder that we pass. What about our wounded?" he asked, turning to their black clad physician.

"They'll keep up," the tall monk said quietly, coming up behind them. "Don't you worry, Gui. Trust me, they'll be fine. I've not lost a man yet whom I didn't expect to. They can always travel in a waggon if necessary."

"They must keep up, Matthew," Gui said firmly to the dark robed Benedictine. "Even if we have to tie them to their saddles, though I don't think anyone is that badly hurt. But it is going to be really hard on everyone. So remind the lads, Fitzurse," he said, turning back to his Master-at-Arms. "That they've all been hand-picked for this trip, and I don't expect them to go soft on us now. We have to get to Narbonne as soon as possible, and smoke that bloody fox from his lair. I tell you, I won't rest 'til I hold Alicia safely in my arms again if I have to wade through rivers of blood to do it!"

"What about that bit of extra for the men, Sir Gui," Fitzurse reminded him. "With a bit of time to 'play' as it were, that would be good for all of them.

"Well thought of, John. And those flagons as well. So wine tonight and silver for the lads tomorrow out of the small strong box. How does that all sound?"

"Good to me, My Lord. Thank you. Now if Jean will come with me, we'll get those lists sorted out before we reach the port." And with a smile he and the tall Burgundian leader turned and walked away, the others crossing the *Mary* to watch their progress from the shattered forecastle, while Thomas and his crew worked her up the river, the *Pride* following.

Chapter 6... Sir Gui defies Sir Alan de Courcy and the Chef Du Port

T wo hours later as the sun slowly dipped below the hills and the trees around them, casting long shadows across the drowsing countryside, they reached Nantes safely at last, crammed with shipping of every sort, the houses crowding down to the edges of the great cobbled concourse that separated them from the quayside. Above them the sky turned a liquid, shimmering gold and scarlet; great streamers of colour that flowed across the whole heavens as if they were on fire, the clouds coming up as evening closed in streaked with orange and crimson flame, and tinged with purple and deep indigo above, and pink and palest yellow beneath.

Here also the river divided, narrower on the side facing the town, but both sides crowded with wharfs, stables and timber yards, forges, with smoke puffing from them, houses of every size, and shops and hostelries of every sort.

It was almost as busy as Brest, and it was here that Thomas finally brought the *Mary* hard up against the long wooden staithes that lined the banks, where they could disembark at last, and the horses could be led ashore to find fresh water and good stabling, and with the *Pride* following behind her both commands could be re-united again and their plans shared.

And with no curfew in place as Matthew had said there were people everywhere: merchants going from ship to wharf and back again, food sellers with trays hanging from narrow cords around their necks laden with pies and sweetmeats, fruit tarts, smoked meats and olives smeared with golden oil; pedlars with ribbons, bows and trinkets; apprentices calling their master's wares, and shop keepers, fariers and stable hands; ostlers from nearby taverns and serving girls in bright cotehardies and pretty aprons; families out to see the ships and the bustle around the port...and whores, with bold, painted eyes and sly, winning ways...children, hounds and wandering pigs; drudges, beggars and thieves; slatterns, scrubbers and crones; old men and striplings, and sailors of every shape and hue. The noise, colour and swirling activity was vast!

With both ships clearly damaged, the *Mary* especially so, with her fothered hull, smashed fore and stern castles, and blood-stained planking, they quickly became the focus of everyone's attention, so there were plenty of idlers willing to grab the hawsers the crew cast over to warp both ships tightly alongside. And when Gui's men began to disembark, carrying their wounded with them, there was even more activity, so it was not long before officialdom duly appeared from within the town.

Small of stature, but large in importance, in a padded jacket of fine red wool, laced across the front over a white cotton shirt, a man came strutting plumply towards Gui in trousers of soft blue leather, feet in well soled boots, and a red felt hat with a two short green feathers sticking from its side on his head. His face was round, mouth prim, and nose pointed, and he had small eyes, black as currants, beneath narrow black eyebrows, and he busily carried a sheaf of parchments in his hands.

Beside him strode a much taller man in long chain mail over a padded gambeson, covered with a short surcoat in the simple colours, Ermine, of the Duke of Brittany, held in with a wide sword belt from which hung both a long blade and a short tapered dagger, both in plain sheaths. He was well muscled and looked both lean and hard, with sharp grey eyes and his mouth grimly closed.

Accompanying him was another man, larger, with a neat red beard and a nasal helmet, grey eyes and a broken nose, wearing the same colours, Ermine, on his surcoat over a tough brigandine overlaid by a coif of thick mail, with mailed chauses and mittens. He alone was carrying a shield, a long, kite shaped Norman shield emblazoned with a dragon azure, armed and langued sable on a field gules…a blue dragon on a red background, with claws tongue and teeth all black as pitch.

With him was a small bodyguard of eight men in light brigandines over leather chauses, two carrying resin torches in iron holders, with chain coifs and round casques on their heads, the Duke's simple colours on their chests and plain swords at their waists; the other six similarly armed, but carrying long spears over their shoulders, and from whom the crowd of cheerful onlookers quickly backed away in sudden silence to let them through. Moving towards where Gui was standing with Sir Richard, idly watching their arrival, while their men began to unload both ships, their sides now open to allow the horses to be walked off and their other gear to be removed and stacked, the small man

43

leading this command raised a plump beringed hand and brought his whole escort to a swift halt.

"I am Monsieur Roland du Clefs," he said sharply in Breton, rolling his 'R's, definitive with his name, and waving his papers at Gui. "The Chief Port Officer for Nantes, *Le chef du Port*," he suddenly added in bad French, tapping his chest, "and the Chief Revenue Collector. All arrivals must report to me at once, explain their business to me and pay their Port Tolls, or they cannot stay here. You have done *none* of those things, and you are late in. The sun has gone down. No-one can enter the port after the sun has gone down. *It is the law here!* This behaviour is unsupportable, and unless you warp your vessels below the Port immediately, they and all their gear will be impounded, and you will be arrested!"

Gui and Sir Richard stood there while the man's Breton words rattled around them in complete incomprehension, then shrugged their shoulders and smiled, both shaking his hand and patting his shoulders before turning to get on with their tasks, while the little man stood and gazed at them in outraged amazement.

But before he could speak with them again, his armoured companion stepped in front of him, and said sharply, in strongly accented English: "I don't think you understood, Monsieur Roland!" indicating the man by his side, body now trembling with affronted dignity. "He is the *Chef du Port*...the Chief Port Officer for the Count of Brittany, and that was not a welcome! That was an instruction!" he growled, thrusting his head forward aggressively. "You have broken Nantes regulations for landing here, and if you do not move your ships immediately everything will impounded til it can all be sorted out, and yourselves, and your men, will be arrested!"

"*Arrested?*" Gui said softly, swinging towards him. "Arrested, and these ships impounded? Are you mad? This is an open port, and we are both belted knights of our realm, as you can see. Men of personal coat armour," he said with icy calmness, indicating the long cyclases both he and Sir Richard were wearing. "How *dare* you address me in so coarse a manner, as if I were a common peasant. On whose orders are we so threatened?"

"By the orders of his Grace the Count of Brittany," the man answered sharply, again thrusting his head forward, tapping his surcoat, bristling with annoyance. "If you do not comply, I will order you arrested."

"*Arrested?*" Gui asked again, his voice rising. "Do you have a brain in that bony lump on your shoulders, you fool? Look around you, man! Do you think my troopers will stand by while you and that rabble at your back, those apologies for soldiers, attempt to lay hands on us? Do you want a bloody skirmish in your town? To lie smashed down in your own blood and that of your men? And who are you to order my arrest?"

"I am Sir Alan de Courcy. This man," he said, indicating his companion, "is my Sergeant-at-Arms, Victor Jonelle. We are both of the Count's personal forces, to assist the Chief Officer of this Port in his duties. Who are you, to question my orders?"

"I do not answer to you, Sir Alan," Gui replied tersely, his voice cold and hard. "Nor to your men, nor even to the Count of Brittany! Not now, not at any time. You are a fool to even think so. My men and I are duty bound for Narbonne, and on the very highest of authority. We were attacked by corsairs just off Belle Île this very morning. You can see the damage! Some of my men were killed and others injured, but we destroyed two of their galleys completely, killing everyone. And in two days time we will leave here, together, unmolested, and in one piece. Neither you, nor your men, nor Monsieur Roland du Clefs," he added rolling his own 'R's as he spoke, "will stop me. Do you understand me…Sir Alan?" And he leaned slightly towards him, like an armoured tower, and put his hand on his sword.

At the very mention of the attack, the words 'Les Corsairs!' flew around the crowd in terrified whispering. All those around them were visibly affected, many with their hands to their mouths in horror, others huddling together or moving swiftly away to put the town's walls between them and any possible attackers.

Up on the *Mary's* deck, Father Matthew and Jean de Beaune listened to the small contretemps with complete amazement, while their men stopped what they were doing and began to reach for their weapons, archers on the *Mary* for their crossbows; Allan-i-the-Wood's men on the *Pride* with Hordle John for

45

their long bows. Beside him, de Beaune said softly to the dark cowled monk, "Father...I think I know those men."

"From where? Who are they?"

"From a sharp skirmish my lads and I had with Mercardier, against some of King Philip's troops in the Vexin. That tall bastard down there was their leader, and red beard is his Sergeant-at-Arms. I took a chunk out of his shield, and broke his nose. His nasal piece saved his life, but he scrabbled away before I could finish him off. We trounced the lot of them! He's a good fighter and leads men well. On his own he's no match for Sir Gui, though, nor Sir Richard...but together they're bloody dangerous, and not to be trusted. If Sir Gui turns his back, either one of them is quite capable of running him through from behind."

"So...they're two of King Philip's men, are they? I wonder what they're doing here in Brittany? The Count is a staunch supporter of Richard's, not least but because he only holds his lands solely through Richard's favour, as Brittany is very much a part of the Anjevin Empire he inherited from his father. He was one of the first to recognising the King as his Overlord! I smell a rat! I had better get down there quickly before this gets any worse. I know Sir Gui well, and these men around us. If those idiots are not careful, and attack Gui and injure him, they will sweep them out of the way and probably sack the town! Stay here, Jean. It might be well for them not to recognise you. Use your imagination and organise these men, while I get on!" And throwing his big leather scrip over his shoulders, and lifting the hem of his long black habit, he raced across the deck, down the dropped sides of the *Mary* and onto the quayside.

Meanwhile de Courcy, with Jonelle, had taken another step towards Gui, coming dangerously close, their men a few feet behind them. "I am no dog for you to address me so," de Courcy growled, face red with anger, cocking his scabbard forward to draw his sword. "I am the Count's leal man. And you *will* do as say, or I will cut you down where you stand!"

"*Step Back, de Courcy!*" Gui then roared at him. "Take your hand of your sword, and take that pompous, bloated popinjay away with you!" Stabbing his hand to wards the Chef Du Port, terrified now rather than affronted, and taking a swift half stride towards them he shouted. "Who is overlord of these

46

lands you stand on, Eh? Who gives orders to the Count of Brittany? Yes? And who is the Count's Overlord in all matters?" But before either man could answer, he added furiously, "and if that oaf, Jonelle, beside you shifts *one* more foot, or hitches his shield *once* more; or one of your pathetic excuses for a soldier so much as touches his weapon, *I will kill you all!*"

Behind him, even as they had watched the strutting figure of the Chef Du Port and his bodyguard arriving, Sir Richard, and Allan-i-the-Wood had swiftly organised their men: some running the horses out of immediate danger, the Verderers moving swiftly to the *Pride's* sterncastle to ready their long bows, Hordle John and his other Lions picking up their weapons, raising their shields and shaking themselves into good order.

Even Thomas Blackwood and the crews of both ships had armed themselves, as they had done against the corsairs, and were loosely forming up behind Gui's whole command. Sir Richard standing, arms crossed before them.

By then the town's people had swiftly retreated to the edge of the cobbled concourse agog to see what would happen next, but equally ready to flee amongst the narrow twisted streets and ginnels of the town for safety, where somewhere a horn was blowing and a great bell tolling.

However, by then Monsieur Roland, Sir Alan and the red bearded Jonelle, were all in a frantic argument. Sir Alan and Jonelle wanting to draw their swords and order their men to the attack, du Clefs desperate to restrain them, all waving their arms and shouting; if the situation had not been so serious it would have been funny.

At this point, in a rush of heavy sandals and flying robes, Father Matthew arrived.

"Is there some trouble, My Lords?" he said moments later in his quiet, commanding voice, calmly looking around him despite his haste. "You all look very belligerent...and sound it too!" he exclaimed.

Then, motioning de Courcy and his big Sergeant to move back, he turned to the Chef du Port, and quietly said in Breton, with his soft Spanish lilt, "You, Monsieur Roland du Clefs, are being very officious. Unnecessarily rude and unpleasant to people who have just arrived in this port. Very unwise of you, Monsieur, *very!* No!" he said, holding up his hand. "*I heard you!* And if you wish to keep your position, I advise you to be eternally careful," he went on ignoring the pompous little man's mouth open in shock.

"Monsieur le Cont is well known to me," he breathed at him, watching his face suddenly lose colour. "Very well known to me…as is King Richard of England who is his Overlord, and whose brother, Count Geoffrey was Prince of Brittany. It is *King Richard's* word that rules here, you foolish little mountebank!" he almost snarled, flicking the man's papers with contempt. "And *I* come with King Richard's personal seal, *on his Royal business*, as do the men with me! And I also come with letters from Rome, from the Holy Father himself! If I were you," he hissed at him dangerously, tapping firmly on his plump. rounded chest with a hard finger, "I would start by begging this man's forgiveness, render him every service possible that you can think of and then pray to God that he does not report your conduct, personally, to Monsieur le Cont, who is with King Richard's army, and then to the King himself! And take that idiot, de Courcy with you, and his Sergeant-at-Arms, before they get you all killed! Look around, you Monsieur du Clefs, *now!*"

And stepping away from him he gestured towards both ships.

Du Clefs looked, saw, and finally dropped his papers in shaking terror. On the *Mary* a dozen crossbows were pointed at him and on the *Pride*, Allan's verderers were standing with their longbows stringed and armed, each clothyard shaft bodkin pointed, and ready to be raised and fired in a moment.

"*You, de Courcy!*" Father Matthew next shouted out, his voice every bit as tough and sharp as any Commander of a Royal Guard. "*Draw back with your men, now!* You and Sergeant Jonelle, both. Be advised that King Richard of England is Overlord of these lands, and these men are on the King's Royal business, *and under his Royal Seal!*" And with a flourish he opened his scrip, pulled open the warrant with all its seals, and thrust it at him, unrolled, the King's Seal huge and beribboned prominently before his startled eyes, and was pleased to see the sudden shock that rippled through them all….the crowd included.

"These men do not pay tolls, do not pay duties and will not be hindered against the King's extreme displeasure, and you *will* assist them in every way while they are in Nantes. *This is the Great Seal of King Richard of England…and your overlord!*" he shouted out to all around him, holding the parchment up for them to see. "Where that seal is, so is the King, and you will bow to it, Sir Allan or be foresworn! *Do you understand me?*"

"Yes! Father," And with gritted teeth he bowed as he had been so ordered.

"All your men, de Courcy! Your Sergeant Jonelle as well, I will brook no mistakes in this matter! Do this or *I* will order your immediate arrest for treason against the King." And he held up the King's seal before Jonelle's face, who with ill concealed anger, and no grace, jerked his head in bitter compliance.

"Good! Lastly, you du Clefs!"

"Yes! F-Father," and he, too, bowed, then stepped back, grovelled for his papers, and practically fled the quay, through the crowds who jeered him, followed by de Courcy, and Jonelle, their faces flushed with humiliation, teeth clenched and bodies rigidly upright as they marched back towards the town, through jeering crowds, their men following.

Behind them Father Matthew turned and held out his arms to Gui's whole command and smiled. "There! That ought to sort things out for all of us. About time I did something to earn my keep. How was that?"

"Matthew!" Gui exclaimed for all of them, as they rushed to gather round him, swordsmen, archers, crews and hound. "I have seen and heard many things since you came among us, but that?...that was beyond simply amazing! That was spectacular...*outstanding!* See, Father, you have stunned us all. But where did you learn Breton? And how did you know those fools names?

"Oh, I am lucky with languages," he said humorously, tilting his head. "I picked it up in my soldiering days from several Bretons in my Command...and as for those two idiots, De Beaune recognised them. And I know you, Dear Boy!" he laughed, patting Gui on his shoulders. "*I know you!* One more word from de Courcy and you would have been at him, and that other, and cut them both in pieces with that great big shaft of steel you love to wield. Blood and slaughter all over the place! Yes?"

"Mmmm. Probably!"

"More than likely," Sir Richard added with a grin, coming up to him and banging him on his shoulders, while the men dispersed to get on with clearing both ships.

"See, Gui?" Father Matthew smiled. "And Richard knows you better than I. But justified or not...and I know things now about those two that they would not be pleased about, and which I will discuss with you later...they are both still Officers of the Count, wearing the Count's colours, and Richard is the Count's Overlord. An attack on those two could have been taken as an attack on Richard himself, and where would that have left us all? Blood shed now would have been just awful!"

Gui smiled and shrugged his broad shoulders, bringing up his hands in a gesture of mock defeat, his eyes going up to heaven under raised eyebrows.

"Where would I be without you, Father? As it is, those two have had the biggest bollacking of their tiny lives. You have made clear from where our orders come, and they must now help us to fulfil them or be in contempt of the King...which they will not dare to be! Truly, Father, you are brilliant and I'm a numpty! Now, let's get all this gear sorted and then find this Angel Inn that Tommy Blackwood has sworn by. I don't know about you...but I am starving!"

Chapter 7...Alicia and Agnes Fitzwalter meet Soraya

For Alicia de Burley and Agnes Fitzwalter, the nightmare seemed never ending!

From the moment Sheik El Nazir's great galley had swept up and hammered the *Pride of Beaulieu* with her artillery...each smashing blow shaking her from truck to keelson, as if she had struck a reef!...before laying herself across the cog's broad stern, they had not known a moment's peace or comfort.

Handed over to the Cousins, whom she believed were true and to be trusted, Alicia had only just stepped out of her cabin in time to see them first hack down the two men standing on either side of the Master in a violent spray of blood, and then, even as she had stood there horrified, next watched Lucas Fabrizan slaughter Robert of Christchurch! One great, swingeing blow that had cleaved his head almost from his shoulders in a rushing, scarlet fountain of blood, making her scream out in absolute terror...only to be smashed unconscious to the deck; and the next moment swept up beneath Fabrizan's arm like a sack of a meal, while the *Pride* had lost all control, flinging her head up into the wind, sails and loose sheets banging and clattering in wild confusion.

That had been the moment the dromond had grappled with them, and a flood of corsairs had leapt on board. And despite all that their men could do to reach them, with Agnes screaming out, "*To me, Lions! To me!*" and kicking and struggling with all her strength, Bouncer leaping and savaging all he could sink his teeth into, and the dozens slain as their men had fought desperately to reach them...they had both been carried off. No match for the two renegade Frenchmen, Jules Lagrasse and Lucas Fabrizan who had held on to them so firmly, and dragged them on board moments before the dromond had swiftly been cut loose and rowed away towards the *Mary*, leaving themselves marooned on her deck surrounded by their enemies.

And, for Alicia, that had been the very worst moment of her life!

Held out across the Galley's rails, while El Nazir had been telling Gui she was destined to be the Baron's bride, her arms pinioned behind her back and shaken like a fine sapling in a storm, she had seen him looking at her. Horror stamped across his belovéd face, surrounded by those who cared for her most as they shouted and raged helplessly at their enemies. She had heard his anguished cries, shouting across to her with all his might, "I love you! *I love you!*...I will come for you! I *will* come for you!" And her final words as they had dragged her below, holding her arms out to him in desperation, and screaming, "Remember me! *Remember meeee!*"

At that moment she had felt as if her heart was breaking, and all the strength rushed out of her.

Then, mercifully, even as the rowers had dug in their blades to the first thud of the hortator's drum, her emotions had got the better of her at last, and she had collapsed in a small armoured heap onto the galley's deck and been swiftly carried away.

★

Hours later she awoke after an exhausted sleep, to find that she and Agnes had been stripped of their armour and cleansed, both now in long, soft, loose fitting gowns of white cotton, with wide sleeves embroidered with flowers in fine ivory thread, Agnes curled beside her, and both lying in a fine cabin at the rear of the ship below the sterncastle. The sea rushing past them, and the heavy clunk of the steerboards making the two brass oil lamps on their gimbals above her head twist and sway, filling the room with pale golden light and flickering shadows.

Here the ship's sides had been panelled with mellow pine, polished so that they shone in the soft lamp light, and on the decking was a huge, thick square rug, deep red with black patterns, fringed in the same colours. The bed was a box bed of dark wood, filled with a mattress of goose feathers covered with canvas and overlaid with soft Egyptian cotton sheeting, a host of plump silk and satin cushions in purple, blue and scarlet at its head and a cotton-stuffed coverlet, embroidered with great blue and purple fronds and flowers on which they were lying.

Struggling awake, her eyes still sore from weeping, Alicia looked at herself and at Agnes, but could remember nothing. Then, pushing herself up against the mass of cushions, she looked around her cabin.

At the foot of the bed was a long padded chest, and against the side, just beyond the door, was a bench seat with a finely polished table surrounded by hardwood fiddles before it, inlaid with coloured woods. On it, in deep wooden fretted holders, so they would not fall over, was a gilt-lined silver jug for wine and one for water, along with three red glass goblets set in chased silver.

Opposite, seated with calm elegance on a cushioned settle, was a tall, deeply tanned girl, looking steadily at her through huge, almond shaped green eyes with long curved lashes, whose beauty was enhanced by thick lines of kohl on her eyelids, and across which she was wearing a yashmak of palest blue silk, tied with fine ribbons behind her head, that also covered her hair. Of the very finest material, it could neither hide the rich, glossy, chestnut waves, now piled up and held in place with ivory pins, nor disguise the fine lines of her nose, and of her warmly curved mouth.

She wore a padded silk jacket, beautifully embroidered with flowers and small birds in iridescent colours, wide open at the front and cut short above her waist, with sleeves to her elbows, beneath which was a white chemise of finest silk, almost transparent, that covered her full breasts, richly crowned with proud nipples set in neat areolas and all touched with gold. The chemise too was short cut, leaving her slender waist bare, roped with a heavy gold chain studded with pearls, and over the swell of her hips and loins she wore long cotton pantaloons to match her jacket, with gold sandals of the softest leather on her feet, the tips curled up and held by the finest golden chains around each ankle.

Her arms were smooth and silky, along which she wore heavy bracelets of red and yellow gold twisted together, studded with turquoise, and her shapely hands had long, tapered fingers, nails tipped with gold paint. Quite simply she

53

was the most lovely and exotic creature that Alicia had ever set eyes on and momentarily she was too stunned to speak.

"Where are we? And-and who are you?" Alicia asked at last, almost in a whisper, giving Agnes a sharp shake.

"You are on the *Morning Star... 'Surah At-Tariq'*, and my name is...Sor-ay-a," the girl replied hesitantly in softly accented English. "Sor-ay-a Fermier." her voice rich and husky, full of the warm south of the Languedoc, of sunshine, red wine and olives, but which Alicia recognised immediately. "I have eighteen years...the same as you, My Lady Al-ic-ia," she said in her husky voice with the hint of a smile. I have served the Lady Rochine de Brocas for six years-and-and now I am yours," she hesitated prettily.

"You are from the Languedoc!" Alicia said suddenly.

"Yes, Lady Ali-c-ia," she replied softly with surprise, her voice trembling around the syllables. "How did you know?"

"Because of Queen Eleanor of England," Alicia answered tersely, running her fingers through her tousled hair. "King Richard's mother. The Languedoc was her home. She also speaks the language."

"Ah...Queen Eleanor of Aquitaine. You know this Queen?" Soraya asked, startled.

"Yes, of course! All who know Richard of England, know his mother," Alicia shot back at her. "And the King is my Guardian. How do you speak my language, and know my name? How is that?"

"Monsieur Le Bar-on, ordered me to learn it, My lady. He was in-sis-tent that I should do so," she shrugged elegantly. "So I did. He also was telling me your name. The Lady Rochine, his daughter, told it to me also. El Nazir himself told it to me as well."

Alicia smiled briefly at her fractured speaking, then seizing a cushion she violently threw it across the cabin. "Those *people!*" she, snarled, swinging her feet to the deck. "Those people, my girl, are murderers! They are my *enemies!*" she exclaimed again," hurling another cushion. "These are *all* my

54

enemies," she added waving her arms around her. Then she snapped: "Why are you here? Who are you?"

"...And-and-what will happen to us?" Agnes broke in, having pulled herself awake and sat up while Alicia had been talking.

"I am here to care for both of you. To see to your needs," Soraya said, collecting up the cushions and putting them beside her on the settle. "To help you...make sure you arrive before Monsieur Le Bar-on safely at Narbonne. And my name is Sor-ay-a...Sor-ay-a Fermier, as I you told"

"Narbonne!" Alicia said, blankly, slumping down on the edge of the bed. "*Narbonne?*"

"Yes. It is a Roman city, very old. The largest in the region, with a busy port. Much wine, much olive oil, many ships. Monsieur Le Bar-on's Château is near there, at Gruissan...you call it 'Grise'. Right beside the Circle Sea. Very beautiful...you will like it there. Both of you, I think?"

"Like it there, Soraya? *Like it there?*" Alicia growled, leaning forward, hands on knees. "Are you moon-mad girl? Do you think I am here because I want to be? *And who are you?*" she asked again, more sharply.

"I have been the handmaiden personal to the Lady Rochine de Brocas, as I said. Since fourteen, chosen *especially* by Monsieur Le Bar-on, and now I am...I am to be yours," she ended simply, with another elegant shrug

"*Mine?*" Alicia replied, astonished. "How do you mean, 'mine?'"

"I am your gift from Monsieur le Bar-on," the girl replied softly, holding out her arms towards her. "I am to care for you, dress you, chap-er-one you, Yes? Serve you in any way you order me to. Monsieur Le Ba-ron gave me to the Lady Rochine in my younger days, as I said. She has taught me many things in-in serving her," she added giving a sudden shudder. "And now she has been ordered to give me to you. A be-tro-thal gift. To...to show his love for you," she ended with a brilliant smile. "It is why I was ordered to learn your language. I am good at it, no? And he has sent me with this letter for you," she said, holding out a sealed parchment she drew from within her jacket. He has signed himself, see it is sealed with his special mark.

55

Alicia, astonished took it and broke the seal, green wax with a great boar's head stamped into it, and flicked it open, her eyes widening as she cast them across the page.

"*Bah!*" She snorted a moment later, seething with disgust, holding it in her hands as if it were poison. "He writes...'*You have imprisoned my heart. Impaled it with darts of Cupid's love, such that I cannot live without you by my side!*' Is he mad that he thinks I should actually believe such appalling rubbish? Oh... '*And for love of you I send you, as a belovéd gift, my daughter's servant, Mistress Soraya Fermier to care for you. Do with her as you will.*'...and so on and so on!" And scrunching it up between her hands she hurled it across the cabin, and stamped her feet in fury on the deck.

"His love for me?" She cried out loudly. "That man is a double dyed, black-hearted, murderous devil in human form, Mistress Soraya Fermier," she swore through gritted teeth.

"I am ward to King Richard of England and already betrothed...before God and with the King's blessing...to Sir Gui de Malwood!" she raged, jumping up. "Now seized from his side, and against my will, by this bloody pirate, El Nazir, and carted off to serve the *so* dear Bar-on's will," she added with withering sarcasm, "by a pair of disgusting French traitors, as if I were of no more value than a piece of common baggage! 'His love for me?...*Arrrrgh!*' And her whole body shuddered. "That man utterly disgusts me!" She raged, and stamped her foot on the cabin floor again making Soraya, and even Agnes, flinch away from her.

After a moment's silence, while Alicia paced around the room in fury like a caged tiger, Soraya asked quietly: "Jules Lagrasse and Lucas Fabrizan?"

"*Ha!*" Alicia snorted. "You know them?"

"Yes, of course. They have been in Monsieur Le Bar-on's pay at the Château for some years. They are not good men, I think."

"Not 'good men'? They are *dreadful* men, Soraya!" she shouted at her, turning to walk across the deck, swaying as she went. "And Lucas is worse than

56

Jules, if that were possible, with a mouth like a rotting sewer! I hope *never* to be near them again without a sword in my hand!"

"You need have no fear of that, My lady. El Nazir will make sure of it..."

"*El Nazir?*" Alicia rasped, her face filled with anger, as she turned towards Soraya, now calmly seated again. "How dare that man, seize us!" Alicia shouted, feet apart as the deck rolled beneath her. "How *dare* he! And as for that...that...*fiend* Roger de Brocas! I would rather *die* than be married to that...that murderous *butcher!*" she ended, spitting the words out in disgust.

Then, suddenly realising the implication behind the language issue, she whirled round at Soraya and demanded of her: "When did you begin your lessons in English, Soraya? When?"

"About a...a year ago, My Lady," she stammered distressed. "Why are you so cross with me?" she went on, tears in her eyes. "I have tried so hard. Please, please do not beat me. Do not hurt me. Please, I beg of you, I will be better, I will be!" And she buried her head in her hands and wept, her whole body shaking.

Seeing the girl's sudden distress and obvious terror, Alicia was aghast, and rushing to her immediately she put her arms round her. "Shh, shh. No-one's going to beat you, you foolish girl. I have never treated my servants so. Never, Soraya. Shout at them, maybe...but strike them? No! I am not cross with you. But I am *furious* with what that...that *Bastard* has done!" She exclaimed, springing up with renewed rage. "He must have planned all this months ago, Agnes," she shouted then, swinging round to face her friend. "He planned this whole bloody charade, from forcing Soraya to learn English, to arriving at Malwood, just so that that...that dyed in the wool *Bastard* could murder all those I most love in all the world and-and...*marry me!* Marry me? *Dear God, how I hate him!*" She shouted, stamping her feet to the beat of her rage: "Hate him! Hate him*! Hate him!*"

"Shh. Shh!" Soraya cried out urgently, hurrying across the room to where Alicia had now flung herself down again on the bed, Agnes' arms around her, her whole body trembling. "*Shh!* I beg you, My lady. I beg you, to be quiet...do not to be alarmed."

"Shh! Shh?" Alicia hissed at her fiercely. "Why should I 'Shh! *Shh!?* Why should I not be 'alarmed'?"

"Please, My Lady. Please!" Soraya begged her again, falling to her knees at Alicia's feet. "There is an armed guard outside this door, one of El Nazir's most trusted men. If he comes in here I will be in dreadful trouble. The Sheik has his orders too, My lady. I may be your gift from Monsieur Le Bar-on, but if I upset you, and that man has to come in here, then he will beat me and beat me. It will be terrible...not to mention what the Lady Rochine will do to me once I am met with her again!" and she visibly shuddered, the tears rolling down her face in sudden black streaks.

"Alright, Soraya. Alright! I am sorry. I did not mean to alarm you so. I will calm down...but I am so-so furious about what has been done to me, so terrified for my life and for Agnes, and feeling so-so helpless to do anything about it, let alone despairing, that shouting is my only release, apart from tears!"

"Soraya?" Agnes questioned her uncertainly. " Soraya. All this talk of you being a 'gift' for My Lady? I do not understand...are you not free to choose? To ask?" she added hesitantly. "To leave, if you want to? I mean...I have served My Lady, and Sir Gui's family, for years and years now, but I am still free to leave whenever I want to. I am not..."

"...Not a slave?" Soraya interrupted her softly, in her rich husky voice.

"Yes...I mean, No! Oh...I am confused."

"Well, Mistress Agnes," Soraya said, still kneeling on the fringed rug at her feet. "I am not a 'slave' as such; but I might just as well be one."

"Explain!" Alicia said, looking down at her, her face softening. "Soraya, bring that water here, and wash your face, and let us have some wine as well. A drink just now will do us all a power of good!"

58

Chapter 8... Soraya Fermier becomes a friend

Moments later, when the wine had been poured, and freely sampled, and Soraya had washed her face and was re-doing her eyes as best she could from a polished silver mirror in the mellow lamp light, she told them about herself.

"My father, Dumas Fermier, was born a Freeman on de Brocas' lands, My Lady Al-ic-ia. But also paying rent for some of them as well. He had also been a soldier in King Louis army, King Louis *Sept? VII?* And went with the King, and the army of the German Emperor, Conrad, on the Second Crusade..."

"But that was a disaster, Soraya," Alicia interrupted her. "I remember Sir Yvo, Gui's father, talking about it. They all set out with great armies from Germany and France, and wasted everything! Queen Eleanor went too, King Richard's mother. She was married to Louis then. They got as far as Damascus, and after a three day siege the Crusaders gave up and came home! Tens of thousands died. The whole thing was an absolute disgrace."

"That is right, My Lady. He was one of the few to survive, and return with gold in his pockets, and more wonderful stories than you can imagine. I adored him. He took over the vineyard from Grandpapa, and with his money he bought some of the very best land. And Papa was a good farmer...hence his name...*Fermier*...His vineyards were successful for many years. His wine was known, far and wide. But, suddenly something happened to the springs he used, and for two years the grapes did not do well and he fell on hard times. By then there were also many little ones at home to care for, and after a while he could not pay his dues. And...and then," she hesitated, looking suddenly haunted as if by some distant memory, "then...there were other things for which he needed money...much money, that I may not speak of. No! Please...do not press me. It is too shameful for me! No matter...at first Monsieur Le Baron was very understanding. Gave Papa more money and time to pay...but unknown to Papa, he added big interest on the payments every month making it impossible for him to clear his debts!"

"But that is Usury!" Alicia said shocked. "Forbidden by the Church. It has been considered a sin for many years. It is illegal and damnable. St Jerome declared it to be the same as murder!"

"Ah, that may be so, My Lady," she shrugged. "But my father would not know that, and he did not want to challenge Monsieur Le Bar-on. *Moi?* I might have done. But Papa? *Non!* He tried always to pay his proper dues."

"How do you know all that, Alicia?" Agnes asked, astonished. "About the Usury I mean?"

"Oh, Sir James told me, Agnes…my Guardian's Seneschal," she added, turning towards Soraya. "He runs all my, and my Fiancé's, lands. The Holy Father, Alexander III, also declared against Usury a few years ago, just before he died. The Church condemns it."

"The Church condemns it? Ha! Monsieur Le Bar-on is to the Church close, like this," she said bitterly, crooking her two forefingers together, tugging them as she did so. "The Archbishop of Narbonne is of his friends the dearest, I think. He gave the Lord Roger a special dis-pen-sation that allowed him to force Papa to sign papers giving me into his hands in exchange for the debts of Papa's, which he could never pay back. Faced with ruin, Papa signed me to bondage."

"No!" Agnes gasped, putting her hand to her mouth

"Mais Oui!… Mistress Agnes. Yes! It is not unknown in my country. By parting with me he thought the farm would be saved. But within months of Papa signing, Monsieur Le Bar-on demanded more payment. Papa could give nothing. So Monsieur Le Baron threw my Papa off his lands."

"All of them, Soraya? Agnes gasped.

"All of them!" she exclaimed bitterly…even those that he held as freehold, which were the very best of all, much of which Papa had bought and some had been *en famille* for generations. He took them as payment. Then, Monsieur Le Bar-on shared the lands with the Archbishop.

"*No!*" Alicia gasped.

"*Mais Oui!...*That is what it was all about, Yes? They took all of them, *tous les landes*, It was of the most, most badness, *trés térrible!* But of the very worst was that once Monsieur le Baron and the Archbishop had the lands...the water that Papa had so relied on all those years, and had disappeared? Yes? Well, it came back!"

"*No!*" Alicia gasped again. "Oh, Soraya...he had diverted the streams. How...how *méchant!* Wicked!"

"Yes, so it now seems. Though how he could do such a thing I do not know? But somehow the springs on Papa's land dried up. So when the vines needed so badly the water...there was none. Then, after Monsieur le Bar-on and the Archbishop had shared it all out...the springs, they flowed and bubbled again"

"Then they were in it together! What wickedness indeed! No!...not just wickedness, real evil! *Dear God, how I hate that man!*" she shouted suddenly, stamping her feet on the deck again in anger and frustration, while Soraya desperately tried to shush her.

Then a moment later she said quietly: "But Alexander...the Holy Father, Soraya... declared that anything taken by a Cleric through Usury must be paid back! Sir James told me that also. Oh, Soraya. If God shines on us, we will gain your freedom and may yet restore *all* your lands. Both those stolen by de Brocas, *Monsieur le Bar-on*," she ended, giving the girl a brilliant smile, "and those by the Archbishop!"

"But what of your family," Agnes asked, slipping her arm around Alicia's waist.

"Well, when all that happened the family was scattered completely," Soraya said very sadly, sitting back on her feet. "I had an elder brother...but..." and she hesitated, her huge eyes filling with tears.

"But?" Alicia prompted her. "What happened to your big brother, Soraya?"

61

The girl hesitated again then, and bowed her head briefly, and when she raised it again tears were just falling silently from her eyes: "I cannot talk of him, My Lady. He was the cause of much trouble. *Plus de malheureux!* Much of unhappiness, My Lady. *Plus! Plus!*" and she broke down then into a wild flood of tearful French: "*Non! Milady. Non! Je ne peux dit pas. La douleur de trop! De trop!*...'I cannot tell you. Too much pain! Too much!' Her sobs shaking her to her foundations. "Please do not make me. In very truth...I do not know where any of my brothers are now, nor my little sister, and a year later my poor Papa died. His heart it was broken.

"And your mother?" Agnes asked, quietly, deciding not to press her any further on her missing siblings. "What of your mother?"

For a few moments Soraya was silent, her thoughts as far away as her eyes, which seemed to stare into nothing then, while she murmured with tears in her eyes: "Ma belle Mère, ma plus belle Mère." Then with a great sigh she said: "It was Autumn time. I would have been about twelve then; two years before Lord Roger took me. Mama was in the forests around us collecting herbs and mushrooms. Monsieur Le Bar-on was hunting *sanglier*...the wild boar?" she explained to Agnes, who was about to ask. "All the mountains and forests around us are famous for the *sanglier*. Big and fierce," she said, using her hands to explain her words. "It was a hunting party, *trés grand*...very big, *plus des chevaux*...many horses, *plus des chiens*...many hounds. *Le Sanglier*...the boar, was a great one. Old, ferocious, male with long tushes. Upon my mother with her basket it came suddenly from the forest, and gored her: then, '*Taroo! Taroo! Taroo!*' the hunt rode right over her. She was very beautiful...*trés, trés belle*, my lovely Mama," she went on, tears now starting from her eyes. "I am like her, very much, people say. She was Persian, slender like me...

"*Persian?*" Alicia broke in amazed. "From beyond the Circle Sea. I had thought her to be from around Grise, or Narbonne, like your father?"

"*Mais non*! My Lady. Mama was from Persia. Far, far away. Papa rescued her from Damascus. She had been a slave to an Arab master killed in the fighting. Papa found her about to be raped by some German soldiers of Conrad's army. Killed them both and brought her back with him to France. He adored her, and she him also. I have her eyes, and her body; but she came back to us on that day most dreadful completely broken, you could not know her. Torn open by the boar and trampled by the hunt. It was terrible!...*Térrible!*' She said, clutching her breast, as her tears streamed down her face. "Me...I could not speak, and my poor Papa? He was of the heart most broken. Crushed. We both cried and cried. Never was he the same after she was killed. The life just seemed to go out of him. It was after her death that everything became of the very worst."

"Oh, Soraya," Alicia said with a deep sigh. "Such sadness...such trials. And now you are in bondage until all the dues are paid. Such bondage deals were made like that at home once, many years ago. Oh dear, you are in as sad a case as we," she added giving Agnes a cuddle. "And with your father dead there is no way those debts can ever be paid and the papers redeemed. Dear God, what an evil man he is. To all of us!"

"The Archbishop also, My lady," Soraya said, dropping her face. "I have shed many tears. Many. But what can I do? Except carry out my orders in the very best way I can, and hope, somehow that things will change. I am well housed, and dressed," she added, sweeping her hands across her body. "And it is not all bad. But how can I ever find a man to care for me? And love me, and have a family, when I am trapped like this?...And as for the Lady Rochine..." her voice trailed away and she just shook her head, tears starting from her eyes, making them glitter in the lamplight. "Sometimes she is a monster!"

"Truly I am sorry for you, Soraya," Alicia said gently, impulsively reaching her hands out to lift the girl's face, still meekly kneeling before her, and kiss her cheeks. "Of course we will do our best not to get you into any trouble. We are both in dreadful circumstances, Agnes and I...and you," she went on.

"We know nothing of what is expected of us, except what El Nazir shouted across at Gui. And that I will resist in every way I can. The Baron, God Blast his wicked soul, may think he has won, but there are many ways they say of skinning a cat, and this 'cat' is not yet ready to be skinned. Not for a while that's for certain! So come, Soraya, be friends with me...with us. Exchange the Kiss-of-Peace," she smiled warmly, pulling the lovely girl into her arms, "and we will do all we can to be good and cheerful partisans against the *so* kindly Baron's evil ways...and those of that scheming bitch, his daughter!

63

Chapter 9...Sheik El Nazir on board the Morning Star

Sheik El Nazir al-Jameel-Aziz-ibn Nidhaal's great cabin, that stretched almost the whole width of the dromond, was immediately above where the three girls were speaking, and was sumptuously appointed with thick Persian rugs both on the deck and hanging from the polished hardwood panels that lined the walls. There were a number of beautiful silver lamps on brass gimbals above him, and horn windows around the stern, beneath which was a long padded seat of green damask, with green and gold silk cushions embroidered with gold thread and great green and silver tassels on each corner.

Along either side were two beautiful, long chests in polished oak and cedar, together with a number of strong X-shaped chairs inlaid with ivory, with backs of scarlet leather and padded scarlet seating. There was also a large, octagonal walnut table inlaid with rosewood and ivory, its fiddles of polished cedar, the underside adorned with the most delicate fretwork.

It was here that El Nazir was seated, pen in hand, on a tall backed armed chair to match the table, a beautiful porcelain bowl of honeyed almonds by his hand, and his galley commander, Raschid el Din standing relaxed before him.

"I thought that all went well, My Lord, considering," Raschid said, taking off his helmet, before bowing briefly, his hand touching his forehead. "Exactly where the Baron said they would be, and his two lads on board couldn't have performed better."

"Yes! But it was clever of their leader to switch ships," El Nazir replied, his voice rich and dark, with a hint of gravel, beckoning him to a chair as he spoke. "Fooled that idiot son of mine, Siraj: cost him his life and his command."

"Those two, Jules and Lucas, used their heads well. That green silk was an unmistakeable marker. The rest was easy. They slaughtered the ship master and his guards and whisked both those girls away in a moment, for which they

64

should be well rewarded. The infidels stood no chance. I thought all our lads did really well."

"But at some cost, my friend," the Sheik replied tersely, tapping his teeth with the stripped quill. "As you said, 'considering'! Those bastard Sons of the Devil fought like all the fiends from Tartarus. How do the Franks do it?" he queried, amazed, pushing the bowl of almonds towards his tall commander. "Two galleys destroyed, and nearly a hundred fighting men slain...not to mention the rowers! And by just a handful... and all for one girl!"

"And her companion!"

"*Shaitan* take the damned companion, Raschid! I hope Lord Roger knows what he is doing? For this morning's little escapade is going to cost him plenty. Where are those two bitches now?" he ended, licking his fingers.

"Below with the girl, Soraya. The one brought on board by the Lady Rochine before we set out from Bayonne."

El Nazir, stood up and moved to sit beneath the stern windows, taking the bowl of almonds with him, rubbing his forehead where his turban had left a mark, his commander moving to sit in his tall backed chair. "That woman is full of more wiles than a Djinn, and can burn just as fiercely. I hear tales of her that make even my hair stand on end."

"Mmmm, you are right, My Lord," Raschid replied. "'The fire of a scorching wind' according to the *Surat al-Djinn* in the Koran. I have seen her both ways. Calm and dovelike, when she can almost coo with sweetness...and moments later a raging fury that would consume anything it touched. But she was most insistent about the care to be given to those two infidel bitches...who fought like cornered leopards I may add. Those two Frenchmen were scratched and bitten all over." And he popped an almond into his mouth with a smile.

"No matter, Raschid. We got the Baron's message before we left Bayonne, and now we have them safe, and will be back there in a few days. Next, you must get our temporary expert to send a pigeon off to Gaston de Vere at first light. He will urgently be waiting for it, but please, Raschid, make sure he chooses the right cage. No good sending a bloody bird to Lord Roger's man in Nantes!"

"This business with pigeons, My Lord? Seems…well madness. Why trust so vital a message to a witless bird."

"Oh, my loyal, hard hitting friend. These are no ordinary birds, I assure you. These come from a long line of racers and are bred for their speed and courage. People have been doing this for ages. Started in India centuries ago, and the Romans used them as well. They can cover five hundred miles in a day…without stopping! Their only enemies are hawks and stooping falcons…oh and ignorant peasants with bows and arrows! We have been using them in the Holy Land for years against the Christians who only see a pigeon as food, truly they are ignorant fools! Each bird takes a great deal of training but once trained the really good ones are worth their weight in gold. Each one of those on board is worth a small ransom. So, Raschid, go carefully, yes?"

"Yes, O Mighty One!" He mocked gently, touching his forehead. "I had no idea they were so special, we have not done this before. And why at first light and not straightaway? ."

"No, my friend, and neither have most foolish Christians! Lord Roger being an exception…and he learned from the Emirs amongst whom he and his daughter trade. And first light? It is something to do with the sun. I don't know. It is just what I was told by the expert who came on board with the Lady. *Allah Be Praised!* Who would have thought those stupid barbarians would not have thought of this message system for themselves? Truly they are mad!"

"It seems a great system. We could do with something like that ourselves, both to warn us of trouble and advise us of good chances."

"Mmm. That is a worthy thought, Raschid. Perhaps we can find an expert of our own to work with us. Train some of our men?

"I will speak with the man, Almahdi. He has come from the Emir of Damascus no less. He is bound to know someone, if you are serious. But what about the Lady Alicia de Burley, My Lord? Will there be trouble from her King?"

"From Richard of England or Phillip of France? Take your pick, my friend. They are all infidels whom the Prophet, *Allah Bless His Name*, will curse from Paradise so we can destroy them once and for all, as Saladin did at the Horns of Hattin! They are of no consequence to me. I do not give a fig for either of them, not even the one known as 'The Lion Heart'. Saladin dished up King Guy and the entire crusader army at Hattin. He will do the same for this King Richard and that weak fool, Phillip of France. None can stand against him. Trust me! *Allah Akbar!*...God is Great!"

"And her young man?"

"A strutting, dung heap cockerel! Let him crow his heart out. In *Allah's Name*, what can he do?"

"He sank two of our ships today and killed many of our men. Without him, that skirmish would have been easy."

"*Pish!*" El Nazir exclaimed dismissively, with a wave of his hand. "By this time that wretched scarlet ship of his will have sunk. Did you see what our artillery did to it? Huge chunks of timber everywhere, and a hole in her side you could drive a camel train through! And the yellow one likewise. Fahwaz and his crews did a great job, and will be well rewarded when we get to Bayonne. No, Raschid. They were sinking when we pulled away. They will surely all be fish food by now."

"And if not, My Lord?"

"*Sweet Allah*, my friend. What ails you? He is no better than any other metal clad madman who comes out here waving a sword. Even if he managed to survive, do you seriously see him assaulting Château Grise with that rabble at his back? The good Baron would make mincemeat of him. And anyway, even if did make it that far, we will be long gone and he has no way of following us. No fat cog would ever be a match for the *Morning Star...Surah At-Tariq...*No, Raschid. I have no fear of such a one as he."

"So…to Bayonne."

"To Bayonne, indeed. And then round Spain and back to the Circle Sea. Lord Roger has paid me mightily to cage his precious pouting 'pigeon' for him…did you see her breasts? Like silver moons. No wonder that bastard lusts after her! And it will cost him even more for me to replace those two lost galleys. All we have to do now is to deliver that infidel bitch, and her companion, in one piece to the *so* kind and caring Lady Rochine, and that sly bastard, de Vere. Collect our money and get back to the war, and some decent trading. *Insha'Allah!…*God Willing" And he touched his forehead with his fingers.

"Will you entertain them here, My Lord?"

"Who?"

"The girls below us. We were specially asked to take 'Royal' care of them."

"What? In my cabin, along with that…that painted Jezebel whom The Lady has placed here to watch over them? Are you mad, Raschid! Just listen to them," he said, cocking his head to where they could both hear sharply raised voices. "Shouting viragos, dressed as men! Did you ever see anything more ghastly, or dishonourable? By God, Raschid," he went on, as the shouting below suddenly increased. "If that stupid French bitch doesn't quell them I'll have that great Syrian bastard, Abdul Aziz, whom you have placed outside their door, drag her up here and flog the back off her!"

"That would not please The Lady, I think, My Lord."

"No…but it might please me!" he snarled. "Take 'Royal' care of them indeed! That woman takes too much upon herself. I owe her *nothing*, Raschid. I have risked the *Morning Star*, my '*Surah At-Tariq*' in these dangerous waters because I owed her father a huge favour, and for the money, which is truly considerable! Not because I am beholden to that raven-haired witch. And anyway, they *are* being 'Royally' cared for: finest clothes, lovely cabin and people to wait on them almost hand and foot."

"So, Lord. No pretty dining companions."

"I will not sully my soul with even the *sight* of them until I have to. The one dressed like a Houri may be enough to enflame any man, but she is just another infidel with no shame. God alone knows why the Lady Rochine has dressed her so? To tempt all of us I suppose? But at least the girl is clean. The others stink! Why do these western infidels not wash themselves? Can you imagine sleeping with one of them? Breath like a wet fart and stinking of stale sweat and sewage. Disgusting!" And both men laughed.

"They think washing too often is bad for their health," His Galley Commander said, standing up. "Some only wash three times in their lives, I am told: once when they are born, once when they marry and once when they die!"

"*Sweet Allah!* They are all mad. No wonder so many die in the Holy Land."

"So, Lord. What do you want me to do with them?"

"They can eat in their cabin. Abdul guards their door; Najid can cook for them and bring them their food; that fool, Zafir, can remove the slop bucket, it's about all he's good for, and the infidel bitch, Soraya, can serve them."

"Fine, My Lord. But they cannot stay below the whole time. That would not be good."

"No…we need to keep them healthy I suppose," he paused then to eat some more honeyed almonds. "They can come on deck before dawn and at sunset, and properly covered! That way their presence will not enflame the men, and they can use the facilities in the bows at the same time. Otherwise they can have a bucket in their cabin. The *Morning Star* is a fighting ship, Raschid, not a fat, lazy, passenger-carrying merchant.

Now, my friend, get off and speak with Almahdi about pigeons and tomorrow's release, we'll be losing him at Bayonne to return to Grise, and then come back here and dine with me. In the meantime tell that lazy bastard, Yussuf, to bring me some coffee before I see his backbone. *Allah Akbar!*...God is Great!"

Chapter 10...The Lord Baron awaits his messages in the Château Grise

Away in Grise, in his fine suite of apartments at the top of the great Donjon, known to all as the '*Tour Barberousse*', the Redbeard tower, because of the colour he'd had the plaster painted that covered it, the Lord Baron Sir Roger de Brocas of Narbonne and Gruissan waited to hear how well his scheme for seizing Alicia de Burley had worked, and whether Sir Gui had been slain along with his whole command as he had planned for.

Seated at the great table in his solar, drenched in sunshine, his crystal on its beautiful cedar stand before him in all its pure beauty, he waited for the news to come in, a full silver goblet of the finest Bordeaux to his hand, alongside a silver dish of delicate sweetmeats.

That they had all set out, he knew. For with Rochine still with him, his crystal had told him so: the ring he had given Gui the night of the fire, and the bracelet Rochine had given to Alicia, making perfect conduits for his mind. And he knew also that the message sent to El Nazir by those two men whom he had placed in Castle Malwood after Alicia's escape, the young man from Oxford and the older man, Henri Duchesne whom he'd sent out there, had arrived safely because his pigeon relays told him so.

He chuckled at the memory.

Those simple fools thought they had escaped his vengeance! *Bah!* He would show them what the Lord of Narbonne and Gruissan could do when he put his mind to it. He was better than *all* of them. Better than the Lord of Toulouse under whom he held Narbonne, better than that fool, Phillip Valois, King of France, and his ridiculous crusade. Better than anyone!

The pigeons had been a brilliant decision. And so easy once you knew how to do it…and they flew swifter than any rouncey could manage, no matter how fast its four hoofs could carry it. A true racer could fly fifty miles in an hour, in as straight a line as possible, and cover five hundred miles in a day without stopping. Wonderful! And all his idea…gained from talking with the Emirs that he traded with across the Circle Sea, who had been using pigeons for carrying messages for generations.

But…you needed experts to do it, and they were not easy to find, because mostly they were Muslims. Somehow the crusaders had largely failed to latch on to the idea, even though they had been in the Holy land for years; most considering the whole idea to be too far fetched for words. Just one more wild tale from the East. Just the sort of stupid thing a bastard infidel would think up to trick an honest Christian! You *ate* pigeons…not used them for messages! Every castle worth its salt had a pigeon loft, but not for any other purpose than to provide food when a change of diet was wanted…and their shit for manure! *Pigeons carrying messages?* What madness!

He threw back his head and laughed, his harsh voice echoing round his room. What fools some people were.

From home to Narbonne, twelve miles by road, less than half an hour's flying; and to Bordeaux, two hundred and forty miles by road, *days* on horse back, but by pigeon, without the delays and all the twists and turns, only a few hours! He could know which ships were going where almost as quickly as their captains did, and plan accordingly. Or to where troops were being sent, or…where an ambush could be set up! And once a bird had been properly trained it would fly to its particular loft from wherever it was released…even from a ship at sea provided it was not too far from land.

And he never overtaxed his birds. While knowing they could fly great distances, he preferred them doing shorter hops when there was less danger of their getting lost, or of stopping, when he might never get them back. Not always of course, but often, so he had set up relays. Town to town and port to port, and where they might be flying over hawk infested forests more than one bird would be released. And God help any peasant who shot one down, or any petty lordling whose falcon might stoop on one of them for sport!

After his family had been kicked off their lands around Toulouse and Lyons, following his father, Lord Thibault's, hopeless rebellion against King Henry of England, in which he had been slain, they had been almost banished to Grise.

71

He growled at that, and drank deeply from the goblet, still full of rage and injustice.

Picking up the dish of sweetmeat beside him, swiftly rising as he did so, he walked across the room to the nearest window and looked across the wide bailey at the great pigeon loft he'd had built inside one of the corner towers. There, around the walls inside it, were a myriad square spaces for the birds to nest in, and wooden galleries so that his Pigeon Masters could care for them in every way possible.

Even as he watched, there was a great wheeling swirl of them now, white, grey and mottled black and white, sweeping and twisting around the far side of the castle. And he lifted his goblet as he watched them, swooping and tumbling, flashing out around the towers and battlements and then winging away across the wide étang in great circles and back again. So harmless to look at…so deadly in effect, and he smiled and grunted in quiet satisfaction, loving the rushing *swoosh* of their wings when they whistled close past him overhead.

Those pigeons had been his salvation. He had brought experts back from Syria and the Lebanon, and they had shared their knowledge with those he had carefully chosen as Pigeon Masters. He'd paid out handfuls of silver for the birds themselves, and then he had set up a series of lofts in those towns with which he most wanted to trade along the coast and inland, and, of course, in various ports along the shores of the Holy Land.

And the money had rolled in.

He was always a jump ahead of other traders, and as long as one was not too particular with whom you traded and what that trade was…then there was money to be made. And by fair means as well as foul he had built up his vineyards and bought, or acquired, olive groves as well: setting up presses for both, so his wine and oil was shipped everywhere and he was now able to indulge himself in every sort of joy that came to mind.

He smiled, thinking of Rochine and the deep sensuous pleasure she gave him, and the power she brought to the great crystal he had left on its delicate carved stand, and he pressed his hand into his loins, wanting her. Then he thought of Alicia, and the pleasure that possessing, and schooling her, would give him, for she would be no easy catch and Rochine might well resent her... and he felt the blood rush through him in a sudden burst of fierce excitement.

He drank again, and bit another sweetmeat, while he looked out beyond the Château and its defences, beyond the town that huddled all around its walls, across the étang that almost surrounded Grise, to the wide, blue, shimmering expanses of the Circle Sea, the beautiful Mediterranean.

No...it was not just because she was such a challenge, that he wanted the English girl, nor because of her beauty, which was ravishing, nor even the children he knew would spring from her womb...but because it was *her* father, Sir Henry de Burley, who had slain his father, the Lord Thibault de Brocas at Cahors all those years ago, and before his very eyes! And then always there was the Crystal!

And it had been Sir Yvo, *Gui's* father, who had fought his father first. Like Tigers they had been until Sir Yvo had fallen. Then, just as his father had stepped up to kill his hated enemy, Sir Henry had attacked him. If he closed his eyes he could see the blows slamming home and hear his father's desperate cry of shock and horror, see his head fly from his body and still feel his hot blood falling all over his face. Possessing Alicia would wipe that particular slate clean, not least because they were the very last of their lines. With Gui dead she would inherit everything, and by marrying her he would get all the Malwood and Burley lands together...and in so doing avenge his father's death.

He ground his teeth with barely suppressed rage.

Well, Sir Yvo and that fucking bitch to whom he had been married were both dead. He had seen to that...and Gui, too, should have been killed...burned to death in the fire he started. He must have a powerful angel indeed to watch over him, he seethed. He had left him with an arrow piercing his shoulder, pinned by a great timber, and almost surrounded by flames...and the Malwood Emerald about to be completely destroyed for ever! How he had got out he still didn't know? But he and Rochine had taken the girl with them anyway, drugged her and ridden off into the night, while castle Malwood had gone up in flames.

He stalked back to the table and banged his fists on it in rage. But the bloody girl had somehow slipped Rochine and escaped them...and he, The Lord Baron Sir Roger de Brocas, had been forced to flee the Old Conqueror's great Forest and take to his ship without her.

And he needed her!

The fact that she was already betrothed, with King Richard's agreement and with God's Blessing was of no importance. He had Archbishop Berenguer of Narbonne in his pocket. There was no way that old pederast and whoremonger would dare to deny him. He would have the good Archbishop dissolve that bitch's betrothal, and then he would get him to marry them out of hand.

As for King Richard, the so called 'Lion heart'...he surely would not make any kind of fuss about one stupid girl and her affairs at this time, no matter how fond of her he might be. No! High politics would take preference! Richard was far too wrapped up in the total madness of his crusade, for which he desperately needed the King of France by his side. And he, de Brocas, had paid Phillip plenty for him *not* to be beside him at Vézalez when he and Richard had set out. And anyway Phillip was also as involved with John's plan for Richard's murder by the Assassins as he was himself! And who had arranged the money to change hands? *He had!* King Philip Valois of France owed him...and one foolish girl was a small price to pay!

He snorted with derision.

Quite apart from revenge for past misdeeds, he needed the girl for a wife! That would give him *all* their combined lands, and with Richard killed and John on the throne, with Phillip's help of course, and the French army under his own leadership, he would be the most powerful man in the Kingdom, next to John: and with John being the kind of useless little *shit* he truly was, then he could be guaranteed to wreck everything; leaving him, Lord Roger de Brocas, free to seize the crown of England for himself!

He grinned then, hugely, and sat down again in front of the great glass orb that was the real seat of his power, and placing his large hands on both sides of it he looked into its crystal depths, wishing Rochine was near him, beneath him, above him, to make the damned thing work!

He gritted his teeth. Alicia-Rochine! Rochine-Alicia! Damn it. He wanted them both! But he needed the girl, first! And that fucking bastard, Sir Gui de Malwood, dead, second! Mother of God! *Where was that bloody message?*

He looked across his room at the sun now slipping down the heavens, the light changing from harsh to soft gold tinged with pink, and sighed. He would have to wait for the morrow now. Almahdi would not make a release until sunrise, then he would fly off the bird to Bayonne first, and from there the message would be relayed to Narbonne and so to the great loft in the far corner tower.

Then he would know! Rochine had left several days ago for Bayonne with de Vere and a strong escort, and without her he could not work the Crystal. He writhed his loins at the thought of her, the blood rushing through him again. He knew he wanted her. But he also wanted Alicia.

Because, above all, he needed an heir!

Someone to carry on his bloodline, something Rochine could never do, even if she had wanted to. What they were to each other was forbidden enough anyway. But a child of such a union? Impossible. Even for him. No! Any child of his had to be born in wedlock and out of a known and accepted Lady of virtue and honour. And Alicia de Burley, from one of the oldest families in England, was the perfect chalice for his seed. And with her connections to his family...she was of the blood! Her grandmother was his grandfather's sister! And the Crystal worked through the blood...he knew that now, so with her...anything was possible!

With Gui and King Richard dead, John on the throne and himself in control of the royal army...she would have no-one else to turn to but him, and he would have the heir he so desperately needed.

He grunted again, with satisfaction. This time it would work, he *knew* it!

In the meantime, he would prepare a message for his people in Bordeaux, and in Nantes, just in case that fucking bastard, de Malwood, survived El Nazir and his *Morning Star*. Either way there were excellent places for an ambush between Nantes and Bordeaux. That was the longest, wildest stretch of their journey…over two hundred miles. Of course, it would need to be carefully arranged, and the troops chosen must be proven fighters and led by men who knew what they were doing. There was now a loft at Nantes; just set up, true, but the men there were keen. De Vere had chosen them himself, and he had arranged for them to be placed in The Duke of Brittany's castle. Port Enforcers in the Count's colours…Alan de Courcy and Victor Jonelle. It was just a pity that the Cousins were on the *Morning Star,* this would have been perfect for their skills. No matter. De Courcy was a Knight and Jonelle his right hand man. Both had fought in numerous skirmishes and escalades together and would know exactly whom to engage to join them. He would send a message out first thing in the morning, and alert them, and Bernard de Vernaille in Bordeaux, whether he had heard from de Vere by then or not.

If that bastard had drowned off Belle Île, with his whole command, so much the better. But if, by some miracle, he had survived…then de Courcy and his men, with de Vernaille's help, would sort them out once and for all. Either way he would be shot of him, of that he was certain.

He chuckled then, thinking of the great Emerald ring that the wretched bastard still wore. What an irony! That it should have survived the fire, where it should have been destroyed…only to trap its wearer even more perfectly than he had even planned for; for once Rochine was back with him at the Château, they would then know his every move. And he chuckled again, not least because he still had his greatest plan yet to look forward to. No fox was ever more cunning! And with that certain smile on his face that all men knew meant trouble for someone, the Lord Baron Sir Roger de Brocas, Lord of Narbonne and Gruissan tipped the last of his wine down his throat and threw back his head and laughed. Then rising he went out of his room to find his Pigeon Master, Raheel al Moukhtara, from the Lebanon, the founder of his feathered fortunes, and arrange with him two urgent releases for the next morning.

This time there would be no mistake!

Chapter 11...Sir Gui leaves Nantes for Bordeaux.

Two days later, in the grey, half light of the morning, cool before the sun had risen, Sir Gui de Malwood and his command left Nantes while the mists were still on the river, writhing like thin smoke and hanging over the fields and around the trees, everything fresh and touched with magic.

A long line of armoured men in two lines, Gui and Sir Richard in front, Father Matthew behind them and then their squires followed by all their own men, all else following: sumpters with their panniers re-packed, some half dozen more than before, and three big tilt carts rather than waggons, two horses to each cart, and with large spoked wheels making them lighter and faster on the road, the girls' mares on long leading reins trotting at their trail. And behind them rode Allan-i-the Wood on Caesar, de Beaune beside him, followed by all their men, and Bouncer running free. With four scouts ahead and four following behind the last man, each alert to any possible danger, and each regularly replaced with another from the main column, so no-one would lose interest or get bored and careless, they were a formidable force, and Gui was immensely proud of them.

★

Days of furious activity had followed their arrival.

The Angel, as promised by Thomas Blackwood, the *Mary's* enormous Shipmaster, had proven to be a friendly hostelry indeed: a long two story building, with a large hall and a staircase along one long wall that led to a handful of rooms above. Each with simple pallet bed and mattress of a bag of hay in canvas wrapped round with coarse linen sheeting, a sheeted bolster and a plain stuffed linen coverlet of blue serge: a covered slop bucket in one corner, jug of water and basin on a wooden stand in another and a shuttered window.

Downstairs, tall wooden posts held up the floor above on wide crutches, with pine tables scattered about, some separated from others by simple wooden partitions, like booths, with benches and plenty of stools to sit on, and even a handful of carved straight back chairs with greasy cushions. Candles of local beeswax from the Abbey hives, and a number of simple oil lamps lit the room casting strange flickering shadows, and there was a wide, empty fireplace along the middle of one side of the building.

The whole presided over by a tall stooped Aubergist, Charles du Vin, scarred from the wars, helped by a handful of busy serving men and cheerful, wide-eyed tavern girls in blue cotehardies over white kirtles.

Tommy Blackwood had been right. It was a good place to be!

With du Vin's help Gui had found good stabling for their destriers and for Sunburst and Gillygate off the *Mary* and for Caesar and the sumpters off the *Pride*; reputable shipwrights and chandlers for Thomas, and an excellent farrier who would sort out all their metal problems. And Sir Richard had found a great wharf nearby where the stores from both ships could be kept safe and guarded, and the men could bed down the following night. It had been a brilliant start.

After a great time out together that first night with Tommy Blackwood and the crews of both cogs...when they had packed the Angel to the rafters, eating the thick meat pottage for which the place was well known, with cheese, olives and fresh bread, and drinking toast after toast in wine and cider, famous throughout Brittany...they had parted company at last. The following morning both ships were to be warped down river; wholly emptied and repaired, then keeled over so their fat bottoms could be scraped of all weeds and barnacles, and re-sheathed with tar, pitch and brimstone. There would be no time then for farewells.

So it had been their last night all together...and it had been memorable: John Fitzurse, Gui's huge Master-at-Arms and Tommy Blackwood, their great rolling bear of a shipmaster, having a rowdy drinking match, with both sides roaring on their chosen champions, but which neither won, much to the assembled gamblers' raucous disgust! It was as well that Gui had spoken with Thomas earlier and secured his willingness to risk the long, dangerous sail around Spain and meet with them again at Grise. God Willing, in a month's time, their repairs would be done and they would be free to journey on from there to Messina and join King Richard's army which by then should safely be there.

"Can you do this, Thomas?" Gui had asked him before the drinking had started. "Will you? It is a long way to go and will be dangerous, and you'll not have us with you round Spain if things get difficult: but I will pay you well."

"*God's Bones, My Lord!*" The big man had roared out giving Gui, large as he was, such a buffet he almost fell over. "I thought you were *never* going to ask! My lads would not miss such an adventure for the world. And with good cargo space now you idle buggers have cleared my ship, and after we are seaworthy again, we'll breeze down to Bordeaux, pick up a good load of whatever's going, and sail round to Narbonne. It is a famous port. We can unload there, at the deep water port, below the canal they call La Robine...we are too deep laden to go right up into Narbonne...and just sit tight and wait for you to finds us!"

"Have you been there before, Thomas?"

""Yes, Lord. Many times on your father's business. Wine here and there, olive oil elsewhere. You father had many interests, Sir Gui."

"So I keep finding out, Thomas. I am sure Sir James would have told me all...but we left in such a harum-scarum manner he never had the chance. Tell me Thomas..." he asked earnestly. "Is there anywhere near Narbonne we could lie up? Someone you could recommend who might help us?"

For a moment, the huge man looked blank, and Gui's heart dropped. Then with a vast smile he turned and smote him on the back with a great roar of laughter that almost sent him flying.

"By all the saints, My Lord, there *is* such a place!" He boomed, with another great shout of laughter. "I am just amazed not to have thought to say so before. One really good place, and a really good man who runs it too. A man I would trust my life to. Armand Chulot at *The Golden Cockerel* at Les Monges. It is a small hamlet about six miles out of Narbonne; noted for its food and its comfort. His wife, Claudine, sees to all that and rules her large husband with a rod of iron. And Armand is a big man, Sir Gui. He and I could be brothers. Get there and he will see you right. He has no love for the Baron, anymore than you do. My word on it!"

"Thomas…You're a Saint! Thank you, for that and we will look for you, and *The Pride,* in a month's time…about the turn of August I expect"

"*Ho!* A Saint am I?" and he threw back his head with a great shout of laughter. "I don't think even my dear mother would have thought that!" and he laughed again hugely. "My Lord, I'll not let you down! My lads and I will be there, I wouldn't want to miss such an adventure with you for a whole hogshead of Burgundy! You're as fine a man as ever your father was, My Lord. I would be proud to, and that's no error!" And reaching out his hand he clasped Gui's in a hard, dry grip.

"And there's my hand on it! Now, my Lord, I'm off to drink that soft-skinned, feeble bastard of a Master-at-Arms under the table. God be with you Sir Gui, for we must be warped from here tomorrow, so I'll not see you again. But my thoughts and prayers will be with you. Just you get that beauty of yours back, and sort out that fucking bastard who's got her. Look for me in August. I'll not let you down!" And with a last solid buffet, he had rolled away with a final great shout of defiance to join Fitzurse and all their supporters.

★

And now, even before cockcrow, they were leaving.

Crossing the wide river on the old cable ferry in the writhing mist, just busy grey shadows with the water sliding by, tall rushes at the edges full of pink and white Milkweed, brown water voles scurrying amongst them; the splash of a fish, the flash of an otter, the ripples spreading outwards, long tail disappearing, the water there deep and clear. The crake of a moorhen, busy amongst the tall rushes, the quack and flurry of wings as a duck sat up in the water, startled by the sudden appearance of the old ferry in the strange misty light of the morning…then rushing silence and the heavy, damp smell of fresh water as they hauled their way across.

The ferry's cable, cold and slimy, the old boat of long planks and dark timbers, with stout rails on either side, was wide and slow, the water running everywhere off their hands and arms, as backwards and forwards they went until all were across, dashing the ferryman a handful of silver for his pains, although they had no need to do so.

And then away towards Vertou and distant Bordeaux. Walk, trot, canter. Walk, trot, canter, the military way of travel. Tilt carts, horses and men, swallowed up by the early morning river mists, just turning from grey to opaque white and softest pink, then golden as the sun finally lifted up behind them to herald the new born day with re-newed warmth and colour.

Chapter 12...How many plans were laid at the Angel.

So...all the next day and the day following had been filled with unrelenting activity, from paying courtesy visits to the Castle, and the absent Count's Seneschal under de Courcy's bitter glare, impotent to do Sir Gui any scathe; to Abbot Hugo Gravier at the great Benedictine Abbey at Vertou, just beyond the town...a thin, ascetic man, with a high cheek bones and piercing grey eyes that missed nothing...together with Father Matthew, to plead their cause, and to the Chef du Port, still shivering in his boots at sight of him, for his continued assistance with Thomas Blackwood and his damaged ships. It had been one thing after another.

Fresh Horses had been bought and bargained for, and fresh stores found to replace those lost in the attack; armour had been checked and dents hammered out, horseshoes looked over and replacements for Beau and Merlin created by the farrier recommended by du Vin. And everywhere they went they found people friendly and willing to assist them, as much because of the silver they had to spend as the sharp manner in which de Courcy and the Chef du Port had been so firmly dealt with, and their defeat of the corsairs that frightful morning.

A whole day of fierce bargaining had secured the horses, with the help of the good Abbot Hugo of Vertou with his own expert knowledge of sound horse flesh, his sharp eyes and no-nonsense reputation, no-one wanting to fall foul of Holy Church! But it was the Abbey itself that had provided them with the three big tilt carts and the bags of meal, oats and huge nets of hay with which to fill them, and earthenware pots of honey, wonderful fat candles from their bees and three kegs of cider for which the area was famous.

As Abbot Hugo had said to Father Matthew when he moved to thank him, both men in their long black robes, "Those carts are of little value to me, Matthew, compared to where you are going. Bring me back a Holy Relict from Jerusalem as just repayment and take it off your mind. When I next write to the Holy Father, I shall tell him of your need, and our loss, and I am sure his treasury will replace them twofold!" And they had chuckled at the Abbot's scheme.

And as for the men?...They had rollicked and strutted round the town like the bold cockerels they were, a girl under every arm, jolly bully boys out for a good time. Their pockets full of silver and their hearts full of desire, and none of them hung onto their money for long as Sir Richard had forecast. They either drank it, ate it, gambled it or cheerfully lusted it away, leaving the girls and the merchants of Nantes better off, their carpenters with plenty to do, and themselves with thick or broken heads and empty purses!

Sir Richard had his two nights between clean cotton sheets; de Beaune his hot meal and a pretty girl; Allan spent time with his verderers, and Gui, Richard and Father Matthew gained a breathing space to talk over the next stage of their journey.

Then, on their last night, Gui called all his commanders together in The Angel.

On that night the place was heaving, the Aubergist and his serving hands dispensing leather jacks of local wine and cider as fast as they could go...as well as trays of local cheese and olives, fresh bread and smoked meats, or rough glazed bowls of pottage, thick with herbs and onions and flavoured with garlic.

Gui and his men sat in a far corner in deep shadow, their table, like some others, shielded with high wooden partitions. With knives and spoons beside them, their table softly lit with small oil lamps, they waited to enjoy the wine, pottage, cheese and cider that had been brought to them and placed around a large wooden platter of fresh baked bread. Around them the room was packed and filled with loud noise and bustle: shouts for wine or food, along with cheerful shrieks and bursts of raucous laughter.

"So..." Gui said, wiping his mouth with the back of his hand, as he looked at them all. "We leave tomorrow at first light, before the sun is up. Is everything done?"

"Yes, My Lord," Fitzurse replied, putting his spoon down. "Panniers packed and ready to load; carts checked over, we had to replace a cracked axle, harnesses too; and loaded with stores from the Abbey, smoked meats from the town, some barrels of wine and the cider from the Abbot, oil for cooking and freshly filled water bags. They also gave us some spare hides for repairs. You did fine work with that Abbot, Father; saved us time and money, loads of it!"

"Abbot Hugo has been very good to us, that's for certain," Father Matthew replied. "For all that Vertou is a brother House, sight of the Holy Father's letters also helped hugely. And he *does* know a good horse when he sees one! With his sharp eyes around the horse market," he smiled broadly, "no one dared to try and over-charge us. We are almost as well provided now as when we set out from Malwood."

"Just a shame we had to ditch so much of our armour and spare weaponry, My Lord," Fitzurse said ruefully. "Where we are going I think we could do with them. Thank God, we hung onto our clothyard shafts. Arrows for longbows cannot be bought in Brittany, that's for certain!"

"Oh...I wouldn't worry too much about that, Master-at-Arms," Sir Richard said lazily. "If the past few days are anything to go by, we're likely to pick up all we need along the way!" and there was a ripple of laughter around the table.

Then turning to Gui and pointing to Allan-i-the-Wood, he added in his laconic fashion. "Talking of which, this lad's been a tower of strength, Gui. Got that young farrier who made those shoes for Beau and Merlin to knock up a great pile of spare arrow heads, both shaped bodkins and broad heads. He and his assistant have been hard at it most of the day. We can cut fresh shafts for them along the way, and there's a good bag of fletchings to go with them off the *Mary*, so the arrows John was concerned about, should now be less of a problem. He also found a tanner to make a load of water skins, remembering what Jean had said earlier about needing plenty of water. He's done well." And there was a general growl of pleasure from them all.

"And what about the lads?" Gui asked, after giving Jean a smile and a further nod of thanks. "There are none in here that I can see. But I expect they're about somewhere?"

"Spoke with Sir Richard, My Lord," Jean de Beaune said firmly, "and they're under curfew tonight. Hordle John has them well organised; he and young Thomas Ringwood along with two of mine. Want them fresh and bright tomorrow...not like they were last night! Those two Bashleys could drink the Loire dry, let alone half a hogshead of Chouchen cider!"

"Good Lord!" Father Matthew exclaimed, laughing. "Chouchen cider? That stuff is made with bee stings...strong enough to knock over a horse; I am surprised they got up at all!"

"Bee stings?"

"Yes, Gui. Bee stings, traditional in Brittany," he added, laughing at Gui's grimacing look of horror. "Gives it added kick, Dear Boy!"

"Anyway, My Lord," de Beaune persisted. "Fitzurse and I will check on 'em later; so they should be fine for early tomorrow.

"Good, well done. Now people," Gui said, with a nod of his head toward the tall Benedictine by his side, dropping his voice as he did so. "Here's the plan."

And pulling a curled piece of parchment from his scrip, Father Matthew unrolled a small crude map across the table, weighting it with a small oil lamp on each corner, and using the point of his knife to show them what he and Gui, with Sir Richard, had decided, they all bent forward to see and hear more clearly what there was to say.

"Here are we in Nantes," Matthew said dropping his voice, "and we need to get here, to Bordeaux. There is no old Roman Highway from here to there, more's the pity. The old Via Aquitaine that will take us to Narbonne starts at Bordeaux. But there is a reasonable route that will get us there starting at Vertou.

I had several hours with Abbot Hugo and he knows it well, as his monks journey from here to Bordeaux about four times a year to sell wine and buy wool. The Abbot's advice is to go from Vertou to Chantonnay, through Clisson, and then to Niort. King Henry built a great castle there, which Richard has strengthened with a huge Donjon, so we can be sure of a warm welcome. From there we go through Saint-Jean-d'Angeley, to Saintes, Pons and finally to Bordeaux.

About two hundred miles of difficult country; but at this time of year it should be dry enough not to slow us down too much. Saint Jean should be a good place for us, Gui. There is a Benedictine Abbey there, said to house the Head of John the Baptist."

"Hence the name of the town."

85

"Yes."

"Wasn't there some trouble there, Father? Years ago?" Sir Richard asked. "Over Henry's marriage to Queen Eleanor?"

"Yes! The town objected to their becoming part of the King's lands. But Henry besieged the place, smashed a hole through their walls, burst in...and-um-the good town worthies of Saint Jean d'Angeley rather swiftly decided that perhaps Henry wasn't such a bad fellow after all!" And they all laughed

"Nevertheless, Father," Allan-i-the-Wood said slowly. "That is still a long journey in what is such unknown country. What do we know of it?"

"A broad mixture, Allan: small villages and little towns scattered amongst great woods and forests; wide areas of wasteland and good cultivation, the soil is good here...much like the Forest at home but on a huge scale, with vineyards, orchards and olive groves. And wild game of course: much boar, '*sanglier*' they call it here, deer, partridge, pheasant. You may feel more comfortable in it than I would. And I have been through it before."

"And bandits and outlaws, beggars, muggers and thieves...and somewhere de Brocas!" Sir Richard snorted.

"Yes," Gui said grimly, looking round the table, dropping his voice. "Sir Richard is right. Somewhere de Brocas! And maybe closer than you think," he added quietly, sitting back. "Remember de Courcy? That idiot who nearly got himself killed, and the other big man with him, Victor Jonelle? Well, they are more than just in the Count of Brittany's pay. They are both in Phillip's pay as well. Jean here recognised them. Fought against them in the Vexin a year back...only they don't know they've been recognised...that's why I wouldn't take Jean with me to the castle yesterday. And we know what Phillip has planned for King Richard...and what part de Brocas hopes to play in that. I think, now, he engineered that whole confrontation just in order to have a crack at me!"

"Didn't realise what they was taking on, My Lord," Fitzurse said, with a chuckle. "You'd've made mince meat of them!"

"Maybe, John. But even the best can make mistakes. They only needed to get lucky once, and then de Brocas would have won everything!"

"No matter, Gui. It didn't happen," Sir Richard said smoothly, leaning across the table, this time with no casual affectation. "And I know you're the best blade in the King's army! However, forewarned is forearmed! So the sooner we slip out of here tomorrow the better."

"I agree," Gui said quietly, rolling up the map and handing it to the tall Benedictine by his side. "I want us to be up and away before sparrow fart tomorrow. No fuss and no farewells, do them tonight. A Roman breakfast to start with, and then off up river to the ferry, and across to Vertou.

Father Matthew has arranged a proper meal break there to see us on our way," he added with a grin, full of mischief. "So don't let anyone be dismayed by a drink of water and a hunk of bread first thing! Now, my friends, no getting up, but a quick toast..." he hesitated, looking round at them. "...To 'Good Fortune and Absent Friends!' And with that they raised their jacks and beakers, clacking them together with a quiet burst of noise, and broad smiles of satisfaction.

"Right, gentlemen," Gui said, wiping his mouth. "I've paid our shot with Charles, and mighty good he's been to us too. So...off with you all, and get what rest you can, for we have an early start tomorrow and a long way to go!" And with muttered conversation and muted laughter, they stood and left. Gui, Sir Richard and Father Matthew up the stairs to their pallet beds...the rest, arms across each others shoulders, and rocking slightly as they walked, to join their men and bed down for as much rest as they could get.

★

And with their leaving, the Angel also seemed to empty.

The men streaming out into the soft warm darkness of that July night, talking, laughing, staggering, in groups and ones and twos, into the streets and alleyways, with the houses leaning into one another full of whispers, and so away to their homes, while inside Charles and his people tidied around the Inn.

But amidst all that earnest talk, no-one saw the small, motionless figure slouched in the darkest shadows of the booth beside that from which Gui and his Commanders had just left; nor noticed the sharp eyes glinting, nor heard the soft shuffle of movement drawing closer. Nor had anyone any occasion to hinder the slim figure, deeply hooded, of Peter Le Croix, the 'Ferret', who slipped out amidst the cheerful farewell bustle of everyone just then leaving, pausing to look up to the shuttered windows above him, before turning up the nearest alley.

Quick and nimble as a questing fox, hugging the noisome darkness, furtive, scuttling from ginnel to ginnel and crabbing round corners, a long cloak hanging from his shoulders, he set off to find the Chef du Port, Monsieur Roland, and the lean, hard authority of Sir Alan de Courcy and Victor Jonelle.

The 'Ferret': ostler at the Angel by day and petty thief at night, had been used by them before. Promised a handful of silver for information about the English soldiers, the Ferret had rubbed his gritty hands together and smiled. But just a handful now for what he had heard? *Non!* He had really good stuff to give them. Red hot from the fire...and this time he wanted more!

★

An hour after the sun had risen the Lord Baron's pigeon relays fluttered into life:

From Sheik El Nazir at sea to de Vere and the Lady Rochine at Bayonne: 'I have the girls. I left him sinking. Two days.'

From Bayonne onward to Narbonne and to the great pigeon loft at The Château Grise: 'He has the girls. Red cog sinking. Bayonne in two days.'

From Grise to de Vere at Bayonne: 'Good news. Bring them to me swiftly as arranged. Unmarked. Undamaged. One week. Be wise!'

★

Backwards and forwards de Brocas' winged messengers flew with their tiny cylinders, each one closely sealed and colour marked to avoid loss of time at each transfer: high and fast and without pause. No hawk or stooping falcon with hungry eyes stopped them, the bells in each loft signalling their arrival, as crooning and bobbing their heads, their messages were taken, replaced or simply transferred to the next carrier. Each pigeon master holding his bird with care and gentleness. Each feathered Mercury worth its pigeon-weight in gold.

From Nantes to Bordeaux to Narbonne and to Grise: 'He survived and has left. Seventy men and three carts. Nantes-Niort-Saintes, via Saint Jean d'Angeley, then Pons – Bordeaux. Suggest, the stream this side Saint Jean!'

From Grise to Bordeaux to de Courcy at Nantes: 'Agree! Liaise with de Vernaille at Bordeaux.'

From Grise to Bertrand de Vernaille at Bordeaux: 'It will be at the stream this side of Saint Jean d'Angeley! Liaise with de Courcy at Nantes.'

Lord Roger de Brocas drank his wine and rubbed his hands. He had the girl...now he would kill her man. The trap would be set, and he like the great black spider he was, would now wait for his fly to become helplessly entangled in the web of his careful planning, and suck his victim dry of every hope and dream.

Throwing back his head he held up his goblet to the sun and smiled.

★

Later, the same day, the notice of the Chef du Port, Monsieur Roland du Clefs, was brought to a body found in the stables that morning, where the two stranger knights had left their horses. A small man, three fingers of his right hand broken, his green woollen cotehardie torn around his shoulders and filled with vomit, the body hidden beneath a great pile of hay...its throat cut to the bone. An obscene, yawning smile in a vast pool of blood. An Ostler from the Angel, Peter Le Croix, 'The Ferret'.

Chapter 13... The White Rose of Malwood on board the Morning Star.

The Lady Alicia de Burley and Mistress Agnes Fitzwalter, were standing near their cabin door waiting to go up on deck at sunset, as they'd been instructed would then be allowed. Both now finely dressed in beautifully embroidered bliauts with wide sleeves of finest blue and crimson cotton, belted at the waist with the softest suede dyed to match and studded with small pearls, astonished by the sheer quality of their clothes: each lovely dress moulded to their breasts and flowing over their hips to the floor in long pleats, with soft leather shoes to match.

Agnes, looking down at herself and running her hands over her hips, had never experienced such luxury, and was amazed by it: "Oh, My Lady...Alicia," she gasped, spinning round making her skirts swirl out. "This is just beautiful!" And she twirled again out of sheer pleasure, her mind completely lost to their situation.

Alicia, very aware of the cost of all they had been given, and the trouble taken to provide them, was anxious: full of fears of the unknown, of how long it was going to take to get to their final destination; about Gui and about how, in God's name was she to cope with the Baron? Concerned also with what might be expected of them in return for such expensive finery.

"Agnes, you...you look just splendid, Sweetheart," she responded, her mind not fully engaged. "We both do. This material is truly delicious," she added, running the soft cotton through her fingers. "Light and soft. And these belts must have cost a great deal too."

Soraya smiled then. "I am so pleased you like them. I chose the material, and Monsieur le Bar-on had them specially made. He said he knew what fitting to give you both. I don't know how? Do... do you like them, My lady?" She added hesitantly.

"Oh, Soraya, very much," Alicia said then with her brilliant smile. "Though I hate the giver! Nevertheless we cannot wear rags...and these are surely better than that. And, please, when we are together like this, please call me 'Alicia'. In public, of course, we must observe all the niceties, but not when we are alone. I could not bear that. Truly, these clothes are very costly. I only hope they do not cost us as well!"

"Money?" Agnes asked puzzled.

"No, not money," Alicia replied softly. "In other ways I can only guess at!" And she shrugged eloquently at Soraya, and turned away.

"What do you mean, Alicia, 'Not money'?"

"Oh, nothing Honeyone," she replied with a smile to Agnes' question. "Just a stray thought," and she looked at Soraya again with slightly raised eyebrows. "Things are not always quite what they seem, are they?" Then noting Soraya's slight grimace, and sideways look, she said: "Greeks bearing gifts don't you think?" and there was a pause then, til she realised her allusion had been lost on both of them, adding with another shrug: "Oh, don't worry about me; I'm just feeling sad, not bad...or mad. Just fed-up not *knowing* anything!" And she turned then and went and sat down on the edge of the bed.

Fed and watered in fine style they might be, but cut off from any normal contact with the outside world, and not knowing what was happening to them, or those they most loved and cared for most, was very frightening.

After their sudden arrival, El Nazir had never called to see his two captives, leaving it wholly to others to do so, treating them as if they carried the plague, concerned that his crew might be infected by the very sight of two such lovely Christian girls. They were not even to be allowed on deck except at dawn and sunset, and even then only if covered with a chador, which having tried on they both hated. It wasn't just the feel of the things, all enveloping and stifling, as much as their unrelieved blackness! Used to fresh air, openness and colour, both English girls felt oppressed. Soraya, who had travelled with the Lady Rochine and her father across the Circle Sea to Syria and beyond, was not so affected.

And they were tightly guarded.

Outside their door stood a huge Syrian warrior, Abdul Aziz, one of El Nazir's most trusted men, pointed black beard and black sloe eyes; Christian mail on thick leather strengthened with extra iron plates across his chest, with steel cuffs to his elbow; mailed chauses on black leather, a mailed coif and a polished nasal helmet topped with a pointed plume holder. Across his arms he carried a great scimitar, which he sometimes rested, point down on the deck. Its broad curved blade, forty inches long and six inches wide at the bottom, was a shimmering terror of sharpened steel, a truly wicked looking weapon that could cut a man in two, and which he hefted as if it were matchwood every time they went on deck, or when he barred the door with his great body should anyone need to leave or enter the cabin. And his voice was dark and full of stones.

So apart from Najid their cook and Zafir their chamber servant, and of course Soraya herself, who was with them almost all the time, they saw no other members of the *Morning Star's* crew. The exception being El Nazir's Guard Commander, Raschid al Din, who had given the orders about their topside visits, and came down twice a day to look them over and ask Soraya if there was anything she needed for her two charges.

And each time he looked at them almost with disgust, as if they were something unspeakable: as if even to touch them would soil him in some way. While very different from what, in all abject terror, they had been half expecting, he never touched them, and each time he came, he only spoke Arabic.

Alicia, watching him watching her, was certain he could have spoken in English if he had wanted to, and she felt subtly humiliated...which was presumably his intention. The second time he came she just shrugged it off. If he wanted to behave in such an ignorant, boorish manner that was his problem not hers, and she determined that every time he came to their cabin she would made a practice of smiling at him. And every time she did so he grimaced and almost shuddered, til she felt like sticking her tongue out at him, like the hoyden she used to be!

"What on earth is the matter with that man, Soraya?" Alicia asked after his second visit. "He looks at us as if we are unclean in both body and soul!"

"He is a high class Arab, My Lady…Al-ic-ia," she said with a smile, her husky voice tripping prettily over the syllables. "And you are both Christians, therefore infidels, and women," she added sweeping her hands over her figure. "And in his eyes 'uncovered', and, so…so shameless," she added struggling for the right word. "He also regards you as whores, because you are showing your arms, and your hair and faces, uncovered. I always wear a yashmak, sheer silk though it may be, and my Huque, when I go from here, that long dark blue cloak with a hood? So I don't have to wear a chador. It is the Lord Bar-on's orders, and I am properly covered, so the man has to accept me. And-and…then-then, you do not wash as often as they do…and-and as I do. So he thinks you stink and are unclean!"

Alicia shrugged her shoulders prettily. "I have noticed that you wash yourself often, or at least try to do. At home we are told too much bathing will make us ill. Gui and I bathe at least once a week, and that is considered dangerous by many. But I do my best with a hazel twig to keep my teeth clean at least."

"You are travelling to a hot country, Al-ic-ia. At the Château, Monsieur Le Bar-on insists that everyone must bathe *every* day! Not only that but that every girl must be shaven smooth…in all places!"

"*No!*" Both girls exclaimed, absolutely shocked.

"I know about the Lady Rochine," Alicia said, ignoring Agnes's open mouth and stunned eyes. "She showed me the night of the fire, before we went to bed. I thought it was just her. The sort of thing she might do to shock; and I was shocked. Well, stunned to be honest never having seen such a thing before. But you say every girl in the Château? Every girl?" she asked again. "*Completely?*" Looking at Agnes' horror struck face, and trying not to giggle

"Yes, Al-ic-ia," Soraya said, smiling at Agnes' reaction. "*Completely!* Underarms and…and secret places, *both!* Monsieur Le Bar-on insists, and in truth there is less sickness in the Château than anywhere else I know. We use special balms to make our skin soft and silky, and perfume to enhance our beauty…not to hide the stink of a dirty body as most women do. And with no hair on us, except on our heads of course, it is much more comfortable in the

93

hot weather. We do not get so sticky...nor so itchy in...in...our secret places," she ended in a rush. "No horrid spots or rashes." Then, taking hold of the rim of her pantaloons, and looking wickedly sideways, she added, "Shall I show you?"

"*No!*" Agnes said, shocked at Soraya's easy acceptance of something so-so intimate and-and shocking. Something she was not used to from someone she hardly knew.

"No, not tonight, Soraya," Alicia said with a chuckle. "I don't think Agnes is ready for that yet, are you, Sweetheart? But we'll get there. I can't imagine what Maude and Judith would say at home?" And they both giggled and then laughed.

A little bashfully Alicia said, "I have my-my 'fur' clipped, as Agnes knows, because she does it. But never shaved. I had never even heard of such a thing until the Baron came to Malwood. Is it difficult? Painful?"

"No - and one day I will show you how, and shave you. Both of you!" she said with a huge grin at Agnes' appalled face. "You will see then how free you feel and how smooth and fresh. Truly," she added, with her husky laugh, "you will both be amazed! Now come on," she beckoned, handing them their chadors, and helping them put them on as the sound of heavy feet came to their ears: "It is time for us to go on deck, and I can't wait to use the 'facilities'. That ghastly bucket? Urrrgh!"

★

From where they were, two short flights of steps took them past the upper deck of rowers, the stench of them strong on the evening air, past the Hortator's great drum and his fleece lined seat, through a small arched doorway, and onto the top deck at last, right beside the sterncastle on which was mounted the Springald that had so smashed the *Mary's* fo'c'sle to pieces.

Beside them were Sheik El Nazir's suite of rooms, lamps being lit inside just as the sun was almost touching the sea in a blaze of yellow and orange glory, the whole sky seeming lit by scarlet and crimson flames, the clouds of night coming down upon them, tinged with purple and midnight blue.

"Thank God, this day is over at last," Alicia said when they had finally reached the bows, where the *Morning Star's* Roman-style Ballista stood unmanned on its turntable atop her forecastle.

"Without doubt this has been the worst day of my life so far! Just so dreadful! I still can't wholly believe it! Only this morning we were happily on the *Pride*, bumbling along towards Bordeaux, Gui just over there," she pointed to where the *Mary* might have been. "Now," she said getting angry, "We've been stolen onto a foreign vessel filled with our enemies – and I am on my way, like some sort of Christmas present, to be placed in the power of the very worst, and most wicked of men, who is intending to force marriage on me! The very thought of which is more hateful than anything I can ever imagine! Oh…oh, *Christos!*" And she stamped her foot on the deck. Then with a sigh, "Where are those 'facilities' that idiot Zafir mentioned to you, Soraya? I need them almost as much as you do…*to be sick in!*"

Soraya, who'd been listening to Alicia's rising voice with great concern, was swift to answer her. "They are close here, near the anchors, Alic–ia," she said. "Low down near the water, behind that wooden screen. When there is a sea running it can be very dangerous. There is a sort of closed–in box you sit on, holding onto some ropes on either side–and–and, that's what you do!" she stammered, suddenly embarrassed. Anxious not to offend the English milady whom she had been so strongly ordered to care for.

"You mean we stick our bums over the edge of this ship, holding onto ropes, and hope we don't get washed overboard?" Agnes asked horrified.

"Yes, Mistress Agnes. And no rags, the sea will clean you!" Soraya replied with a laugh, as if it was the most natural thing in the world. "Look, I will go first and you can see what I do. I'm bursting, and I *hate* using a bucket! You will see, this is not so bad…not so difficult as it seems. Just don't get

95

caught short in the middle of the night when it's pouring with rain and the sea is running high!"

And with amazed looks on both their faces they watched while Soraya almost disappeared from view down a few steps, lifted up all her garments and squatted on the wooden box provided, hanging onto two thick rope handles that hung from either side over the gunnels of the *Morning Star*, while the sea playfully smacked her naked buttocks.

Agnes followed very nervously, and there were plenty of shrieks which made them all laugh. And then finally Alicia, no less anxious but absolutely refusing to show it to either of her companions, and actually relishing the sudden cold freshness of the sea as it rose up and suddenly sloshed over her exposed tail, and between her legs, making her shriek almost as much as Agnes had done!

By then they were all giggling, and moving away to the port rails pointing out across the bows to where the distant shore appeared to be floating past them, a long, dark undulating line of land, the black shadows of woods and forests, the twinkling of lamp light where there were houses, farms and villages. But the sight of the shore so visible, yet so far way, flattened Alicia's spirits and she walked away to lean across the rail on her own.

Where are they now? She thought, looking past the distant shore line and beyond into the far blue yonder with unseeing eyes as the sun slowly disappeared behind her, the gold and crimson after glow a vast sheet of colour across the sky, turning softly pink and buttercup yellow. Where were they? Gui, Richard and Father Matthew…and all the others? Had they really got away safe from the Mary? That dreadfully smashed up wreck? She was so sure she would know if anything really bad had happened…if Gui were dead! But her very soul shuddered at that, refusing even to contemplate it, and she hugged herself fiercely.

How she loved him…and missed him! Not just for the loving…but for himself: his humour, the sound of his voice, the crunch of his tread, the feel of his hands when he hugged her, the touch of his lips: the strong, musky very *maleness* of him! That smell of leather, armour and stables. He made her feel so safe…and special, and she felt the prickle of tears behind her eyes. O, my

96

darling! Her heart shouted. Where are you? I love you *so* much it hurts. I need you so: don't forget me. Don't forget me! A cry from the very depths of her soul, as lonely and forlorn as that of the passing gulls, planing and turning so closely above the waves.

"Are you alright, my...my Alic-ia?" Soraya asked softly, coming up beside her with Agnes.

"No...not really," she said with a great sigh, turning her face towards her and back again. "I was just wondering where they all are?" She added, putting her arm around Agnes. "Gui, Sir Richard and all the others. Your Allan, too, Sweetheart," she said to Agnes, giving her a cuddle. And she dashed her hand across her face with a soft sob, as the tears fell from her eyes. "And what will happen with us? How am I to confront that...that *bastard*, and his witch of a daughter? *How?* When he has been responsible for so much wickedness and—and misery to those whom I love most! I don't know. I don't know!" And she wept as though her heart was breaking, burying her face in her hands, while the others moved swiftly to comfort her.

For a moment, as they clung together, they were all silent. Then, taking a deep breath, Alicia stood back, wiping her eyes with the back of her hands to brush away her tears and gaze out across the railings at the darkening sea.

"How silly of me," she sniffled briefly, giving them a wan smile. "This will never do! Lady Margaret would be brisk and cheerful about something like this, wouldn't she?" she said turning towards Agnes.

"Yes, my love, she would," Agnes replied. "Sir Gui's lovely mother," she added turning towards a puzzled looking Soraya. "A wonderful Lady loved by all....murdered by the Baron. 'No point in crying over spilt milk, young Agnes,' she would have said with a smile and a swift pat on the back...and then got on with sorting things out. That's what she was like when things went wrong!"

"And so must we!" Alicia said, taking another deep breath. "Gui would expect it of us...of me; no matter how much he might sympathise with our situation, or hate what has happened. All we can do is the best we can. And

97

that does not mean dissolving into a hopeless puddle of grease when things go bad. 'Things' just happen sometimes…and we'll just have to make the best of everything. Gui is coming for us, I am sure of it!"

And she turned away for a moment, listening to the sea hissing down the ship's sides, the calls of the crew at the stern, the creak of her timbers, the groans of her slave rowers below decks and the muted rattle of their chains…and then she looked up and around her.

At the *Morning Star,* oars drawn in, flying free with the wind behind her whistling across her deck, and through her rigging, as she barrelled into the warm July darkness. Ploughing through the short rollers, each topped with foamy white, she swooped down the darkly blue and green troughs, then up again. And as the *Morning Star* rose up, so Alicia's eyes were drawn the whole length of her tilted deck to the very sterncastle where El Nazir's great cabin, right above theirs, was filled with golden light and sudden laughter.

And to the steersmen by their great steerboards, one either side of the ship, lit by two huge lanterns at her stern, with other crewmen around them. Then up to the masts themselves, soaring into the midnight-blue darkness, their great lateen sails let-out as far as they would go, powering the *Morning Star* forward, two crewmen just glimpsed at the base nearest the stern, behind some great coils of rope, waiting for further orders…and all beautifully backlit by the last dying light of that awful day, as the western horizon finally faded to a long, broad band of palest crimson and gold, beneath the gathering velvet of the night, where the first stars were just blinking into life high above her.

Turning then she opened her arms to Agnes and Soraya, so needing the touch and feel of human love and kindness.

"Oh, My Lady," Agnes said in a whisper, burying her head into Alicia's shoulder, as Soraya moved to put her arms around them both. "I think of them all too: my Allan and his gurt hound, that Bouncer, and the lovely burr in his voice, and his kindness and his kisses. Makes me go hot just thinking of them, my love," she smiled. "Then - then I think of that poor busted up ship, with a

98

hole in her you could drive a tilt cart through-and then I'm not sure of anything any more? If they survived?...or what?"

"Don't you dare think otherwise, Agnes Fitzwalter!" Alicia said firmly, turning the girl and giving her a shake. "I won't even let you think it. They were still afloat when those two bastards took us off the *Pride*. And the *Mary* couldn't have a better Master or crew. If something awful had happened I would know it! *I just know I would!* Nor will I believe otherwise until I am told so by someone I know and trust. So, my girl, cheer up. No megrims from any of us! Remember, all is not over, til the minstrel's last song, or the jester's tumble! Dear God," she added, pulling at her chador. "What I wouldn't do to take this beastly thing off!"

She turned then as they were hailed by Abdul Aziz, their huge Syrian guard, and ordered below. So, with a sigh all round, Soraya led them back down to their cabin, where Najid was waiting with their evening meal, and a great carafe of fresh orange sherbet, only missing the ice to make it a perfect drink: not regarding the two figures that had just flitted away from up forward, where she had noticed them earlier behind the mast nearest the steersman, to disappear down a nearby hatchway.

Chapter 14... The Cousins discuss the virtues of Alicia and her friends.

Jules Lagrasse and Lucas Fabrizan, knowing that the girls would all be on deck, had come up after them, and now watched them from behind the mast nearest the starboard steersman, concealed as much by the falling darkness as by the heavy coils of sheets and halliards that hung from all the cleats around it. Watched them walk along towards the bows, back-lit by the glowing sunset, and as they ducked down behind the partitions that concealed the ship-board garderobe, they both grinned.

"Just think, Jules, of those lovely smooth fucking arses hanging off the sides of this fucking tub!" Lucas grunted, his eyes leering sideways at his cousin. "Like soft, ripe peaches," he added, squeezing his fingers into his hands, as if there was half a lemon in each. "What I wouldn't give to get my hands into any one of 'em!"

"You're always such a crude bugger, Lucas. Is there no refinement in you?"

"What, you sod? Crude bugger, am I? I suppose you've never rolled a hot bitch in a hedge and fucked the arse off her then? What about that Cristobel outside Narbonne? Didn't see *you* being bloody refined then, you idle bastard. Nor with her Ma! At them both like a fucking fiddler's elbow!" And they laughed.

"Listen Cousin! You stand as much chance of laying a hand on any one of those beauties as you do of becoming King of Jerusalem...especially after what happened on board that ship! Shame about those chadors though. Was hoping I might get a glimpse. No bloody chance!"

"Did you see that Alicia's fucking tits when we flung her on the bed? Gorgeous! And that Sheik El Nazir, bloody infidel, gawping at 'em, miserable sod. His eyes were falling out of his fucking face! On bloody stalks they were! Mind, he's not been anywhere near 'em since. And that other bitch of the Lady

Rochine's? That Soraya…whom we've seen around the castle? She is a prize bit of cunt too…would love to stuff her one I can tell you, Coz. She's ripe for anything from what I hear. She and that fucking bitch, Lady Rochine. Right sodding goings on! And there's that other silly cow, that Agnes, whom you was sweet on talking with at Malwood. She's full of luscious firmness too, that's bloody certain, I had my hands all over 'em when I was carrying her on board. Fucking lovely!"

"Proper dished her up, poor little filly! 'I'm saving myself for the King of France' indeed! Stupid bitch! Are all English girls so bloody useless? Still, she gave us what we wanted. Frankly that Under Sherriff's welcome to her. She's tighter than a Jew's arse. He'll get nowhere with her!"

"Don't you believe it, Jules! Give her to me for half an hour and I'll have her suck all the sweetness out of me, before I give her the solid sorting she deserves," and he gave a coarse, grunting laugh, pumping his fist up and down. "A shame for her not to have the sodding joy of being fucked by me from all angles! A proper sin that'd be."

"Well, we might just get lucky there, as long as you keep that great prick of yours under control between here and the castle! That Rochine…and she's a fine piece too I might add!…She has a plan for forcing that stuck-up tart, Lady Al-ic-ia de Bur-ley," he mocked, "to give herself to Baron bloody Roger, and no questions asked, that might be good for us yet."

"So he can give her a proper 'Rogering' eh?" And Lucas guffawed at his own crude humour, grunting like a boar rooting for acorns in the forest.

"Oh…very witty, you bloody moron," his cousin replied with a wry grin. "How you have survived all these years, Lucas, without my aunt throttling you, I'll never know!"

"That's because I'm her proper little soldier, with angel's wings!"

"Dear God, aid me!" he muttered, casting his eyes up, adding: "Anyway, this plan's not about Lord Roger, 'Rogering' you ignorant peasant! It's a quite different plan.

"What plan's that then, you tight arse?"

"Tell you, Lucas? Are you fucking crazy? Three good clacks of wine in your belly and you'd spill bloody everything! No, you stupid bastard, I'll tell you when it's necessary, and not before. In the meantime keep that fat prod of yours buttoned up, or you'll ruin everything and I'll be forced to cut it off myself! Now, come on, Coz, those girls are moving this way, time to leave. I'm ready for our scoff too anyway, so let's get about it. I could eat a horse!"

"And knowing this fucking country," Lucas growled, spitting over the side as they turned away, his arm on his cousin's shoulder, "that's just what we will bloody get, fucking horse! What I wouldn't give for a great, oozing chunk of roast pig!"

Chapter 15…*How Sheik El Nazir created the Company of the White Rose*

wo mornings later, as the *Morning Star* turned in towards the Adour Estuary, they were finally summoned by Raschid al Din to go to El Nazir's great Cabin beneath the sterncastle with Soraya, accompanied by Abdul Aziz, to receive their instructions: knowing from the previous evening that they were now approaching Bayonne at last.

With their hearts somewhat in their mouths to say the least, and covered with their black chadors, Soraya by her dark blue Huque, so that only their eyes showed, all three women came and stood before the Dromond's great Master and owner, famous across the whole Circle Sea, Sheik El Nazir al Jameel-Aziz-ibn Nidhaal. He, in complete contempt of them both, remained seated, leaving them uncomfortably standing before him while he ate honeyed almonds and drank freshly squeezed orange sherbet from a beautiful tall goblet of green and blue blown glass on a fine twisted stem.

"I have brought you here as we shall shortly be entering the River Adour that leads to Bayonne," he said in Frankish, in his usual dark voice. "Soon we will furl our sails and my rowers will take over. *Allah be Praised,* we have made a swift passage, and I shall soon be finished with you. It was not my desire to make this journey, and it has cost me the loss of two fine ships, the deaths of many of my men…and of my son, Sharif."

"That was no fault…." Alicia started to say, stepping forward.

"*Be silent you Infidel bitch!*' El Nazir suddenly roared at her, rising to his full height and making all three women flinch, and Agnes cower. "*No-One speaks when I do!*…least of all a Christian Houri. Next time I will have that strumpet whom the Lady Rochine put on board my *Morning Star* stripped and flogged for not educating you better!" And he sat down again, fanning himself with a huge whisk of stiff peacock feathers lying on the great octagonal table before him.

After a pause to collect himself, and staring into Alicia's blue eyes, more outraged than frightened, he said: "You might not personally have been at fault, La-dy Al-ic-ia de Bur-ley,"… emphasising the syllables of her complete name to Alicia's surprise…"Never-the-less your capture has been very costly, and handing you over will be a total pleasure, if not one of great enjoyment to The Lady into whose charge I will shortly be placing you, along with the two Frenchmen who brought you on board! For certain she will have to pay me greatly more to do so!"

"*No!...Please…*"

"*Silence, you Nasraani whore!*" he bellowed again, making the whole cabin quiver. "*Take that one,*" he shouted at Abdul Aziz, stabbing his hand towards Soraya. "Strip her now and beat her with this," he ordered handing over a pliable rod of thick cane, "*until I tell you to stop!*"

Instantly Alicia fell on her knees, pulling Agnes down beside her as Matthew had once long ago advised, heads bowed and her hands thrust out through her chador in desperate, silent supplication, even as the giant Syrian seized Soraya to tear off her Huque.

Without speaking El Nazir threw up his hand like a knife blade, stalling the man completely. And coming to stand over Alicia as she strove not to tremble he snarled: "One more word from you, Infidel! *Witch!* Just one more of any sort, and not only will I have this pathetic creature flogged, but your friend, Mistress Agnes Fitz-wal-ter, will be given to Jules Lagrasse and his cousin for their amusement. Do you understand me?" he snarled at her. "And this time you may speak."

"Yes! I understand you, My Lord." She replied as calmly as possible. Then, raising her violet-blue eyes to his hot, black ones, she said quietly. "Please do not give my friend to those…those *animals!* And do not raise your hand to Mistress Soraya. We will do as you ask," and she bowed her head. Then looking up again, she added: "My Lord Sheik El Nazir ibn Nidhaal. I have been in the presence of many great men. Men greater than you, My Lord Prince. There is no need to shout at your humble servant." And she dropped her eyes and bowed her head again, hiding her smile at his astonishment for knowing how properly to address him, and for her courageous defiance.

Following her spoken words there was a deathly silence, as no woman had spoken so to the Sheik before, least of all a Christian woman. So they waited, breath held, for the sky to fall in on her as he scowled down at her, head bowed as Soraya had also taught them the day before, and still meekly kneeling at his feet.

Although he knew of her exploits during the fire, and how she had escaped from the Baron and his daughter. He was still stunned by the reality of this *Nasraani* woman the Baron had decided on for his bride. He had seen no fear in her eyes…only courage and defiance. No Muslim girl would have dared to face him in so…so bold if shameless a manner.

Nor so bravely either, and in all truth, *By the Beard of the Prophet,* she was very beautiful, her deep blue eyes piercing, penetrating, her body lusciously curved as he had seen when she had been dragged on board…such magnificent breasts, and so richly crowned! No wonder the Baron had been so determined to seize her. She was a true rarity. Had she been Muslim, he would have desired her for himself, and throwing his head back he laughed, as much at her demure boldness as his own unbidden lustful thoughts that had suddenly coursed through him like fire, and on an impulse he reached down for her hand and raised her up, Agnes following her.

Such an action startled everyone, apparently even El Nazir himself who, after a moment's stricken pause, conducted her to the long stern window seat, motioning the other two girls to join her there, as he moved to his high backed chair, ordering Jussuf to adjust it to face them. At the same time Abdul Aziz moved to stand across the closed door, while Al Raschid strode behind the Sheik, sending two of his men to stand guard outside, and El Nazir ordered Jussuf to bring more goblets and more fresh orange sherbet.

For a moment there was silence in the great room, broken only by the shipboard noises beyond and below them, and the distant cries of gulls above the estuary, as everyone mentally shook themselves over what had just happened.

Then, to the absolute astonishment of Alicia, and others around him, his rich voice switched seamlessly from Frankish to lightly accented English: "You are a very remarkable woman, My Lady Al–ic–ia. You fear me, I can 'feel' it. …yet you do not show it. There is only courage in your defiance and purity in your answers, and you are very beautiful…*Jameel*. You also have knowledge and wisdom which, in a woman, is rare. I can see why men can love you. Why the Lord Bar-on Sir Roger has set his heart on seizing you, and…why his daughter fears you! You may speak, My Lady," he said, seeing her sudden astonishment, and he deferred to her with the very slightest of head movements.

"You-you speak English, My Lord Prince!" She stammered, amazed at his grasp of her own native language which even the King couldn't speak.

"Yes, My Lady," he said with a smile. "Your people are being found everywhere. Your language is useful in trading as well as in warfare, as is Arabic and Frankish. In my trade you need clearly to be understood," and he gestured towards her, and to all the others around him.

"You do me great honour to reveal so 'secret' a skill. I am astonished."

"So am I, My Lady," he replied, again slightly inclining his head towards her. "It is your eyes, I think. They are…very compelling," and he smiled again, lighting up his hard face with sudden, unexpected humour.

"Why, Sheik El Nazir ibn Nidhaal," she said then, reverting to formality, "do you say the Lady Rochine fears me? I am astonished. It is I who fear her."

"Not so! She sees in you a deadly rival for her father's affection. Be warned, My Lady, she is not what she seems!"

"I know what nature of woman that *witch* is, My Lord Prince, She has had me in her power before."

"After the fire, you mean."

"You know about that?" She replied, astonished again.

"Of course. Why else have I had to seize you so violently? The Bar-on failed. I have not. And remember, when you escaped from the forest the Lord

Roger was still with The Lady. He would not have allowed her to destroy something he so desired!"

"Is my life in danger then, My Lord Sheik?" She questioned him urgently, adopting a more Frankish approach to his name.

"Only if the Bar-on is not immediately present."

"But is he not here to view his 'captive' personally?" She asked with a flash of disgust, gesturing towards the port they were approaching.

"No, My Lady Al-ic-ia. He has sent his daughter, The Lady Rochine, to do his greeting for him, along with an escort led by his own Guard Commander, Gaston de Vere, with the added company of two of his men...Jules Lagrasse and Lucas Fabrizan...currently on board my ship. Together they will conduct you, and your companions, to the Lord Bar-on at Gruissan."

"*No!* My Lord Sheik!" she almost cried out in shock. "Not those two French *animals!* Not them along with just the Lady de Brocas and her men as my escort. They are not to be trusted, *any* of them. Least of all de Vere whom I believe rests in *her* pocket, *not* the Baron's as he might choose to believe. I had thought the Baron, himself, would be here to view me...us," she added, pointing to Agnes beside her, "and gloat over his success. If what you say is true, we will *never* get there alive. Please, is there nothing you can do?"

He paused, considering her and sipped his drink, turning his eyes away to look beyond them all to the furthest distance of his mind: To the time Lord Roger had saved his life from the rocks that had ripped his boat in pieces, slaughtered the men trying to kill him, soothed and healed his wounds and introduced him to his beloved, beautiful Constance; to thoughts of the Lady Rochine, his daughter, whom he was certain had poisoned her mother to acquire her father's love; to her continued use, with her father, of the Crystal, which he knew she relished hugely; her plotting; her murdered lovers; her obsession with her father...and her truly deadly jealousy wherever the Baron was concerned. And to what the Baron had persuaded him to do.

With a sudden grunt his mind snapped back to the present, to the Lady Al-ic-ia de Bur-ley seated before him, and turning towards her he smiled: "Of Course…My Lady Al-ic-ia! I am not Sheik El Nazir al Jameel-Aziz-ibn Nidhaal for nothing. Before this morning I would not have cared. But now I have met you, and for the love *I* have for the Lord Bar-on Roger, I will send you under an escort of my own."

"*You?*" She exclaimed, startled. "You have a care for the Baron Roger? *An Infidel Lord?*"

"As a brother, My Lady. For no-one else would I risk my ships on so dangerous a mission. Especially not my '*Surah At-Tariq*'…my *Morning Star*…He saved my life in exceptional circumstances when others were trying to kill me. And he cared for me, introduced me to his wife, the Lady Constance, and took me safely back to my family. We have been close friends now for many years."

"And his daughter, My Lord Prince?" she said reverting to her earlier use of his title.

"No…My Lady! I do not care for his daughter. His wife, the Lady Constance, was a true beauty, exotic and amazing….and true. The daughter has since taken her place, and in ways I can neither condone nor approve of. It is a blasphemy before *Allah!* And, I believe, is turning her mind."

"My Lord Prince," Alicia implored him again. "Will, you help us…at least to get safely to Grise."

"Gruissan, My Lady."

"Even so, My Lord Prince. After that…"

"After that, my Lady, *Insha'Allah!*"

"*Insha'Allah!* My Lord Prince El Nazir al Jameel-Aziz-ibn Nidhaal," she replied putting her hands together and bowing her head towards him.

"My Lady Al-ic-ia de Bur-ley, "he said looking down at her with a surprised smile. "You never fail to amaze me. Who taught you that?

"A Benedictine Monk who has travelled even to India, a Black Monk. He is a very wise man, quite unlike any Churchman I have ever met. His name is 'Father Matthew'. He has travelled amongst your people, and advised me of many things before we all set out to join King Richard's army."

"Father Matthew? I am impressed that even among the Black Monks there are cultured Nasraani Churchmen who speak the language of *Allah.* I have never met such a man, though I have heard of him. He was a friend of one of our Emirs I believe? A shame he is not with you now. His teaching makes me even more willing to help you."

"At least to Grise…Gruissan, My Lord Prince."

"My Lady Al–ic–ia, I was engaged to carry out your capture by The Lady Rochine's father, The Lord Baron Sir Roger de Brocas of Narbonne and Gruissan, to whom I am indebted as I said. Not by his daughter whom we call 'The Lady'. She is nothing to me. I am *not* one of her creatures, though she would dearly like me to be so. Indeed I almost fear for her father at her hands. He seeks absolute power through her…and absolute power corrupts absolutely! My promise was to my friend…*not* to his daughter!" and turning he called out, "Abdul Aziz, come here!" Then, turning to Al Raschid, with a nod of his head and raised eyebrow, he said. "Send for Mhaktoun Aquib to come here to me also, my friend. Do not be so astonished; all will be well. Now, Abdul Aziz," he said as his Guard Commander went out. "Come to me. I have a special task for you."

"Yes, My Prince." The huge Syrian replied in Arabic, coming to kneel before the Sheik, touching his forehead with his fingers and then his lips as he did so.

"Abdul Aziz aal Suriyyan," El Nazir said in his accented Frankish. "You see these three ladies whom you have been guarding these past few days?"

"Yes, My Lord Prince," he replied similarly.

"You are to guard them as if they were myself, and I am sending Mhaktoun Aquib with you to ensure that all goes well. I know he is your friend, so I will expect you to work together at all times to keep these *Gamila*

Nasraani...these beautiful Christians, safe and in your sight whenever possible. At night you and Mhaktoun will stand guard over them, turn and turn about. And Najid will feed you all. No-one else must prepare your food. Even after you have all handed them to the Lord Bar-on de Brocas of Narbonne, at his castle in Gruissan, your duties will not end. They will not end until I come for you in the *Morning Star*. I will write to the Lord Baron today to say so, Abdul, and this Lady will give it to him. Do you understand?"

"Yes, my Prince. These are good ladies," he said rising and turning to the three women on the long window seat, his voice strong and light, his black eyes steady, with a glint of humour Alicia had not seen before.

"I and Aquib will care for you. *By the Beard of the Prophet* we will make sure you are safe," then he put his hands together and bowed to them and to Sheik El Nazir: "*Salaam Alaikum!*"... 'Peace be unto you'... And he stepped back towards the door, moving swiftly to one side as it opened to allow Al Raschid to enter, followed by another soldier, who walked soft footed to where the Sheik was sitting and knelt down before him touching his forehead and his lips also.

"You called for me, My Prince" he said in Frankish.

Soraya, who knew the man, just smiled, but Alicia and Agnes had actively gasped because, quite simply, while Aziz was big...this man was massive!

Taller than either Gui or Abdul Aziz, and perhaps twice their bulk? With arms like knotted tree trunks, thighs sculpted pillars of hardened muscle and a chest like that of the Colossus itself, he towered over everyone. But like many very big men he was surprisingly light on his feet, carried his chainmail armour as if it were tin, and in his hands his sword was more like a bodkin than the forty inches of clouded steel it truly was. He had a strong face, with a square chin and deep nose, and very dark brown eyes that also hid a certain twinkle. Alicia liked him at once, not just because he was so large but because he had about him an air of trust and dependability.

"Yes, Mhaktoun Aquib," El Nazir said switching effortlessly to English. "I have a task for you to share with Abdul Aziz, but under your command.

"Yes, My Prince. It will be as you say." He replied in like manner, in English, to Alicia's complete astonishment, and that of her companions.

"Very well. That is good. I want you to go with these three ladies, and Abdul and Najid, to the castle of the Bar-on, my friend, the Lord Roger de Brocas of Narbonne, and make sure they are safe and well at all times. You will take your orders from Lady Ali-ic-ia de Burley, and use your common sense. Do you understand? But you are in command and all must do your bidding or be lost."

"Yes, My Prince. They will be safe. *By the Beard of the Prophet,* I promise this!" He said, raising El Nazir's hand to his forehead in ritual acceptance of the man's authority.

"So! That is very good," the Sheik said with quiet pleasure in his deep voice. Then, turning to Alicia he smiled. "I understand that some people call you 'the White Rose of Malwood', My Lady? That white roses are your favourite flower both for beauty and for scent...as are they mine also, when I am not on board the Morning Star."

"It has been said, My Lord Prince," she replied bowing her head towards him. "But it is a private name between me and my family. In Jest and not generally known."

"No matter. Today you leave the *Star* together as one company. You three," he said gesturing to her, Agnes and Soraya. "With Aquib, Aziz and Nijad to guard and guide you. All for the one purpose of getting you, the 'White Rose of Malwood', safely to Gruissan and to my friend The Lord Baron, Sir Roger de Brocas. And, knowing The Lady, it may not be a safe journey. That is why I am sending my two most trusted, fiercest warriors with you. So...you will be one Company together, I think. Yes?" he asked then, the word shooting out of him tersely.

"Yes!" My Prince, Aquib replied swiftly.

"So, with what you are doing," he said then with a smile at Alicia, and a subtle tilt of his head towards her. "You shall be the 'Company of the White Rose'!" And he raised his glass of sherbet to her as those around him gasped and suddenly clapped their approval.

"If that is your wish, My Prince?" Aquib said then, bowing his head.

"It is!" Sheik El Nazir said, standing; his eyes bright and glittering in the sunlight off the water. "I wish it...so it will be. And with a good name like that to believe in you will all be the stronger for it, and will bind together better when you need to most!"

"It is a good name, My Lord Prince El Nazir," Alicia said smiling, bowing her head towards him again. "I wish I had thought of it myself!" And they all laughed, a light ripple of sound that ran round the great State Cabin, and startled the guards standing outside the door.

★

All this time Soraya had been sitting, astonished, to one side of the long settle. In all the times she had known the Sheik, never had she witnessed such kindness or generosity. And not just because he had chosen to be wooed by Alicia's beauty and spirit...but because of his close affection for the Baron.

Lord Roger wanted Alicia, that much was plain. And El Nazir had risked everything to deliver her to him, even to the point of sacrificing one of his sons. Now, clearly he believed that Alicia's life was threatened by Rochine...as well he might for The Lady could, indeed, be maniacally jealous, beyond all reason. So, by assigning two of his most trusted soldiers, and a much valued cook to support them, he truly was nailing his colours to the mast for all to see. And the name he had so suddenly assigned to them simply bore that all out. And she was amazed by it. Aquib and Azziz, and little Najid, were all men whom Rochine would not dare to assault; but The Lady was so uncertain a quantity that Soraya felt she must do something more to help her new friends survive the coming journey. So, dropping to her knees before Sheik El Nazir, head bowed and hands held out she begged leave from him to speak.

Chapter 16... More plans are made... and others secretly revealed!

Turning his sharp, black eyes towards her, Sheik El Nazir paused and studied the lovely girl kneeling silently in front of him, head down and hands out in supplication...before ordering her to raise her head. And looking into her green eyes with the penetrating stare of a falcon, he gave a slow gesture of his right hand for her to rise: "What is it you want of me. Mistress Fermier?"

"Please My Lord Sheik," Soraya said humbly in the warm voice of the Languedoc. "Before we all leave, may I speak?"

For a moment longer El Nazir looked at her steadily again through hooded eyes, before saying: "Yes, Mistress Soraya. You may speak."

"My Lord Prince," she said quietly, raising her face to his. "For your men to carry out the orders you have given them, the new Company of the White Rose, I believe it is imperative that they do not speak anything but Arabic *at all times!* Neither The Lady, nor any of her people...especially not her Guard Commander, Gaston de Vere... must know that either Abdul Aziz or Mhaktoun Aquib can speak different languages. My Lord Prince," she said, hesitating, "will you ask them if they speak Farsi?"

"*Farsi?*" He said astonished. "*Persian?*"

"Yes, My Lord. It was my mother's tongue. I learned from her and have never forgotten it. None of The Lady's people speak it. Indeed very few do anyway around the Circle Sea, but both the men you have chosen have travelled widely before entering your service, and may just do so."

"How do you know this?" He asked her severely.

"I am an expert, silent listener, My Lord Prince. Those who serve The Lady, as I do, have learned to be! Amongst The Lady's guard, and she always travels with the same men, some speak Arabic, all know some English and of course all speak Frankish. But none speak Farsi. If either of your men can speak it, then we can converse in a manner that no-one else can understand. And if they only ever speak Arabic around her guards, and no other language, then anything that may be planned against us in ignorance of their skills...may be revealed."

Leaning back in his tall chair he studied her in silence, his great peacock fan moving gently from side to side as he did so. "I am impressed, Mistress Soraya," he replied at last. "You have thought of something both Al Raschid and I have missed. I will ask them," he said, turning to where both men were standing. "Abdul...Mhaktoun? You heard this lady. Do either of you speak Farsi?"

"A few words only, My Lord," Abdul said, with a wry smile. "But none that a lady would want to know!"

"Mmmm, Guardroom language!" He grunted. "You are right, my Abdul...not helpful for us now. Mhaktoun?"

"Yes, My Lord Prince. I do speak Farsi...not fluently perhaps, but enough to be useful and more I will catch onto quickly, I am certain."

"How do you know Farsi, Mhaktoun Aquib?" El Nazir asked, fascinated at finding so unlikely a skill amongst his fighting men.

"In my younger days, as Mistress Soraya says, I travelled a great deal. I wanted to be the greatest wrestler of all time. They have many cunning wrestlers in Persia, so I travelled there...and then...and then...

"...There was a girl!" El Nazir interrupted with a deep laugh at his enormous guard's embarrassment. "Be not ashamed, Mhaktoun. *By the Beard of the Prophet*, when was there *not* a girl about you somewhere? You are so huge I sometimes think you hide them about your person!"

"Even so, My Prince. Being so large seems to encourage them to come to me," he added with twinkly grin. "But this one was very special to me. Leila," he said. "So I was as keen to learn her language as she was to learn mine," and to much laughter he added. "I found I learned quickly!

114

"And the girl, Mhaktoun? Your Leila?" Al Raschid asked him, still grinning.

"Sadly, my Lord, she was bitten by a black scorpion in the desert lands near Tabriz, as we were travelling home, and died. In truth I loved her greatly. Her name means, 'Beautiful with dark hair', and so she was…and she was with child…so I lost them both. *Insh'a Allah.* But I could have wished it otherwise."

"I am sorry for that, my Mhaktoun," Al Raschid said, briefly laying his hand on the man's massive shoulders. "I had no idea any girl had ever come so close to your soul."

Sheik El Nazir, watched the confusion on his giant guard's face and was moved by it. Then he looked at them both and smiled. "Very well, you two. You have heard all that Mistress Soraya has had to say, and I believe it to be both wise and sensible. Do not speak any language other than Arabic unless you may be certain of being neither observed nor overheard. Najid can only speak Arabic anyway, so he is not a problem. If anything else needs to be discussed, then speak in Farsi with Mistress Soraya, except in private when you are sure no-one else is near to hear you. I put her and her companions in your charge, both of you. But it is to be Mhaktoun's responsibility to ensure their ultimate safety. Your balls on a plate before me if any harm comes to them! Understand?"

"*Yes, My Prince!*" They both replied, bowing before him, touching their fingers to their foreheads and to their lips as they stood up again.

"I will speak with you all, before you leave the *Morning Star*, my new 'Company of the White Rose.' You may both go. *Salaam Alaikum!*"

"*Salaam Alaikum*, My Lord Prince!"

El Nazir watched the men leave, and turned to the two English girls and smiled, pleased with their astonishment at his munificence and at the new name he had given them all…as much as the wide eyed surprise on the faces of all those around him. He liked to do the unexpected; it kept everyone on their toes!

"Mhaktoun Aquib is a good man, My Lady Alic-ia," The Sheik said turning to her. "The name 'Aquib' means '*Protector*'...in fact he is a great wrestler as you may have gathered, as well as an amazing swordsman. 'Abdul Aziz' means '*Servant of the Powerful One*'...And so he is," he added with a grin. "He serves me...and has been with me for many years, and has never been beaten in a fight. They will care for you...and they will obey you. They will keep you safe. And Najid will ensure that only the best, and safest, food is served to you. You must eat only what he has prepared!" He added, with a hard stare and a sudden quirked eyebrow. "Even so, My Lady! Even so!" he ended, looking into Alicia's eyes, as the import of what he had said sank home.

She then rose, with Agnes and Soraya beside her, and while Soraya bowed deeply to the Sheik. Alicia and Agnes, encumbered as they were by their chadors, still managed to give him a truly Royal curtsy.

Alicia, stepping forward slightly, her blue eyes glittering behind her Chador said: "My Lord Sheik, when we were so violently seized off my ship three mornings ago I hated you with great bitterness and anger. I feared for my honour and that of my companion. Yet you and your people have treated us with great generosity and care on your *Surah At-Tariq*...your *Morning Star*. She is a fine vessel and I can see why you are so proud of her. There are many Christians who would not have been so generous nor so caring, were we to have foundered in a like manner.

I thank you also for the great kindness in providing us with such unexpected protection in the face of one whom I now know to be an even more dangerous enemy than I had expected. And for the lovely name you have chosen for our little Company. I have no wish to be allied to the Baron in any way, and while deploring him as a murderer and a man of evil deeds, I respect your friendship for him and hope that if I was faced with the same situation, I would behave towards my enemies in the same manner in which you have behaved towards me and my companions.

We may be of different religions, My Lord Prince. But we both honour the same God. We are also People of the Book...*Ahlul Kitaab*...as I learned from the Black Monk who is my fiancé's friend, and has journeyed as far as Persia and the Arabian Sea in his travels, and has taught me many things as you know. May *Allah* protect you, *El Nazir-al Jameel-Aziz ibn Nidhaal*, as I pray

116

for God to protect me, and I thank you, from the bottom of my heart." And she rose and, bowing deeply, said. "*Salaam Alaikum!*" Before stepping back beside her friends, everyone astonished by all she had said.

Standing, Sheik El Nazir looked directly into Alicia's violet-blue eyes, and once more gave her the slightest inclination of his head, touching first his forehead and then his lips with his fingers as he did so. "*Insh'a Allah*, My Lady," he said in his dark, rich voice, before gesturing for her and her companions to leave his great cabin, along with everyone else except his cabin servant, Jussuf.

To him he gave a written order for Almahdi aal Suriyyan, his Pigeon Master, to send a bird to the Baron immediately informing him that Alicia had arrived at Bayonne and his plan was in operation, before waving Jussuf away about his master's business.

★

No sooner had the door softly closed behind him, than Sheik El Nazir leaned back against it with a sigh of relief and breathed out deeply. So, that was that, the Baron's careful plan was now in motion and he could move forward at last, master of his own destiny again! No longer in Baron Roger's coils. All he needed to do now was collect his men from Grise in due course, and get back in the war!

And moving towards the wide stern seating, collecting his glass of orange sherbet from the table as he passed, he paused first to listen to all the shipboard sounds going on around him, before bending to slide the oak panels that held the horn windows in place to one side. Then, sitting down, he turned to look at the blue sparkling waters of the great Bay behind him as he drank, and giving a another huge sigh of relief, he smiled.

Above him, with a sudden bang and clatter he heard the great double banks of oars lifted up and outboard on either side of the ship; the first deep, reverberating ***thuddd!*** of the Hortator's drum…and the great shout of the rowers, all two hundred and fifty of them, as they made that first deep pull into the sea. On deck, he knew that the sails would soon be tightly furled, their halliards coiled and sorted and the two anchors readied to drop if necessary, while his two 'captives' and all their gear, and that of Soraya and the men he was sending with them, would soon be gathered together and taken up there also. The 'Company of the White Rose'. He liked it. It pleased him, and he smiled at the shock his words had caused that morning.

Her oars beating together as one, like gulls wings he always thought, the *Morning Star* would make a powerful sight as she swept from the estuary into the River Adour itself, passing all the many smaller ships like a great shark amongst a shoal of simple herrings.

It could not be often that a great fighting dromond from the Mediterranean ever came into a Christian port like Bayonne on the Atlantic Coast. Frightening for some…even terrifying. What a panic she would cause if she entered with her artillery manned, her great siphon in place and her marines all armoured-up on deck!:…'*Les Corsairs! Les Corsairs!*'…he could almost hear the screams. And he grinned mischievously at the thought of it, then laughed. But he had a special pass for this visit. From the Lord Baron, his friend, signed by King Phillip of France himself no less. And he had ordered the white flags of peace to be flown from both mastheads and from her stern. So…no panics today! He sighed, and sipped again from his glass.

How the Baron had managed such a thing was beyond him? But he had it, and it was real! And he laughed again, gazing without processed thought, to the far, far distant horizon where the azure sky and the deeper blue of the Atlantic finally met in one long, dark line.

It had been an extraordinary time…and what an extraordinary woman, the White Rose of Malwood.?

A battle as fierce and bloody as any he had witnessed, or fought in. By *Allah*, but those Franks, could fight! And their women too! And what a girl?…no, a '*Lady*'…that one had proven to be! He was astonished. Both at her boldness under pressure, and at her courage, and pride…and her learning, extraordinary! Who would have thought any woman could read, let alone use Arabic at him? No wonder the Baron had been so impressed.

He drank again, watching the local shipping bobbing in the *Morning Star's* wake. He had started this expedition with a profound contempt for all Christian Franks, especially their women. And all just to serve his friend, The Lord Baron Roger de Brocas! He had ended not just touching one, but offering her hospitality and the services of two of the most trusted and ferocious warriors in his command…and that not just because he had already agreed to do so with Lord Roger…but because he actually wanted to! And he suddenly rocked with laughter.

It was such a cunning plan that the Baron had devised…and he had *loved* the role of bestial, roaring, infidel Pirate…after all that's what he was! And then, next moment, to show himself to be suddenly caring and understanding…soo friendly? It had all been masterly, and he chuckled again, pleased with himself, especially as none of the men leaving him knew a thing. Not even Al Raschid knew the truth of why he had changed his mind about the two *Nasraani* women. And poor Lady Al-icia?…He smiled. The White Rose…she had been properly fooled, and no mistake.

But the Lord Roger needed a wife. His friend needed an heir, he understood that, and Rochine knew that too, and had planned and schemed with her father to seize hold of the girl he wanted, no matter what the cost, expecting to control everything as she was used to doing. She had thought she would be grabbing hold of a silly pigeon ripe for plucking…but she had found instead a wild, bating Goshawk, with a wicked beak to tear and the sharpest of talons with which to pierce and bind on! And their plan had been foiled, *Insha'Allah*, and so Lord Roger had turned to him for help.

Well…he, Sheik El Nazir, had now done his part for his friend…and more! Not only had he succeeded where Lord Roger had failed. But he had made sure the girl had the support she would need when the time came for her to flee from The Lady again. And two of his best men too! And little Najid. Such planning had gone into all of this that surely, *By Allah's Mercy*, it must succeed?

And if Roger's Guard Commander, Gaston de Vere, played his part too, *and* did the right thing with what he'd told him about Najid's pretty sister, Faridah, and the powdered roots he would be bringing from Grise; then The Baron's plan might work really well. For if they all fled from Rochine's men, as the Baron had planned for…and he then rescued her from de Vere and The Lady in hot pursuit of them; then she would see him in the light of blessed rescuer and not of hated jailor and enforcer.

And the Baron could be so very charming when he wished to be…and so dissembling! Now was the time to see if his friend could hold on to what he had stolen. He couldn't wait to see Rochine's face when they docked, and her 'pigeon' walked off the *Morning Star* with her own little coterie of servants and her two giant bodyguards. The Company of the White Rose!

And he smiled and raised his glass to the morning. *Allah Akbar!...'God is Great!'*

Chapter 17...The White Rose and The Lady meet again.

O n the upper deck all was tremendous bustle and noise as the *Morning Star* swept up the river towards the long quays that stretched away both up and down it on either side of the town's battlemented walls and towers. Everywhere there were ships of every size loading and unloading; carts and waggons arriving and leaving; strings of pack horses, laden donkeys, porters and dockers carrying loads on their backs and busy cranes, their huge wooden tread wheels in constant motion, dipping their hooks deep into the bellies of a number of great cogs that had recently arrived, laden with huge hogsheads of wine and casks of oil. And people thronging everywhere.

Even with her white flags streaming from masts and stern, so that all could see she came in peace, the *Morning Star's* sudden appearance had brought wild consternation to almost the whole waterfront. And in the town the bells were tolling. Had she arrived with her vicious artillery fully manned, her armoured men on deck and her siphon for spewing out Greek Fire properly mounted, the terror and confusion could not have been any greater.

So no-one noticed Almahdi carefully choosing a bird from one of the two wicker cages that had been brought up onto the high sterncastle, playing with her legs briefly before throwing her up into the air, where she circled the *Morning Star* briefly before flying off like a feathered arrow to the South. Nor did they see him dipping in again amongst his crooning, fluttering charges to choose a second message carrier, and releasing that one too. And no-one heard him say: "'Ware Hawk, my Lovely! 'Ware Hawk!" as he threw her upwards.

Up on the her deck Alicia, Agnes and Soraya, with their baggage and new belongings beside them, stood watching in amazement at the sight of so much pandemonium along the dockside: people running in all directions, many screaming; bundles dropped, donkeys kicking and braying, packhorse trains being run up the streets of the town, horns blowing dogs barking...even some ships desperately trying to cast off before they could be seized and boarded. All expecting 'Les Corsairs' to pour out amongst them, with all the terror and violence for which they were so well known.

With their two huge warrior guards behind them, and Najid and his collection of pans, ladles, baskets of spices and special provisions close beside them, the three girls laughed and pointed out to one another all the chaos going on as their ship made her dramatic approach, drums and oars beating in quick time, a bone of boiling white in her teeth, nakirs rattling and trumpets blowing from her raised sterncastle.

But it was not a universal panic.

Others stood in fascinated groups as they watched 'Surah At-Tariq' swooping down towards them: spray flying from the great iron ram at her beak and water running in sparkling rivulets from her oar blades as they flashed in the bright sunlight, moving all together in spectacular rhythm, churning the river, beating it into fierce whirlpools of white water every time they dipped up and down; the *thudding!* of the Hortator's drum, the bang and groan of her rowlocks never ending as she swept past them all less than half a cable from the quayside, with a fierce tattoo of nakirs and a blast of wild, brazen music,

Then, as if by magic, the oars suddenly rose up as one, level with the river, the noise stopped, and both sets dropped down and held water, forcing her rapidly to lose way. Then, with a great *thudd!* on the Hortator's huge kettle–drum, while one bank of oars dipped down again and rowed forward…the other held and backed water so that the whole vessel spun around as if on some amazing hidden turntable, all one hundred and thirty feet of her, losing all speed as she did so, til with another *thudd!* She began to paddle quietly towards the quays, both sets of oars still in the water to hold her steady till the way came off her completely and she could sidle gently with the current against the sprung staithes that were waiting for her.

Truly it was a bravura performance and many actually clapped as the spin stopped and the *Morning Star* began to move again.

But clearly someone had been watching for her, for even as she had appeared, and the bells had tolled out, a whole company of soldiers had trotted out of the town gates and formed up around what was clearly an agreed space for her to moor up to, creating a human barrier between the Dromond now being tied firmly to the quay with great ropes fore and aft, and the town itself. Flags of peace there might well be flying from her mastheads…and her artillery might well be covered, but this was a great fighting dromond from the Circle Sea…and no-one was taking any chances!

With the ship finally at rest, a long ribbed gang way, with rope sides on spaced stanchions, was rushed forward by four of the soldiers who made up the sudden dockside guard, and from behind where Alicia was standing two trumpets sharply blew, and two dozen of Sheik El Nazir's men ran out, down the gangway and formed up on either side of it.

Each wore pantaloons of white silk, with a quilted jacket of white serge, sleeves embroidered with gold thread, under a short breastplate of polished steel, and each also carried the curved scimitar for which the Corsairs were famed, wore a white tarboosh with a great gold tassel on its crown, and looked both magnificent…and clearly ceremonial.

Behind them came Al Raschid in glittering mail that fell below his waist over mailed chausses on black leather. He wore a pointed helmet, green feathers at its top, over a shining chain coif. A long jewelled sword, of Christian pattern, hung off a glittering belt of scarlet leather, studded with disks of pure gold, and a long cloak of green satin shimmered from his armoured shoulders.

And behind him strode *Sheik El Nazir-al Jameel-Aziz ibn Nidhaal*, in white and gold like his guard, only all of purest silk, with a long cloak of cloth-of-gold hanging in glittering magnificence from his shoulders in the sunshine, and a white satin turban with a huge sapphire in its centre on his head. Around his waist, from a gold leather belt studded with sapphires and rubies, hung a jewelled scimitar on one side and on the other a great *Khanjar*, the curved dagger for which his people were famous, its hilt encrusted with jewels, its scabbard of gold chased with silver and rimmed with emeralds, the colour of Islam. Quite simply he looked every inch the Prince he was. Gleaming…outstanding…dazzling! No-one in Bayonne had ever seen anything like it before in their lives!

At a sign from the crew manning the deck, Alicia and her small party quietly made their way to the head of the gangway and stopped.

Below them the Sheik's personal honour guard were still drawn up in two lines either side of it, himself not yet having actually stepped onto the Quayside. Before them, well spaced out, stood the soldiers who had trotted from the town at the *Morning Star's* arrival, equally still and silent; the crowd behind them murmuring, gabbling, pointing and jostling; pushing amongst themselves for the best view of all that was happening...then came a sudden stillness.

The only sound that of the gulls as they swooped and wheeled, filling the sky with their mewling cries, while the sun blazed down, its summer heat making the roof tops shimmer, and the sweat flow. It was but a momentary frozen tableau: the wind fluttering tassels, feathers and silk alike as it whispered amongst them, flacking loose halliards against the *Morning Star's* tall masts, scuttering small fragments of hay and straw across the cobbled ground. An unreal stillness that was as swiftly broken by the sudden clatter of shod hooves, the scrunch of wheels and the snort of horses, and the scramble of booted feet as a whole section of soldiers around the dockside swung open like a gate, through which a small party of nine men on horseback, fully armoured-up, weapons at their side...four with crossbows on their backs, and one woman, accompanied by two large tilt carts, two horses to each cart and a number of horses on leading reins, slowly made their way.

At the foot of the gangway, in all his magnificence El Nazir stood with his guard around him. At the top, still in her chador, stood Alicia, with her new household around her, her Company of the White Rose, her blue eyes chips of ice.

Below, on her white mare, in a scarlet bliaut, embroidered with swirling patterns of gold and silver thread over a white silk kirtle, sat the Lady Rochine de Brocas, belted in with enamelled panels of scarlet and blue edged with gold, Her black hair covered by a white satin caul, threaded with gold and studded with pearls, above a brilliant scarlet silk coif that flowed from her shoulders like flames, and a long scarlet mantle that fell right over her horse's back, even her feet were clad in scarlet leather. She looked imperious...untouchable.

Alicia thought she was dressed in blood, and shuddered, glad of the black chador that covered her.

Kicking her horse forward, her Guard Commander by her side, her personal guard fanning out in a semicircle around her, the Lady Rochine's emerald eyes were as hard as jade, her mouth a scarlet slash. She had come to collect her father's bride-to-be. A week's journey if all went well. She grunted, looking up at the women standing above the gangway, and her eyes glittered. She *knew* which one was the Lady Al-ic-ia de Bur-ley! Not even that ridiculous chador thing could hide her! She swayed delicately in her saddle, her thoughts venomous, her stomach suddenly griped with bile, and she turned to look up river.

Over two hundred miles lay between Bayonne and Gruissan. By river first to Peyrehorade, then all the rest by road and trackway: mountains, forests, wilderness and streams; deep valleys, small villages, little towns and rough tracks; bandits, murderers and thieves! Nothing civilised until Carcassonne. She had just travelled it.

She kicked her horse forward some more and smiled. A lot could happen over two hundred miles…and she smiled again!

Chapter 18... *Gui leads his men on the long road to Niort.*

They broke fast at Vertou, with the mists burning off as the sun rose gloriously into a duck-egg blue sky filled with great streamers of pink and gold, just as the lay brothers were setting out for the fields, and the monks to the cloisters.

As they approached the great Abbey gates, the ground still wet with dew, the air clear, Abbott Hugo Gravier came out to greet them, his arms open wide, first to clasp Father Matthew, and then Gui, while their men flung themselves off their horses to make their way to the trestle tables that the Abbot had ordered prepared against their coming. Bread still fresh and warm from the Abbey's ovens, cold meats, cheese and olives all on polished wooden platters; crocks of butter, and golden honey from the Abbey's hives…and wine, French ale and cider. And while they ate and drank in the Great Courtyard before the gates, some standing some sitting on the verges nearby, the horses were watered by the lay brothers, and those still too wounded to ride were comforted, and their dressings changed.

"Where to next, My Son?" Abbot Hugo asked of Sir Gui, as he stood with his Commanders, drinking from a horn beaker.

"As you suggested, Father: Clisson, Chantonnay, Niort and Saint Jean d'Angeley. The same route your monks take with their waggons to Bordeaux. Then Saintes, Pons and Bordeaux at last. One week!"

"That will be hard going, Sir Gui. The road is not smooth and there are many streams and fords. You may need more than a week…but there are some small towns along the way, and castles, which will always take you in of course, especially at Niort, where King Richard is building a massive donjon, and re-arranged the castle his father first commissioned."

"Who holds there Father?" Sir Richard asked.

"Count William de Forz holds for the King and is very much Richard's Leal man; which, sadly, cannot be said of all the Poitou Barons. He and I have known each other of old, and I have a parchment for him that might be of help," he said, handing Gui a short scroll tied with blue ribbon, secured with blue wax and stamped with the Abbey's Great Seal.

"Thank you, Father. Is there anything else you can add?"

"Not more really than I told Father Matthew, yesterday. There are a few inns where you might get shelter," he added. "Not perhaps The Angel...but good enough," he smiled. "And once you reach Saint Jean d'Angeley you are nearly there. It is a cheerful place and will serve you well. They are good people there, and another brother house, famous for having the Head of John the Baptist...well so they say! The town has good walls and a tall tower the merchants there are very proud of."

"Thank you, Father, for this parchment," Gui said smiling, tucking it into his saddle-bag. "And for all your kindness...and for your advice," he added sweeping his arms around him. "God Willing, we will come back through here and bring you the treasures you seek from Jerusalem."

"A Blessing, Father," Sir Richard drawled, dipping his fingers in a bowl of warm water. "And then, Gui, we must leave. We have stayed overlong as it is, and have plenty more miles to cover today before we can stop. I don't trust de Courcy, and we are still too close to Nantes for comfort!"

"I agree, Richard!" then calling to his men: "*Fitzurse, Jean, Allan-i-the-Wood*, mount-up, we are leaving. Change the scouts around, Master-at-Arms. Father Hugo, my warmest thanks," Gui bowed to the Abbot, who briefly laid a cool hand on his forehead in silent blessing, before he swung himself back onto Beau, as with a clatter and grind of wheels, they all began to leave. What the men couldn't eat they took with them, stuffing it into the small leather bag that each man had hanging off the back of his saddle, together with a small flask of watered wine for each man, that Abbott Hugo had also provided.

Then, while he stood in his long black gown, with its cowl down, and his arms up and open wide to give them all the Blessing Sir Richard had asked for, they pulled off all around him and were gone, the last scouts behind the column turning in their saddles to wave a final goodbye to Abbot Hugo and his brothers, all clustered around him like a Parliament of Rooks.

★

Throughout that remaining day they travelled south, the track they were on busy with travellers in some places, and barren and empty in others. Sometimes, on the edge of far clearings, deer could be seen at gaze from amongst the trees, or leaping across the track as they approached, only to vanish as swiftly as they had been seen. And there were those amongst them who twitched to draw a bow at venture and shoot one down, all eyeing Bouncer to see of he would give chase. But Allan had trained him well, and he stayed close to Caesar when called to heel.

There were pedlars with heavy packs on their backs, bulging with trinkets; farmers with solid wheeled carts laden with vegetables, chickens and piglets in wooden crates; a farmer with a calf on a rope bawling for its mother; a tilt cart with family belongings, father leading a horse, mother and children piled amongst the furniture; a boy with a dog and a small flock of sheep; players and musicians, tumblers and groups of sturdy peasants trudging between fields, tools across their shoulders; a wandering grey friar; a Palmer in his wide brimmed hat, his scrip full of relics, fragments of the True Cross, no doubt culled from a local carpenter, or the nails from Christ's hands and feet stolen from a nearby blacksmith! Even a lady in a covered horse litter, an armed guard at her head and two at her side. But they pushed past them all in a jingle of spurs and bridle irons and a thunder of wheels and flashing feet, and with such determined faces no-one chose to try and stop them.

The trackway, hot and dry under the relentless sun, and deeply rutted in places, was hard under their hooves, as they barrelled on their way. The dust of their passage floating like pale smoke above them, whitening their faces and their armour, making those at the very end of the column spit and choke, tying masks across their faces, and cursing their Commanders for not allowing them to stop.

Walk, trot, canter! Walk, trot, canter! Walk, trot, canter!

128

Everyone joggling in their saddles, or swaying from side to side: those leading the sumpters straining with their long reins; those driving the tilt carts watching the traces and head collars for any signs of breakage, and doing their best to keep up the pace. Hard on the men...but even more so on the horses pulling them in the cloying heat and dust of that first day.

At noon Gui flung up his hand and they bounced wearily to a stop beside a small stream, pulling off the road under the shade of some trees to refresh the horses, which stood heads down in the crystal running water, as much to cool their feet as to drink their fill. All around them the men sat or lay flopped with tiredness, eating from their packs that which they had saved from the morning, and drinking from their flagons, before going upstream to re-fill them. Many relieved themselves amongst the trees...all grateful for the rest.

"You were right, Jean," Gui said to de Beaune a while later with a grimace. "It *is* different in France from at home. Greater empty distances and much harder and drier...and hotter," he finished, wiping his face with a linen cloth wrung out from the stream.

"You think this is hot?" Father Matthew chuckled, flapping the loose neck of his woollen habit as he joined them. "You wait til you get to Grise...or even more, to the Holy Land! Now...that really *is* what one might call *hot!*"

"God willing we will be more hardened to it by then," Gui grunted. "How are the lads doing?"

"Oh...fine. Hot, bothered and dusty. Especially those at the rear of the column. We ought to change them round more often. And the horses are suffering a bit."

"Yes, my Lord," de Beaune nodded. "Especially those pulling the carts. They need more care or they'll not make it. Trying to get them to drink from a waterskin wastes too much...and a helmet isn't big enough."

"And we have no buckets from which they can drink," Gui groaned, levering himself off the ground. "Silly of us not to have thought about that sooner. So simple really! We must try and buy some on our way through the next town, or market we come to. Come on, O my noble Guard Commander, it's time to move."

"Can't think of everything, Dear Boy," Richard said with his lazy grin, as he gathered his things around him. "Must have something to moan about, don't you know, or where's the fun in life?" Then, standing up he shouted: "Master-at-Arms! Get the lads moving. We can't stay here all day...*Mount Upp!*"

And banging the dirt from his cyclas and off his steel chausses, Sir Richard pulled his squire, Philip, to his feet and went to inspect Merlin. Lifting each enormous foreleg in turn, checking the frogs on each hoof for stones or damage, and testing his shoes for movement. Then with a swift ruffle, a pat on his withers, and a foot-up from his squire, he was back on Merlin again and together with Gui, their scouts already ahead of them, he led the column back onto the road and away again.

Fording streams and wending down valleys, helping with the tilt carts where it was most needed, the ruts deepest from the winter or where the trackway was badly broken up, they pushed forward til the sun was beginning to fall, and they came to the Sevres River, from where the battlements of Clisson Castle could be seen poking up above the trees ahead.

Gui stood up in his stirrups and stretched himself, and leaning forward on the high pommel of his saddle he looked about him. Twenty miles a day a Roman army could cover, Father Matthew had told him when they had all set out. And they had done almost twenty five since leaving Nantes...and that had included the long river crossing before Vertou.

He looked up at the sky, still blue and clear, the occasional bird passing high, high over head like an arrow. A pigeon probably from the way it was flying, wings beating fast and continuously. It would take a rare hawk to catch that one! And watching it speed away he suddenly thought of de Brocas, and looked again at the bird, now fast disappearing...and, for a moment, he wondered, his face creased with a frown.

All around him, as well as great acres of vineyards, were vast open fields filled with wheat and barley, some with a mass of scarlet poppies amongst them and tall, Ox Eye daisies. Purple Vetch and Meadow Sweet thrust out from the verges, along with Toad Flax and pink Valerian, and the hedgerows were thick with Old Man's Beard, Goldenrod and red and white Campion. And he breathed deeply and relaxed.

But even as Beau pushed forwards he disturbed a great covey of partridge that leapt up with a frantic whirr of wings, almost from the feathers around his feet, making the great horse snort and toss his head as they rocketed away into the nearest wheat field, and as they landed a startled flock of sparrows and goldfinches suddenly rose up, tiny wings blurred with speed, and flashed across his path to settle in the hedgerows, swinging and chattering fiercely from the bushes as he and Beau ambled past, making him smile.

Drawing another deep breath he turned round, his eyes flicking past Sir Richard on Merlin just behind him and studied his long column of men and horses, sumpters, carts and all. Tired faces, plodding beasts, dust covered and weary. They could keep going til almost dark, find a bivouac and hunker down…or they could call a stop here. Cross the river by its bridge and beg a bed for the night from the castle. Then they could check again for loose horseshoes, stable the destriers properly, hobble the rest…and start again fresh in the morning. Not so early as today…but early enough to get to Chantonnay tomorrow night…and that was much closer to forty miles than they had covered that day.

Stop now…or press on? He reached down and patted Beauregarde on his neck and pulled his ears gently through his hands, making the big horse shake his head and hurrumph through his nostrils. "So…that's it is it, old chap?" he said as he reached forward and patted his withers. "Had enough for today then?"…and Beau tossed his head and hurrumphed again.

"Talking to that great lump of horseflesh are you, Dear Boy?" Richard drawled at him, with a grin. "At least it's yr horse and not yr sword! That really would worry me!"

131

"Don't you insult Beauregarde, like that, you affected apology for a Christian Knight! He's very sensitive. See he added," as Beau tossed his head again. "Much more of that and we'll push on till dark!"

Richard laughed, and bent his head forward. "O, worthy horse," he intoned solemnly. "O great wise one! What is your wish today? Go on...or stop?"

At which question, without further ado, Beau thrust his head forward into the nearest bush, pulled out a great mouthful of long grasses and nodded his head again, and they both laughed. "Well. I think that settles it," Gui said. "We stop here for the night and move on tomorrow."

And turning to his own Squire he said, "Simon, ride back up the column and tell Fitzurse and the other commanders we will be stopping here at Clisson. Then go with Philip, unfurl our colours, and ride on to the castle and call for aid for tonight. Father Matthew is with the wounded on the carts, so make sure he knows too. Now...I wonder what kind of reception we'll get. I don't know who holds here, but he is on King Richard's lands, so we ought to be alright!"

And with every anticipation of a pleasant evening they both kicked on, their column following, their two squires, with the colours of Malwood and L'Eveque bravely streaming from their standards as they galloped ahead of them towards the castle, from which brazen trumpets were already calling.

*

Four days later they reached Niort.

Four days of hard travelling and frustration, for despite their care at Clisson, Merlin cast a shoe half way after leaving, as had two of their sumpters. A truly maddening delay, while they paused at the tiny village of Saint Fulgent to get them fixed, dealing with the dumbest farrier it was possible to imagine, who had to be dragged out of the nearest alehouse and threatened with castration before he would pick up his tools!

Even then he had been too drunk to do the job, falling all over the place like a witless clown, until Fitzurse had hurled him into the village pond in disgust, to the huge amusement of his men and half the village, while Hordle John pumped up the forge, and Pierre Leclosse, one of de Beaune's Burgundians, sorted out Merlin's shoe and hammered out two more for the sumpters.

A job well done…but it had all taken time, so they'd bivouacked for the night alongside a small stream they'd come to, and then started out again at first light to reach Chantonnay early enough to push on to Niort, still hoping to reach there two days after leaving Nantes. But, two miles out of the town, while negotiating some vile ruts on the trackway, littered with jagged stones, the wheel on one of the tilt carts cracked, the whole iron rim spun off amidst a medley of vile curses, the heavily laden cart collapsed on its side…and they'd lost a whole day!

But Chantonnay was a market town, and having trailed back in, found a wheelwright who could do the job properly…who was neither one of 'God's Children' nor drunk…Gui decided that they would stay there properly, and leave the following morning.

"God's Blood! Matthew," he cursed, tearing off his helmet and throwing it down onto one of the packs. "What a damned mess of pottage this is. First Merlin, and now a bloody cart's wheel. I thought we'd fixed all that up before leaving Nantes?"

"Remember what I said, My Lord?" Jean de Beaune said in passing, with a grin. "France is not England! Hotter, drier and harder. The more we try to hurry, the more likely it is we'll break something."

Gui laughed ruefully. "More haste less speed, you mean?"

"Something like that, Sir Gui. But I tend to look at things in the light of 'things happen when they're meant to'! In this way, as it's Market Day here, we ought find those buckets we need for the horses, and some fresh eggs as well," he added with a hungry look. The horses need the buckets…and I like a hard boiled egg with my smoked meat…"

"And a flagon of cider with which to wash it down," Sir Richard interrupted, with his lazy voice. "Father Matthew's chasing up some Milfoil and Vervain he saw some on one of those stalls in the market, and he's collared the local priest about some shrine or other we passed earlier. Gui, Dear Boy, just bend to it. We can't move on without the damned cart, so you might as well take it off your back and enjoy it!"

And so they all had. Found the buckets they needed, fresh eggs and fresh vegetables…and lots of local red wine!

The arrival of so many strangers, with money to spend, and some time to spend it was good for everyone, and before long the men had dispersed amongst the market stalls, and the houses, shops and bothies that made up Chantonnay, arm in arm with a cloud of girls who had suddenly appeared amongst them, gaily dressed as for a festival.

The horses were hobbled by the stream that ran along the edge of the little town where they would bivouac for the night. The local inn was thronged, and the townsfolk produced the best they could, especially fresh bread from the town ovens…and the men drank, spent their silver, squabbled and boasted cheerfully amongst themselves…and fought the local lads over the local girls, who shrieked and laughed and fled amongst the barns and bushes in the warm night like so many fireflies.

★

In the morning they left again at first light, with the sky clear, but soon after the sun had risen in a blush of crimson and gold it began to cloud up from the North West before a flustering breeze, the clouds casting great drifting shadows across the long ridge of hills that ran along the horizon on their right. And as the day progressed, the cloud cover grew denser, the sun disappeared and rain threatened, the wind now scurrying amongst them, and Gui pulled the column over so that the men could dig their hooded cloaks out of the packs they had rolled up against the high cantles of their saddles.

"Rain...and soon, I think." Father Matthew said, looking up into the darkening sky. "Those clouds are getting lower. I've lost sight of that long ridge over there already."

"That'll cool everyone down," L'Eveque drawled. "Specially all those with a thick head this morning. By God, that local red wine was rough! Certainly left my mouth full of moths this morning!" He ended with a wry grin.

"I expect there'll be a few blue eyed strangers amongst that lot too come the Spring," Fitzurse laughed, pointing back along the way they'd come. "Some of our lads were in amongst those girls like rats up a pipe. A fair number of Hail Mary's in Chantonnay today I'll warrant!"

Richard laughed too and Gui grunted, shifting in his saddle. "All the more reason to press on now!" And standing up in his stirrups he waved his hands in a circle around his head, calling them all forward again and kicked Beau back onto the road, while his Master-at-Arms waited to let the column leaders go past, before spurring back to his chosen scouts at the rear.

Ten minutes later the rain started, a fine driving mizzle that soon became a steady fall, first laying the dust and then pooling in the ruts that scored the track. All around them the trees shook their heads in the wind, rattling more drops over them as they passed, and the birds flocked from the fields to shelter in the woods and hedgerows. And so it was all that long day.

Worst when the trackway wound amongst the vineyards and the great open fields, where there was no cover at all, the wind driven rain making the men hunch their shoulder in under their cloaks and drop their heads, pulling their hoods further forward as they did so. Their horses too tucked in their tails whenever the wind squalled across their rumps with a sudden extra blast of rain, and plodded forward, heads down and miserable. Nor was it much better amongst the woods where wet branches, in full summer leaf, smacked them as they went by, each time giving them all an extra soaking. And as the day progressed, so their passage slowed as the carts got into trouble amongst the deeper ruts and the trackway turned from hard passage to sticky mud.

Twice they stopped briefly to change scouts around and rest the horses, but Gui was determined that they would reach Niort that day, no matter what, and so it was a very weary, sodden Command, that crested the road that led down to the bridge across the Sèvres at last, and to the town beyond and the great castle that towered high above it.

Chapter 19...The Lord Baron makes his plans with care.

In Nantes the Baron's pigeon message arrived safely at midday. The bell that de Courcy had arranged in the tower loft the Baron had set up two years before, when he had bought the manor in which Sir Alan was living, rang sharply to tell him so, and it was only a few minutes later that his Pigeon Master brought the tiny cylinder through to him.

Freed from Castle duties as he was, he and Victor Jonelle, his right hand man, were together in the house's modest Great Hall when they received it.

"So...Lord Roger wants us to set things running with Bernard de Vernaille in Bordeaux. That's good. I expect we'll get a message from him too shortly. But I do not intend for us to miss out on all the fun, Victor. What did you do with that little rat who came sneaking to us last night?"

"After I smashed-up his hand, and threatened to cut his throat?"

"No...after that. After he told us all he knew."

"I dragged him down to where those two bastards had stabled their horses and cut his throat, of course! Lovely mess. Blood everywhere! Covered him with hay and straw and left him for someone to find. He has no family, so next stop the river!"

"Good! I'll arrange for that idiot du Clefs to find the body...and then we'll both shout Blue Murder and rouse the Hue and Cry against them."

"But we have no Warrant to arrest them, My Lord, nor ever likely to get one...not least because they didn't do anything! And you know as well as I do that the Hue and Cry is only strictly local."

"Are you going soft on me, Jonelle," de Courcy rasped.

"No, Sir Alan!" He replied tersely, straightening his shoulders. "I want those bastards as much as you do! They shamed me as well as you, and our men. But we swore on King Richard's Seal...and I like my job here and value a whole skin! A shame we couldn't have done for that fat fool Roland, that really would have given us a lever against them!"

"No matter! King Richard is on his way to Marseilles, and we are the Count of Brittany's 'leal' men, or so he believes, and the Hue and Cry will enable us to mount a strong party at the Duke's expense. His Seneschal is down with the bloody flux, and can do nothing to stop us. Be bold, Victor. We have done this before...there is no reason it won't work just as well again now! So...how many men do we take?"

"Thirty, I think. And if Sir Bernard brings swordsmen and archers...we'll bring lancers with re-inforced chest pieces, shields on their backs and long swords. We can draw rations for five days, and be on our way before Vespers."

"We need to fix the ferry for our use. So send half a dozen of your lads to seize it now. And if that stupid bastard who runs it complains, break his fucking head for him! A little blood spilled now will save us hours later."

"What about Roland?"

"Leave him to me! He's in as deep as we are. If he knows what's good for him he'll keep his trap good and firmly shut. He has made a mint out of working with us over the Port Tolls and Revenues, and I have kept a record of *every* penny he's taken out of the Count's proper dues. He'll be no problem; values his fat skin far too much for that. Any real nonsense and he can join the 'Ferret' in the bloody river...and so I'll tell him!"

"Right, My Lord. I'll get on and sort out the men I want with us. No new ones. Just the hard bastards who know what cut and thrust is really all about, what will you do?"

"Send a message to the Baron Roger at Gruissan, and another to Bernard in Bordeaux. He'll need eighty men at least...and he'll have to be careful where he gets them from and how he musters them. That bastard Sir Hugh Willoughby is the High Constable of all Aquitaine, *and* Guard Commander at Bordeaux. He *is* a truly Leal man to King Richard, and as hard as bloody nails. If he gets even a whiff of what we are planning, there will be a dreadful reckoning to pay. He can cut de Vernaille, and any command he has, in bits before he's even gone a mile!"

"Let's hope Sir Bernard has as much sense as we do, then?"

"Victor…I hope so too! Now, those fuckers left at first light this morning, and they have carts with them which will slow them down. We don't, and can travel fast and light. In five days at most they should be at Saint Jean d'Angeley. Plenty of time for de Vernaille to close in on them from the South, and for us to catch up with them from the North. Then, between us, we'll take them to pieces and feed their bits to the bloody crows! We leave in four hours!"

★

Just before Vespers, the bell in Bernard de Vernaille's Pigeon Loft on the southern edge of Bordeaux also rang, and moments later he held de Courcy's message in his hand, having already received an earlier one from the Baron in Gruissan, and sent one on to Nantes as well.

A tall rangy man, with a loping stride and narrow shoulders, his face smooth, with dark eyes to match his hair and eyebrows, and a mouth made more for smiles than frowns. But his soul was bitter, and his humour sour, not matching the smiling face he showed to strangers; and his prowess was with ill-tutored townsmen, loose women and the wine for which Bordeaux was famous. His father, Sir Rupert de Vernaille, had been a famous warrior. A man of a steel whom all men could trust. His son seemed not to be of his father's making, and the old Lord had turned him off his lands, not given him authority over his estates…nor of any part of his inheritance.

So he had come to the Baron's notice, and had joined his faction; and Lord Roger had fed his esteem and built up his meinie with soldiers of his own, and now the old Lord was dead at last, he had inherited all that his father had so carefully built up, had thrown out all those who had worked for Lord Rupert without a penny...and installed his own people in their place. He was a mean master, and good men would not work for him.

Now...waving the tiny message in his hand, he fancied himself a warrior in his father's mould. A cunning fighter; a man for tomorrow whom men would follow into Hell's mouth itself and he viewed the coming skirmish with relish. An ambush, near Saint Jean d'Angeley? Good thinking. He knew that area. There was thick forest all round there...apart from the great fields that edged the town...and nothing much in between, and several fordable streams and a river with a proper bridge just this side of the town where they would be sure to draw up for the night. From Saint Jean to Niort was the best part of forty miles. So they would not push beyond the town. If he got moving as soon as he could muster his men, they would have time to do some useful scouting. Pin things down properly...as his father would have done!

Should get there with a day to spare, maybe more!

Eighty men! That would not be easy...especially as he must be certain that that cunning bastard, Sir Hugh Willoughby, didn't get wind of anything. He had eyes and ears everywhere, especially just now with King bloody Richard about to set off for the Holy Land, everyone a bit uncertain about what might happen behind his back once he'd gone! Not all his Barons could be trusted...not even his brother, so it was rumoured? So...difficult, but not impossible!

"Geoffrey, you idle bugger," he shouted over his shoulder. "Get yourself here straightaway! We have had our orders from the Baron at Grise...and advice from de Courcy at Nantes. He's setting out with thirty lancers today...and advises us we'll need eighty men from here. Come on dear brother; we need to put our heads together, and send for that Master Sergeant of ours to join us!"

Moments later both men were seated at the long table in Sir Bernard's hall, wine to hand in tall silver gilt goblets, both elegantly dressed in long gowns with wide sleeves, coloured hose, and suede half boots on their feet; Sir Geoffrey de Vernaille, square where his brother was lean, and more broad shouldered, but with the same dark hair and eyebrows, and the same smiling face with the evil intent hidden behind it.

Shortly after that, with a brief bow, their Master-at-Arms, Martin Riberac, joined them, a tough, burley man with a weathered face like tooled leather, piercing grey eyes, and great butcher's hands that could wield an axe as if it were of wood, not hardened steel. In tough, riveted mail and leather chauses, plain sword and dagger at his waist he looked what he was, a hardened, professional soldier.

"Wine, Riberac?"

"Thank you, My Lord."

"We have had the message we have been waiting for, Martin. We need eighty men, horsed, fully armoured-up and ready to leave by tomorrow. No fuss, no arguments…and no boasting!"

"Where for, My Lord?"

"Saint Jean d'Angeley in four day's time. Mixed forces, Sergeant. Half archers, half swordsmen. No spears. They are coming from elsewhere."

"We have half of those already under arms several miles outside the city walls, at Saint Savin, My Lord. Your father held land there in the days of the old King, Henry Plantagenet. It was a kind of training camp for the old King's wars. We just kept it going."

"The Sergeant's right, Bernard," his brother said swiftly, putting his drink down in surprise. "I had forgotten that. And it's been a while since we rode out there and gave the old man's lands the once over. That bastard, Willoughby, would never question us doing so now we have inherited…nor taking a guard along with us."

"What, Geoffrey? Twenty men apiece? He would have to be both blind and stupid not to question such a large bodyguard. And while Sir Hugh Willoughby may be many things we both deplore…blind and stupid he is not!"

"You are forgetting that Richard of England is gathering an army to fight the Saracens in the Holy Land. Troops are moving around all over the place just now, leaving many manors vulnerable...and we do have many lands hereabouts, as Sir Hugh knows."

"And not all the Poitevin Barons are as secure as our noble King would like. So taking a good guard, with what men we can muster, to visit our newly gained lands in Saint Savin...since that miserable old bastard, our late and unlamented father is now finally dead and buried thank God!...Willoughby will not think that surprising."

Geoffrey de Vernaille, looked at his brother and grinned. "A particularly useful idea, Bernard, as Saint Savin just happens to be towards Saint Jean!"

"And if I set out with half now, My Lords, and you two follow tomorrow individually with the rest, but from different gates and at different times, I doubt anyone will be any the wiser. Not least because you have lands in both directions! It might mean a slight detour to join up together...but that would be a small price to pay, My Lords. Don't you think?"

Bernard de Vernaille looked at his brother across his wine goblet, and then up to his powerful Sergeant-at-Arms, standing with his hands on his hips. "Yes, Geoffrey. That could work. How would you sort it, Riberac?"

"Well, My Lord. If the men play their part, and ride out with plenty of jokes and laughter, all light-hearted like, and full of bounce...saying they're on a training exercise, who would question that?"

Sir Geoffrey stood up: "Martin Riberac!" He laughed. "There are as many rogues in this city as there are rabbits in a pie! We, on the other hand are both belted knights about our lawful business, with no-one to say us nay! You are right...no-one will suspect a thing!"

"I agree, brother. We'll do it. I'll go and see Sir Hugh about the necessary passes; you, Geoffrey, get a message off to Grise to tell Lord Roger what we're doing. And you, Martin, get the lads organised. We travel light, understand? Rations for five days, and weapons only.

We'll take four sumpters with us to carry our armour, and for spare strings, bolts, extra food and sundries, and we leave by stages as discussed. Just pray the weather doesn't turn really foul. Meet me back here in four hours," he ended briskly, banging his hands together, "and we can sort out all the finer details.

You, Riberac, will leave with a third of the men as soon as you can. Night bivouac exercise is what I'll tell Sir Hugh. You and I, Geoffrey, will leave at first light," adding with a laugh, "So no staying with your favourite doxy tonight, brother. If I must do without the so luscious Miranda…you can do without your vulpine Leonora! Up at dawn, and away the moment the gates are opened…and the Devil take the hindmost!"

Chapter 20...Sir Gui arrives at Niort.

After such a long, bruising day in the saddle, by the end of which there was scarcely a dry bit of flesh on anyone, the welcome they received at Niort was every bit as warm as the absent sun. And draggled as they were, the flags that Gui ordered Simon and Philip to unfurl as they approached the long stone bridge over the river, snapped and fluttered in the gusting wind as bravely as any could have wished.

The Scarlet Lion Rampant of Malwood, and the Sable Lion Rampant-Gardant of L'Eveque, both snarled and swiped with their great clawed feet as their two young squires carried them forward with as much pride as if they were bearing the King's own colours on their standards! Over the bridge they clattered, forcing all others to the sides as the long column of mounted men, carts and sumpters entered the town and rode up to the castle gatehouse, all taking note of the long crenellated walls and the twelve well spaced towers that reared up out of them.

The moat, fed by the River, separated the walls from the rest of the town, a serious barrier in itself, but completely dwarfed by the truly massive donjon that King Richard had ordered to be built. One part was already at its full height of nearly a hundred feet, the other still only half built, the whole further protected by a ferocious dry ditch, twenty six feet deep, and nearly as broad, that separated the donjon from the castle bailey and the walls around it.

Gui and Richard halted their column before the gatehouse, its heavy drawbridge open, its portcullis raised, and just stared up at its immensity, the very fighting tops almost lost in the low misty clouds that had bedevilled them all day, the standards flacking wetly in the rain-laden wind and trumpets blowing.

"Well, it was worth the bloody journey just to see it!" Gui said almost breathlessly. "That thing is simply stupendous! Those walls must be twelve feet thick at least...probably twenty at the base, and I hear the ditch is just a nightmare. God help anyone trying to batter their way into that...let alone try and scale it! Amazing!"

"You like my castle, then?" a soft voice broke in unexpectedly. "Sir Gui de Malwood...and...and Sir Richard L'Eveque? By your colours and your blazon?"

Gui, completely taken aback, looked down astonished at the slight figure before him, who must have walked out from the Gatehouse and across the drawbridge to greet them while they had been talking, and was reaching his hand up in welcome even as he spoke.

Immaculately dressed in a long flowing, pleated bliaut of finest green cloth, with narrow sleeves down to his elbows; and on his chest, in beautiful silver thread on a scarlet background his own blazon of three Escalopes Argent on a field Gules, over a blue chemise with silver sea shells all down the long sleeves. He was open faced under a green chaperon, with a long liripipe wrapped round beneath it and a sweeping cloak of red wool around his shoulders, lined with blue sendal, held by two ouches of worked gold and his blazon in beautiful silver orphrey all across the back of it. His face and style was that of a man very much of Sir Yvo's age, with bright blue eyes that twinkled even in the rain, a short pointed beard and a wide smile; his Chaperon held in place with the staring eyes of three enormous peacock feathers. He looked magnificent.

My Lord...Count - William - de Forz?" Gui asked hesitantly, clasping the man's outstretched hand.

"Yes, Sir Gui; the very same. I am the constable of this castle and have been watching your approach for some time. You are welcome indeed, but please kick-on out of this rain. You look soaked!"

Gui laughed. "Soaked indeed...since eight this morning when we set out," he said, shaking the rain off his helmet. You are most generous, My Lord Count," and swinging off Beauregard's broad back he clasped the Count's hand again, leading Beau forward as he did so, while Sir Richard came down off Merlin as well and also took the Count's outstretched hand.

145

"In truth we have all been looking forward to getting here since leaving Chantonnay at dawn. It has been a long, bitter day and we must leave tomorrow again at first light, for we have a long way still to go. But, My Lord, you speak as though you know our colours with more than passing interest?"

"I am King Richard's Leal man here in Poitou, Sir Gui, and there are not many knights who can knock the King out of his saddle without their names becoming known...and that of his closest friend," he added with a friendly nod towards Sir Richard. "Quite David and Jonathan I understand."

"Oh!" Gui exclaimed surprised. "Yes. I suppose so? Sir Richard and I have rubbed together well for some years now. He's an idle hound," he added with a grin, "and I'm impulsive...so we complement one another I suppose. As for the other, the Christmas Tournament in London? I am surprised you heard about that."

"Indeed?" He smiled, his eyes fairly sparkling. "Who has not heard how the young Sir Gui of Malwood of the King's Guard, with the scarlet lion rampant on his chest, dumped the mighty Lionheart on his royal armoured bottom in front of all London!"

"A lucky strike, My Lord, I assure you," Gui answered with a laugh. "The King was not trying!"

Count William chuckled: "Wisely said, young man. Kings can be of a very uncertain temper...and Richard is famous for being less...shall we say 'temperate' than some others I can think of?"

Gui looked into Count William's eyes, saw the twinkle and smiled. "Mmmm, some might say so, My Lord...but *very* quietly!" And a further ripple of laughter ran around them.

"In fact, Lord William, the King roared his head off, as only he can," Sir Richard said in his usual laconic style. "And rewarded this miserably bedraggled fellow with a ring off his own finger." Then, pausing to give Gui an arch look with a raised eyebrow, he added: "Next moment he gave him a thumping royal buffet that almost sent him sprawling, just to remind this young sprig of fancy here, that he was no weakling!" And they all chortled at Gui's embarrassment,

146

swiftly at ease with one another, even though they had only just met, all knowing *exactly* what it was like to be dumped off one's horse at a tournament...but better there than on the field of battle!

By then they had walked through the long gatehouse passage and were paused, out of the wet, just at the end of it before a huge open bailey, smirred with rain, from the far side of which the King's new donjon sprang up in all its power and strength, the enormous ditch that went all round it every bit as frightening an obstacle as Gui had been told. There were also a large number of additional buildings within the bailey: stables, storage barns and slate roofed lean-tos; a large, busy forge and sleeping quarters for the garrison, some with families; chapel, kitchens, castle well, and an elegant hall for visitors; even an inn, with its own stables and hay barn, as well as numerous other outbuildings.

"As you can see, Sir Gui," Count William said expansively. "We have plenty of space for all your men, and your horses. King Richard did not stint anything in the re-building of this fortress, and the kitchens will supply you with plenty of hot water for a bath for you and your principal officers if you so wish. Frankly you look as if you could do with a long soak and a large goblet of Burgundy! I bring it in specially as it is a true king among wines." Adding softly with a wry grin: "We have nothing so noble here in the Vendée."

"My Lord Count, a king among wines indeed; you never spoke a truer word," Sir Gui replied, shaking the water off his mailed hands. "A good soak, a goblet of your finest and a chance to get out of this damned armour and into real clothes for all of us would be just wonderful."

"That is all as good as done, Sir Gui," he said cheerfully. "My steward will see to all those details, show you to your rooms and ensure your squires know where to find you. He will also send some pages to help with hot water and things, so you can be comfortable. My Master-at-Arms, and yours, can direct the men. I see you have a Benedictine with you?" He added, as Father Matthew rode through beside one of the tilt carts.

"Yes, Lord William. That is Father Matthew, on special assignment from the Holy Father himself. He is both friend and confessor, as well as a brilliant doctor. We would all be lost without him. His skills saved my life!"

"On assignment from the Holy Father?" Count William queried astonished. "From the supreme Pontiff himself? He must be a rare man indeed. My chaplain will be delighted to find another of his calling in the castle tonight. I will make certain he is both properly housed and seated at the High Table tonight. I cannot promise you a feast, Sir Gui," he said warmly. "But I can promise you an evening of cheerful friendliness and good food, for your whole command, with which My Lady Beatrice will be certain to provide us. She is my Heart's Ease…but frightens the life out of me," he said with a certain smile, as a bell began to toll across the bailey, "so do not be late! That is the Vespers bell. We shall eat in two hours in the great hall."

Just as he finished speaking a number of castle varlets, all in the de Forz livery of silver sea shells on a scarlet background, came running up, accompanied by a tall man in hauberk and cross gartered leather chauses, followed by a small retinue of servants, chattering like magpies, led by Count William's Steward, himself in a long red gown, split to the waist, and blue hose in long red leather boots, silver scallops on each shoulder, and carrying the long black polished rod of his office.

"Here are my people now, Sir Gui," Count William said, clapping his hands for immediate silence. "They will care for you, and later will show you where to go. So, I will see you then." But, just as he moved to leave, he stopped and turned back towards them again.

"Forgive me, Gentlemen," he said, quietly, looking at them steadily. "But I feel there is a tale yet to be told, as to what two belted knights, one clearly of the King's personal retinue, are doing in the Vendée, fully armoured-up and with so professional, and powerful, a body of men…and in the company of a Benedictine under the auspices of the Holy Father himself no less? Moreover, a clearly tired command, who must all leave again tomorrow at first light? As Constable of this Royal castle I am intrigued, My Lords. I am sure it will be a most illuminating tale," he added with a firm glance up into Gui's face, in which there was no sign of a twinkle. "I shall look forward to it!"

And with a bow from his guests, and a tilt of the head from himself, he was gone.

L ater, when all the food had been cleared away by Count William's varlets, the Great Hall mostly emptied, and the long tables that everyone below the dais had been seated on removed and replaced with wool stuffed pallets for sleeping; Gui, Sir Richard, Father Matthew and Count William remained seated at the huge table of polished oak planks at which they had eaten.

Lady Beatrice, a lady as large and bountiful as her husband was small and lean, with irrepressible humour and sound common sense, had left her husband with their guests to retire to her own private solar, taking her two daughters with her, and her tire-women. Count William's eldest son was away learning his Squire's duties with a neighbouring baron, as Gui had done in Yorkshire, and his younger son, James, had gone with Simon and Phillip to clean armour and help prepare them for tomorrow's journey.

With the summer darkness now upon them, the huge hall, lit by lamps and flaring flambeaux in iron holders on the walls, was a mass of dancing shadows warmed by the great fire the Count had ordered against the unexpected chill of that wet rainy evening, the clouds still low over head dampening the natural light.

With a wave of his hands, and a quiet word with his steward, Count William dismissed all the servants, preferring to care for his guest's needs himself, rather than have even a page left standing nearby to serve them. So after filling their glass beakers in their silver holders from a beautifully chased silver-gilt carafe, he first moved a huge multi-branched candelabra closer for better light, then sat down in his great armed chair and looked at them, their faces half in shadow and half lit by the fire and the candles.

"So My Lords," Count William said firmly after a while, with a gesture. "As you see, I have dismissed all my servants and my pages, and there are armed guards at every door," My Steward has seen to that. "We will not be disturbed I assure you. Now…I think you have a tale to tell me?"

Gui, looking at his host's face, fully lit by the candles, was not under any illusions. This was a man, chosen by his King, to guard this whole area of the Vendée against attack. Mild as he might seem, he had a core of steel…and this great castle could as easily become a daunting prison, as it was a pleasing place of rest and friendship.

But how much to trust this man whom he hardly knew? How much to say of all that he knew? How much help might he get for his quest? Questions that he, Richard and Matthew had asked themselves before entering that great keep for dinner. Gui looked briefly into the flickering shadows, at the flames in the massive grate leaping and twisting, at the flaring flambeaux now beginning to die down…and back again into the sharp, concentrated gaze of those two bright blue eyes looking at him. Trust…or Secret? Honesty or betrayal?

He smiled, "Indeed I do My Lord Count…"

Count William relaxed, and smiled in turn, his eyes losing their hardness. "Please, Sir Gui," he interrupted, "there is not the need now for such formality. Not now you have made your choice, yes?" he added with a tilt of his head and a flick of his left eyebrow.

"Yes, My Lord Count. I will tell you all I can, and please be advised that I and my whole command are the King's Leal men too, as you are too."

Count William studied the young man before him, and looked into the hard, tense faces of those around him and smiled.

"You make a wise choice, Sir Gui," he said tersely, looking hard into his eyes as he spoke. "Just as our King has made a wise choice in you! And I would rather, by far, have you as my guests than as my prisoners, for we live in unquiet times. The Vendée is not the safe haven for Richard as he would wish it to be. And it is good for a wise man to be prudent! Please call me, 'William' and I will use your given name as well. And you, Sir Richard, if that is agreeable? At times like these I feel titles are not helpful."

Gui looked at him and nodded his head. "Very well...William...thank you, and thank you and Lady Beatrice for your enormous kindness and generosity this evening, and at such short notice..."

"Gui. Please," the Count said a firmly. "Keep your many 'Kindnesses' for tomorrow. It is your 'tale' I wish to hear...and learn how it may affect me here in Poitou, and the King's absence from his lands at this time. And how I may help you."

Gui smiled and bowed his head, then turning to his black robed confessor and friend, he said quietly: "Matthew, show Count William the Holy Father's Commission and Writ of Passage...and the King's Warrant for de Brocas, and we'll take it all from there." Noting as he spoke how the mention of Lord Roger's name had brought a sharply indrawn breath from de Forz, and a very fierce look indeed from those blue eyes, now shorn of any hint of amusement, but only piercing interest.

"You have the King's Seal, Gui?" He asked, completely astonished. "Here in my castle?"

"Yes, William. Along with other...special papers, some of which Father Matthew will show you. Others we cannot."

"I understand, Gui," he said leaning forward into the light. "I *am* the King's Leal man in Poitou, I told you. Now, I am agog to hear you tale...and will render all assistance where I can!"

And so Gui, and Sir Richard, with Father Matthew's help, told Count William of all they knew, and all that had happened to them since the terrible night of the fire at Castle Malwood...while the candles burned down in their sockets, the carafe was emptied and owls were calling beyond the castle garth.

They told of the foul murders of Gui's parents to Greek Fire; the deaths, the treachery and the plots against themselves and against their King by both Philip of France and Prince John; the desperate battle against the Corsairs, and theirs to save the *Mary*...and the dreadful loss of Alicia to de Brocas after all. And they shocked the Lord Count William de Forz to his very core.

151

"My God!" He exclaimed at the end of it. "And you have the proof of your claims against Philip Valois and against Prince John?"

"Yes, William. Father Matthew has them. If you like…?"

"No! No! I have no wish to see them," he exclaimed, almost in fear. Even to know of such things was bad enough. To know actually where they were…or to see them without the King's permission to do so, almost terrifying. "I only wished to know you had them. This is a very bad business. Roger de Brocas is a most dangerous enemy, Gui. He has the French King's protection anyway, as all men know. And is allied to Count Raymond V of Toulouse who is Richard's sworn enemy at this time. But I did not realise he was so thick with Prince John as well?

That is not good! And with Richard away in the Holy Land on his damned Crusade…Yes! Yes!…" He said, waving his hands as Gui broke in to defend Richard's decision. "…I know it is all very honourable, and re-claiming Jerusalem is every Christian Knight's true ideal. But Richard is but two years a King, and the land is unquiet. John and Philip plot, and we, Richard's Leal men, cannot be everywhere."

"Are you in danger here, My Lord?" Father Matthew asked, leaning forward across the table.

"From those petty Lordlings who hold around here? *Pish!* They are nothing. But from greater Lords further afield who have greedy eyes for chunks of Poitou, if they join together? Maybe.

Niort is wealthy, and important. That is why Richard has commissioned such a powerful new Donjon. I can hold Castle Niort, and the town, in the teeth of Richard's enemies for as long as it takes, have no fear of that. But if the King is absent for too long or, God Help us, he should be killed, then there are those who may change sides sooner rather later. But de Brocas? That is another matter altogether. He is as bad a man as ever spoke our language. He certainly needs to be taken down, as the King's Warrant declares. What do you have in mind?"

And for some time they discussed all their options, but came back again and again to their one real difficulty.

"The simple thing is, Sir Gui, you need more men!" The Count said, leaning back. "I agree," he said, gesturing with his hands, "that a sudden assault is the only way you can get in. No siege will work. You have neither the machinery nor the time for that. Slam, bang and in y' go! Is the way to do it…but you need three times the men you have as a hard core no matter what, and you can expect high casualties."

"I am hoping that when we arrive we will find those who will join our standards against the Baron. There must be many who want him dead…but lack the leadership, or fighting skills to give that bastard a real run for his money!"

"You may be right, Gui. But you need more good fighters to make an impression!" And standing up he called two of his men over. "Philip, Stephen. Go now and find de Fontenay. Tell him I want him here immediately. Go now, quickly!" And seizing a nearby torch from its iron sconce they trotted off across the darkened hall.

"De Fontenay is my Guard Commander, Gui. As Sir Richard is to you, so Sir Russeau de Fontenay is to me. Charles Fouissy!" He called to another of his men, "Bring us another carafe from the Buttery, and another silver glass beaker. If that fat fool Gisgard wants to know who, tell him your Lord commands it!"

Moments later there was a bang and a clatter and a tall, rather square man strode into the room dressed in a long pleated bliaut of red wool over an amber chemise, a short surcoat carrying his own colours, belted in with a long sword off a stout blue leather belt and blue leather half boots on his feet.

"Ah, Russeau. Thank you, for coming so quickly. I am sorry you could not have joined us earlier. I hope all is well?"

"Yes, William. A fine foal, sturdy like his father," he said, excited. "Dark with a white blaze like his sire, and four white socks like his dam. A real beauty, already finding his milk and his mama is doing well. I am sorry,

Gentlemen. But this a most favoured mare, and it is her first foaling…I always like to be there if I can. I sent my Sergeant-at-Arms to meet your men when you arrived, I hope that was satisfactory? Robert Bourchier is a good man. I hear he and your Jean Fitzurse are getting on well!

"A first foaling," Gui replied with a broad grin, as the tall soldier sat down beside him. "That is always an occasion. Practically the whole castle turned out when my Beau was dropped, all wobbly legs and his dam snuffling him all over with many blowings and licks. Just beautiful! 'Gui de Malwood'," he said extending his hand. "And this is Father Matthew, our Benedictine Saving Grace. Stitches our wounds, absolves our sins, and generally keeps up our spirits. He also stops me from being impulsive," Gui added with a laugh. "I would be lost without him!"

"'Richard L'Eveque'" His own Guard commander responded, with a smile, thrusting out his hand as well. "Yes, I heard that Fitzurse and your man, Bourchier? were as thick as thieves," he said in his lazy drawl. "Had a run in with the same gal in Normandy some years ago so I understood when I went to check on them all before dinner. They were knocking it back heartily. Have some of this wine," he said filling a glass beaker. "It is excellent!"

"Rousseau," the Count chipped in. "We have a problem that I think we might be able to help solve for our friends. Come, sit down, and let us see what we can do to help?"

And without further ado, while the long, wet, summer night settled around the castle like a large towel dunked in a pond, filling the water butts, pouring out of the lead shutes all around the towers and roofs in small cascades, flowing in swift runnels across the Bailey, and soaking the men on guard along the battlements and up on the top wall-walks of the massive donjon…Count William, Gui, and all those gathered around the long table on the top dais wrestled with the problem of more men.

★

"How many do you think they need, William?" Rousseau asked after everything necessary had been explained to him.

"How long is a piece of string?" the Count replied with a shrug. "And is it a question of numbers, or quality? Numbers we have…there are always plenty of farm boys who want to go for a soldier! The money is better, it's constant and there's always the chance of a bit extra if things get interesting. But quality? That is much harder to find so quickly."

"Fifty, William?" Gui asked, raising his eyebrows. "Sixty? Enough to replace those who've been killed and a good handful more.

"Half and half," Sir Richard drawled. "Half, good, hardened fighters who know the difference between a sword and a falchion…and which way to stick the damned thing. And half green 'uns. Who aren't sure but are damned willing to give it a bloody good try…with a smile!"

They all laughed at that, then settled back on the benches, while Count William, in his great armed chair idly rolled his silver drinking beaker between his hands.

"Can we find sixty, Rousseau?" he asked his Guard Commander a moment later.

"*Fwoough! Sixty?* " his Guard Commander queried, the breath hissing out of his mouth as the Count's sudden request rattled round his head. Then he smiled. "Yes, William," he said after a further moment's thought, and a long look at Gui and Sir Richard. "Yes! I think I can find them sixty."

"And have them ready to leave straight after Lauds?"

"Not Lauds, Count William," Father Matthew said quietly, tugging his cowl further back off his neck. "I know Gui would like to be off at daybreak. But no-one will be ready by then. It must be getting on for Matins now, and none of us is abed yet. But if we all rise at Prime, Gui," he said, turning towards him. "About 6.00am…and leave two hours later…that should do us all well. That way we should reach Saint Jean about sunset, with plenty of time to bivouac before a proper daybreak start in two morning's time."

"Good, Matthew," Gui replied swiftly. "That sounds good. But can you really spare sixty 'half and halfers' William!"

"Oh...Gui," de Fontenay said with a smile, hesitating slightly over his name. "I'm sure I can find sixty 'half and halfers' for you. But they may not all be the easiest men to handle!"

Sir Richard guffawed quietly. "Mmmm, know what you mean, you hound!" he drawled, with his lazy grin. "I saw that sudden smile too! Bloody good fighters all the way round! Fighting their bloody selves as well as the bloody enemy! All those whom your man Bourchier would most like *not* to see every morning on parade!"

"Mmmm, probably," de Fontenay, replied with another sideways grin.

"Probably, you shameless rogue?" L'Eveque laughed, banging him on the arm. "*Most likely* you mean! Well, as long as they can fight when they need to do most, then I'll not be complaining. Do you want 'em back, Dear Boy?"

"Only if they're all in one piece," de Fontenay laughed. "I can't do much with bits and pieces!"

"And I'll pay the ferryman, William," Gui chipped in. "I won't be adding any salt into anyone's injury, that's for certain.

"Lancers, bowmen, or just plain fighters with sword, shield and gisarme?"

"Half and half again...Rousseau?" Sir Richard asked. "We have excellent bowmen and swordsmen...but no lancers, and no specialist spearmen either, and the gisarme is a wicked weapon: long as a spear with a bill on one side for hooking, and an axe blade on the other for chopping. Lovely!"

"Can we do that, Rousseau?" Count William queried. "It would certainly balance Sir Gui's command nicely. And we are definitely not short of horses."

"Yes, William we can do that. Who should go as their commander?"

"Whom do they most respect?"

156

"William of Bergerac," de Fontenay said immediately. "He is a first class soldier, and as hard as bloody nails when he needs to be. He has hands like a side of beef, and rides a horse as if he were moulded to it…and he is worthy of promotion. Put him up to 'Sergeant', and the men will be as delighted for him as we are…as well as not wanting to get the wrong side of him. He has a voice to shame the Abbey Bells, and a boot like a thunderbolt! Him I *do* want back in one piece if possible!"

"Sounds just John Fitzurse's kind of man," Sir Richard laughed. "Like a thunderbolt, eh? That I must see! And 'Sergeant' is good. Outranks all his troopers…but of lower rank than Fitzurse, so he'll have no problem with taking orders. Are you happy with that, Rousseau. There can only be one leader of any armed expedition…and that is Sir Gui. We follow him…and your men must follow us."

"Quite right, Richard. I would expect no less myself. There will be no problems, I assure you. And thank you, My lord for your generosity over their pay."

"Excellent!" Gui said, and standing he clasped de Fontenay's arm in a Roman salute, before turning to the Count.

"William, for a man whom I had never met until today, you have proven to be the most amazing host and Companion-in-Arms. I bet when I knocked Richard out of his saddle that afternoon in London, he could never have guessed what a spectacular result his gifted ring would bring him! Thank you, *so much!* And please thank the Lady Beatrice for her kindness around this table tonight, and your Steward for all he has done for my men."

And stifling a yawn, he added: "Please, if it does not seem too churlish to you, I crave your indulgence for me and my fellows to leave and get what sleep we can before cockcrow. As I said this afternoon when we arrived, we need to be on our way at first light as we have a long way to go!"

And bowing to their host, Count William de Forz and his tall Guard Commander, Sir Rousseau de Fontenay, Gui and his fellow leaders stepped down from the dais, and with two of the Count's soldiers to lead them with flaring torches, they made their way back to their quarters and so to bed at last.

Chapter 22... The road to Saint Jean d'Angeley.

They left the next morning with the clouds still low across the far hills, and the horizon grey and drear, but at least the rain had cleared, driven south before a stiff breeze that fluttered the standards Gui had ordered be unfurled and again carried at the front before him by the two squires.

All had broken fast with chill water from the castle spring and fresh bread, warm from the ovens, a drizzle of spiced oil and a handful of olives. More than a Roman breakfast of just bread and water, but still strange to the English troops who found the olives bitter, and moaned for the hard cheese they were more used to at home. But with cold meats cut and packed for them in panniers slung across some of the sumpters, along with a score of fresh loaves, wheels of soft cheese and fresh picked peaches and cherries...each man with a flask of watered wine to carry with him, they were all well enough prepared.

True to his word, and much to Gui and his commanders' delight, Count William and de Fontenay had found the sixty 'half and halfers' they had discussed the previous night, and they halted to watch them coming up from the stables: first William of Bergerac, with his new sergeant's colours stitched on his right shoulder, and a new standard carrying the de Forz blazon of three Escallops Argent on a field Gules bravely carried beside him...followed by a long double line of troopers, the lancers and spearmen they had hoped for, together with a pair of their own tilt carts for all their spare equipment, their spears and their bivouac material, and pulled by two horses each.

Every man was clad in stout ringed mail, over a red padded leather jacket with steel bracers around each wrist, and a polished nasal helmet. They also carried the traditional kite shaped shields across their backs over long cloaks, and a plain sword, or mace in a shaped leather bucket, at each man's side.

Behind the flag rode the lancers, with their nine foot shafts tipped with long, lethal pointed heads, flanged for extra weight and penetration, each butt-end carried in a toe bucket at the right stirrup edge. They were true specialist forces trained in the use of the lance in battle, whose impact could be decisive if wisely used. And each lance carried a fluttering pennon bearing the de Forz blazon. Following, behind their carts, their long gisarmes upright in long racks all round the carts' sides, came the spearmen, shields on their backs also, personal weapons by their sides.

And they were all proud.

Despite having been roused at Lauds, just as daylight was pushing out the night, and then being buzzed about furiously by Bourchier and others, like frantic bluebottles in a privy…the whole castle an ant's nest turned over with a stick…they had been chosen, sorted, fed, horsed and armed, and were now leaving. Standing upright in their high saddles, straight-backed and heads held high, booted feet thrust into in their long stirrups, they felt like the best of the best and looked it, despite the fact that many would be going into action for the first time.

They represented their castle, their friends and their families, who had flooded out across the bailey to watch them go with cheers and much weeping from those whose loved ones had been torn from their arms when called to muster before dawn that very morning, and were now leaving under a leaden sky.

But with double trumpet blasts from above the gatehouse, and from the great donjon high up above them, the Silver Shells from Niort and the Scarlet Lions from England clattered and rumbled over the drawbridge and took the long road south to Bordeaux and to Gruissan beside the Circle Sea.

★

All day Gui and his command pushed South towards Saint Jean d'Angeley, the weather steadily clearing from the North West as the brisk wind of the morning drove the clouds away at last.

By late afternoon the sun finally broke through, melting the last vestige of grey from a burgeoning azure sky, and throwing dappled shadows through the leafy branches of the trees hanging over the trackway. The light danced and sparkled off every hedgerow, each rain drop turned into a dazzling array of tiny diamonds that dangled from every leaf and bush like earrings, glittering pear drops just waiting to caught, as they plunged once more into dense woodland, leaving a vast span of open fields behind them.

And as the sun's warmth caught up with them, so the trees and bushes steamed, like pans held over a fire to boil, and coming to a sudden clearing, Gui halted the column so that the men could take off their cloaks and roll them up again behind their saddles, take a short breather and relieve themselves, and check hooves and harness, bridles, bits and leathers before kicking on again.

★

Once more they stopped to water the horses beside a small stream, now rushing wildly along the edge of the woods they had just cleared from, gurgling and leaping as it sped amongst the ferns and rushes, lilac water mint and yellow loosestrife growing strong amongst them, and as the men dismounted and clustered round one another, a laugh here a joke there, so all the leaders came together as well.

"God's Blood, but I thought it was never going to stop!" Sir Richard swore, shaking out his cloak. "I really thought we'd be bivvying in the rain tonight! This is the first time I've felt warm in two days! Much more of this and my armour will rust solid!"

"I'm more worried about our lads' bowstrings than about your rusting armour," Gui said with a frown. "I hope they've kept 'em well greased, John," he said turning to his huge Master-at-Arms. "There are few sorrier sights than an archer with a limp bowstring!" and he waggled a limp hand as everyone laughed.

"No, Sir Gui. All strings will be as tight as bow strings should be when the need comes, and every man's blade is sharp and rust free. Made sure of that this morning!"

"How about your men, Allan?" he asked, turning to the young Under Sherriff. "How are things with them?"

"They are fine, My Lord. Of course longbow men carry their bows in leather cases, and their strings in their hats to keep them greased. So they are fine. But something has come up, My Lord, that I think you should know about. I haven't spoken before because I have only just found out...but two of my lads think we may have been followed yesterday."

"Followed, Allan?" Father Matthew broke in puzzled. "When?"

"Yesterday afternoon...just after it had really started to throw it down. They weren't back- scouting, some of Bergerac's men were on that duty. But my lads were just forward of them, when a flurry of pheasants came bursting out of the murk straight over them, cock-cock-cockling their heads off and then swung into heavy cover on their right. Not long after that, the same sort of thing happened, only it was young boar that time, shoats apparently, still in their stripes, a dozen running close behind two old sows that broke cover behind them fast, Sir Gui...and I mean fast! Now you see them, now you don't?...so they were gone in a moment. But the lads were so busy being excited about seeing game they know so well at home..."

"...That they didn't think of the implications!" Gui finished for him, with a real frown of concentration across his forehead. "I heard the pheasants...I mean, who wouldn't, they make such a bloody cackle when they take off? But I thought it was just one of us. Like those partridge Beau almost stepped on at Clisson. A pity we didn't know about it sooner?"

"Why is that such a concern, Gui," Father Matthew asked.

"Because, Father," he said, reaching for a peach out of a nearby pannier. "Pheasants aren't as stupid as some might like to think. No pheasant will fly unless it has to...especially in foul weather like this. They really don't like the wet, and they won't easily be startled by a fox or a weasel. They'll run first and

161

fly later if they have to…and they won't scream about it. But if a man steps on them, then they *will* take off! Straight up into the air…and then you *will* hear them go, as Allan's men did yesterday"

"The same with wild boar, Father," Allan-i-the-Wood said, leaning back against Caesar, Bouncer by his side. "Boar lie up during the day and those old sows with their little ones wouldn't go anywhere near humans if they could avoid them, know they mean trouble! Least of all a great long column like ours. They are very protective mothers, and lie up close with their babes, their shoats, often in sounders, several sows in a group, and will not let them move into danger unless forced to do so. And boar have no natural enemies in the forests, save us!"

"So…if they shot across our paths yesterday," Sir Richard said, picking up Alan's words, "With their little ones close beside them, then someone scared them. Not something, Father. *Someone!*"

"Hmmm," Gui muttered. "So that was twice that game was startled in what…half an hour?"

"Yes, about that, Sir Gui. Do you want to check with the lads?"

"No, Allan. I don't doubt them for one moment."

"I told you you'd find yourself at home in these lands," the tall Benedictine said with a grin, shaking his long habit. "And by Saint George you have too. The thing is? What does it mean?"

"Do you think someone's following us, Sir Gui," Fitzurse asked him, crossing his massive arms across his chest.

"Well…it would have to be a bloody desperate poacher to be out after game in weather like that," he replied with a chuckle. "It will all be closely laid up in the dry as we should have been!"

"Has anyone reported seeing anything on our tail?" Sir Richard asked, picking at a roll he had taken from his bag. "We've kept changing the scouts about so no-one gets bored looking…but the weather has been truly foul. So they may have missed something that otherwise they might not have done."

162

"Well who would? Follow us I mean?" de Beaune asked just then, having listened to the conversation. "We are still hundreds of miles from Grise…so it can't be the Baron."

"But not so far that a pigeon might not have been sent somewhere with a message to intercept us?" Father Matthew said quietly. "Remember what I said about pigeon carriers? Flight times and distance? And whom do we know to be a likely traitor whom we've met along our trail?"

"Alan de Courcy!" De Beaune exclaimed. "And that bastard Victor Jonelle, both of whom I fought against in the Vexin when they were in Valois colours; fighting for King Philip against Mercardier, Richard's Master of Mercenaries!"

"Well," Gui said, shaking his shoulders to settle his armour more comfortably. "There's nothing we can do about that now, Gentlemen. But forewarned is definitely forearmed, so very well done, Allan, and tell your two lads I will see them to thank them properly later. Meanwhile we must move on, but keep alert. Another hour, maybe two, will see us at Saint Jean. John," he said briskly to his Master-at-Arms, "go forward now and have a word with your scouts. Yes?"

"Yes, Sir Gui. Extra vigilant, and report immediately if they see, or hear, anything wrong." And he left at once.

"Allan, I would like to put four of your best men forward towards Saint Jean. They may even need to dismount and screen the town on foot when they get there. And we won't enter until they have safely reported back. Now…*Mount Upp!...*" he shouted, waving his hand twice around his head…and swinging himself back onto Beau's solid back he led them all off again and back onto the trackway.

Chapter 23...De Courcy comes down like a Wolf on the fold.

Seven miles away, that daybreak, as Sir Gui and his men were leaving Niort, Sir Alan de Courcy and Sergeant Victor Jonelle sat their horses at a small crossroads that would lead them either to the village of Benet on their right, or straight to Niort. Their command, clustered in behind them, wet, weary and stiff from bivouacking in the barns and sheds of Oulmes, a few miles behind them, and beneath the trees and hedges around it, wrapped in their cloaks, their saddles at their heads, now awaited their orders, their horses stamping their iron shod feet and shaking their heads in the grey morning light.

They had arrived there the evening before, almost at last light, having pushed hard all day to be within easy thrust of their quarry's route the next morning. And having hobbled the horses on a long line beyond the village, bought food from the people for themselves and their men, not wanting to cause any trouble so close to Niort, they had themselves slept in a rude inn just off the roadside. The food might have been a simple pottage with bread and wine, and the two small rooms kept for the purpose meanly furnished, but at least they were dry, and though the wide grate smoked foully it was warm enough on that suddenly chill summer's night, and together they had laid their plans.

★

All that day they had tracked Gui and his men, having caught up with them just as they were leaving Chantonnay the day before. Not in close company of course, but from a distance with a pair of cunning trackers, who had kept Gui's own scouts, themselves riding some way behind their main body, just in sight. And that had been enough. They knew the make up of the English knight's command from seeing them at Nantes. The only thing that mattered was where they were!

And all day it had rained steadily, the wind gusting and sighing, filling the eyes with water, chilling the hands, and stopping any dust from rising to give their movements away…as well as preventing Gui's men from keeping the sharpest look-out, deterring them from riding back across their line of march which otherwise they would have done. So, as Gui and his command had left Chantonnay, so Sir Alan had skirted it with his lancers sufficiently far off for them not to be seen, but close enough not to lose touch with their quarry either.

By dusk they had reached Oulmes and bivouacked in the rain, their men huddled in their cloaks wherever they could find shelter, making desultory fires as far out of the wind as possible for warmth and mulling wine in deep billies, with a handful of spices brought with them from the Duke of Brittany's own table, and having seen their men settled they had then retired to the ancient inn for the night.

"Well, Victor," de Courcy said, as he wiped his rough glazed bowl of pottage with a piece of bread. "At least we know where those bastards are…*and* where they are going. The lads have done really well, those brothers, Marcel and Antoine Renard, particularly."

"Fox by name and fox by nature," he answered with a grin. "But poachers or not, there were one or two times I thought they'd gone too near and were bound to be spotted…but it seems the luck was with them and they managed to get away with it."

"When those pheasants leapt out from underneath their feet and went off like shooting stars right over those bastards, cock-cock-cock-cockling their heads off?"

"You saw them?"

"No…heard them! And Dan Massif told me the rest. Those English scouts must have been dreaming!"

"Marcel said they'd been lucky!" he replied getting up to kick the fire into life.

"Mmmm. Well, one more good day and we can lie up and wait for them at Saint Jean."

"Do you know this bit of country then, My Lord?"

"Enough to know that we can avoid Niort completely by taking a faster route to Saint Jean through Benet. Small village just off this main trackway, a few miles from here. Cuts off a good dog's leg round Niort, and will lead us straight to Saint Jean. Niort is one place we do not want to go near if we can avoid it!"

"Mmmm. Count William de Forz!"

"Just so, Victor. He holds it for King Richard, may the Devil take him! He has very sharp eyes and a heavy hand, the good Count...and he may remember us from our time in the Vexin? I do not intend to put us anywhere near his executioner's grasp. Let's just leave it at that!

"Right, My Lord," the big sergeant grunted, sitting down again. "So...How long to get there do you think...to Saint Jean?"

"At the rate we have been travelling? About half a day! We have no carts to slow us down remember. So even if we have to walk the horses a while, we'll still get there long before those bloody English."

"It'll mean another early start, My Lord. We need to be away from here at first light in order to rest up before we have to go into action. And we will need to be careful not to alarm the people at Saint Jean," he added, pausing to drain his horn beaker. "We don't want them to alert those fucking bastards coming through the town later, that there might be trouble. How do you want to work this?"

"Well, firstly we can skirt the town completely, and cut back in towards it from the west. The place is well protected, and has a famous Abbey, so there will be people about...but they will not bother us. The main trackway leads through the town towards Bordeaux through quite thick woods and then a huge open space of Common Land before the river where there is a strong stone bridge. Before that there are a couple of streams with fords. From the

166

bridge the track goes through more woodland til it meets up with wide open fields and vineyards, and so on until Saintes."

"You know it well!"

"Went on escort with those bloody monks and their wine to Bordeaux a few times…while you were off with that busted arm a while ago. So, yes, I do know it. And the best place to hit them will be just after they've have bivouacked for the night. The river is about half a mile from the centre of the town, and the land is quite flat right across the clearing, with a few dips and hillocks, before dropping down to the river.

If Bernard can block off their route across the bridge with his spears, and pour in concentrated fire from the surrounding woods, he'll have them in bloody chaos in no time. Then we'll hit them with our lancers from behind, and push them onto Bernard's spears at the bridge. We'll make mincemeat out of them. They won't know what's hit them. It'll be the fastest action in living memory! There are only seventy of them anyway, and some of those are too wounded to fight! It'll be a piece of apple pie !

Now, in the chill dampness of the early morning, the clouds still low overhead but moving with a brisk North Westerly behind them, de Courcy and Jonelle took the right turn off the main trackway and spurred their mounts away across the countryside, empty of travellers at that time, though they passed many small bivouacs as they rode, clods of wet earth flying up from their hooves, spattering both horse and rider as they pounded at an easy canter towards Saint Jean d'Angeley.

Chapter 24... De Vernaille comes also in Azure and Gold.

Away to the South, travelling steadily up from Bordeaux, Sir Bernard and Geoffrey de Vernaille led their men up the main roadway to Pons and then Saintes as swiftly as their horses would safely carry them, having been delayed by over a day in setting out from Saint Savin.

Getting the necessary passes out of the city from Sir Hugh Willoughby had not be so difficult, though he had asked some penetrating questions that had left Bernard sweating as he felt Sir Hugh's fierce grey eyes on him every time he lied! Nevertheless, even though he had still looked askance at him, Sir Hugh had granted him the passes he had asked for, so all his men had left the city as they had planned. And despite having to detour a long way round to meet up again, they had managed to do so without a problem, and had arrived at Saint Savin as expected.

But once there things had not gone so well!

The man whom Martin Riberac had placed in charge was sick of a sudden fever, and the men were out of control. Their equipment dirty and ill cared for, several of their horses in urgent need of shoeing; many out at grass, eating their heads off, and had to be rounded up and sorted before anyone could do anything; and the panniers for the sumpters could not be found!

In short, since the old Lord de Vernaille had died, and his two sons had stayed amongst the wine booths and doxies of Bordeaux, the estate at Savin had been allowed to drift and the place was a shambles. No proper organisation and no good leader to follow, so far from a disciplined, well practised command, the men of Savin were an ill disciplined rabble, and it took several immediate hangings and the ample application of Riberac's boot and fists to sort things out, so it was a sullen and thoroughly chastened command that had finally set out on the long road for Saint Jean d'Angeley.

168

At first, with the sun on their backs and the men in better heart having had the worst of the Savin Command weeded out from amongst them, they made good passage and a brave sight as they trotted or cantered along the dusty high road. The Vernaille blazon of a Lion Passant d'Or on a field Azure with Etoiles d'Or, was sufficiently bright and gay to bring people to the roadside to watch them ride by, a long column of armoured men relaxed enough to wave back and catch the fruit and rolls that many threw up to them as they passed by with smiles and laughter.

The golden lion the men wore on their surcoats, with his one great paw raised, on his azure background dotted with golden stars was very eye-catching, and they had no difficulty in finding lively girls to keep them company at Pons when they got there, the inn keepers only too willing to have so many cheerful spenders come suddenly amongst them.

But after Pons the weather changed. Clouds came up, with a chill wind behind them from the North West, hustling round the backs and rumps of their horses, and by afternoon on the third day the rain came. A steady drizzle at first that found its way into everything, followed by a thorough downpour that turned the hard roadway into a foul muddy soup, splashed everyone and filled the ruts and potholes so they had to slowdown rather than risk losing a horse to a bruised fetlock, or worse, a broken leg.

By the time they reached Saintes, sodden wet and swearing, the men sullen and complaining, the horses with their heads down and plodding, they were nearly a day behind their expected arrival at St Jean. So instead of stopping in Saintes as all had hoped to do, with its two spacious inns and good stabling for men and horses alike, Sir Bernard had led them forward a further ten miles until the wet summer darkness was almost upon them, arriving at the tiny hamlet of Saint Hilaire de Villefranche with little light left to see by.

Almost everyone in his command was weary and saddle sore, cursing the weather, cursing the lack of comforts and cursing their leaders, as they swung off their horses at last to find what shelter they could from the weather. And in truth it was a mean place. A handful of hovels and bothies, no manor house as such, just a huddled collection of larger cruck houses with a small collection of barns clustered around them. Nearby was an ancient smithy and a broken wine press in a large thatched building with rough stone walls and an open front, the whole roof space now a great hay loft, with a rickety wooden ladder leading up to it.

With two of their men carrying their saddles, the Vernaille brothers climbed into the loft space and spread themselves around, while below them others tended their horses, or struck a fire in the round space where the pressing stone should have been, and began to heat up some wine in a deep pan.

"What a completely vile day, Geoffrey," His elder brother growled later, holding a large horn beaker between his hands. "I had forgotten what real campaigning was all about! If it hadn't been for those fucking morons at Saint Savin, we could have reached Saintes yesterday, and covered the last bit to Saint Jean in a single easy stage with almost a day in hand!"

"As it is we shall have to be up with the bloody larks in order to cover the distance and have the time to seek out the best places to mount this ambush. God's Bones, Bernard, I could have slaughtered the lot of them! Stupid ignorant *bastards!* That idiot, Georges Le Breton, is lucky to be alive. Fever or not, I'd have hung him along with the rest! Dear God, I *hate* the rain!"

"Yes," his brother said getting up and looking out into the pattering darkness, leaning against a great roof truss as he did so. "That damned stuff gets into everything, and ploughing through all those muddy ruts and ditches has left my boots saturated. If I take them off now, I might not get them on again! Come on, Geoffrey, we can't stay up here like this. That old bastard was right…"

"Which old bastard?" His brother queried him at once.

"The Old Lord…our bastard of a father! Who else…Moses?"

"Might just as well be, given all this bloody rain just now!"

"That was Noah, idiot! Moses was the Red Sea and the damned Egyptians!"

170

"Well...let those bastard English whom de Brocas wants so badly killed be the Egyptians, and by the time we get to Saint Jean let's hope the stream we want to pin them against is so bloody swollen the whole bloody lot of them will bloody well drown, like Pharaoh's lot in the Red Sea! Then we can bloody well go home and get bloody dry!"

His brother laughed. "Don't be such a misery! As I was saying...it was always the Old Man's contention that men won't fight well if their leaders don't show they care...So, come on, let's go find our noble Sergeant-at-Arms out there somewhere in that wretched, soaking darkness and show our lads, who have had just as bad a day us, that we are all in this together. Then he can come back and join us for another beaker of hot wine, and we can decide who is to do what tomorrow!"

"Do you have a plan?" His brother asked, getting up with a groan, as Bernard began to go backwards down the ladder.

"Yes. Of course," he said, looking up into his brother's face. "A combination attack using our bowmen from concealed positions and our spearmen to hold the ford, while de Courcy's lancers drive that fucking English rabble onto our spears...and if that stream *has* swollen into a rushing torrent so much the better. We can then hold it from this side so they can't get away...and then they might well all bloody well drown! What do you think?"

"Sounds good to me," he said starting down the ladder himself. "Have you discussed it with Riberac?"

"No...not yet. I thought we could do that over some more hot wine...as I suggested. Then it's heads down as best we can, for we must be away as early as possible. *Sweet Jesus!* But this is a miserable place," he exclaimed bitterly, throwing his wet cloak over his shoulders. "At least we will be dry tonight in this hayloft...those poor bastards we are leading are mostly out there under the hedges, poor sods. So let's see what we can do to cheer them up, eh? And pray for better weather tomorrow!"

Chapter 25...*But the Lion will never be clay to their mould!*

All day Gui and his command pushed forward towards Saint Jean d'Angeley, the weather steadily clearing from the North West as the brisk wind of the morning drove the clouds away at last.

By late afternoon the sun finally broke through, melting the last vestige of grey from a burgeoning azure sky, and throwing dappled shadows through the leafy branches of the trees hanging over the trackway. The light danced and sparkled off every hedgerow, each rain drop turned into a dazzling array of tiny diamonds that dangled from every leaf and bush like earrings, glittering pear drops just waiting to be caught, as they plunged once more into dense woodland, leaving a vast span of open fields behind them.

And as the sun's warmth caught up with them, so the trees and bushes steamed, like pans held over a fire to boil, and coming to a sudden clearing, Gui halted the column so that the men could take off their cloaks and roll them up again behind their saddles, take a short breather and relieve themselves, and check hooves and harness, bridles bits and leathers before kicking on again.

Once more they stopped to water the horses beside a small stream, now rushing wildly along the edge of the woods they had just cleared away from, gurgling and leaping as it sped amongst the ferns and rushes, lilac water mint and yellow loosestrife growing strong amongst them, and as the men dismounted and clustered round one another, a laugh here a joke there, so all the leaders came together as well.

"God's Blood, but I thought it was never going to stop!" Sir Richard said, shaking out his cloak. "I really thought we'd be bivvying in the rain tonight! This is the first time I've felt warm in two days! Much more of this and my armour will rust solid!"

"I'm more worried about our lads' bowstrings than about your rusting armour," Gui said with a frown. "I hope they've kept 'em well greased, John," he said turning to his huge Master-at-Arms. "There are few sorrier sights than an archer with a limp bowstring!" and he waggled a limp hand as everyone laughed.

"No, Sir Gui. All strings will be as tight as bow strings should be when the need comes, and every man's blade is sharp and rust free. Made sure of that this morning!"

"How about your men, Allan?" he asked, turning to the young Under Sherriff. "How are things with them?"

"They are fine, My Lord. Of course longbow men carry their bows with ready strings attached in leather cases, and their spare strings in their hats to keep them greased. So they are fine. But something has come up, My Lord, that I think you should know about. I haven't spoken before because I have only just found out...but two of my lads think we may have been followed yesterday."

"Followed, Allan?" Father Matthew broke in puzzled. "When?"

"Yesterday afternoon...just after it had really started to throw it down. They weren't back- scouting, some of Bergerac's men were on that duty. But my lads were just forward of them, when a flurry of pheasants came bursting out of the murk straight over them, cock-cock-cockling their heads off and then swung into heavy cover on their right. Not long after that, the same sort of thing happened, only it was shoats that time, apparently, still in their stripes, a dozen running close behind two old sows that broke cover behind them fast, Sir Gui...and I mean fast! Now you see them, now you don't?...so they were gone in a moment. But the lads were so busy being excited about seeing game they know so well at home..."

"...That they didn't think of the implications!" Gui finished for him, with a real frown of concentration across his forehead. "I heard the pheasants...I mean, who wouldn't, they make such a bloody cackle when they take off? But I thought it was just one of us. Like those partridge Beau almost stepped on at Clisson. A pity we didn't know about it sooner?"

"Why is that such a concern, Gui," Father Matthew asked.

173

"Because, Father," he said, reaching for a peach out of a nearby pannier. "Pheasants aren't as stupid as some might like to think. No pheasant will fly unless it has to...especially in foul weather like this. They really don't like the wet, and they won't easily be startled by a fox or a weasel. They'll run first and fly later if they have to...and they won't scream about it. But if a man steps on them, then they *will* take off! Straight up into the air...and then you *will* hear them go, as Allan's men did yesterday"

"The same with wild boar, Father," Allan-i-the-Wood said, leaning back against Caesar, Bouncer by his side. "Those old sows with their little ones won't go anywhere near humans if they can avoid them, know they mean trouble! Least of all a great long column like ours. They are very protective mothers, and lie up close with their babes, their shoats, often in sounders, several sows in a group, and will not let them move into danger unless forced to do so. And boar have no natural enemies in the forests, save us!"

"So...if they shot across our paths yesterday," Sir Richard said, picking up Alan's words, "With their little ones close beside them, then someone scared them. Not something, Father. *Someone!*"

"Hmmm," Gui muttered. "So that was twice that game was startled in what...half an hour?"

"Yes, about that, Sir Gui. Do you want to check with the lads?"

"No, Allan. I don't doubt them for one moment."

"I told you you'd find yourself at home in these lands," the tall Benedictine said with a grin, shaking his long habit. "And by Saint George you have too. The thing is? What does it mean?"

"Do you think someone's following us, Sir Gui," Fitzurse asked him, crossing his massive arms across his chest.

"Well...it would have to be a bloody desperate poacher to be out after game in weather like that," he replied with a chuckle. "It will all be closely laid up in the dry as we should have been!"

174

"Has anyone reported seeing anything on our tail?" Sir Richard asked, picking at a roll he had taken from his bag. "We've kept changing the scouts about so no-one gets bored looking...but the weather has been truly foul. So they may have missed something that otherwise they might not have done."

"Well who would? Follow us I mean?" de Beaune asked just then, having listened to the conversation. "We are still hundreds of miles from Grise...so it can't be the Baron."

"But not so far that a pigeon might not have been sent somewhere with a message to intercept us?" Father Matthew said quietly. "Remember what I said about pigeon carriers? Flight times and distance? And whom do we know to be a likely traitor whom we've met along our trail?"

"Alan de Courcy!" De Beaune exclaimed. "And that bastard Victor Jonelle, both of whom I fought against in the Vexin when they were in Valois colours; fighting for King Philip against Mercardier, Richard's Master of Mercenaries!"

"Well," Gui said, shaking his shoulders to settle his armour more comfortably. "There's nothing we can do about that now, Gentlemen. But forewarned is definitely forearmed, so very well done, Allan, and tell your two lads I will see them to thank them properly later. Meanwhile we must move on, but keep alert. Another hour, maybe two, will see us at Saint Jean. John," he said briskly to his Master-at-Arms, "go forward now and have a word with your scouts. Yes?"

"Yes, Sir Gui. Extra vigilant, and report immediately if they see, or hear, anything wrong." And he left at once.

"Allan, I would like to put four of your best men forward towards Saint Jean. They may even need to dismount and screen the town on foot when they get there. And we won't enter until they have safely reported back. Now...*Mount Upp!*..." he shouted, waving his hand twice around his head...and swinging himself back onto Beau's solid back he led them all off again and back onto the trackway.

175

Chapter 26...And so the scene is set!

Two hours later, with the sun beginning to slip away to the west, firing up the clouds left behind from yesterday's rain with gold and crimson streamers, they came within sight of Saint Jean d'Angeley at last.

A small walled town athwart the road that led from Niort to Bordeaux, it nestled against the right bank of the river Boutonne, from which two small streams flowed around the west side of the town, both crossed by fords masked by heavy woodland, the roadway running straight to the bridge that spanned the river itself, before stretching out across more great open fields carved out of the wild that reached out all around them, heavy with wheat and barley, peas and beans.

Thrusting up above the main entrance to the town was the great tower the merchants of Saint Jean had built to show off their success, and beyond that was the abbey that gave its name to the place...and all round were the walls that protected all who lived there, and which the Old King, Henry Plantagenet, had assaulted with such overwhelming vigour forty years before.

And just off the trackway, carefully hobbled and picketed, were the four horses of the men whom he and Allan-i-the-Wood had sent forward to scout the whole area. Quietly cropping their way around their pickets, they were calm and settled, but of their riders there was no sign at all.

Throwing his hand up, Gui brought the whole long column to a halt and called his commanders forward to join him. With night drawing on this was no place to linger. They needed to get the horses watered and settled, and the men fed and bedded down also. Above all, they needed to be sure of their safety...yet the very men sent ahead to ensure that were nowhere to be seen.

"Well, Gentlemen," Gui said tersely, gesturing to the horses near by. "Here we are...and no sign of the men whom Allan and I sent forward. The sun has not yet set, so the town gates will still be open to us, but I am loath to enter without being sure we will not be set upon. I know these men of mine well. If something goes badly wrong, and we are attacked, they will not hesitate to take this town by fire and storm…and that would be a disaster!"

"I agree, Gui," Father Matthew said quietly. "If Allan's men do not appear soon, I will ride on in to the Abbey and see what I can find out. After all it is a Brother House, and I hold the Holy Father's Commission, which will give us the most powerful aid. The Abbot would not dare to refuse us. But the Abbey is not large, and could not take in so great a force as we now have with us…nor do I wish to advertise our strength. But knowledge is power, and if there is anything untoward within his bailiwick, the Abbot will be sure to know of it!"

"That is a good plan, Matthew," Sir Richard drawled. "But even you cannot go in alone. Take the cart with our wounded with you and two of my troopers as escort. They can take off their surcoats so as not to be of much notice, and that way you will gain ready access to both town and abbey, and few questions asked by the town guard that is sure to be beside the gates."

But before any such move could happen, and with little more than a rustle, Allan's four verderers appeared before them, eeling out from amongst the trees that crowded over the trackway, their faces streaked with black, ferns and twigs tied around their helmets with bow cord, and their clothes grass stained and muddied….and they were breathless with excitement.

"Report!" Gui exclaimed swiftly, as he swung off his horse, the others following; Fitzurse, de Beaune and William Bergerac pushing theirs closer, eager to hear the news.

"Peter of Minstead…My Lord," the first scout said breathlessly. "Be warned! The river is alive with men. Spearmen and archers, mostly, but some with sword and shield, dozens and dozens of 'em; led by two belted knights and all wearing the same colours: big golden lions with one foot raised, on a blue background covered with golden stars. Most are mingled in the woods between two small streams and the river itself. There's quite a lot of water, My Lord. Soft going after all that rain; not good for horses."

"Mostly between the streams and the river?" Sir Richard interrupted.

"Yes, My Lord. There are two streams, not one, all swollen and running fast…and then there's the river itself. None of the streams are very wide, but too much for a horse to jump, so they have to be forded. The river is different, wide and deep, but there is a good stone bridge over it, more than a big wagon's width, across stone piers. Beyond the town gates, and before the first of the streams, there is a huge area of common grazing land, more than four furlongs, across which the trackway runs, with thick woodland around its edges."

"My Lord?…Roger Fox, came with the Sherriff. It looks as if they plan to hold the bridge with their spears! They were moving those men back across the river as we slipped away, must be thirty or forty of 'em at least. But grumpy they were, Sir Richard. Slumped like, spears at the trail. And wet, too. Not much like the golden lions they're wearing!"

"Do you know that blazon, Gui?" Matthew asked, urgently. "You've been to more tournaments than I have."

"No, Father!…Richard?" But his tall Guard Commander said nothing, just shook his head, his mind busy with the logistics of fighting a swift, brutal action in poor light.

"Those are the colours of the de Vernaille family, My Lord," William of Bergerac rasped, nudging his horse forward: "I'd know them anywhere. They hold lands all around Bordeaux, and beyond. Their father, the old Lord, Rupert de Vernaille, died not two months back. Count William went to his funeral; I was in his honour guard. He was a fierce old bugger, the Old Lord, but straight. Knew whose side he was on. Supported the Old King: swore allegiance to Richard. Those must be his two sons, Bernard and Geoffrey."

"Up to much?" Sir Richard drawled.

"Don't know, My Lord. Had more of a reputation for wine and tavern wenches, than hard campaigning and cold steel; though the older one is supposed to be a fighter. The old Lord wouldn't have them near 'im! Kicked 'em off his lands: didn't trust 'em his own self! The Count held their fealty to be more likely towards Phillip of France than Richard of England."

"Easy prey for de Brocas!" Gui said bitterly. "Just the kind of weak, greedy men he would choose to use against an enemy he needed slain!"

"My Lord," another of Allan's scouts said urgently. "They have also been joined by a strong body of lancers...this side of the river and the streams.

"*Lancers?*" Gui exclaimed. "Where did they come from?"

"Must be from Nantes, Sir Gui!...David Coulter, Joined at Malwood. They are led by those two you met with just as we landed, about thirty of them. Riveted mail, and long shields. They look weary, but seem keen enough."

"De Courcy!" Sir Richard exclaimed. "And his man, Victor Jonelle."

"I bet it was his scouts who startled that game yesterday," Allan said, reaching down to fondle Bouncer's head. "Takes a rare forest ranger to move across wooded ground without startling the quarry off in all directions!"

"If they are de Courcy's men, they'll fight, and fight hard," de Beaune said firmly, banging his fist into his open hand. "He only ever leads the best he can find."

"How many, Master Coulter? Altogether?"

"Thirty lancers and about four score of the others, My Lord. Couldn't tell you exactly how many bowmen or how many spears...but certainly no heavy foot."

"Bows?"

"All cross bows, My Lord," Peter of Minstead replied. "You'll not find a longbow archer this side of the channel. Those Frenchies don't know 'em... can't use 'em. And have no idea what they can do!"

"Anything else lads?" The Under Sherriff asked, urgently. "Anything else Sir Gui ought to know that might help?"

"Well, Master Sherriff. As Foxy said, I don't think those lads with the golden lions on 'em are that keen...Ben Tiley, joined at Malwood, Sir Gui. They looked pretty beat up to me. Lots of grumbling, and bad feeling.

179

O'course, I don't know what they was saying, like. But definitely not happy…and their gear wasn't in good order. Bow strings wet, winders not working properly, quivers not filled. Bloody mess, My Lord. Their sergeant was going berserk with 'em! Those lancers looked as if they were up for it, though. Good equipment and well organised. But that other lot? Nahh!" he said with disgust. "One real taste of steel and they'll be off like rabbits from a fox!"

"However did you get so close?" Sir Richard asked, amazed.

"Practice, My Lord," David Coulter said proudly. "If you want to catch a Hampshire poacher in the great forest, you have to be as quiet as fox and swift as a weasel, or you don't get bugger all! That lot! They wouldn't have seen anything even if we'd danced in front of 'em! And that Foxy pretty near did on one occasion. Stupid bastards…we ran rings round 'em, My Lord."

"Well done, all of you! Your information is really worthy. When this is over come and find me and I will make sure you are all properly rewarded. Now, off with you and find your mates."

"Well gentlemen," Gui said, leaning back against Beau as he looked around him. "Now we know…thing is, what do we do about it? Those bowmen will not be easy, and I could have done without a squadron of lancers on our tails, that's for sure."

"Nevertheless we do have the element of surprise," Matthew said, throwing back his cowl. "Firstly, they don't know we know about them. Second, they don't know we've got more men, *nor* that we have any lancers at all! Remember, de Courcy saw us in Nantes. He *knows* we don't have any, and they never saw beyond our rear scouts anyway…and, thirdly, they *don't* know how lethal the longbow is in expert hands!"

"Yes, Gui, those are excellent points that Matthew's just made," Sir Richard said, as if he had no care in the world. "Those longbows really are an ace up our sleeves! I've seen those men of Allan's at work, and those we brought with us with Dickon Fletcher. Twelve arrows a minute they can fire…and at two hundred and fifty paces too. We may only have twenty five of 'em, but they can lay down nearly three hundred shafts a minute on those boys

180

out there…that's why we brought so many more clothyard shafts than bolts with us. If we can get those lads properly placed, and well balanced, they will slaughter those bastards before they can strike a single blow!"

Gui paused then and looked up at the sky, the sun now sinking behind a high bank of cloud that had wandered up across the horizon, the edges rimmed with purple against a crimson background shot with golden fire; listened to the birds beginning to fly home to roost in the gathering dusk; crows carking and squabbling high in the tree tops, the clap of a wood pigeon as it swooped into a nearby beech, the screech of a questing owl quartering for voles across a distant field.

"Well…Gentlemen here's what I would like to do. It's risky…but if we can make it work we'll win the day. William…I want your spears to lend their spare surcoats to twenty five of my crossbows. Then, with all the courage you can muster, and as much noise as you like…I'll give you one of my trumpeters! I want you to take the whole lot of them…your lancers and my crossbows…and march through the town and out the other side as if you didn't have a care in the world! Straight up the main track, through de Vernaille's men, over the bridge and away as if you're off to Saintes!"

"Then what, My Lord?" The big man asked, appalled, looking as if he'd been asked to march them off a cliff.

"Spears are good against horses…but hopeless against bows. Sir Richard and I will assault those men amongst the trees with all the lads we have, making as much noise as we can. Trumpets, shouts anything. When you hear that, you come back and attack those spears like fury with my crossbows! And when my lads shoot…they don't miss. But hold your lancers back until you hear three clear blast of our trumpets: '*Tan-tan-tara-tantaraaa!*' repeated three times. You won't miss them, I assure you. Then come like all the devils of Hell were after you!

"You're mad, My Lord!" The big sergeant said grimly. "We'll be cut to pieces before we've gone a hundred yards, let alone cross that bloody bridge. We'll be shot down like rabbits!"

"Well...of course that is possible," Gui said, taking off his heavy helmet and fratching his head with the palm of his hand. "But I don't think so. Firstly, they don't know you are with us, their scouts *never* got close enough to see. And, secondly, as Father Matthew said, de Courcy will be bound to tell 'em it's not us...because *he* knows we don't have any lancers! But, Vernaille will recognise the de Forz colours...and he won't want to make a terrible enemy out of the Lord Count of Niort! If you are bold enough, you will bluff your way past them. They will see what they won't expect to see...a body of men, in the colours of one of the most powerful Poitevin Barons, marching through the sunny evening countryside, looking as cool as a maiden's kiss!"

"God's Bones, Sir Gui, but you're taking an awful risk!" de Beaune said, his horse skittering beneath him. "That's almost a third of our troops."

"Well, Master Jean," Sir Richard drawled up at him with his lazy grin, his hand on his bridle, "'Faint Heart ne'er won Fair Lady!'" Then, turning towards the horrified Sergeant Bergerac, he added: "Everything Forward and Trust in the Lord, Sergeant, and the Devil take the hindmost. Don't fear so, man, and it will turn out better than you think. Trust the Lord of Malwood...he has done this sort of thing before against the Scots, and they don't come much tougher than that! Now, Gui. What about the rest of us?"

"Well, Richard, remember, they don't know that *we* know both where they are, and what they are. So...Allan, take your bowmen, with Dickon Fletcher and his men, he's the finest shot in the Forest, and make your way round the town. And they are to take *off* their surcoats! In fact," he added swiftly, looking round him, "We'll *all* fight in plain armour, no colours for any of us. Far too easy a target in the coming dusk!

Anyway, Allan, eel your way round the outside of the town to this side of that clearing, find a good place and lie-up and wait. When the time comes, I want you to stand up and be ready to drench their lancers with arrows, because attack us they will...and anyone else you see who is not one of us! I will put the Niort spears in front of you with their big shields and wicked gisarmes. Horse won't charge home against a line of pointed steel...and their long shields will help protect all of you. Will your men stand, Sergeant Bergerac?" he asked suddenly, turning towards the gnarled sergeant. "Have they practised to do this?"

"Yes, My Lord. We have practised, but not for a while. But they'll stand, Sir Gui! Never fear. *My lads'll stand!* I'll put Robert de Fer in charge of them. He'd stand against a charging bull, that one. And the men will follow his lead."

"Good man," he said, with a warm smile, and a pat on his stirruped boot. "I never doubted you!"

Then turning back to Sir Richard: "As for you and me, Richard…Fitzurse, de Beaune and Hordle John…we'll attack on foot. I'm not risking Beau and Merlin, nor any of our horses, to flights of crossbow bolts across a darkening field. We can picket them here, along with these others, and the tilt carts.

If Sergeant Bergerac does his stuff, and our lads shoot the living daylights out of those spears across the bridge, then when he charges with his lancers, they must drop their bows and pile into those bastards potting at us from behind the trees and cut them to ribbons. Give them the whacking they deserve. If all that Allan's men have said about Vernaille's troops is true…then they'll run for their lives, rather than be hacked in pieces by our Lions on the rampage: and my guess is they'll bolt right into Allan and Dickon Fletcher's sights. They will be beautifully back-lit by the sunset's afterglow …and they *will* fall like bloody rabbits!"

"And me, Gui?" The tall Benedictine asked, his head tilted slightly, with his deep Spanish lilt.

"Do almost what we suggested before Allan's lads came back, Matthew. Take the cart with the wounded, and go to the Abbey…but get two of them as much on their feet as possible to act as an escort. This will not be an easy fight, Matthew," he said, turning to face him closely, "despite all our courage and a good plan. We are going to need your skills this night for certain, and the Abbey is perfectly placed to be our headquarters. Remember, we still have to reach Bordeaux, let alone Grise. So ready your salves and your bandages, and your needle and thread…and God be with us.

Right, let's get to it before it's too dark to do anything," and he strode off with his huge Master-at-Arms, his other commanders following, to get their men ready for battle.

Chapter 27......*Now let the players take their stand.*

What followed next was an intense period of re-arrangement, as all the men from Malwood took off their distinctive surcoats, those with crossbows put on the de Forz colours that Count William's spearmen had taken off, all the rest being bundled into the spare tilt cart from which sheaves of extra clothyard arrows were taken and handed out to Allan's men, and those under Dickon Fletcher, Malwood's famous Master Bowman. Then, while Gui and all those going with him picketed their horses by the stream, Allan's verderers filled their quivers, taking two extra sheaves per man on their backs. And with personal weapons at their waists, and de Forz's spearmen with their long shields and wicked gisarmes beside them, they slipped off into the trees and disappeared.

On the track, Father Matthew climbed up onto the other tilt cart, with two of their walking wounded by his side, and prepared to follow Sergeant Bergerac and his standard bearer, one of Gui's trumpeters blowing mightily at his side.

With the great house flag of the Lord Count de Forz of Castle Niort floating above his head, Gui's mounted archers all boldly wearing de Forz's blazon as they walk-marched towards the town, and his lancers, with forked pennons fluttering from below every shining steel tip, it looked, and sounded, very much as if a travelling fair was come to visit. And before long people began to cluster round the town gates to see what all the fuss was about, running out of their houses or thrusting their heads out of their windows and all to shout and wave at the brave parade entering Saint Jean d'Angeley.

And all the time that Bergerac and the tilt cart were cheerfully distracting the townsfolk and the town's guard, Gui, Sir Richard and all the remaining Lions were swiftly making their way around the eastern walls of Saint Jean, weapons free and shields now firmly on their left arms.

In ones and twos and little groups, they slipped from corner to corner along the base of the walls, hidden by the long shadows they cast across the many tracks and pathways that criss-crossed the ground beneath them. And all the time they could hear the braying trumpet and the shouts of the townsfolk as William of Bergerac led his men through the narrow streets of Saint Jean d'Angeley.

With no moat, or town ditch, to be bothered with, and pressed against the mortared stones of the walls, Gui and his men were hidden in the deep shadows cast by the sun, now setting behind the trees at the far side of the clearing…all of half a mile away, and quite beyond the sight of anyone looking out for them. Especially as anyone looking would be seeking white surcoats with leaping scarlet lions all across them…*not* men in plain armour and dark brigandines, their shapes lost in shadow.

★

Overhead the sky was awash with gold and crimson, the air warm and lazy with high summer, the wind light and playful, the scent of new mown hay heavy on the senses. Bees wandered busily from flower to flower and the two de Vernailles and their men, dozed in the late evening sunshine.

All day they had been stood to arms waiting, their horses picketed to a strong rope line along the river side, while the sun had risen over their heads getting hotter and hotter.

Waiting for de Courcy and his lancers; waiting for their scoff; waiting for the bloody English…Just waiting for *something* to happen! They were hungry, fed-up and wanted to get back to the wine booths and taverns of Bordeaux, to their doxies and their gambling. Not stuck out in the middle of nowhere playing soldiers for the two armoured-up fancy boys who'd brought them here! Sod the lot of 'em! And they lounged at their posts…and waited.

Those by the river looking for fish in the deep clear waters, still rushing past full of the recent rainfall; those amongst the trees and bushes that ringed the great clearing, leaning back half asleep in the cool shadows out of a sun that had been getting hotter all day and was now, at last, sinking to its rest. Four days they had been on the road, and they were weary, bored and sleepy.

Across from where Bernard de Vernaille and his brother were lounging, sharing a flask of burgundy, De Courcy sat with his lancers and fretted. Pulled right back under the overhanging trees of the thick woodland to the left of the rutted roadway that led to the town, and mounted on his favourite bay, he could see that de Vernaille's command was dozing on their feet.

"Victor," he said fiercely, pointing across the clearing. "Those fucking bastards over there are practically asleep. Look at them!"

"Yes, My Lord," the big sergeant grunted sourly. "Just inviting a swarm of hornets to fly straight down their bloody throats!"

"Send Valentine across with a message from me to Sir Bernard to get his men to wake up before they get their fucking throats cut! The English fight like tigers. Tell him if he's not careful he will get well and truly mauled!" And he jagged his horse's mouth in frustration, making it twitch sideways and skitter its hooves.

"*God's bloody Bones!*" he exclaimed sharply a moment later, as the sound of cheering and trumpet calls came faintly to him from the town, getting louder by the moment. "What is that hellish noise?"

"I don't know, Sir Allan. It's coming from the town. Sounds like...like a fair, or wandering players. Shall I move out a little and see?"

"Yes, Victor. Just you. A single horse will not cause any alarm. Leave me your lance and shield, but take your sword of course."

And gently twitching his reins, Victor Jonelle kicked his horse forward and onto the track. Geoffrey de Vernaille, who had also heard the commotion coming from Saint Jean, was similarly sent forward by his brother, so both men broke cover together, too busy to notice the sudden movement of men falling flat, far away to their left as they rode forward...and de Courcy who was also

187

mounted was too busy watching Geoffrey de Vernaille, and cursing him for a fool, to notice either.

★

Allan-i-the-Wood, who had eyes like a hawk, had missed neither of them, and hissed through his teeth to drop his men the moment that Jonelle had kicked out of the woodside, almost disbelieving his luck when the other man joined him. Now he knew exactly where the ambush was laid, and where he should best place his men to support Sir Gui's attack without endangering his Lions with their arrows.

With the long shadows as they were, and being over two hundred paces from the trackway, it was not difficult for them to eel their way backwards into the wooded verges of the clearing and move stealthily towards a small area of raised ground he had spotted earlier where he could make his stand when the time came. And once in the deeper evening shadows of the trees he quickly called the leader of his spears together and with simple signs and gestures, and broken French, he told him what he wanted.

"*John-Paul*, when Sir Gui begins his attack...*Quant Sir Gui commencer l'attack*...I want you and your men to run out and make a line around the edge of that little hillock," he mimed with arms pumping and pretending to run. "*Pres cet petit mons... la bas!*' ...'There!'...He said jabbing with his finger until he was certain the big Niortian sergeant knew what he was on about. "*Et puis...* 'and then'...I want your men kneeling, with their gisarmes pointed up and out and your big shields across your bodies!" He urgently mimed again. "My archers," gesturing frantically with his hands, "will stand in a block...*un carré*...behind you...*vous derrière*...and you will see such shooting as will astound you...*c'est sera encroyable, mon vieux!* Now, down all of you," he said gesturing fiercely with his hands as he spoke. "Down and wait...*Attendez vous, mes braves!*"

188

I n the town, the streets were narrow and twisted, the houses timber framed and leaning towards each other so closely as to make any light struggle to break through, but the way forward was quite clear and before long William of Bergerac's men were passing the Benedictine Abbey of Saint John that gave the town its name on their right, and before him a deep stone archway bathed in light, showed the other gateway leading directly to the streams and the River Boutonne beyond.

Here, giving them the sign of the cross and a silent Blessing, Father Matthew left the column to seek aid from the Father Abbot, leaving the big Sergeant to make his way out of the town, pursued by a crowd of shouting people, barking dogs and running children, with the trumpeter by his side red in the face and still blowing fit to bust.

Next moment they were passing out of the shaded streets, through the shadow of the gateway entrance and into the rosy glare of the setting sun…with Geoffrey de Vernaille in his golden lion and stars on their blue 'field,' and another armoured man in the Ermine colours of the Duke of Brittany, coming slowly up towards him from the far side of the clearing.

Behind him, flitting from cover to cover as best they could find it, Gui, Sir Richard and the rest of his English command were just breaking away from the town walls, their movements masked by all the furore going on: the trotting hooves of William's men as they sallied out from the gateway, and those of his own horse that he had sent curvetting prettily sideways down the track, as his men rode down towards the River Boutonne and beyond.

Of Allan-i-the-Wood, his archers and their spear men, there was no sign at all. For all Gui could tell they might as well be in Bordeaux as anywhere near Saint Jean d'Angeley. All he could do was pray they would turn up when he needed them!

★

With their hands on their swords Victor Jonelle and Sir Geoffrey de Vernaille, having forded the first stream, now reined in across the track at the head of the second, amazed at the sight of William de Bergerac, the great house standard of de Forz waving over his head, the de Forz blazon fluttering around the points of the lancers behind him trotting unconcernedly along the track towards the second ford, even more mounted troops behind him, all in de Forz colours.

Seeing them coming on relentlessly, Jonelle went to draw his sword, but De Vernaille pulled him back: "Hold back, man! *Hold Back, I say!*" he shouted as Jonelle struggled to draw his sword. These men are known to me. Their leader is one of the Lord Count of Niort's men. I know him: William of Bergerac. He came to my father's funeral, in the Count's Honour Guard. Put up your sword, you fool! Count William is one of the most powerful Barons in Poitou. Let them by…these men are not English!"

"Sir Allan said *no-one* was to be allowed past, My Lord!" Jonelle raged, kicking his horse round in a circle. "*No-one* is to pass without challenge, Sir Geoffrey!"

"Allan de Courcy does not rule here Jonelle. I am a belted Knight, and you *will* do as I say…*these men may pass!*" And he swung his horse off the track to let the riders by, his men amongst the-tree line behind him standing up to watch what was going on, while Jonelle rode back to de Courcy, furious with Sir Geoffrey's decision.

Meanwhile Bergerac kept his whole column moving steadily forward, his heart in his mouth, but enough sense to signal his gratitude to de Vernaille with a simple nod of his head and a terse, "Thank you, My Lord!" as his men clattered by, all sixty of them. Lancers first, crossbowmen behind, each horse's hooves making small swirls of dust in the dried up trackway. Hearts pitter-pattering like mad in every breast, all trying not to look sideways at the other horseman now cantering away from them, they crossed the ford and rode on towards the bridge, just less than two furlongs further on; every moment expecting to get an arrow in the back.

A t the bridge, the spears holding it had also heard the trumpet, but no sounds of fighting or yelling, and many of those there also recognised the de Forz blazon, and knowing the Vernaille brothers were both ahead of them, made no challenge, but opened their ranks and let Bergerac's men through with a few shouts and gestures of friendship as they did so, before returning to the boring duty of waiting for something to happen. And many propped their spears against the stone walls that ran either side of the bridge, while they watched the long column of riders bounce and joggle out of sight.

★

G ui, watching them go past Jonelle and de Vernaille, saw the row of heads and bodies raise themselves above the bushes, and where Jonelle was making for, and wormed his way further forward, sliding his shield across the warm tawny grass and slithering behind it, until he dropped down into a slight dip in the ground he had been making for. This was a sort of long fold that ran across the huge clearing, into which he could gather his men before launching his attack...which must be soon as by now the light was definitely fading...and without light his archers would be useless. But he still couldn't see where Allan and Dickon Fletcher were, and he raised his head in desperation.

★

De Courcy, joined by Jonelle, was seething at Vernaille for allowing the column of men to pass without challenge…if only because they shouldn't be there! What were sixty armed men doing riding out of a town just before sunset when the gates were about to close? Why be out so late, when they should have been settling in there for the night? Their leader was not a belted knight…he could tell that from his equipment. So what was going on? And it was as he turned to rage again at Jonelle about de Vernaille's decision, that he caught a flicker of light and movement ahead of him and he stiffened in his saddle, like a hound at quest, standing up in it to look out across the whole area, now heavy with shadows.

"What is it, Sir Allan?" Jonelle asked urgently as de Courcy's voice died and he stood up to shade his eyes.

"I saw something, Victor. Out there in the middle. A flash of light, a waving hand…something!"

"An animal, My Lord?

"No, Victor. An enemy!" he shouted, settling himself firmly into his saddle. A fucking English enemy. Look, man! *Look!*" he shouted, gripping Victor's arm. "We've been fooled. Those bastards are out there! *Look!*" He pointed furiously, as a long line of soldiers leapt to their feet, almost as if they were bursting out of the ground. "There they go! The bastards! *There they goooo!*" And as the leaping, thrilling sound of an English trumpet shattered the evening, he turned to his command and roared, "*Attack!* **Attack!**"

Chapter 28…Alarums and Excursions in Saint Jean d'Angeley.

G ui, hearing De Courcy's wild shout, realised he had been seen and knew it was now or never, so trusting Allan's men would be there, he grabbed his trumpeter by the arm and they both leapt up. Gui raised his sword and roared, William Bell put his trumpet to his mouth…and all hell broke loose around them!

"*Tan!-Tan!-Tara!-Tan-Taraaa!* **Tan!-Tan!-Tara!-Tan-Taraaa!**" Three times William Bell blew his heart out, as Gui had promised Bergerac he would do, the bright, shining notes shrieking out their desperate call: "*Come to me! Come to me!* **Come to meee!**…*Come to me! Come to me!* **Come to meee!**" until the whole clearing seemed to be filled with its wild brazen screams, that went on and on and on! Until William slung it across his back, picked up his shield and raced to join his Lord in their sudden ferocious attack.

And as the trumpet blew, so Allan-i-the-Wood, Dickon Fletcher and their men rushed out from the tree line and covered the small hillock he had spotted earlier in a crescent shaped formation, thrusting a dozen arrows each into the soft ground around them, each man with enough space to draw and loose. Some standing half way up, some across the top so they could shoot over the heads of their friends below, and all round the base facing their enemies, the spearmen from Niort crouched behind their big shields with their gisarmes thrust out before them, butts to the ground, with every man's heel behind them. A ring of pointed steel no horse would choose to challenge.

And not a moment too soon, because by the time Gui's trumpeter blew the second ringing blast, de Courcy and his lancers were already on the move, sweeping forward in a thunder of flying hooves, their nine foot, steel-tipped shafts already couched beneath their arms as they dropped them towards their running enemies.

"**Loose! Loose!**" Alan shouted as de Courcy's lancers swept down towards Gui's running men. "**Loose!**" And in seconds the air was filled with the **twang!** of strings and the soft *Swoosh! Swoosh! Swoosh!* of shafts, as the first flight leaped into the sky, springing off the bows in a constant bright stream that flickered in the sun's fiery light as they soared up and turned, followed by another and another and another, as the bowmen got into their stride; bending and loosing, and bending and loosing with seemingly effortless ease until all the arrows they had laid out for their first strike had been fired.

They didn't look to see where their shafts were going, they didn't need to, they knew by instinct and fierce, constant practice exactly where; and in one minute three hundred arrows shot up into the glowing back-lit sky of pink, orange and gold...and fell on de Courcy's lancers like a sleet of death, horses and men riddled with shafts, the first line of men going down like ninepins, the rest floundering into, around and over them, the screams and howls of the wounded and the groans of the dying filling that great clearing with agony and death.

In one minute of concentrated effort a proud squadron of well mounted and armoured lancers had been turned into a terrifying, bloody shambles of smashed men and horses, broken legs and shattered bodies. Those not killed outright staggering and crawling around in mindless pain and fear, arrows sticking in them like cloves in a Christmas orange. Some horses stumbling with broken fetlocks, others screaming and trampling in pain and terror, some running free, arrows sticking in their flanks and rumps, the blood running down them in thick dark streams. In one minute, de Courcy's whole command had simply ceased to exist!

No did the horror cease, for a minute later a further douche of steel sleet fell upon them as Gui's archers let loose a second deadly flight that skewered to the ground any who might have survived their first assault, followed by the fierce '*Hee! Hee! Hee!*' of the longbow archer's traditional cry of success.

Only a few right at the very front were spared and recognising Gui from his size, his great fighting helm and his long coat of mail de Courcy hurled his horse towards him, lance lowered, feet thrust downwards into his stirrups and leaning back in his high saddle ready for the strike roaring in anger as he came.

Hearing the thunder of hooves and the bellow of hatred, Gui turned and stood foursquare, shield held high and sword held in front of him across his body, left to right, as de Courcy hurtled down on him, his eyes fixed on the gap between Gui's shield and his neck. He could imagine his lance tip bursting through that guard, the great spout of blood as his lance tore open the throat, and the scream as his enemy fell beneath his hooves. He was exultant, and as he rushed upon Gui still standing there, apparently paralysed with fear, he leaned forward and thrust his lance down for the kill!

It didn't happen!

Gui waited for that final thrust, parried the lance point away from him on his shield, turning as he did so and smashed his sword across the horse's legs as it rushed by and with a scream the bay fell, catapulting its rider onto the ground in a tangle of legs, lance, helmet and flying equipment. But de Courcy rolled as he fell and came up onto his feet, sword in hand, dazed but fighting, and Gui was on him like a tiger, while crossbow bolts flickered around them and Fitzurse led his men into the attack, bellowing like the great bull he was.

Crash! Crash! Crash! Gui mercilessly hammered de Courcy, still reeling from his fall, driving him backwards with every blow, his eyes glittering with the joy of battle, concentrated, deadly, marking his prey as Gui stalked forward, every parry that de Courcy made weaker, his legs less stable until he could barely stand. And so Gui finished him, a smashing, overhead blow that cleaved his skull in a violent spray of blood and brains and cut him to his pelvis, hewing through his armour as if it were paper, eviscerating his body, lungs heart and entrails falling out onto the torn ground. As de Beaune had said to Father Matthew at Nantes, de Courcy was good…but no match for the Lord Gui of Malwood.

As for Victor Jonelle, Dickon Fletcher shot him through the neck, his blood fountaining out of his wounds like a gargoyle spewing water in a violent storm.

★

D own by the river, de Vernaille's men heard the shining notes of the trumpet and were electrified, fizzing with sudden life as they rushed to grab their spears, galvanised by the desperate screams and yells coming from the other side, grinning and nudging each other in their eagerness for the hunted rabble they could hear being massacred to come running down towards them. Relishing the prospect of hurling them backwards over the stone balustrade and into the swollen waters rushing by below them, they stood with their spears thrust out and waited.

Nor were they dismayed when they saw marching back towards them, now on foot, their crossbows in the crook of their arms, the same men that had passed through their ranks not half an hour earlier, all wearing the de Forz colours as before, and behind them the lancers, who halted to address their lines, while the crossbows continued towards them. It wasn't until the marching men stopped, shook themselves into two loose lines and raised their bows that anyone realised that something was wrong…and by then it was too late.

A crossbow, unlike a long bow, has a flat trajectory, fires a short thick bolt, often with leather fletching, from a composite bow strengthened with steel, that the archer has to bend down to wind up, his foot in a kind of stirrup, because the bow is too stiff to be pulled by hand. It fires like a gun from the shoulder and is deadly!

Twang! Swoosh! Thunk! Like a butcher hacking into a great side of beef. The bolts flashed across the distance and hammered Vernaille's spearmen into a terrified rabble. Blood and brains splattered, muscles ripped and tore, bodies punctured to the very hilt of the fletching, and the men fell about like shot rabbits.

Within seconds over half were killed, others wounded, the rest too shocked to do more than stand with their mouths open. But not for long, because having fired their one volley, with a fierce, triumphant '*Tan!-Tan!-Tara!-Tan-Taraaa!* from Sir Gui's trumpeter, the Lancers drawn up behind the crossbows thrust their rowels into their horses flanks and charged into the attack.

196

And de Vernaille's men did not stand...they took one look at death on the hoof thundering towards them, dropped their spears and fled. But no running man is any match for a lancer! William Bergerac's men hurtled over the bridge with wild shouts and cries and hunted their quarry to destruction, thrusting their lances into backs, sides and chests without mercy. Their hardened steel points ripping and tearing the lives out of their enemies. Like hunting the wild boar they ran each man down, thrusting their lances into them with controlled fury, riding by to let the horse pull the lance free before driving on to stick the next one and the next one, shouting exultantly with every kill.

Behind them, the Malwood Lions, dropped their bows, rushed over the bridge and plunged into the woodlands beyond with drawn swords to hunt down the enemy crossbows lurking there, striking down the men they found without pity, flaying their bodies with sharpened steel, thrusting into their bellies and flensing their flesh away in gouts of blood and brawn; shoulders, heads and arms cleaved through til their armour ran red and their blades with thick with it.

★

In the great clearing the fighting was over.

With the death of de Courcy and the arrival of William Bergerac and his lancers, the fight went out of their enemies, and with desperate cries for mercy those still alive fell on their knees and begged for their lives. And while Gui looked around at the carnage his men had wrought, at the piles of bodies of both men and horses where Allan and Dickon Fletcher's archers had mown down de Courcy's lancers, some poor beasts still struggling and heaving for life, others staggering, heads down, their flanks pierced with arrows...and at the fallen bodies of his own Lions who had lost their lives in the attack, he looked and felt very grim indeed.

And it was in this spirit that the two Vernaille brothers were dragged before him, caught trying to flee the stricken field by two of de Bergerac's lancers, their bridles seized in an iron grasp, themselves heaved from their saddles and now hauled before Sir Gui to face his fury, their standard in de Beaune's tough grasp.

"These are the two Vernaille brothers, My Lord," he said, casting their standard at Gui's feet, disgust in every word he spoke. "Two of William's lads caught them trying to flee. This one," he said, shaking one by the shoulder like a terrier with a rat, "is Sir Bernard   I found this in his saddle bag, Sir Gui!" And with a grim face he handed Gui a tiny roll of parchment.

Gui took it carefully from his hand and read it, before handing it wordlessly on to Sir Richard, who hold it up to the light, the better to see the tiny writing more clearly.

"Bones of Christ, Gui. De Brocas! Another of his messages. Sent five days ago, the day after we landed at Nantes. That means de Courcy..."

"...Also had a message to come here," Gui interrupted him savagely, and he looked at both men with such anger, their faces visibly paled, turned to stone, while he was seized with an almost uncontrollable urge to kill them where they stood so arrogantly before him.

Meanwhile Gui's command gathered around him, many wounded, several badly so, leaning on their friends, their wounds roughly bound with blood soaked rags, their faces dark and sour as they looked at the handful of survivors thrown at Sir Gui's feet where they cowered on the bloodied grass, hands tied behind their backs with the whipcord every archer's bow case carried. All waiting to hear what their Lord would say to the men who had led the attack against them.

"You two miserable wretches deserve to die, for what you have done today," He growled at the brothers, through gritted teeth. *"And, by God's Bones I have a mind to slay you both!"* he suddenly roared, his bloodied sword whirling over their heads, making them flinch and step away from his anger.

"How *dare* you stand there before me, with your heads in the air you…pathetic *cowards!* You…*Nithings!* Men of no honour and no courage. At least that bastard over there," he shouted, pointing to where de Courcy's shattered body still lay amidst its burst offal and bloodied entrails, "had the courage to fight. He led his man bravely and bears his wounds to the front. You…you brought your men to the ring, and left them to hop! Abandoned them. No wonder your father detested you both so greatly!" And he glared at their shocked faces, as his words struck home.

"And for what?" he derided them. "To curry favour with King Phillip? To please Roger de Brocas?" And snatching the message from Richard's hands he seized Sir Bernard's face, squeezed his mouth open and forced the crumpled parchment into his mouth, stuffing it in to the back of his throat, the man's eyes goggling at him in terror as he gagged and choked on it, falling to his knees and scrabbling desperately to pull it out with trembling fingers, his brother hiding his face in his hands unable to watch.

"So…the good Lord Baron Sir Roger de Brocas put you up to this! You are in his pay, you miserable worms. You are both no better than dog shit! Belted knights? Yes and so you should be, stripped and flogged through Saint Jean d'Angeley at the cart's tails with stirrup leathers, like the common felons and murderers you are, til your backs are bloody while everyone pelts you with rubbish…because that's all you are!!"

And stepping towards them he ripped their surcoats off them and trampled them under his feet, tore their standard apart at the seams, stamping on it, and heeling it into the ground til it was indelibly soiled, while his command looked on with bitter faces in full agreement with their Lord's actions.

"*You are not worthy of the colours you bear!*" he roared into two faces white with shock and fear. "I hold you both responsible for this…this carnage scattered around us. You will come with me to Bordeaux, in chains if necessary, where I will hand you over to Sir Hugh Willoughby, the Guardian of the King's Peace where you hold your lands, for him to do with you as he sees fit. But be certain that when I meet with King Richard of England…which I will do, I will seek to have you banished from all Aquitaine, and *all* your lands held forfeit to the crown."

199

Then dropping his voice completely, he walked right up to them and almost whispered in quiet, seething rage: "I assure you, *both*, that you will rue this evening's filthy work, and any allegiance you might have had with that Man-of-Blood, till your dying days. Now take them out of my sight and feed them. Any attempt to escape…cut them down without mercy!"

Then turning to Sir Richard beside him, he pointed to the handful of men still crouching on their knees: "Release those men, Richard. Give them five silver pieces each and send them home. There has been enough killing today. There is no need for more!" And ignoring the pardoned men's cries of gratitude and prayers for God's Grace upon him, he walked away to meet Father Matthew now coming towards him from the town with his tilt cart, a large group of monks and assorted town's people in his company, all bringing help and succour for any who had survived the battle.

★

Far away in Château Grise the Baron waited to hear that Gui was dead and his command scattered…and how his other plan for Alicia's 'rescue' from his daughter was working. He knew that El Nazir had seized her, and that she had arrived at Narbonne. Now it was up to de Vere to play his part. The man had all he needed…he just had to set the ball rolling.

The Lord Baron rubbed his hands together fiercely with sudden pleasure, and grinned. Good so far. Excellent! But where was his message from Bertrand de Vernaille, or de Courcy? What had happened at Saint Jean d'Angeley?

Chapter 29...Alicia begins her journey to the Château Grise.

The Lady Alicia de Burley had never taken twelve more difficult steps in her life, than the ones she took that morning at Bayonne, when she, with her small household behind her, stepped onto the gangway that led to the quayside...and the Lady Rochine de Brocas waiting beyond. Her enemy, and the daughter of her enemy, now down from her horse and standing tall, her long scarlet silk coif swirling in the breeze, her red cloak covering her right down to her scarlet booted feet, her face smiling a welcome, eyes bleak as midwinter.

Alicia looked at her and stretched her shoulders...her eyes sharp with fierce determination. Two could play that game...and her face was masked. Rochine might see her eyes...but she could not see her face!

And coming across the quayside Alicia greeted her French cousin with a smile, holding her hand out through her black chador as she did so, such that Rochine could do nothing except receive it.

"Welcome, Cousin," Alicia said, her eyes a-glitter from between the black material that covered her head and the lower part of her face. "I had expected the Great Baron himself to be here to greet me...after taking such trouble to 'collect' me," she added gesturing towards the *Morning Star* and El Nazir, standing not twenty paces away from them. "No matter, I suppose if the blade himself cannot come, my dear Rochine...I must make do with the oil that keeps it bright!"

Rochine's green eyes stabbed at her with fury, and gripping Alicia's arm above her elbow she hissed viciously: "How *dare* you! How *dare* you insult me! Had I had my way you would have been delivered to me in chains!"

"But I *am* in chains...Madam!" Alicia bit back at her sharply, her eyes like sapphires, hard, unblinking. "*Bound by them,* my *so* dear cousin! Chains of truth and honour and everlasting love that you will *never* break. Even if your father drags me up the aisle and nails me to the altar, he will *never* possess me. All he will ever have of me is my carcase...my heart and my spirit will always lie elsewhere. Now...unhand me!" she snarled, tearing her arm out of Rochine's grasp.

"If you have not noticed, I am not alone!" she said, directing Rochine's furious gaze to her two enormous guards, and to Najid standing near them. "See those men there? They are my Household and my guardians, and the smaller one is our personal cook. They are on loan to me from the Sheik, your so dear father's dearest friend. And will travel with me to Grise. *All the way*...for my added safety, and yours too, dear coz.," she added sweetly. "To ensure that nothing surprising happens to prevent our safe arrival beneath your father's walls? Yes? Just so that no sudden accidents happen between here and Grise?...and no-one would want that...would they, Sweet Coz!" she ended with a lift of her eyebrows. And she gave her cousin a swift bob, and walked back to where Aziz, Aquib and all the others were standing.

The Lady Rochine de Brocas stood rooted to the spot, almost shaking with rage.

How *dare* she speak to her...The Lady...in such insulting terms, and with such contempt! She looked at her as she walked back towards her 'Household' and snarled. Her '*Household*' indeed! Two great lumps of humanity, one small cook, whom she knew all about, and two stupid girls...one of whom she had personally trained in her ways! Just wait til she had Soraya Fermier under her hand again!

The thought almost made her purrr.

De Vere would deal with them in short order. Once they were clear of the quay, and on board the barge her father had commissioned for the river journey to Peyrehorade, she would see about her pathetic 'Household.' No-one...but *no-one* could be allowed to treat her like that...that English *putain!* That whore whom her father so desired. She had given him everything...heart and body! What need did he have for *une salope, une trui!...une conne Anglaise!*' She almost stamped her foot and spat she was so angry...panting with suppressed rage

But swirling her long scarlet cloak around her she turned, steadied her breathing, and then stalked slowly towards the Sheik El Nazir, striving to calm herself, when she almost wanted to run, surprised at how easily the wretched girl had disturbed her. She smiled...just give her half an hour alone with in her chamber and she would soon make her sing a different tune!

El Nazir, who had watched the little scene with Hawk like eyes, grinned quietly to himself. The little one had shown too much spirit too soon! She should have played The Lady on a string for much longer; not have declared herself so soon in the game. Dissembled more. Instead she had done exactly what he hoped she would do! Stick the knife into The Lady and then twist it, and his eyes wrinkled with another quiet smile of satisfaction.

He had seen how rigid Rochine had gone while they had been talking, and that look on her face would turn milk sour! The rest he could guess, and looking across at Abdul Aziz and Aquib, he shrugged. He had done his bit for the Lord Roger, as he had been asked to do, and she'd had first throw of the dice. Now she and The Lady would have to sort it out between them, with de Vere to help things along if he could. 'Insh'a Allah!' And he turned and walked towards The Lady Rochine de Brocas with his hands held out to her, a welcome smile on his sun-hardened features.

Alicia watched them greet, and then grimaced as she walked back to Soraya and the others, while some of Rochine's guard swung off their horses and ran out to load their things onto the tilt carts: chests of clothes for the girls and all their essential belongings, bundles for the men, and baskets of tools and spare armour, grinding stones and oil, along with all Najid's pans and ladles; fresh eggs, smoked meats of fish and pork, bags filled with fresh lemons and oranges, and his precious boxes of rare spices. Sugar from Cyprus, peppercorns and turmeric from India and even cinnamon and nutmeg from the magical Spice Islands of the distant East, brought by caravan to Damascus and Egypt from across the top of the world...many were beyond simple price, along with rice from the Jordan river, bundles of dried herbs and a great box of salt crystals. And last of all, accompanied by their Master, *Almahdi aal Suriyyan*, came the Baron's precious pigeons in their large wicker cages

"I think I overplayed my hand," she growled to Agnes and Soraya, when she reached them. "I was too cross for my own good. Thought I'd give as good as I might receive." Then she chuckled, and pulled a wry face. "I don't think my French Cousin likes me very much...and with two hundred miles to go, I'm not sure that was too clever!"

Soraya sighed, and put her arms around both girls. "She *hates* to be crossed, Alicia. She always has to be '*right!*' When things go well she can be as warm as the sun itself, loving and generous. You would be surprised. But there is a vicious 'twist' in her...almost evil, that she cannot control, and her moods can change like lightning; cooing like a turtle dove one moment and a spitting virago the next...then she can be *truly* dangerous! And she has great power over her father.

I have heard of terrible things they have done together, and when she is jealous her temper can be horrifying. Yet she has a 'way' with her even I have found hard to resist, and have done things with her that I could never have dreamed of!" she said, her face ashamed, suddenly pale in the sunshine. "I told you...on the *Morning Star*? She can be a monster...and she loves her silken lash!" She added with a shudder.

"Right now...she is in a fury! I can tell. By tomorrow, after proper food and rest, she could be your best friend for life. Thank God, we are not reliant on her for protection, or for our food, and can avoid her completely."

"She will not be pleased about that I think." Agnes said quietly.

"No...I told you, she likes to control things. But she will not go against El Nazir. She would not dare. He is her father's greatest friend, as he said, for many years. And she is afraid of him. Afraid he knows a terrible secret about her, that she dare not risk her father *ever* finding out."

"What secret is that?"

"I do not know. But I am certain she had two girls murdered who tried to find out!"

"*Murdered?*" Alicia and Agnes whispered, aghast.

204

"*Yes!* I am sure of it. But I have no proof. One moment they were around her chambers and close with her father...the next moment they had disappeared. *Poofé!* Gone...and their bodies were found two days later almost eaten by the castle swine."

Agnes shuddered. "Pigs will eat anything! They're almost as bad as goats."

"But not flesh, Sweetheart. Clothes and such...but not bodies," Alicia added. "Sweet Jesus, Soraya. But you have served a dreadful Mistress...just be careful I don't turn out to be like her," and leaping round in her chador, making sudden claws of her hands, she growled like a tiger... "*GRRRRRR!*"...so that everyone laughed.

"Right...that's enough doom and gloom for a while. As long as we stick together, and have Abdul and Aquib to watch over us," she said, looking up at them both with a smile, "and Najid to cook for us...and I don't irritate her any more, then we ought to get by. Oh, Soraya...Agnes...how I *wish* Gui were here. I do miss him sooo much!" And her eyes suddenly flooded with tears.

"I know, *ma pauvre petite choux*," Soraya said softly as she would to a child, drawing her into her arms and kissing her cheek. "*My poor little honey cake,* he will come for you, your so brave Sir Gui, on his great charger. Me, I am certain of it. We must just hang on until he does...and do all we can to keep things smooth in the meantime. Now...no more tears. They will make your eyes red," and she laughed. "Right now I can't wait to take off my Houke...and you your chadors. They are impossible to ride in!"

Chapter 30… *The White Rose twists The Lady's tail.*

F our hours later and they were all on the great barge that Lord Roger had commissioned for the first part of their journey, and well on their way up-river to Peyrehorade from where they would strike across country towards Carcassonne and the Via Aquitania; the great Roman road, that still linked Bordeaux with Narbonne. Once it had carried the eagles swinging through Gaul at the head of the Legions at twenty miles a day, meeting the Via Domitia coming up from Rome, having crossed the Alps where Hannibal had once driven his elephants all those years before.

They were the two great High Roads that joined Italy to Spain and to the Atlantic coast through Narbonne, over the long bridge with its five great arches that still stood over the Robine, the canal that the veterans of Caesar's Xth Legion had dug to join up with the River Aude. It was what had made Narbonne a great port, ships sailing all over the Old Empire with oil and wine in great amphoras…now in great casks and hogsheads to all parts of King Richard's Plantagenet Empire, including Toulouse, an Empire put together by his father, King Henry II, and was so important a source of the money Richard needed to fight the Saracens in the Holy Land.

And the mighty County of Toulouse, the greatest single County in all France, whose ruler Raymond V was a mortal enemy of Richard Lionheart, included Narbonne and Gruissan ruled by the Lord Baron Sir Roger de Brocas who was his closest ally!

Sweet Wine of Christ! What a dreadful tangle to be caught up in?…And it was to Narbonne they were going now, Alicia thought, as she looked along the boat they were in, at the rowers on long sweeps either side, now resting, and at the great square sail spread above them, its broad, brown belly filled with the brisk North Westerly that had carried the *Morning Star* down from Nantes. Narbonne first…then Gruissan: Grise as she had always known it.

Twenty miles of gentle sailing against the current, always pushing East, the river curving and bending through the warm, sundrenched countryside, past great open fields of wheat and barley, busy with groups of hoers. Past long rows of vines, that stretched in all directions, bright green lines against the darker woodlands, the rich red earth lightly dug around them, thick with grapes hanging from them in a welter of great fruity clusters...and past the silver-grey leaved olive groves, the trunks and branches gnarled and twisted with age, heavy with green and black fruit, the wind making the leaves turn and flicker silver bright in the brilliant sunshine.

Dressed in the blue pleated bliaut she had worn three days ago, her hair brushed out and piled beneath a snood of golden thread, matching blue leather half-boots on her feet, Alicia felt elegant and comfortable, delighted to be free of the hated chador, and she looked at Soraya, now similarly dressed, but in deep green to match her eyes, no longer like a Houri from an Eastern harem, and smiled...reaching out to tap the girl's hand gently and draw her attention away from the drowsing countryside.

"You look lovely like that," she said, taking her hand with a wide smile and giving it a shake. "You could not go across half of France in the way Rochine had dressed you, Soraya. You are a part of my Household now, Honeyone...not hers. She cannot control you any longer...no matter how much she may wish to. Her father ordered you to serve me...gave you to me as a gift of 'Love'," she added dryly. "So I will have you dressed as it suits me, not her...as I told her. Do you not like the clothes I have chosen?"

"Oh, yes, My lady...Alic-ia," she replied instantly, with her stunning smile. "They are lovely. Not as free to wear as my Yashmak and half jacket...and my breasts feel squashed," she said giving her body a shake, "and no-one can see my golden tips, which I quite liked," she added with a shrug and a swift grin. "But they give me an elegance, and...and...so-ph-ist-ic-ation," she said stumbling over the word, "that I have not enjoyed before. They make me feel...to you special," she added softly looking down.

"But was it worth that awful, awful row, Alicia?" Agnes asked quietly. "I thought she was going to kill you where you stood. And those two cousins? Did you see their faces afterward? Maybe you are pushing The Lady too hard, my pet," adding with a wry smile: "I thought you were going to try *not* to irritate to her so much?"

★

They had arrived at the barge earlier, having waited for the *Morning Star* to sail, de Vere chivvying his men to get every last thing loaded on as swiftly as possible…especially the large wicker cages of pigeons that were the special responsibility of their Syrian Pigeon Master who was also coming with them off the ship.

And finally Jules Lagrasse and Lucas Fabrizan, who'd come last off the *Morning Star*, and were then by his side waiting to assist the Lady Rochine up the rough gangplank off the stout wooden pier against which the barge was moored: Alicia and her Household bringing up the rear, not wanting to be any nearer to any of them than was necessary.

The boat itself was large, with long sweeps on both sides and a single tall mainmast that carried a great square sail of brown canvas. Half decked, with a number of cabins at bow and stern, and a huge long empty belly for cargo, the space now only partly taken by their many packs and saddles and the contents of both tilt carts, so the barge was quite spacious: horses and tilt carts having been left behind ready for the next travellers to come that way.

At first all had been well, with both parties settling into their little cabins at either end of the boat, prior to sailing, until Rochine, with a mouth pinched as if she'd been sucking lemons, and a face to match, had sharply ordered Soraya to come to her quarters. Soraya, used to such peremptory handling, and knowing what would happen when she got there had looked terrified, but was still about to do as instructed when Alicia had stopped her.

"Where are you going, Sweetheart?"

"The Lady has ordered me to go to her. But I am afraid!"

"Of course you are afraid, Soraya. But I am not…and you are in my Household now, and she cannot order you about any longer without my say so. And I don't say so! Tell Aquib what we are about and ask him to speak with Aziz and then both must come and join us. Agnes, we will be back

208

shortly....ask Najid to prepare some orange sherbet for later. Now...you two, come on," and Soraya, having spoken briefly to Aquib, then said in Farsi, '*Ba man bia*'...'come with me'...and had moved to join Alicia.

Aquib, after first speaking with Aziz had padded along behind them like the great soft-footed bear he was, and together they had gone up to speak with Rochine.

"I understand you have ordered Soraya to come to your quarters, cousin?" Alicia had asked quietly. "Why is that? She is not your servant to give orders to any longer. Not without my say so. Please, if you need her for something, I would be grateful if you were to ask me first!"

Rochine, who'd been momentarily speechless at her presumption, had then lost her temper completely and shouted: "*How dare you interfere!* She is *nothing* to do with you...*cousin!* She is mine to control. *Mine!* You understand? And has been since she was given to me by my father six years ago..."

"But that was six years ago, Rochine," Alicia had interrupted sweetly, smiling into her cousin's raging face. "As I understand it she has been given into my sole care, by your father, as my 'Betrothal Gift'...because he 'loves' me? I have it here in a letter Soraya gave me when I was brought on board the *Morning Star*," she added waving the crumpled piece of parchment in her face. "So please do not interfere with my Household again!" And thrusting her father's latter into Rochine's hands, she had turned her back and walked away, saying sharply over her shoulder: "Soraya. Come with me...*now!*"

"*NO!*" Rochine had almost screamed, hurling the letter tempestuously onto the deck and stamping on it in her fury. "*NO!* I say. That girl shall stay here, as *I* have ordered. Jules, Lucas...take her to my cabin now and strip her! De Vere, remove this...*this person*," she had raged, stabbing her finger at Alicia. "And have her conveyed to her quarters and keep her there. Kicking and screaming...*I don't care!* And you! You great *lumpen oaf!*" she had snarled up at Aquib, standing before her, his arms crossed, while she had gestured at him violently. "*Get out of my way!*"

But Aquib had not moved.

His face impassive, his body enormous and seemingly immoveable, he had just stood there, completely calm in the face of her unbridled fury, while he had waited for Soraya to tell him what to do...all the time watching the two Frenchmen as they had rushed to carry out Rochine's orders, and de Vere as he had stolen up behind Alicia to seize her and carry her away.

But the moment Soraya had felt the Cousins' hands on her she had shouted in Farsi: "Aquib! *Ahay anha!*"... *'Stop Them!*...and absolute mayhem had followed.

With two great strides Aquib had seized both Frenchmen by their arms and simply hurled them overboard behind him as effortlessly as if they had been sacks of feathers, sending them soaring over his head, in a wild cartwheel of arms and legs, their cries of shocked alarm brutally cut off as they had hit the river bank with a terrific *thump!* Landing amongst the reeds and rushes, half in and half out of the water, all the stuffing knocked out of them, unable to move.

De Vere, seeing them spin through the air had stopped dead in his tracks, awed by the ease with which the huge soldier had hurled two fully grown men, armour, weapons and all, straight over his head...and had backed away immediately to give himself space to draw his sword.

But Aquib, who had been expecting it, did not give him the chance to do so.

Moving more swiftly than de Vere could possibly have imagined, he had pounced on him, clamped the big man's sword arm in his enormous hand and then shaken it till de Vere's teeth had almost rattled and, willy nilly, he had been forced to drop his sword with a clatter on the deck. And before he could speak another word, Aquib had seized his head in such a fierce grip under his arm, with his other hand twisting the far side of it, that de Vere had stopped struggling immediately for fear his head would simply have been torn from his shoulders...as he felt was surely about to happen.

With the two Frenchmen still flat on their backs just shuddering back to life like a pair of ancient cripples, her Guard Commander completely immobilised and his horrified soldiers, with no bows to hand, too scared even to move, there was nothing else that Rochine could have done save to accept defeat with as much grace as possible…which was not much!

"*Very well!*" she had almost spat at her cousin, her fists clenched in humiliated fury. "Soraya stays with you as my father seems to have ordered…at least until we reach Grise, then we shall see, *cousin!*" she had snarled viciously, poison in every word. "He needs me in ways you cannot even begin to guess at…ways that may bring *us* together sooner than you think, you foolish girl! And you are not even married yet, my *so* dear Alicia…nor have we reached home. You have drawn the lines, Coz. Pray God *I* do not cross them to find you!

Now, take that *putain* with you!" she had hissed with venom at Soraya. "That cheap whore…that *conne Francaise*, and dress her how you wish. They say that revenge is a tree that bears sour fruit," and she had thrown back her head and laughed. "But I do not have a sweet tooth in my entire body, *ma petite choux* ," she had sneered at Soraya, chucking her under her chin. "I prefer my food to have lots and lots of lovely, salty savour…*ma pet-ite lap-in…*" she had growled, bitter sarcasm dripping from every syllable. "*My lit-tle bun-ny rabbit…*as you know soooo well. And savour you I will, *ma mie…to the very last, precious..tasty..drop!*" and pausing to plant a soft kiss on Soraya's cheek with her sweetest smile, she had turned away to rescue de Vere, gesturing fiercely to Aquib: "Now, you big *lump!* Put my man down and get about your business…your mistress has more need of you than I do!"

And so everyone had parted, while the dust settled, the boat was quanted from its moorings, the captain seizing the heavy tiller as the rowers heaved on the long sweeps against the current, 'til the great sail had been raised and their journey east to Narbonne had at last started

Chapter 31...And the Morning and the Evening were the First Day! (Genesis 1:5).

So...was that awful row worth it, Agnes?" Alicia asked her in rhetoric, sitting on one of their long clothes' chests with a padded top, "For that—that wicked Harpy, that Medusa, to know how I feel? That she is my enemy...and the daughter of my enemy? Father Matthew always says that '*knowledge is power*'...and that '*to know something is better than to know nothing.*' He also says that '*to enjoy ignorance is the opinion of fools!*' And, before God, Mistress Agnes Fitzwalter, while I may be many things my love...I am no fool. So, *Yes!* Sweetheart, it *was* worth it...if only to force that bitch, that '*salope*' to show her true colours."

"The colours you saw the night of the fire?" Agnes said coming to join her on the long chest, putting her arm around her waist. "When her father killed Gui's parents and she drugged you and helped him steal you away?"

"Yes, Agnes! Oh, I heard what you said, Soraya," she added turning towards the lovely girl with a smile, "about her being warm and generous and loving? I experienced that also after the banquet, when we shared a room together...and before it...when I am sure she tried to make love to me. Wanted me to play her games...only I would not...could not, even though I was tempted. She seemed so sophisticated, so much a 'woman of the world', and I a simple country bunny! But country bunnies have claws, Soraya, and teeth...and know when to run and hide from the fox...and I escaped her."

"And today, *ma mie?*" Soraya asked, reaching out for her hand. "When she threatened you...screamed at you, weren't you afraid?"

"Yes. Of course I was afraid. Only fools have no fear, Sweetheart. And no...I was *not* looking forward to meeting with her again. Walking down that gangway off the *Morning Star* today was one of the most difficult things I have ever had to do. But I was far more afraid of showing it, of letting her *know* such a thing of me. Of giving her that kind of power over me. So, yes, I taunted her a little," she said with a grin.

"After all she is my cousin, we share a certain blood, and I know what a murderous creature she is...and how her father so wants me in his bed!...Not as his *salope,* his 'bitch' - his piece of *conne Anglaise,* his 'English cunt!'" she said shocking them both, Agnes putting her hand to her mouth with a sudden squeak, Soraya's eyes popping out of their sockets. "*But as his legal wife!* To bear his heir, as he hopes! Sweet Jesus what a ghastly prospect? The man must be mad even to think of such a thing! So El Nazir was right - she is *far* more afraid of me than ever I will be of her. For that is the one thing she can *never* do for him, give him a child, and I can guess the rest...and dreadful that is too. So, yes, she fears me."

"Thank God for Mhaktoun and Abdul," Soraya said breathlessly.

"And little Najid, with his pans and baskets and spices," Agnes added with her gentle smile. "He will need caring for too, it would be dreadful if anything happened to him because of us."

"And thank God, for the Sheik," Alicia said, standing up, and leaning against the smooth gunnels of the barge, as Najid bustled about with the orange sherbet behind her, while Mhaktoun Aquib, her 'Protector' and Abdul Aziz aal Suriyyan, her 'Servant of the Powerful One', stood nearby, their hands on their huge swords, their eyes looking everywhere.

"Before today perhaps we could have dissembled. Played The Lady on a long line with a mask of sweetness and light...and watched our backs. Pretended respectability - while harbouring rebellion. But we have two hundred miles to go, and I would rather *know* of her personal hatred and her anger...of her jealousy and spite, and mine for her, and for her to know that I will not be suborned nor trifled with...nor have my people ordered about without my say so, than play her game with lies and deceit and dishonour, and in the end be no better than she is!

213

After today's experience she will know not to interfere with our arrangements…and that Aquib is more than a match, *single handed* for any of the men she has with her. And of Aziz's abilities she still knows nothing…but she will secretly fear him, for what she doesn't know! As I said, 'Knowledge is power'. We have it…she does not…and nor is she to find out either how devastating Aziz can be when necessary. Anyway, we are safe enough on this barge, with us here and she over there," she added pointing across to Rochine's cabin at the other end of the long barge. "Good arrangement!"

Then turning to look out across the countryside she added: "The real trouble will start when we reach Peyrehorade, and start across country. That's when we will need to start watching our backs with a vengeance. Til then, let's just enjoy ourselves. Oh, look!" she called out, pointing; we're mooring up for the night. Well done the captain, we might get a hot meal after all…how lovely! Soraya call the 'boys' and let's see what they can get for us from the so dear Lady Rochine de Brocas' people for our food tonight. You'll have to go with them…they can't speak the language, remember? Agnes, my love, pass that sherbet, I am thirsty!

★

Later, after de Vere had done his rounds and all had settled for the night, seated on sacks and woolfells beneath where The Lady was lying amongst the cushions his men had brought on board for her, Gaston de Vere, Jules Lagrasse and Lucas Fabrizan plotted their revenge…and the relief of all The Lady's troubles, with a couple of wineskins and two small brass oil lamps, while they chewed on the remainder of their dinner.

"That fucking bastard will pay for what he bloody did to me and Jules," Lucas swore, as he rubbed more ointment into the massive bruises that were now blackening his back and shoulders. "Tossed us overboard as if we were a pair of bloody maidens! And as for that sodding piece of English shit, if I don't stuff my fat prick up her fucking arse, my name's not Lucas Fabrizan!"

"You're welcome, Coz," Jules snarled, tearing a piece of bread between his hands. "I want the other one. That Soraya. Dark meat is always delicious, especially after a good smacking! Tenderises it like prime beef…makes it even more juicy. You can have that other English bitch, de Vere. That Fucking

214

Agnes. I swear she's dying for it! And she's whole...untouched by human hand. A virgin hole is always tighter, more springy," he leered. Then chuckling hoarsely he added: "And there's *nothing* like popping a fresh, young cherry...always that lovely sweet burst of bloody flavour!" And they both laughed, a vicious gasping sound that made their bellies shake.

"It's not the fucking girls I want, lads," de Vere growled, drinking from an almost flaccid wineskin, the red wine splashing over his face, before tearing at a piece of smoked meat with his teeth. "It's that sodding great lump of infidel muscle pretending to be human...that Aquib. *No-one* does that to Gaston de Vere. He may be big, and quick...*Jesus* was he quick!...but cold steel, or a well heated iron from the fire, in the right place will quell any fighter faster than a bucket of water on hot coals!"

"Just shoot the fuckers," Lucas swore. "Him and that bloody Aziz. You brought some sodding bowmen with you in your guard...I saw the buggers."

"Yes!" Jules agreed, reaching for the wine skin to fill his beaker. "Wait til we get off this damned barge. There'll have to be some hunting if these people are all to be fed...then wait til we are all away up-country, or somewhere lonely, and shoot some bolts hard into 'em! Nice, barbed, broad-head hunting quarrels, and they'll go down like shot rabbits. *Shhiew!...Thump!*" And he banged his right fist into his hand. "The bigger they are, harder they'll fall!"

"No...can't do that," de Vere growled again, looking at them both sideways. "Though that would work a treat, for sure. But they are off the *Morning Star.* Two of that fucking Sheik's best men I gather. The Baron would have our guts for garters. No...it has to be cunning! So no-one can blame either us...or The Lady."

"Well how the bloody fuck do we do that?" Lucas sneered. "With fucking magic?"

"The man's a bloody mountain!" Jules cursed bitterly, pouring the wine down his throat. "None of our lads want to get near him. "They both are. If the lads can't shoot the buggers from behind a rock; they're sure not going to stick bloody cold steel in 'em!"

De Vere smiled and leaned forward, his voice dropping to a husky whisper as he sneered: "Don't you worry, lads. I know something about that little cook, that stupid bloody 'Najid' that will put him right in our frame!"

"*What?*" both men exclaimed sharply, leaning towards him.

"*Shhh!*" He hissed at them urgently. "Softly! Keep your voices down. Do you want the whole bloody world to know what we are about? Especially as it's something The Lady doesn't know," he husked, leering at them. "Remember, we have travelled on that sodding *Morning Star* before, she and I...and with the Lord Baron, several times. And I happen to know that Najid has a sister he's devoted to; got the word secretly from a friend," and he tapped his nose and winked. "'Faridah' she's called...means '*Precious Pearl*'," and he snorted in derision. "Pretty as a picture she is, all sloe-eyed and slender; only twelve, and that stupid, fucking little cook dotes on her!" And he paused to take another swig from the wineskin.

"Well, go on!" Jules urged, drinking from his beaker and wiping his mouth with the back of his hand.

"So...their parents are dead," de Vere went on, turning his head one to the other, his eyes glittering in the lamp light, sly, full of secrets. "And that Najid is her only real protector. She lives with an aunt, his Papa's elder sister, a real miserable, sodding bitch of a woman. Bitter as stale piss in a bucket: she'd sell her grandmother if she could find a buyer...and Najid knows it! It's only his money that keeps the old bat caring for the child at all, or she'd be out on the street...and she's *just* the sort of young meat that The Lady so likes to trade with!"

"So?" Lucas, sneered, and spat across the deck. "He is also part of that bloody Sheik's crew. We're no further forward"

"Does this stupid sod have any brains at all?" De Vere snarled at Jules. "Or are they all in that sodding prick he carries dangling between his legs?"

"Coz?" Jules asked with a sigh. "Do you suppose that Najid, *knows* what The Lady is really like?"

216

"Yes!" he said quietly, after a moment's thought, his brow creased. "Yes...he must do."

"Well suppose, then, that our beloved mistress learned...somehow?...that Najid had a problem about his darling little sister, and she suggested to El Nazir that she should care for the child herself? Yes? Well, Nazir knows what a vicious old hag the aunt is, that she doesn't want the silly little bitch...and that Najid can't take her with him on the *Morning Star*...so, suppose Najid found out about it? That someone told him of The Lady's interest, and that she'd spoken with El Nazir?...well, Najid might easily think the Sheik would agree, seeing as he and The Lady are always as thick as bloody thieves, and gave the girl to her...or sold her...then his *'Precious Pearl'* would be well and truly stuffed. Literally, knowing The Lady's tastes! Yes?"

"Yes! So?"

"Dear God, it's like wading through bloody treacle with you sometimes, Lucas. You tell him Gaston!"

"So...if Najid thought that The Lady might *really* get her hot little hands on his sister, with El Nazir's blessing...what might he *not* refuse to do to prevent it...eh??"

"And he does *all* their cooking, Coz!" Jules added, looking at his cousin with his head on one side...finally sitting back and smiling as the lights came on at last behind his cousin's eyes.

"So...So...the stupid bastard could slip something into their fucking scoff to prevent that happening, and..and then, when they all bloody died...or...or something... *he'd* fucking get the blame and not one of us!" And he looked so pleased with himself the others laughed.

"Brilliant, Lucas!" And Jules gave his cousin a cheerful thump on his shoulders. "I knew you'd get there in the end! What will you tell him?"

"He's only a dumb fucking Arab," Lucas sneered. "Tell him it's a fucking powder to make that stupid bitch forget her boyfriend; that sodding Gui! He's fucking stupid enough to believe anything, that fucking cook!"

217

"My God, Lucas!" de Vere exclaimed, astonished. "Now that *is* a good idea...I didn't know you had in you? That is just the sort of thing he might well believe, the silly bugger. A 'Forgetting Potion,' something real 'Special' from distant lands. Good plan! Good plan! And if The Lady had any sense," he added, shaking the wineskin hopefully, peering down its open end, "which she has plenty of, she would then kill off the little shit as well - have us stick a knife in him, or garrotte him, saying it was done in passionate grief for her father's *so* sad and unexpected loss!"

"That would solve everything neatly," Jules said quietly, passing him another wineskin. "No witnesses! So, Gaston. You'll speak with the Lady in the morning?"

"No!" he exclaimed softly, looking at them from the corners of his eyes, half closed. "No, I don't think so, lads," he murmured, drawing them closer. "I think this is something we must do ourselves. Leave The Lady out of it until it's all fixed. One whiff of her personal involvement at this stage will frighten him off. He'd have to get permission to speak with her, and that fucking English bitch will smell a rat straightaway. No...I have enough Arabic to speak with him myself. Remember, the stupid little bastard doesn't *know* that I know about Faridah. One hint from me that The Lady would just love to help his *'Precious Pearl',*" he drawled suggestively, "...and had spoken with Sheik El Nazir about her, will be enough to make him shit his pants!" And they all guffawed, eyes bright as berries.

"What will you give him to use on those fucking buggers then?" Lucas asked.

"This!" Gaston whispered, his voice slow, deep; and reaching behind him he pulled out a handful of twisted roots, dried black and dark brown, with a faint tangy odour to them. "This is what they're going to get."

"What's in the devil's name are they?" Jules asked in a hushed voice, while Lucas just gaped, his eyes narrow slits.

"*Black Hellebore* and *Belladonna*...Deadly Nightshade." de Vere murmured darkly, holding them up in the faint lamp light for the others to sniff at and touch. "Gathered at dead of night, and dried over a slow fire...real witches' brew stuff, got them from that old Greek perfume seller in Grise whom The Lady uses from time to time."

"Stanisopoulos," Jules said softly. "He's a bad one."

"What the fuck do you do with them?" Lucas asked slowly, awed by the sight and feel of the hard, blackly twisted roots.

"You grind them to a powder and mix it in with food," de Vere grunted. "In very small amounts either of these can be used in all sorts of good ways. But in quantity, it is the most deadly powerful stuff!"

"So, what does it do?" Jules whispered. "If you give too much?" And he reached out to touch it.

"*No! Don't!*" de Vere hissed fiercely, knocking Jules' hand away. "Not even the tip of your finger. The stuff's bloody lethal. It will gripe your belly horribly; make you vomit blood and squit yourself like pissing shit, and you'll foam at the mouth and go mad before it paralyses you and you die.

"Fucking Hell!" Lucas exclaimed softly, with a wide grin on his face. "So, if that fucking Najid mixes that stuff in with their sodding scoff, they'll get fierce griping bellies, go bloody green and purple in the face, froth at the mouth, roll about like lunatics and fucking shit themselves to death. Lovely!"

"Yes!" de Vere said grimly, shaking the small box at them both, and then closing it. "And after what those bastards did to us, that's just about how it should be for those fucking shits! Can't wait to see Najid's little face when I tell him about his sister, poor little sod. It'll ruin his day, that's for certain!" And he laughed, grunting like a hog. "Now, bugger off you two," he added, thrusting the remains of the wineskin at them. "Piss off. I need my beauty sleep. We've a lot to do in the morning…and I need to be fresh for it!"

Chapter 32...*Sleep that knits up the ravelled sleeve of care:*

(Macbeth II:II)

Gaston de Vere watched through slitted eyes as the two Frenchmen left for their own sleeping pits, their arms over each others' shoulders, and he held up the box of powdered roots in the flickering lamplight and laughed.

What they had all forgotten was that he was *not* The Lady's Guard Commander...he was the Lord Baron Sir Roger de Brocas of Narbonne and Gruissan's Guard Commander! And as such was as close to his Lord, as any man of his rank could be. And it was Lord Roger who had sent him to Stanisopoulos for the roots, planned with him to have the two Frenchmen placed on the barge...and had told him what he had already asked the Sheik to do.

The Baron knew how ferociously jealous Rochine could be when pushed to it...and how unstable her temper was. And he had also known about the little cook, that fucking Najid, and his pretty sister. And he grinned. The moment that poor little sod knew *that*, he would be terrified. The Lady's trading tastes were well known. Once let her get her hands on the girl...and he would never see her again! He would promise *anything* to prevent that...and then he'd blab! Even if he really did think it was only a 'Forgetting Powder' he'd still blab. No fucking oyster that one...known for it. Heart like melting butter, he'd no more poison that lot than fly. He would be in despair, sick with it...and those girls would get it *all* out of him. Be sure to!

He tossed the box of ground powder between his hands and grinned. Powdered Hellebore and Belladonna root indeed...more like powdered toast crumbs! And he chuckled again. As if he'd let the silly sod really poison them! Oh...the roots were real enough...but the powder? Twice toasted breadcrumbs ground up fine. He'd done them himself with a pestle and mortar. Got the bloody stuff everywhere! But only he and the Baron knew that! And he chuckled into the darkness, pushing the box carefully under his cloak as he did so.

Sort that lot out, get the girl away from The Lady and into the Baron's waiting arms…and maybe he'd give him Soraya for himself? That would be good, he'd always fancied her. Gorgeous body, lovely smile…that'd be good on his pillow every morning!

He lay back on the great bolster of woolfells that he had provided for himself and blew out the lamps, looking up at the stars, the sky full of them, a million, million lights blinking down at him from the soft, velvet darkness of the warm summer's night. And laying there, as he thought of Soraya beside him, he listened to the creak of the barge as she pulled at her moorings and the soft rushing of the river as it passed them by, the croak of a frog, the sudden quacking of a startled duck, the splash of a leaping fish in the river, a dog barking far away across the sleeping countryside, and he smiled.

Tomorrow they would reach Peyrehorade, then off the barge and onto horses again for the long haul to Carcassonne and home. And he thought of Najid and of Alicia…and The Lady's fury when, one day, she found them gone. And get away they would…he would fix that too. After Foix probably, and he thought of the Baron's face when he'd get the pigeon message that they were on their way for him to 'rescue' them, and he laughed again. Now that *would* be worth seeing…and with that thought in his head he turned on his side and fell asleep.

★

And as the moon finally rose in silver splendour, The Lady Rochine de Brocas lay back in her cabin on the great pile of satin cushions she'd brought with her, in a short chemise of cream embroidered silk. Her raven hair unbound around her head, and sipping a deep red Burgundy from a great silver-gilt goblet, she delicately picked honeyed almonds out of a silver dish, unable to sleep, still seething with inward rage as she planned the

221

death of the two women who had opposed her will that day: the Lady Alicia de Burley, her *so* sweet English Cousin…and that *connes Francaise*, Soraya Fermier, whom her father had given to her after he and the Archbishop had stolen all her family's lands…and she clenched her hands til they were white with suppressed fury!

Those two she would have begging for her mercy….And that they surely *would* do before she was finished with them! As for that silly bitch, Agnes Fitzwalter? The Cousins could have her for their amusement… And as she dipped her long fingers in the wine to suck the honey off she smiled.

Her father was such a fool at times!

He had planned the thing so carefully…but she had heard and seen almost everything! He kept forgetting that she had many secret spy holes around the Château from where she could watch him. She'd been doing it for years. First watching him, goggle eyed when she had been a just a little girl, making love with her mother…and then with the various whores who had gone to his bed…until her mother had died and she had taken their place…and she giggled at how shocked her mother had looked when she had finally realised what she had done to her. So simple! And she wriggled her body sensuously, feeling fresh warmth flooding into her.

And of course Stanisopoulos, the little Greek perfumier in Grise, was her creature of the night. That's where everything had come from! So she knew about the roots he had given de Vere, and how he had set out to fool the little cook; and she laughed again. Twice toasted bread crumbs ground up and put in a box! *Bah!* They might trick a stupid Arab…but not her! And, of course she knew about 'Far-i-dah'…his *'Precious Pearl'*…too. And she giggled softly. She knew everything! But that particular beauty could wait. That would be a pleasure yet to come! It was that *conne Anglaise* she was really after! And she snorted in disgust.

So she had bided her time and then, at the right moment, she had changed the stupid powdered crumbs for the real thing, that when sprinkled on their food would give them all a horrible death: a wicked combination of violent emetic, madness and paralysis! And she chuckled at her cleverness and her father's simplicity.

She sighed, and touched her breasts, pinching her nipples beneath the sheer silk that covered them. Such a shame they both had to die so soon, because she so would have liked to 'play' with them first. Have some fun. Twist their flesh, pour hot wax on their breasts, shave them, thrash them, cut them til the blood flowed as much as their tears. *Anything* to hurt them, make them cry out, beg for mercy as those two wretched sluts had done at Grise, trying to find out her secret, til she had slit their throats in a violent spray of blood that had spattered all over her naked body...and de Vere had later thrown them to the pigs!

She shivered at the delicious memory: at the horror on the girls' stricken faces, at the *feel* of her knife slicing into each so deeply, cutting right to the bone, the flesh springing open beneath her blade in a great bloodied yawn, their cries becoming helpless gurgles as the hot blood fountained over them both...and the rough grating of her blade against their neck bones...and she giggled, her eyes wide and staring, her thoughts running wild.

She smiled and sighed, and stroked her breasts and thighs more firmly, feeling them grow hard and wet...as she 'saw' in her mind the Frenchmen rape Alicia, while the other two *salopes* were forced to watch, their voices joining with her cousin's frantic screams. Before they also were seized, one after the other, held down on their hands and knees and well and truly *fucked* like the stupid bitches they were!

Oh...that would be good!

And she thrust her hands between her legs, curling up over them as they pierced her loins. Those two cousins on her Cousin together?...and she laughed, *Yes!*

Then she shook her head. *No!* Not because she did not want them dead...but because she had not sampled the bitch herself while her father watched. He always liked that, before plunging into her himself...and she almost purred, rubbing her breasts with her hands at the thought of such fun together, feeling her nipples harden beneath her silk shirt, peaking against the palms of her hands, and she stroked the lips of her wet loins with her long fingers.

Mmmmm...the girl had *such* a luscious body...as she'd seen the night of the fire. Her father would love it. Would love to thrust his strength into her again and again...as he did to her!...and she moaned, feeling her body quiver at the very thought of him doing so...of them both...of Alicia!

Such magnificent breasts - better even than Soraya's, fuller, heavier...but so proud, so upstanding and thicker teats, longer! And she squirmed amongst the satin cushions, feeling her loins open, her own breasts tighten under her questing hands, her dark nipples standing out like stiff soldiers on parade til every movement of her silk chemise was such a torture that she had to tear it off, tossing her head from side to side, drawing her breath in with a gasp, as she moulded her breasts with her hands, squeezing them, milking them, grasping her swollen teats with her fingers and twisting them fiercely til the blood pounded and they were almost black with pressure.

And then...and then...she would sell her! Had already agreed the price with Wazzim: Six thousand Bezants! And she cried out at the thought of it. Of all that money and of how shocked Alicia would be to be sold! To be examined and tested. Her naked body abused by de Rombeau, her Enforcer, so that it would be in very peak condition before Wazzim...and she moaned at the delicious thought of it, caressing her loins fiercely, pressing her hands into them til they were on fire yet soaking, as the fierce, rampant desire she so longed for rushed through her at last.

Seizing her hard nipples between her thumb and forefinger, she rolled and crushed them fiercely, pulling her breasts upwards into taut, swollen cones, shaking them as she did so, spiralling her emotions upwards as she moaned and tossed amongst the cushions, her whole body ragingly flushed with heat. And suddenly her loins gushed and flooded at last, her whole body liquidising in violent heaves, like a salmon leaping and twisting on a gaff, as she jerked and spasmed, and flew up amongst the stars...to float down softly into exhausted oblivion, as with a sigh her whole body relaxed and sleep finally claimed her, a sweet smile of satisfaction on her lovely face.

Chapter 33...Najid's terrors break The Lady's spell.

La Bastide de Serou.

A tiny settlement of hardy folk, warm hearted and well satisfied with their lives under the Count of Foix, perched high on a long ridge with the Arize River foaming at its feet, that would lead them down at length to the walled town itself.

And it was there that Soraya found him weeping, sitting with his back to a rock over looking the river as it bustled under the old stone bridge below the tiny village in a steady rush, fast and clear this high in the hills. In his hands he held a plain wooden box, and his whole body was shuddering with his sobs, as if his heart were breaking.

Soraya was appalled, and plumping herself down beside him she put her arms around him, speaking soft Arabic in her husky voice: "Najid! Whatever is the matter? Come tell me, I am your friend. You know, you can tell me anything," and she rocked him in her arms as she would a child. "Come. Sah! Sah! Little One. Nothing can be as bad as that, surely?"

"O-Oh, Mistress Soraya!" He stammered, his words broken by his sobs. "I-I can-not tell you. My sister...my p-poor little Fa-Faridah. S-She is all I-I have le-ft. I-I cannot tell you. I-I-can-not! They will...they will ki-kill me! T-They will take my-my Far-Faridah...and-and then I am sure they will ki-ll you...*all!* Oh-Oh *Allah!* He-help y-your so H-Humble Servant!" And he turned and buried his head in her shoulder, his distress just too much even for words.

Holding the little man in her arms as she comforted him, Soraya looked out across the countryside, at the great hills all around them, and the thick forests...and the high, high snow-capped mountains of the Pyrenees away in the distance that marked the boundary of Spain, and back up towards La Bastide de Serou. Here they were bivouacked for the night after leaving Saint Girons early

225

the previous morning, the village being too small for any wayside inn worthy of the name, so they were all looking forward to journeying on to Foix, with its great castle on a huge knotty crag and a whole busy town to enjoy for a day.

And now here she was with Najid, their dear little Arabic cook: small, slender with a shock of black curls, large brown eyes and a mouth made for smiles and laughter, but who had been like a stranger ever since they had stopped at the market in Saint Girons two days ago. From light-hearted happiness and silly jokes to an almost silent figure, stark in his unhappiness and yet refusing to talk! And now this!

And giving him a final hug, she pulled him to his feet and said briskly: "Najid. You are a very silly fellow. We have all seen how unhappy you have been, and now you talk about death! I have had enough of such nonsense! You are coming with me to the Lady Alicia now, and you will tell her everything!" She said firmly, giving him a shake. "*Everything!*"

"We all love you...and we love your cooking, and there is nothing that cannot be put right if we try. But no-one can help unless you tell us what the trouble is. I have had enough of rotten meals from you these past two days...so come on," she added, tugging him almost bodily up the hill. "This time you will tell us all!"

So, with the sun tilting down into the West, with the sky filled with gold and crimson bars, up the hill to the village they had gone, Najid snuffling miserably at her side, Soraya wondering what on earth had gone wrong this time?

★

 nd it was all so-so...wretched...so frustrating!

Since that awful struggle on the barge on the first day of their Journey east towards Carcassonne and Gruissan, everything had actually settled down into a real spell of smooth travel and a fair truce between Alicia and her French Cousin.

They had got off at Peyrehorade, with de Vere's men helping where they could, but giving quite a wide berth to Alicia and her small Household – her Company of the White Rose - which seemed to please everyone. Even The Lady Rochine had seemed delighted with their progress, though they were obviously slowed by the two large tilt carts they had found waiting for them, each pulled by two horses either side of a central yoke and loaded with all their goods, the wicker cages that held the Baron's pigeons right on the top of all so that the birds had plenty of air.

Every night their pigeon master, Almahdi the Syrian, would take each bird and examine it closely, holding it in the palm of his hand with firm gentleness, while he stretched out its wings, one by one, to test the muscles and check its flight feathers, feeling each bird's breast to be sure it was in perfect flying shape and weight…just as one would with a hawk or falcon.

And as a falconer would check his birds of prey's long legs and pounces - its sharp talons - so Almahdi checked each pigeon's legs for strength and fitness. For while it was the beautiful sickle shaped wings that gave each bird its speed…it was the legs that carried the vital messages…and every bird was different: some for long haul, some for short; some for carrying weight more slowly…others ideal for the tiny, light brass message capsules and for enormous speed. And he also looked each bird in the eye to check for brightness and colour and to ensure there was no damage or scratch on each brilliant lens. And all the time he crooned to them and murmured soft words, just as they crooned and bobbed their heads back to him.

And they were all different colours. Beautiful soft grey and white, slate grey all over with white wing feathers, white and a kind of ruddy orange…even almost dark blue with black wingtips, and some were white all over.

The girls were fascinated, and clustered round him to watch and gently stroke the beautiful feathers and feel the taut strength in the wings as Almahdi stretched them out and showed what he was looking for in each of his winged Mercuries, while Soraya chattered to him in Arabic and they all laughed and giggled light-heartedly together.

227

Most days they had pushed on hard, adopting the long haul tactics of the military…Walk, trot, canter! Walk, trot, canter! Half of de Vere's men riding far ahead to check the way, the other half hanging behind to make sure no-one tried to make a break and so escape. And where the roadway divided, or others joined it, two of his men, with their bows armed and ready, would dismount and watch them all go by before re-mounting and cantering forward to the next point along their way and the next beyond that.

Then there were lazy days when the men had gone hunting up into the hills for small game. Pheasants and rabbits, shoats still in their stripes…even two brace of geese on one occasion, bought from a smallholder up in the wilds somewhere. And on those days the girls had gone wandering themselves, sometimes to find mushrooms, sometimes to walk into the nearest village for fresh vegetables, sometimes just to dangle their feet in a stream and watch the fish flashing by amongst the reeds and rushes. And always with either Aquib or Aziz in company to watch and guard their backs.

Then there were gold and azure days, when the sun shone bright from a cerulean sky and the air was as fresh and cool as chilled wine, as it so often is in the high lands close to the great mountains that reared their snow-capped heights into the heavens. Then the only thing to do was clap heels and gallop away up the track with shouts and laughter, giving de Vere's men nightmares of escaping prisoners as they chased after them, hurtling along at breakneck speed, only to find them all waiting by some vantage-point drinking in the view, chuckling and smiling at the men's fears and mocking their taut, sour faces when they caught up with them, as only girls can.

Even Rochine had joined them on two occasions, and for a moment both she and Alicia had laughed together at the sheer exhilaration of being young and beautiful and *alive* on a wonderful, fresh summer morning in the high foothills of the Pyrenees. Up here the streams cascaded off the hills in all directions, running fast and white, the water cold and fresh on their flushed faces when they stopped to water their horses, and delicious to drink it from cupped hands, themselves cooled beneath the rushing flow, with the sun warm on their backs and the larks singing high up in the sky above them.

And all around was bursting with life: the green of wood and forest; or the distant patchwork quilt of strip fields heavy with wheat and barley, orchards of quince apples and apricots; peaches, plums and damsons...and small silver-grey groves of olives, black and green; and the dark twisted branches of cork oak that sometimes lined the trackway, their dark leaves hanging over them, small fields of purple lavender beyond. And dotted about up on the high pastures the white and mottled forms of sheep and goats with their clonking bells, and cattle too lower down, sometime bulling in the evenings when they were called in for milking, their hoarse cries echoing around the valleys.

The first time Rochine had joined them, Alicia had been quite startled, had even been about to speak when Rochine had suddenly realised what she was doing, her face had fallen and she had swiftly turned and walked away, head down, clambered into her high saddle and ridden back down the track.

Alicia had watched her go and sighed.

It would have been so easy to like her. That was the real sadness! The Lady was quick witted and had a bright, gay spirit. And she was as well read as she was herself, with a wealth of experience that it would have been such fun to have shared. And they were cousins...the only real family she had left since her parents had died so many years ago.

In different circumstances she was sure they would have been friends. But after what had happened at Malwood: that dreadful fire, the awful murder of Gui's parents by her father, his attempts to kill Gui, and her own actions that night towards her...such friendship was impossible. And now she was her jailor! So all that was left between them was a strange kind of 'armed' truce: Rochine would leave her alone...and she would not try to escape. And in God's Truth, she cursed silently, where would they go to? And how?

They were almost in the middle of nowhere, three unarmed girls and three stray Arabs, only two of whom could fight! And mighty as Aquib and Aziz were...they could not fight all de Vere's men, half of whom were armed with bows. And no man, no matter how big and strong he was could take a bolt and stay upright for long. Look at what had happened to Gui? And the arrow that had struck him was tiny by comparison with a full size quarrel...especially one with a barbed hunting broad head at its point!

And where was he? Where was her Gui? And Sir Richard, and Father Matthew and all the other Lions whom she had set out with from home? Bones of the Saints…it was only a few weeks ago…yet it already seemed like ages! And she dashed away the sudden tears that had sprung unbidden to her eyes making them glitter in the sunshine.

Were they alive? She so devoutly hoped and prayed so. She didn't 'feel' as if her beloved Gui was dead…and she was certain she would *know!* That 'something' would tell her it was so…some dreadful lurch in her heart or sudden blackness of spirit would *tell* her she had lost him. And she had not felt that-yet-in any way. So she must still believe and keep going. Until when? Until Grise? And the bloody Baron and his ghastly wedding plans? Until her cousin's spirit finally twisted so wickedly that she tried to kill her?

Christos! What a dreadful tangle. How lovely to be Alexander the Great with the Gordian Knot, and just take a sword and hack through the beastly thing in one great swipe of hardened steel! And with another sigh of frustration, she had re-mounted and kicked on after her.

And now, out of a clear blue sky, when everything seemed to be going so well…*this!* Some unknown terror about his sister that had so gripped poor Najid as to render him speechless with grief! And with a grunt of exasperation Soraya dragged the little man up the hill to find Alicia, and Aquib, and sort the whole beastly thing out!

Chapter 34...How Gaston de Vere ruined Najid's day.

Through Ortez, Pau and Tarbes they had ridden along the main roadway that led from Bayonne to Toulouse, staying in Inns and small castles where they could, by-passing all travellers whom they met with studied indifference and forcefulness: packhorse trains, each animal piled with goods in great panniers on their sides, mounted armed guards close by; parties of pilgrims on their way to Saint James of Compostella; merchants on their way to Bayonne or Toulouse, beautifully dressed, with huge ox-drawn wagons of wine and olive oil; jongleurs, ladies in wimples and long capes, with their grooms by their sides, men trudging from town to town for work, scholars in black gowns, messengers on fast horses, thundering by in a blast of dust and fury...and young knights off to the wars in velvet caps brave with bright feathers, and flowing bliauts of orange, green and scarlet satin, embroidered with gold and silver, long capes billowing out from their shoulders and jewelled swords and daggers at their sides.

Sometimes on their own, at others in pairs, caracoling and titupping across the road in the joyous excitement of youthful high spirits, boasting of the conquests they would make, the girls they would love and the enemies they would slay, often accompanied by small troops of armed men, brilliant in each family's blazon.

Then, at St Goudens they had cut across country to St Girons, across the ridges and along valleys that seemed to twist all around them, sometimes clip-clopping alongside the rivers, which in high summer were slower and lazier, as they flowed towards the distant sea; not rushing wildly in a boiling mass of white foam, brown with silt and filled with melt water and spring rain, making bridges dangerous and fords deadly. And sometimes right across the very tops of high ridges from where it seemed you could see the whole world in a single glance.

And so they had come to the town of Saint Girons, crossing the River Salat, broad and deep, with shoals of great fish black and silver beneath the surface, fins and tails working to hold themselves almost motionless against the current, before dashing off to do the same thing further up the river, the sun sparkling off the blue waters.

As they approached the bridge they found it was packed with people coming in for the Saturday market, bustling, jostling, chattering; every kind of food imaginable on the move towards the town, from live pigs and chickens, and goats on strings, to fresh vegetables, scallions, shallots and lettuces, fruits of many kinds, strings and strings of smoked sausages, great bundles of herbs, cheeses, butter, breads…everything.

Najid's eyes had lit up at the sight, and as soon as they had found a suitable Inn, with space for their men and stabling for their horses, he had come running to Soraya to ask permission to go to the food market that was even now taking shape amongst the plane trees that shaded the central square of the little town. And he had been boisterously excited, his Arabic so fast that even Soraya'd had to ask him to slow down, while Aquib stood by and smiled at the little man's enthusiasm for his cooking, and Aziz helped to find the pots and pans he needed for their evening meal.

"Mistress Soraya! Mistress Soraya! Did you see all those herbs and those chickens? And the fruit? Apricots as big as plums, peaches as big as..as big as my hand!" he exclaimed, waving his hand at her and smiling. "And cherries and onions and beautiful bunches of red and orange carrots, celery too and fresh bread and butter in great crocks, and oil to cook with. I may even find some spices…and we need salt as well. Please, will you ask the La-dy Alic-ia if I may go to the market…and will she give me some silver as I have none left to buy with?" he ended breathlessly, almost bouncing with excitement.

"What is all the to-do?" Alicia asked laughing, coming up to them, seeing Najid almost hopping from one foot to the other.

"It is Najid, Alic-ia," Soraya said with a grin, laying her hand on his slender shoulders. "He is desperate to go to the food market; they hold it every Saturday I gather. And he has seen such lovely things for us that he is desperate to go and see what he can buy. How are we for money?"

"Oh, My Lady...Alicia," Agnes said pleadingly, her large hazel eyes wide as a fawn's "This looks such a pretty place, and we have barely stopped anywhere for days. A market would be just lovely to go to today. Especially in all this sunshine, and the river and all those trees for shadow. I know we don't have much money, but I have a bit hidden and I know Sir Gui left you with some when we..we parted in Brest....oh come on, Alicia," she pleaded, and seeing Alicia hesitate she took her hands and asked again, adding: "And Najid, needs things for us...and we need things for ourselves too!"

Alicia looked at all of them, at Najid, hopping about like a herring on a griddle, and at both Soraya and Agnes, their eyes shining, saying everything their mouths surely would have done...and she laughed again.

"Oh...very well! We will *all* go to the market, just as soon as Aquib and Aziz have finished, and you too, my Ladies," she added with a raised eyebrow. "Fun and games are lovely...but I don't want to come back and find our things in a mess. So bustle about and we'll meet here before the sun has passed the steeple.

Soraya," she added, holding Najid back as Agnes hurried off. "Please tell Najid he must go to the market now...and not wait for us. I know all about markets, and some of the best things that he wants may be gone by the time you two have finished. I have a small purse of silver here which should be plenty. Gui also left me with a few gold coins as well...but they will not do here! Tell him to take a basket with him, and that if he can't find us amongst the stalls, we will meet him later...by the bridge we came across, by the time the sun is near the roof tops. Now, come on," she urged Soraya, as she spoke in swift Arabic to the little man, both laughing as he ran off to find a basket off one of the tilt carts, "Now...I simply must get out of these clothes!"

★

233

Unnoticed by everyone, all being so busy talking, Gaston de Vere, standing not twenty paces away in a deeply shaded doorway, had watched the whole little scenario play out before him: saw the little cook run off towards the tilt carts, and Alicia and Soraya turn back towards the Inn chatting happily together.

He grinned, his mouth crinkling in silent satisfaction, his eyes hooded. For some time he had been wanting to have words with that damned cook. But every time he had found the time to do so, the wretched man had either been with Soraya or Lady de Burley...or in company with the two huge men whom El Nazir had sent with Alicia to protect her. Now however, in the midst of this bustling, thronging market...and with his protectors all cheerfully busy elsewhere...now was the perfect time to put the frighteners on him...give him a real belly trembler!

Foix was the next substantial town and beyond that was a really wild country of thick forests, twisted tracks and open spaces. Ideal for flight, and if they knew where they were going they could evade pursuit and capture until the last moment...which was exactly what he had planned with the Baron all those months ago!

And waiting til the girls had disappeared, he signalled to the Cousins who'd been waiting near an empty courtyard for his sign, pushed himself away from the door he'd been leaning against and casually sauntered after Najid.

He, happily bouncing along amongst the stalls without a care in the world, beyond what to cook for dinner that night, a small Ali Baba basked strapped to his back for all the good things he was hoping to find, was humming as he went, his dark brown eyes flashing with excitement and simple pleasure. So it was a terrible shock when he felt a tap on his shoulder, turned with a smile, expecting to see either the ladies or his two Arab friends...and found instead that he was looking up into the leering faces of Lucas Fabrizan and Jules Lagrasse, and found himself totally unable to speak.

"Here you little *fucker!*" Lucas exclaimed, grabbing him by the arm before he could bolt. "There's someone who wants a quiet word with you, you sodding little squit. So just come along with me and you'll be alright!" And he pulled him towards him, clamping his hand over his mouth so he couldn't cry out.

"*Ta'ala alaan!*" Jules growled at him, grabbing his other arm. "Come with me now! *Asre'!* Hurry up!" and together they picked the little cook up under his arms and ran with him through the crowds to where de Vere was waiting in a grimy wine booth down a shaded side alley at one edge of the market, with some stoups of wine in tin beakers and a dozen tired slices of soft cheese on a red glazed platter. And dumping their captive on a coarse wooden bench that lay against one side wall, the Cousins picked up the beakers de Vere had left for them and loomed over their prize, full of evil intent.

"Well, well, well," the big guard commander growled at Najid in Arabic, a wide grin on his heavy face, while the little man trembled, terrified, like a tethered goat before a tiger. "Look who you've found, boys? How good of you to drop by. And so unexpected...especially as I have been wanting to have a quiet word with you for some time, laddie," he snarled, poking Najid in the chest with one hard finger, while he looked into Najid's quivering face, and at his eyes wide with fear, before added quietly: "It's about your sister, Najid, your 'Far-i-dah!'" And he grinned sweetly as he saw the frightful shock rush across the man's face, the colour draining from it till he looked washed out, almost grey with the horror of hearing those words from his mouth...almost fainting with it.

"Now, Najid," de Vere went on quietly, after Lucas had slapped him about to bring him to his senses. "You love your sister don't you? Don't want the aunt to kick her out do you?" he went on remorselessly, watching Najid wobble about on the bench, nodding his head all the time, too terrified to speak. "That sour old witch. No! Course not. Don't want the old bat to go to El Nazir, do you? Ask him to sort her problem?" He shouted at him, while Lucas smacked his face again, and Jules kept guard at the entrance to the booth.

"No, Master! No...please. Do not hurt my sister!"

"Hurt your little sister? Me? Do I look like a monster? No, Najid. Not me," he hissed at him..."*The Lady!*"

"No!...**No!**" Najid gasped, his hands scrabbling in his lap, even his feet shaking. "**No!**...she will do terrible things to her. People talk, Master. I have heard. Please, I am a poor man. I have nothing to give you. No money. Nothing. Wh..what do you w..want?" he stammered desperately as de Vere leaned closely towards him. "I w..will do anything! *Anything!*"

"Now...isn't that good to hear, lads?" de Vere said sitting back and looking up at Jules and Lucas with a satisfied smirk on his face. "How loving! This poor lad will do anything for his little sister. Isn't that sweet? Ahhh!" and they all laughed, the sound harsh and brutal. Then, tapping the little cook on the shoulder he grinned into his terrified face and snarled quietly: "That's just what we wanted to hear, Najid," and he tapped him on the shoulder again. "Anything, Najid?" he queried heavily. "Rather than have me talk with El Nazir and The Lady about your little problem 'baby'? She's just the right age now for The Lady to be interested in her. Your Far-i-dah...your '*Precious Pearl!*'"

And he sat back and grinned again, as the tears sprang to Najid's eyes, and he bent his head forward and cried, his shoulders shaking. Then sitting back he dashed his hand across his face, eyes reddened and said limply, utterly defeated: "Anything, Master. For my Faridah, anything! I promise!" And he slumped back against the wall, exhausted.

"Right...now you listen carefully, my lad," de Vere said briskly, leaning forward again. "And your little lass will be as safe as a castle in a storm," and reaching into the bag at his waist, he took out a small wooden box, and while the two Frenchmen took up guard outside the booth, having kicked the owner out with a few well chosen words and the threat of serious damage to himself and his wine booth if he didn't '*Fucking, Hop Off!*' for a moment, de Vere told Najid exactly what he expected him to do...!

Chapter 35...The Company of the White Rose decides to flee.

So...just as de Vere had predicted that long ago night on the barge, between bouts of sobbing and broken sentences, and with encouragement from everyone, Najid told them all he knew...and all that had happened to him at St Girons, while Aziz took his turn to stand guard outside their covered bivouac.

And as the little man's tale unfolded an intense feeling of anger, and dismay, flooded out from those who were gathered there that summer's night. An anger displayed in growls of suppressed rage, small cries of horror and clenched fists for what had been said and done to Najid...and dismay for its implications, and the added distrust that it would now mean between themselves and the Lady Rochine de Brocas.

A distrust only heightened when Najid finally showed them the box he had been given, and the black and cream speckled powder it contained, with its dark tangy odour and its promise of uncertainty at The Lady's hands.

Alicia looked at the powder in the box and shivered, goose pimples suddenly appearing along her arms. Forgetting Powder? Poor Najid. What was he to know of such things? What did she come to that? But whatever it was...it was not going into anything they might eat. If her Cousin had had anything to do with it was safer to treat it like the poison it probably was. Try it on a passing stray dog if they ever found the time; meanwhile she would keep it safe! And without a word, her eyes slitted with disgust, Alicia took the box from him and held it closed tightly in her lap.

In the golden lamp light beneath the canvas sheeting over their camp-site, with the stars bright overhead, sparkling in the cool clear air of the mountains, the moon rising in glorious silver splendour, just a few days off being full, they sat on cushions and leaned back against their saddles. Wine to hand and light blankets around them against the cool night, they had listened as if spell bound as Nijad's tale of St Girons unfolded, and then finally came to an end, his voice

237

tailing off into a profound silence. Each one of them thinking about the full meaning of all that they had heard.

Soraya moved first to comfort poor Nijad, standing utterly dejected, tears in his eyes not just for his sister whose life was still in such danger...but also because of what he might really have done if he had been alone...and not with people whom he had come to care for and who cared for him.

Then, as her face relaxed, Alicia had looked to them both, and smiling at Najid for encouragement, she spoke the words everyone was expecting: "Well...that's it! That's enough! We made a kind of bargain, she and I. She wouldn't raise a hand against me, nor any of my Household...and we wouldn't try to escape. But if she thinks I am going to sit by and do nothing while she uses her power to terrify one of my people into a possible act of mass murder with this stuff...and God knows what it really contains? Then she doesn't know who she's up against!"

And it was with an act of supreme force of will that she didn't hurl her goblet and the box into the night she was so angry. "That double-dyed, murderous, black hearted, wicked *bitch!*" And then she really did swear: "*Cette conne Francaise!* Urrrgh! And to think I almost liked her! God preserve my sanity...but I could murder her!"

"So, My lady," Aquib rumbled at her, as she collected herself. "What do we do now?"

"Well...we can't fight them, Aquib," she said resignedly. If we had some bows we might have given that some thought...but we don't and none of us are trained in their use anyway. So...if we can't fight them...then we must run from them, and as fast and as far as we can before they find us missing."

"But where to, Alicia?" Soraya asked. "We are in the middle of nowhere here, and we have no friends nearby."

"And no–one knows where Sir Gui is," Agnes said quietly.

"Or even if he is still alive," Alicia finished for her, looking across at her with a sad smile. "I know, Sweetheart. I know that *I* believe he is still alive, somewhere...but it isn't as if we can just set out to find him, as we have no way

238

of knowing where to look. And I'm not forgetting your Allan either, Honeyone."

"So where, My Lady?" Aquib rumbled again

"And when?" Soraya asked. For once she finds Najid has failed them…they will surely kill us all anyway…and say it was outlaws or bandits!"

"Well," Alicia said, drinking from her goblet before shuffling herself up against her saddle. "And forgive me for this, because you will all think I have gone completely mad, but the only place we *can* run to, where we will be safe…and where Gui will *know* where to find is…"

"…Is to Monsieur le Bar-on in Grise!" Soraya interrupted, her voice almost soundless.

"Yes! The bloody, murdering old bastard himself," Alicia said through gritted teeth.

"You *are* mad! "Agnes exclaimed, appalled. "After all that man has put us through, to throw ourselves on his mercy now seems…seems completely insane, my love. You have bats in your belfry!"

"No…Mistress Agnes," Aquib said calmly in his deep, gravelly voice. "The Lady Alicia is right. Only the Bar-on can control his daughter. Our Prince said so. Only the Lord Baron can protect you all. Right now The Lady is racked with jealousy, and is acting without thought or reason. Sadly, Aziz and I cannot fight all these men together, as the Lady Alicia has already said, much as we would like to. But they are armed with bows, and bows of great power…so we must run. And there is only one place we can run to and that is to the Baron's Château at Grise.

"*Sweet Jesus!*" Agnes exclaimed, horrified. "What may that man not demand in return for all of that?" She asked, her face suddenly drawn.

"What indeed, Agnes?" Alicia said, looking at her grimly over the rim of her goblet. "Let us hope it is not such a price as we cannot easily pay, because if he rescues us from this deadly peril…he will have earned it!"

"Well," Soraya said a little sharply. "You may be right in that, Alicia, but while Monsieur le Bar-on is one thing…you can at least reason with him. But his daughter is quite another! If we are to flee…and I am sure that Alicia and Aquib are right in that, it is to Grise we must go, if only because Lord Roger is the only one who can control The Lady when she gets like this. But then how are we to do it? And when? We are foreigners here, with no knowledge of where to go; no map and we can only go with what we can carry. And very little money!"

"Well," Alicia said quietly. "Actually money is the very least of our problems. Before Gui left us at Brest to board the *Mary*, he gave me a money belt…"

"But there was nothing like that on you when you were brought on board the *Morning Star*," Soraya said, astonished. "I searched you myself."

"No…it was stitched inside my armoured jacket, which Aziz rescued for me before we left her five…six days ago? Knowing that El Nazir would not just throw anything of such good use away, I guessed it must be somewhere safe and it was, hanging in the armoury. And, '*Insh'a Allah*'!" she exclaimed softly with a smile and a subtle nod to Aquib and Najid. "There should still be a hundred and fifty golden Bezants hidden within it…" And everyone just gasped, for it truly was a great sum of money.

"No wonder it was so heavy, My Lady," Aquib said with his quiet smile. "Because it was to me that Aziz gave it after Mistress Soraya had changed you."

"Thank you, Aquib. Agnes can you bring it to me please? It is in the bottom of the clothes chest that came off the *Morning Star*…beneath yours, which Aziz also rescued. So…Soraya," she said grinning, as Agnes bustled off. "How are you with sums? One Bezant at home is equal to two silver shillings, and there are twelve silver pennies in each silver shilling. So…how many silver pennies does that give us for our one hundred and fifty gold Bezants?"

"Plenty, My Lady," Aquib said with a laughing growl, watching the tortured look on Soraya's face as she struggled with the strange figures, while

Agnes brought in Alicia's armoured jacket; handing her a small pair of beautifully made spring shears as she did so

"See!" Alicia crowed softly after snipping at the back of it. "My money belt!"

And pulling out a long canvas belt into which had been stitched tiny pockets, each one containing a hard disk, she looked around at everyone and with a great smile she cut one open and squeezed out a beautiful golden coin that simply glowed with rich, fat colour in the soft lamp light. "Wheee! Abracadabra! One golden Bezant!" and she held it out on the palm of her hand for all to see.

"But I'll not take out any more…that'd be the quickest way to start losing them. But they are all there, and that actually gives us…*three thousand six hundred silver pennies!*" And she was delighted with the further gasps and looks of complete amazement on all their faces. "So, as I said. Money is not really the problem! And as for the 'when' you have asked me?…then…" she hesitated, looking round at them for a moment. "Then…I think we must leave from Foix; in three morning's time. But we need a proper journey plan and a good map!" she added as they flustered at her decision. "So, tomorrow, when we get there and have settled in for the night…and we are not going up to the castle de Vere tells me…which I hear is magnificent…

"Why not to the castle, My Lady?" Soraya interrupted.

"Because, Mistress Soraya," Aquib chipped in with his dark, rumbly voice. "The Lady would have to answer a lot of very awkward questions about you all to the Count of Foix who is no fool, or to his Seneschal in the Count's absence…and neither are lovers of her father either. The Count supports the Crusade which the Baron has refused to go on…and he is neither deaf nor blind to what goes on in Grise."

"You are well informed, Aquib?" Alicia said, surprised.

"I am a good listener, My Lady," he chuckled deeply. "With Sheik El Nazir, you learn to be!"

"As I have learned to be also, with The Lady!" Soraya exclaimed softly. "As I told you on the *Morning Star.*"

"Well, that is actually better for us, isn't it?" Alicia said looking around at them. "Getting away from a town with lazy town guards is infinitely easier than getting out of a powerful castle with sealed gates and efficient professionals to keep them safe. No, my friends, outside is infinitely better, and if we can find good stabling for our horses near the ford out of Foix…then so much the better.

Anyway, once we are well settled in we can all go into town, and have a thorough mooch about the place. So, keep your eyes sharp and ask questions. And we will need tougher clothes than these to flee in. Leather kirtles, chausses and jackets and simple woollen cloaks at least; all sorts of things I expect. We have to get to Carcassonne and onto the main roadway, the old Via Aquitania that runs from Narbonne to Bordeaux. Once on that and we should be safe from outright attack, and away from these small roads and distant country places…yet we will also have to go across wild country to escape easy pursuit…and to get there.

One thing is for certain…the moment we are missed there will be a frightful uproar, and de Vere and his men will be on us like wolves after sheep. If we set off up any main trackway, they will have us as quickly as chasing deer at home with a pack of rache hounds!"

At that moment Aziz put his head around the wide canopy that had been stretched over their bivouac. "Be warned! There's movement over by The Lady's encampment. Some men are leaving and De Vere is arranging his guards."

"Right, Aziz," Alicia said quietly. "Council of War over." And turning to Aquib, she touched his arm: "It is your turn to take over the watch: Aziz must rest. But call us if there is anything you are concerned about. He will relieve you later. And remember' she added to them all. "Tomorrow, we do everything exactly as normal. Everything, and Najid, you must continue to be miserable," she gestured with a long face as if her eyes were weeping. "Because for certain they will be watching our every mood. Especially de Vere and those two bloody Frenchmen…so if he suddenly becomes cheerful again," she said to

Soraya, "they will surely smell a rat and we will lose the advantage. So make it clear to him, please.

And all of you...don't get caught in dark corners when we get to Foix...stay in pairs! That was always Gui's advice to his lads whenever they found themselves in an unknown place. Soraya, Honeyone, tell Najid he is to stay with either Aquib or Aziz at all times...and to decide what he must take with him when we go, and what he can most easily leave behind. And remember, I have that box of powder which we will need to keep hold of til we can give it over to the Lord Bloody Baron himself in Grise! Now...sleep all of you. We have a lot to do tomorrow. I don't know about you?" she said to them with a weary smile and a stretch of her shoulders. "But I am feeling exhausted!"

Chapter 36... Foix!

F oix!

A lovely, ancient walled town nestling in the space between two rivers, the Ariége and the Arget: the Arget crossed by an old wooden bridge below the castle; the Ariége by a ford close to the ancient Benedictine Abbey church of Saint Velusien that had stood there for nearly three hundred years.

Both crossings had their own gateways into the town and Abbey through the walls where they ran beside the two rivers; and to the South, facing Spain, where the greatest danger lay, a further battlemented wall, with its own strong gateway, that ran back to join up with the town's Northern entrance below the great castle of the Counts of Foix. High on its massive pinnacle of rock, its twin towers linked by curtain walls and surrounded on two sides by foaming water, the great fortress was impregnable, and had dominated the town and countryside since Roman times.

Battlemented town and castle; Abbey, church and bustling market...truly Foix was a little gem.

The narrow, winding streets of shops and timbered houses, their red pantiles glowing in the sunshine, were broken up by little squares with trees scattered amongst them for shade and beauty, stone benches to sit on and a lovely open square next to the ancient Abbey Church of St Velusien. Here, every Wednesday, it was packed with traders, farmers, pedlars and local villeins come in to sell their wares, a market so popular it spread out amongst the twisted streets around the Abbey church, and would be held the second day following their arrival.

Lady Alicia de Burley, paused on the high ridge overlooking the long valley that led to the distant town, was breathless both with the view and the excitement of their coming escape. From where she was seated on her horse, she could see for miles: great rising ridges dark with forests, and a wild panorama of distant mountains and twisted valleys, blue smoke from the tiny settlements hidden amongst them winding upwards, and nearby the flash of sunlight off the two rivers between which Foix had been built. And far to the South the vasty high mountains of the Pyrenees, snow capped and shining, that marked the barrier between the lands of the Franks and those of Moorish Spain.

And high up above the town, its crenellated walls seemingly built into the very rocks themselves, stood the mighty fortress of the Counts of Foix, its two great square towers rearing up into the summer sky, just as they did on his own Great Seal. With the massive mountains of the high Pyrenees to the south, it was like an eagle's eyrie, from where the Count of Foix, Raimond-Roger II and his lovely wife, Philippa of Montcada, could view all that moved for miles around them.

★

All day they had travelled along the high ridge on which La Bastide de Serou had sprung up, stopping only for food right on its crest, Alicia and her little Household on what Najid could find for them, and The Lady Rochine and her guards on supplies that de Vere had gathered from the tiny Auberge before they had left that morning.

With his troops ranging both far ahead and behind the tilt carts, and Almahdi close to the Baron's precious pigeons, de Vere had kept everyone moving at a steady pace, so it was just as the sun was beginning to slide down the heavens, that they had come at last to the old wooden bridge across the Arget. From there it was just a step to the stone gatehouse that guarded the Western entrance to the town, as a gatehouse had done since the Romans first fortified the place over a thousand years before.

And on that Monday evening, still glowing with late sunlight, warm and golden, dappled with lengthening shadows, the townsfolk were already walking out to take their ease after a long day. And while the river slipped by in one long crystal stream beneath the great timbers that carried the bridge, bubbling and frothing amongst its piers, the handful of guards who lazed near the archway, their long spears propped against the warm stone work, chatted with them happily.

Others Foixians paused to look down into the clear flowing waters of the river to watch the ducks. Lovers strolled hand in hand, or leaned over the bridge sides to watch the fish that swam and darted in the crystal waters. Still others, with children and hounds at heel, walked and gambolled along the wide river bank, pleased to be away from the close, hot air within the narrow streets, rejoicing at the end of yet another busy day...with all the excitement of the Wednesday Market still to come.

Nothing could have appeared more peaceful as De Vere, The Lady Rochine and his whole command, pigeons and all, clip-clopped and rumbled over the bridge with a casual wave to the guards lounging there; just another small party of travellers coming for the Wednesday Market. Yet despite the seeming calmness of their demeanour, there had already been a further violent clash of wills between Rochine and Alicia over arrangements for their brief stay in Foix, which had come just as they were setting out.

★

"So! Almost packed and ready I see, Cousin?" Rochine had sneered, sidling her horse close to where Alicia was helping Agnes and Soraya to sort out some of their things, while Aquib and Aziz loaded up their tilt cart.

"Well, Rochine," Alicia had replied tersely, looking up at her cousin, her hands on her hips. "You have twelve men to run about and do your bidding. I have three, including Najid, who is as sulky as a bear just now. I have no idea why? And is almost worse than useless," she added, looking sideways at her cousin's face. "So I think we have done rather well. By the way, I understand we are not staying beneath the Count's roof tonight. Why is that? We have

246

stopped in far smaller castles than Castle Foix before now. And it is supposed to be magnificent."

"It does not suit me to do so!" Rochine had stated baldly. "We shall stay in *L'Auberge de le Roc*...the Rock Inn. It is spacious and I have stayed there before with my father. There will be no problems about rooms. And we will all stay together there. I cannot allow you to be on your own in the town. It would cause comment."

Alicia looked up at Rochine sitting comfortably on her mare, looking self-possessed and supremely conceited and had an almost irresistible urge to seize her elegant booted foot and pitch her straight out of her saddle onto her elegant pleated backside!! Instead she simply said dangerously: "Cannot allow? You dare dictate? No!"

"No?" Rochine said astonished. "You will not comply?"

"Comply? No, Cousin! I will not 'comply'! I do not intend to stay anywhere nearer to you and your men than I can throw a stick! Foix is a very well organised, smart little town, and though its ruler may not be present, as I can see no house flag waving above the castle, his seneschal certainly will be. If you will not accede to my request for separate accommodation, I will instruct Aquib to accompany me directly to the castle and throw myself on his mercy."

"The Seneschal of Foix! Hubert Le Grange? That old fool?" her cousin mocked, her eyes twitching sideways at Alicia. "My father bought him years ago. Why else do you think we are here? He will not lift a finger to help you!"

Alicia looked at Rochine and shook her head. "I do not believe you, Cousin. The Count has a reputation for straight dealing, fidelity and honour. No man such as you suggest would last in his Household for five minutes. And if not the Seneschal...then there is always the Abbot! Mother Church would not turn down anyone who could claim the Holy Father's protection!"

"*Fough!*" Rochine snorted with disgust. "Now *you* lie! You have no such protection. You were searched, remember...to the skin, Cousin; which is as wrinkled as an old prune and withered as your parts!" she sneered. "The Abbot would not let you near him."

"Try me!" Alicia said in deadly earnest. "Just try me…and we will see who lies and who tells the truth."

"You would not *dare!*" Rochine snarled, her face suddenly fierce with anger. "I would have de Vere seize you immediately. You would not get twenty paces."

"And what then – Cousin?" Alicia mocked her. "The moment you try to do that, Aquib and Aziz will defend me. Your men are no match for them at any price…they will be slaughtered."

"No…they won't. If those two infidels draw their swords, or attack my men, I will have them both shot!" Rochine snapped back, flourishing her whip, making her horse rear its head and shuffle its hooves. "And you, I will have bound in chains as I have always wanted."

"In chains? My men shot?" Alicia laughed at her, arms akimbo, eyes flashing. "Then what, my so clever Cousin?" She sneered. "This is not wild, empty countryside, Rochine. This is a well travelled trackway in a well ruled land…and murder will out! Two arrow riddled bodies in the Count of Foix's domains, and one English noblewoman, Royal ward to King Richard of England, in chains to the Baron Roger de Brocas' daughter? I think not!

What on God's Earth would you say to the Seneschal about *that*, My Lady? And when his men arrest you for bringing death into his town, what then? And do you think I will stand there mute? And how will you explain their deaths to your father? And to Sheik El Nazir? You, dear Cousin, are a fool!" And she laughed again, while Rochine almost foamed at the mouth with rage and frustration.

"Don't you *dare* laugh at me you…you *bitch!*" she hissed down at her venomously, whisking her hand up to strike at her with her whip, immediately pausing to lower it again as she saw both huge Arabs take a determined pace towards her "Fine!" She snarled viciously. "Have your wretched accommodation then. Wherever you please. It is *nothing* to me what gossip you arouse with your dusky Arab followers. But you still have to get to my father

248

Cousin! And I rule him, my sweet, *Not you!* And one day...one day, I promise you, I will give you the thrashing you deserve!" And viciously twisting her horse around, she thrust in her heels, pulled her horse onto his hind feet, spun him around and thundered off, while Alicia laughed.

"My lady, you push her too hard." A harsh, gravelled voice quietly admonished, and Gaston de Vere pushed his horse forward from behind her. "She is not used to being crossed...and she is not easily reasoned with," he added. "There is only one man who can control her...and he is not here. Be advised, Lady Alicia de Burley. Do not lock horns with The Lady. That way always leads to bitter sadness." And with a shake of his head, and raised eyebrows, he gave her a look almost of pity and then, after a pause, to her complete astonishment, he leaned over her and said softly: "*L'Auberge de L'Abbéye*...The Abbey Inn, is said to be good," and with a slight bow, and sardonic smile, he turned and cantered slowly away, leaving all three girls open mouthed.

Chapter 37...How the Company of the White Rose escaped from Foix.

Two mornings later and they were ready to leave by the ford that ran from just below the Abbey across the Ariége, then up river, away from the main route to Carcassonne and Toulouse, and into the wilderness beneath the huge escarpment that loured over the town and then stretched Eastwards for miles across the countryside, a good day's journey from which lay the village of Roquefixade, their first stopping point.

There the village was overlooked by a remote stone fortress built on the very crest of huge limestone cliffs, where eagles flew and only mountain goats could find a way. Then they would journey through the edges of the great Corret Forest, completely by-passing the usual trackway by miles and miles...and then away towards Lavalenet, Chalabre and Limoux...and at last to far distant Carcassonne.

★

It had been a day and a half of intense activity carried out under the very eyes of de Vere and the Lady Rochine's guards; when bit by bit they had gathered all the things they needed into the large room that Alicia, Agnes and Soraya had hired in a small inn close to the ford itself, opposite the open square on the south side of the lovely stone Abbey church of St Velusien, where the market would be held, the many stalls and booths crowding into the narrow streets all around it.

Close by, the walls of the town curled towards the stone gatehouse that guarded the ford across which everything moved, goods, animals and people, both to visit the Abbey and to enter the town itself. While this was nothing like the great gatehouse that guarded Castle Malwood, it was sufficient for Foix, for the walls were thick, the ashlar smoothly laid, and all properly crenellated, the merlons rising strongly above the wide parapet walkway that stretched around them, the defences completed round the Northern end by the Abbey walls themselves as they curved past the confluence of the two rivers...where the Arget met the Ariége. And to the South, to guard Foix against any possible attack from Spain, a further battlemented wall ran between the two rivers, with a stout gatehouse midway along it to protect the entrance to the city and the great southern highway that ran through it.

Alicia viewing the defences as a whole...as Gui had taught her, sighed. Altogether it was a really neat little town, only somehow they would have to get out of it, and Alicia silently thanked the Good Lord that indeed they were not in the castle.

She smiled. Clearly the place was confident of its own safety, otherwise the town guards would have been much more circumspect towards any travellers entering its walls, market or not... but they had been relaxed and sloppy as she had suspected they would be, employed by the town rather than by the Count himself. They should be grateful that they were not at Castle Malwood, Sir Richard would have had them hopping about in no time! Castle Foix, however, would have been a very different matter altogether, with guards and careful checking everywhere. Not good. And it was just as well the Count was not at home, because he would have been bound to have wanted to meet with them, and he was allied to the Count of Toulouse, himself an ally of de Brocas and no friend of King Richard of England. And Alicia had no wish to fall into his hands. Better Lord Roger de Brocas, from whom she might escape...than the Count of Toulouse from whom such a thing would not be possible at all!

God Willing the town guards would be just as relaxed and sloppy on Wednesday morning?

★

L'Auberge de L'Abbéye... The Abbey Inn, was typical of the town: red pantiles, white plastered stucco on lath between tough oak frames and built on two floors, the second story leaning out over the ginnels that ran between the other houses and over the church square with its drainage channel down the sides running towards the river: small set of stables, hay barn and outhouses, with well and kitchens at the back and the usual midden in a far dark corner.

After what de Vere had said, there had been quite a free discussion amongst them, with much general dismay... and complete amazement that so kindly a suggestion could have come from such an unexpected source? It was as if a wolf had shown a sheep how to escape his pointed teeth!

And while Rochine and her party had settled into the Rock Inn almost beneath the castle, as she had said they would do, they had tried to find a different place to stay other than that suggested by de Vere. But in vain, as with the market opening early on the Wednesday morning, almost everywhere else was full. So, in the end, the Abbey Inn it had had to be, and Alicia was surprised to find a large single large room for herself and her two ladies was still available, and good stabling for her horses and for her three men.

But it had been quite funny in a way, because Monsieur Gerrard, the Aubergist, had been very unwilling to deal with Alicia, or her companions at first, finding it very strange that three such Ladies should be out on their own...until his doorway had actually been darkened by the appearance of Abdul and Aziz behind her. One look at either being enough for him to fall over himself to help her. As Soraya said laughing to the others later, she had heard one local merchant say to the Innkeeper: 'By God's Teeth, Gerrard. It looked as if the tower of Saint Velusien itself had walked into your bar today!"

But at least the place was theirs to command...and they did not continuously have to check on Rochine's whereabouts...because she came with de Vere to check on theirs. Sweeping in behind him, two of his men left outside as guards, a long cloak of azure damask lined with sky blue sarsenet, pinned to her shoulders by great ouches of burnished gold, the centre of each holding an enormous garnet, which flickered in the sunshine every time she moved, making her the very image of arrogant hauteur.

And seeing the surroundings Alicia had chosen she laughed with derision, even more so when she saw the people amongst whom her cousin had been forced to stay: visiting pedlars and common market traders, even several farmers with special produce to sell like cheese, Pâté de Sanglier and Foie Gras for which the area was famous.

"My dear Cousin," she had mocked. "How positively rural! And the smell...so disgusting. Of swine and the byre...and no bathing facilities either I should think!" And she gave a tinkling laugh that reeked of utter disdain. "But then it is no wonder you are happy here, Cousin," she had said, turning to Alicia with an angelic smile, adding with dripping venom. "So like that pigsty my father and I had to endure at Malwood...just asking to be burned down, don't you think? Along with the common farmers who owned it!"

And smiling at the rage that suddenly suffused Alicia's face, she ignored her cousin completely while Aquib seized Alicia's shoulders in a vice-like grip, watched by The lady with a curling lip from beneath an arched eyebrow before turning with a shrug of elegant distain to de Vere: "Post two of your men to watch this...this *midden*, and the three sows within it!" And she had swept out again, leaving Alicia more angry than distressed, tears flooding into her hands as she buried her face in them and wept as the pain of Rochine's vicious comments about the murder of Gui's parents swept over her...while Agnes and Soraya rushed to comfort her.

But the Aubergist and his plump wife, Mathilde, who'd heard what had been said, did their best to make up for Rochine's wickedness with small kindnesses of their own and much understanding, and the food had been good...food they could all eat and enjoy And that last night a delicious lamb ragout had been served, with green vegetables, shallots and some of their precious rice that Alicia persuaded Monsieur Gerrard to allow Najid to cook for their final meal before leaving; followed by a wonderful deep peach and apricot pie and custard from Mathilde, who had beamed at them when she had presented it.

And that last day the girls, and Aziz had scoured the little town for more suitable clothes to wear, leather hats and chausses against the rain that could come sweeping down the mountains, tougher boots, warm cloaks and woollen chemises against the cold mists that were sometimes a problem in the high lands,

253

even in summer, where cool air off the mountains met the warmer air off the land. While Aziz and Najid sorted things out at the Inn.

But though they managed to plan some kind of route across the countryside to Carcassonne, it was only sketchy at best. Nowhere near as specific as they really needed, so by late afternoon they were seated together on a stone wall above the river across the cobbled Inn yard, feeling pretty grim as they pooled their knowledge.

"Well, we have all that we need…except any sort of map!" Alicia muttered darkly. We can't take the tilt cart…but we can take the two horses as pack animals, and I have quietly purchased off Monsieur Gerrard some pretty ancient panniers, the crooks to hold them and the leather harnesses the horses need to bear them which, after Rochine's little display yesterday, he was very happy to do. The panniers are a bit ropey…but Aquib has had a good go at them with some of the wicker we bought this morning, and he says they will be fine. Yes?"

"Yes, My Lady," the huge man replied, in his calm manner. "And I have replaced the worst of the leather strapping," adding with his wicked grin. "Something I am used to doing after my travels through so many places in the Persian wilderness."

"And Madame has agreed to give us all a pack-up meal to take with us," Agnes chipped in brightly. "All wrapped in linen, and half-a-dozen old wineskins we can fill with water. She was really sweet," adding with a grin, "especially as I did my best with her language, poor love. She even gave me a kiss!"

"I have found some old sacks we can use to muffle the horses' hooves," Aziz said quietly. "We can cut them up and tie them on with some of the twine Mistress Soraya bought for us."

"Actually, Aziz, I don't think we'll need them," Alicia said, laying a hand on his arm with a smile and a swift word of thanks. "It is the Market tomorrow, and people will be flooding in from all around here from well before dawn to set up their stalls and be ready for the market bell at 8.00 o'clock. There will be carts, drovers, pack horses, loose animals and people everywhere.

It is the very best thing for us…for who will notice just one more string of travellers amongst so many?"

"What about the Gatehouse, My Lady?" Aquib asked quietly.

"I cannot see any problem. The town guard here are wholly relaxed and undemanding. No-one asked us for papers when we came in. Didn't even bother to check us, and I am sure that leaving will be no different. Agnes and I have been watching them down by the Abbey gateway. The men there are so 'not alert' it's untrue, they've even put out a bench for themselves to sit on, spears propped against the walls, helmets on top. Sir Richard would have them skinned alive were they at home!"

"That's right," Agnes chirped up as she saw the men's eyebrows rise. "Alicia and I went down to check things out. Very cheerful guards completely relaxed. Oh, don't worry we didn't talk with them! We just sat around and listened, and threw pebbles in the river. Just like home really," she added wistfully.

"The Count and his wife are away with their children visiting family," Alicia said, looking around her. "And there's no alert anywhere nearby. We must have been there a good hour, and they didn't bother to stop anyone. Crack of dawn tomorrow," she continued, stretching her shoulders, "there will be many others crossing that ford, both coming in for the market…and leaving to get away before it becomes too crowded. We will just be some of many."

"But still no real map!" Agnes said.

Alicia sighed: "No, Sweetheart. Soraya and I searched everywhere, and asked as well. But no joy. What we really need is…"

"…Is a friendly pedlar, Milady," Mathilde said coming across the yard in a floured apron, dragging a surprised young man with her, an enormous pack across his shoulders, stuffed with every imaginable trinket one could think of: bundles of brightly coloured ribbons, rag dolls, carved wooden soldiers and horses on sticks, clumps of wooden spoons, kitchen knives, little silver charms, and rolls of parchment, quills for pens and small pots of black ink sealed with waxed corks.

255

"This is Louis," she said, giving Alicia a big smile. "He comes from Carcassonne every year, across country, through Limoux and Chalabre and often stops off at some of the smaller places along that route that don't often see a pedlar. He will help you I am sure...the more so if you buy him his supper tonight!" And she gave the man a playful cuff across the top of his head.

"But Madame," Alicia said shocked. "How..."

"...How did I know you were a Lady?" she asked with a smile. "Because of how you *are*, Milady Alic-ia. The way you speak with people...*sans hauteur*...without pride. And the way they look to you, your own people, and how you walk. Nothing escapes the eyes of Mathilde. Nor Monsieur Gerrard...and after that one yesterday? *Poufe!* No-one! but no-one insults this house like that but I do something about it! Yes? A Pigsty indeed!" she exclaimed enraged. "She is *La cochonne...La Trui!* So...I help you, Milady. It is the pleasure of the house. Now, Louis," she said briskly these people need your help and you are to give it, yes? Good! *C'est Bon!*" And without giving him the chance to object, she turned and walked briskly away rubbing her floured hands together, leaving Louis seated on the ground, a piece of rolled parchment spread across a large flat stone, a fresh quill in his hand and a screwed-up expression of great concentration on his cheerful face.

★

And now they were really leaving, with the stars still shining form a clear sky and the light grey, everything formless and without colour, hidden in a fine mist writhing off the river as the day slowly crept into life, the dawn chorus breaking out all around them. And as they prepared to leave, so a host of others were already beginning to flood into the town for the Wednesday Market.

Up in the stables the two guards whom de Vere had left at the Inn to keep watch were laid out flat, unconscious from Aquib and Aziz's gentle ministrations: rough wine forced down their throats and poured all over them, gagged with strips torn from one of Alicia's kirtles, trussed like chickens, old sacks over their heads and hidden behind a huge stack of hay. Also ready were their rounceys, and their two pack horses, panniers stuffed with all they had decided they must take with them, including the armour that both she and Agnes had worn on the *Pride*, with the precious money belt firmly stitched back in place.

And while Najid and the girls were dressed in simple country clothes, Aquib and Aziz wore their half armour under their plain woollen cloaks, bought the previous day, their monstrous swords in their deep scabbards strapped across their backs, hilts and quillons hidden beneath their cloaks, their hoods pulled well over their heads to shield their faces; but no chain mail to chink or suddenly sparkle in a stray shaft of light.

In her saddle bag, carefully rolled, Alicia had the precious map that Louis had drawn for them with the names of the places they must go through, a track to follow with simple directions...and advised cautions: places that were dangerous or absolutely to be avoided, places to beware of...and places where they could be sure of a ready welcome. The little map was a joy, and much joking and laughter had gone into its creation, with little drawings of special features and stick people doing funny things. And they had invited Louis to join their little farewell meal in heartfelt thanks as well as giving him two silver pennies for his pains. To Monsieur Gerrard Alicia gave one of their precious Bezants and to Mathilde his wife, all the fine dresses she could not take with her...for which she was more than delighted.

So, with caution, they swung up into their saddles and gently clip-clopped on their way as they pulled out of the Abbey Inn's little yard and towards the small gatehouse that guarded the ford across the Ariége, the river bubbling over the bar of rocks that marked it, black and white in the pre-dawn, the tall rushes and yellow irises still closed up for the night swaying in the current, a pair of swans paddling majestically against it, dipping their long necks into the clear water as they searched for food. And as they passed under the arch, the two men on guard looked up and smiled calling out 'Good Morning' and shouting to be careful as the river was higher that day due to rain further south in the mountains. And with a casual wave, their hearts hammering as they gently urged their horses forward, fearful at any moment of a wild shout for them to stop, they pushed forward into the rushing stream. But no call came. And so that morning they left Foix behind, as did many others that day, plashing through the ford already busy with traffic: horses, carts, driven animals and people. Many flooding in as Alicia had expected, as people did everywhere there was a market…and many others leaving.

Faces blurred by the early mist, cloaks wrapped round them against the morning chill – they were just another string of riders on the move, and once across the river they turned up-stream, away from the town, and about a mile or so later they left the main roadway altogether. Kicking-on up a narrow, isolated trackway they had chosen with Louis' help the day before, overhung with trees and bushes, the thick wayside sedges muffling their hooves, they silently disappeared.

With unexpected help from good people they had slipped their leash at last, and were on their way towards the tiny villages of Caraybat, Soula and Saint Cirac; riding along the base of the vast escarpment that ran right across the countryside steep and craggy above them as far as the eye could see, with little more than goat tracks leading up it: and thence to the village of Roquefixade below its rock-bound fortress.

Then, in the grey pre-dawn tomorrow, after a simple 'Roman Breakfast' as Gui would say, and a hard ride through the Forest of Corret, they would re-join the distant roadway that today they were avoiding, that would finally lead them to Carcassonne, still a fair week's journey through the wilds.

Alicia leaned back in her saddle and jagged her heels in with a smile. De Vere would need a good lymer to catch them then…a really good scent hound…and she knew he didn't have one!

★

From behind one of the great stone buttresses that held up the walls of the Abbey church, despite the ghostly mist off the river, de Vere watched them leave and grinned. Soon be time to find those two fools he had left on guard and rescue them from wherever they'd been dumped. And rubbing his hands with quiet satisfaction he went to join Louis, Mathilde and Monsieur Gerrard for breakfast, and pay them for the arrangements he had made with them for room and board and Louis' help. It had gone well. The Baron would be pleased. What he needed now was some of Mathilde's fresh baked rolls, with butter, apricot jam, fresh peaches and a glass of wine. Lovely. And he smiled.

Next the message to the Baron: '*Your pigeons have flown! Make for the Fox and Goose at Rouffiac-d'Aude. 4 days!*' And then to tell The Lady…who would be livid. Wine first and Rochine second…and he laughed. It was going to be an interesting day!

Chapter 38...The Company flee into the wilderness.

Alll that day they travelled hard, and as fast as it was possible to go along the twisted trackway that ran along the base of the enormous escarpment they were following. Aquib led, with Alicia close behind, then the other two girls, Najid with one packhorse and Aziz, behind him at the trail with the other; both tough beasts, with shaggy fetlocks and strong hindquarters. They had been good on the tilt cart, and were excellent as pack horses, delighting in having panniers evenly weighted, and not the great, heavy yoke from which the long shaft of the tall-wheeled tilt cart would have been fixed between them.

And as the morning progressed so the sun burned off the early mists and they began to climb up the sides of the first ridge below the great escarpment that would take them all the way up the deep, flat bottomed valley to Roquefixade. Past fields of wheat and barley; cattle on the lower pastures and flocks of sheep scattered like stray bundles of wool across the hills, their bells clonking as they moved: every horse stride taking them further from Foix...and further from the hot pursuit they were all certain would be raised against them.

At first they looked often behind their trail, but soon concentrated more on covering the ground safely, than on anyone who might be following, and as the sun rose higher so it got hotter, becoming harder on man and beast as they kept moving. So it was with enormous relief when they reached Caraybat that Aquib called a halt, both to water their horses, and to fill the empty wineskins that Mathilde had given them with fresh water from the deep well in the centre of the village, that was fed by one of the many springs that bubbled out from below the escarpment.

But though it was intended to be only a brief stop, enough to run cool spring water over their faces, wash off the dust and pull a soft roll to pieces, fresh baked by Mathilde that morning early before they had left...they'd had to wait while others used the well first, for by the time they reached the village, the world was waking up. Colour had flooded back into their lives with the light, the sky turning from blush pink to scarlet and gold as the sun leapt up into a clear, cornelian sky in one gorgeous bound. First the women came out to draw water for their families, and while some men left for the fields, their bait in simple carry-sacks over one shoulder, others came in from milking, some with small flocks of sheep to water at a great stone trough put there for just that purpose, while the communal goats and geese were herded out to pasture under the watchful eyes of a handful of small boys whose job it was to guard them.

And all looked at the six strangers suddenly come amongst them with a mixture of awe and fear, the dark faces and hawk-like eyes of the three Arabs stunning them to silence.

Aziz laughed. "They don't know whether to run or make friends. I am sure if I said '*Boo!*' really loudly, and flapped my arms they would all flee like monkeys up a tree!"

"And that, of course, Dear Friends," Alicia said with a wry smile, leading her rouncey to the water trough at last, "funny as that would be...is also a problem because we cannot just melt into the local background. You are all too noticeably different. However, as we move further south that should be less of a problem, as the people there are more used to having Moorish traders amongst them. Up here you three stick out like blackbirds in the snow. Very handsome blackbirds I hasten to add...and I am *so* glad you are with us," she added gripping each huge man by the arm with a smile. "But...you are still...noticeable!" And they all laughed, including Najid as Alicia smiled at him also, just to be certain that he was not allowed to feel left out in any way.

"Hot work, My Lady," Aquib said as he led his rouncey to the water. "And like to get hotter," he added looking up at the sun. "We must be careful not to push these beasts too hard in these empty hills. We have a long way to go, and no spare mounts. We may have to stop more often."

"How far have we come?" Agnes asked coming up, wiping a cold, wet rag over her face and around her neck. "My haunches are feeling worn already."

"About six miles, maybe seven," Alicia answered. "It is hard to tell with so many twists and turns, and so much woodland around us. It could be more…I could wish it were twenty! We must have been missed by now, and we are not nearly as far forward as I had hoped. We have had to travel such a wide loop to get here."

"That is true, My Lady," Aziz said coming up to them. "But from what Louis said yesterday the next bit of the journey is fairly straight all the way to Roquefixade."

"But higher up this enormous ridge!" Agnes exclaimed, tearing into a roll with her neat white teeth. "And it is so hot. Can we not take off our cloaks now? I am roasting."

"Aquib?" Alicia asked. "You are our guide and leader on this journey."

"It is a pity we don't all have *djellabas* to wear," he sighed. "Arab cloaks of light cotton, or wool depending on the season. Light brown ones right now would be ideal both against the heat and to hide us against all this rock. Especially as we go higher. So, we must keep cloaked-up for the moment, until we have gone further. At least to Saint Cirac, which according to Louis' map is the last but one village before Roquefixade. By then the sun will be right on top of us. The main trackway to Lavelanet and Laroque-d'Olmes runs behind that long ridge on our right. While up here we are several miles distant and moving slowly. Anyone riding as if *Shaitan* himself was after him will show as a plume of dust; but of us they should see nothing!"

Alicia sighed and shuffled her shoulders under her cloak. "Right, if everyone has watered themselves and their rounceys, let's get going again before anyone plucks up the courage to start asking questions; lunch when the sun is right above us. Kick-on, Aquib, before we all melt into pats of greasy butter!"

★

In fact it was about the time that Alicia and her small company were leaving Caraybat, that Rochine was told that her birds had flown their coop…left the Inn she had visited and disappeared into thin air.

No-one had seen them leave, and no-one knew in which direction they could have gone either. With the Wednesday market now in full swing, and people coming and going everywhere, trying to find anyone who knew anything was an impossibility…and The Lady was incandescent with rage! Not only had she trusted the little *conne Anglaise!*…but the guards she had put to keep watch over them all had failed her. Like two soused herrings pickled in alcohol, they had been found trussed like chickens for the market behind a huge stack of hay! If she could have slit their throats then and there she would have done so…as it was she satisfied herself with watching de Vere flog them with a stirrup leather til their backs were bloody.

As for the Auberge, '*L'Auberge de L'Abbéye*', she ordered de Vere and his men to turn it inside out, and string up Gerrard to one of his own rafters by his wrists and submit him to the bastinado, tie his big toes together and beat the soles of his bare feet with a thick rattan, while his wife was forced to watch…and was even more angry when he refused to do so!

"You cannot do this, My Lady," he had said calmly in the face of her tumultuous rage. "The Aubergist, Monsieur Gerrard, is an important citizen of Foix. How do you think the people here will react to such a brutal act? The Abbot himself is in the market today…and no matter what you may have said to Lady Alicia, Sir Hubert will have you and me arrested immediately word reaches him, and we will all be imprisoned. And do you think he will release us because your father asks him to? Or the Count of Foix? No, My Lady…let me question them, and I will see what news we can gather elsewhere." And he had marched off before she could say a word, leaving her biting her leather quirt, stamping her feet with rage and shouting at everyone in her household.

Calm de Vere may have sounded, but he had rarely seen her in such a fury, and there was cold sweat on his brow as he thought of what would happen if she discovered the trick that had been played on her. Worse…that he had assisted in her captives' escape and even now knew where they were headed, and what tracks they were taking to get there. He might indeed be the Baron's

Guard Commander…but even he would not countenance any harm coming to his daughter…so God help him if he ever actually had to draw steel against her!

Still, Almahdi had sent off his message…the next thing was to send out his men to scour the gateways and the roads: North towards Toulouse; back the way they had already come towards St Girons and, of course, East towards Carcassonne across country, but along the main roadway towards Saint-Antoine and Celles and Canalot…and not the tiny, almost hidden trackway south of the town that led towards the huge escarpment that ran for miles.

Eventually, of course, he would have to do so. But fast messengers sent along the three most obvious routes for them to have taken, given their obvious ignorance of the countryside, would keep The Lady on side for a while. And by the time he did 'find' the correct route they had taken, Lady de Burley and her party would be at least a full day ahead of them, maybe more. And unless something drastic happened, they should meet up with Lord Roger this side of Carcassonne…and all would be well.

He just had to keep all his balls in the air…and gripping his crotch lightly he grinned. Except those of course…the air was the last place he wanted them to be in, and certainly *not* on a silver platter cooked like doucets with roasted garlic and a source of white wine and cream, when The Baron would then expect him to eat them!

Chapter 39...The White Rose and her command reach Roquefixade.

The Lady Alicia de Burley and her small company reached Roquefixade just as the dusk was settling around them, swifts screaming on scimitar wings both high and low across the darkening fields as they hunted for moths and insects still a-wing in the soft dusky light. The castle perched like an eagle's nest high above the village, its battlements part-lit by flaring flambeaux stood out stark against the last light from the western sky, as the first stars blinked into life.

And those last few miles had been almost the hardest, the three girls drooping in their saddles by then and all exhausted from their early morning start so they were delighted to have got to the Castle Inn...*L'Auberge du Château*...at last. Clean and bright, with rooms for all to share and, because of the castle, a warm welcome: the Aubergist used to stray travellers, and to travellers from hotter climes than his, so their little Arab entourage did not startle him.

They had time to settle their horses, curry their hides, check their shoes, and relax a while before their supper which was excellent: delicious baked rabbit pieces beneath a crusty topping of cheese and herby breadcrumbs with fresh greens and peaches to follow. That left them all pleasantly sated and very ready for an early rest for which they were desperate, having had little break all day, except a short time when the sun in all his glory was right above them and they had stopped at Saint Cirac.

★

And Saint Cirac had nearly been the end of them!

There Aquib had taken pity on them and had at last allowed them to take off their cloaks, and they had flopped in the shade of the nearest group of trees just above the village, almost panting like hounds on the chase, while with a big smile Nijad brought round tin beakers into which he poured cold sherbet made the night before from the last of the oranges off the *Morning Star*. And for everyone there were chicken thighs stuffed with cheese and herbs, wrapped in lettuce leaves; with hard boiled eggs, also cooked that morning by Mathilde, and the last of the rolls; all double wrapped in cheese cloth in the middle of his food pannier…together with a fresh apricot pie as tasty as the one they had so enjoyed the previous evening.

"I know you told us Mathilde had given us a pack-up to take with us today," Alicia said to Agnes. "But I was expecting a cheese roll at best…not a real diner's delight like this…and no bones in my chicken to bother with either. Delicious!"

And seated right up against the slope of the hill, the main roadway between Foix and Lavalenet that ran below them about a mile away was perfectly laid out for them to see, and though traffic was moving along it, it was more solid wheeled farm carts and groups of peasant workers, with the occasional horse litter accompanied by a groom or man-at-arms, than a furiously riding messenger with a plume of dust behind him. And for nearly an hour they sat and lazily lunched there, while their horses cropped the grass around them and the bees buzzed amongst the wild marjoram, bell flowers and wild carrot that were growing in profusion all around them, with blue cornflowers, scarlet poppies and brilliant corn marigolds dotted about throughout the wheat fields below.

With the sun casting dappled shadows through the trees, and a soft breeze blowing up the long valley below it was hard to remember that they were on the run from real enemies who were seeking their deaths, rather than their safe delivery to Grise! It was not good enough. Much more of this and they would all fall asleep…and then where would they be? With a grunt of effort Alicia dragged herself to her feet just as Aquib was coming across to her, Aziz helping Najid to pack up his food pannier again; and everybody stirring from their midday torpor.

266

"Next stop, or little market we come to, we must buy some sturdy buckets, My Lady," he rumbled at her in his dark voice. "Aziz and I have watered the horses as best we can with the help of two of Najid's pans. But that really wont do. Like today at Caraybat; if we'd had buckets we could have been on our way much more quickly. And for us, time is something of which we have very little to spare."

"You are right of course, Aquib. In all the rush to get away, no-one thought of it. When we stop for the night, I will see what can be found. Sweet Jesus, my bum is sore!" she exclaimed to laughter as she rubbed her buttocks briskly. "If I don't get moving again soon, I may never want to!"

Minutes later they were on their way again, dropping down fifty yards or so from where they had rested and back onto the long twisted trackway that led first to Leychert, and finally to Roquefixade with its castle poised right on the very edge of huge limestone cliffs that over looked the village, and which could clearly be seen against the cornflower horizon, still miles away, made dusky blue by the distance.

Then, when they were less than half way towards Leychert, just as they were negotiating a sharp bend in the track, they heard what they had all secretly been dreading all morning, the faint thunder of hooves in the distance. At once all looked towards the main roadway now just half a mile distant below them, closer than it had ever been since setting out. Here the ground was sloping open pasture on fallow land, a mass of flowers and long grasses, with a great open field of swaying barley, golden in the sunshine just beyond, hiding flocks of small birds that whirred from one part of the field to another as the fancy took them. And they were all in plain sight.

Immediately, Aquib threw up his hand and they all stopped.

"Everyone, off your horses, fast. Aziz, Najid, run your packs back down the track, and shelter them behind that huge hedgerow we passed a few minutes ago, no-one will be able see you from the road through that...but hold their muzzles. Everyone else, pull your horse's heads and make them lie down. Then lie across their faces, eyes and ears particularly. If they can't see they

267

won't struggle and they won't call out. And once you're down stay down until I say move. If he's one of de Vere's men he won't be looking for us here, he's going too fast for that. If he was ambling I would be far more concerned. But that is a pounding, fast gallop. Now...down you go! I will help you...and whatever else you do...keep your pale faces away from the road!"

In fact it only took moments once all three girls were out of their saddles. While Alicia had done it before with Gui, not so Agnes or Soraya...but with Aquib's great strength to help, there was no horse on earth that was going to resist him, his own included, and with less than a minute to spare all four were down, their riders lying across their heads, their faces buried into their horse's manes.

Closer, and closer the hooves raced til with a muted thunder they rushed past below where they were lying in a whirl of dust and small debris off the road and disappeared into the distance. Then...suddenly they slowed...and stopped, and with the wind blowing towards them up the valley, they could all hear the rider clip-clopping slowly back along the road. Something must just have caught his eye: some flicker of movement, something out of place that had made him stop and walk his horse back to try and find it.

Even though they were lying flat in grassy wasteland the track they were on was on sloping ground above the line of sight of anyone on the road below...especially if they were mounted, and to say their hearts were racing was to put it mildly, Alicia especially as she had the most to lose.

"What's he doing?" She hissed to Aquib, who was lying across his horse's withers, face towards the road.

"I can't see, My Lady. There's too much grass in the way. But my face is dark, and I am shielded a bit by those bushes behind us. I will take a slow look." And raising his head very gently he lifted his eyes above the tall grasses all around them.

★

Beyond the fallow pasture sloping away from him, was a huge open field of golden barley that almost swept down to the road where a man on horseback was stopped, his hand up to his eyes as he looked up towards them. At first Aquib felt sure he was looking directly at him, but just at that moment he moved his horse and it became clear that the man was searching a different part of the field. For quite a while Aquib could not, for the life of him, see what it was that had caught the man's attention, and in fact he had to kneel up in the end to find out, his head and shoulders draped with his cloak swiftly pulled from his pack to disguise his shape. And then he laughed. A quiet chuckle, that almost drove Alicia mad, because she could not see anything funny to laugh at!

Below them to the right, a very rough cart track from just beyond Saint-Cirac ran down one long side of the barley field, and two thirds along it, part hidden behind a clump of trees was a tilt cart, one solid wheel in a ditch, its horse happily cropping the wayside flowers while those who should have been on it were thrashing around in the barley chasing pigs! This way and that they fell, their wild shouts coming clearly up to them on the wind...now they had one, now they didn't... as the wretched animals dived this way and that to avoid capture, rushing between their legs, standing still, then dashing in opposite directions, and squealing as only pigs can, giving the two lads after them the complete run around.

Down on the road the rider was falling about with laughter, almost out of his saddle, as he rollicked from side to side, his great hoots coming faintly up to them on the wind, then, clearly wiping tears from his eyes, he kicked on his horse, picked up speed and hurtled on his way once more.

"Pigs, My lady!" Aquib exclaimed, laughing properly, pulling his rouncey up as the horseman disappeared from his view. "Listen! You can hear their squeals! And look!" He pointed, and in moments she too, and the others who quickly joined her, were all in stitches at the frantic activity going on below them, as the two boys desperately hunted down their escaped charges and finally carried them kicking, wriggling and squealing back to their tilt cart, furiously arguing as they did so, completely unaware that they had reduced a small group of adults into a state of writhing, comic stupidity, tears rolling down their faces, hands clutching their bellies and gasping for breath as they mimicked the wild antics of both pigs and boys…

So…by the time they reached Roquefixade, and were finally seated for supper, with wine and cold lemon water to hand, it had been a long, long day, the first of many; and the first of many early starts too before they would reach their journey's end.

Chapter 40... The Lady and de Vere take up the chase.

For Gaston de Vere in Foix the initial turmoil had settled down to a more controlled wait as his messengers came and went throughout the day, and the Lady Rochine, after her opening burst of violent rage, had also settled down to await results, her anger cold but none the less potent for being so!

And the Rock Inn was ideally placed to be such a headquarters, as the crossing points over both rivers were easily accessible, being well within the town wall that joined them up along the south side. And while there were gatehouses in front of both crossings, and to the south, with the market in full swing, and the guards wholly relaxed in their duties, their comings and goings had not caught the interest of the town commander; especially as de Vere had expressly told his troopers *not* to gallop their mounts within site of the castle for any reason. Not even if all the devils in hell were after them!

But by the evening of course there was still no news, and by then The Lady was getting very restless indeed as messenger after messenger returned with nothing to report. No-one had seen any such party leaving; at neither gatehouse had anyone passed over of their description, and along all the obvious routes leading North, East and West, *for miles*, no-one had seen anything either. Travellers and market traders had been asked, innkeepers questioned, and stables along the way searched. Their tilt cart lay abandoned at the Abbey Inn, and almost all their clothes. They had paid their shot the night before and simply disappeared.

Monsieur Gerrard and his plump, cheerful wife, Mathilde were as mystified as any one else: They had been quiet guests, kept themselves to themselves, been polite, and their Arabs had slept in the stables with the horses. No...they had not talked with anyone else they could think of. They didn't know anyone, did they? The ladies were all very pretty. The one called, 'Alicia' especially so. Very kind to her servants. Very like a proper Lady. Had they been ill? From her food? '*Non! Non! Non!*' The very idea! '*Quelle horreur!* Yes, they had paid. The money was in their rooms, and a bit extra. *'Formidable!'* One moment they were there…the next, *'poufe!'* they were gone. Like magic, like witches on broomsticks! And she and her husband had laughed at the idea.

So it was a gloomy, frustrated gathering that had met for food that night, de Vere sharing a table with The Lady in a room separate from the rest of their company, she in glowering silence; he contemplative and aloof. Her anger was not so much because de Vere had defied her earlier…but because his men had found no sign of her fugitives! Dead was one thing…but alive, and on the run? Maybe even to her father? Was a prospect far from pleasing, unless that ridiculous cook used the 'spices' that she had poured into his box…in place of the powdered toast crumbs that de Vere had given him in St Girons.

Or thought he'd given him…and she looked at de Vere from the corner of her eyes, happily stuffing his face with Foie Gras and lettuce. Now that *would* be good…and she suddenly chuckled, her eyes sparkling at the thought of what de Vere had actually given the little Arab in his plain, wooden casket. One good spoonful of food with that in it would do for them all, and she smiled again.

"You seem suddenly more relaxed, My Lady," de Vere said wiping his mouth. "What has amused you? I could do with a good joke just now. This day has not been exactly glorious!"

"No, Gaston," she grimaced, her smile disappearing. "It has not. Those fools of yours should surely have found something by now? They must have been looking in all the wrong places. And my smile? Just thinking how horrified those thrice damned *canaille* will be when we catch them. That rabble…that rabid pack of dogs! Now what is all that noise?" She demanded fiercely as the men eating their meal in the Great Room nearby suddenly burst into raucous laughter, beating their hands on the tables and stamping their feet. "What do those idiots have to be so amused about? Go and find out. They are disturbing my meal!"

But it was not necessary. Almost as swiftly as the noise had erupted, it had fallen away again, and moments later there was a knock on the door and de Vere's second stepped into the room.

"I am sorry to disturb you, Sir...My Lady, but one of my lads may have stumbled on the very news we have been seeking all day."

"You know where they are Sergeant?" De Vere asked his troop leader tersely...quite sure he didn't!

"No, Commander. But I think I know where we should have been looking today"

"And where is that, Sergeant Duclos?" The Lady demanded of him, menace in every word.

"The lad we sent to search towards Lavelanet, Pierre Rouge, saw something that caught his eye on the long stretch of road just past the hills near Celles..."

"*What?* What did he see, Duclos?" Rochine snapped at him, exasperated.

"It's not what he saw, My lady. That was just riotous...what we have just been laughing about. It's what he didn't see, My Lady..."

"*What he didn't see?* Gaston, is this man drunk or mad? What stupid riddle is this you have brought me tonight Sergeant. Get out of here!"

"No, Sergeant!" de Vere crisped at him. "Stand your ground, and explain. We will listen."

"Well, Sir," the man continued somewhat abashed. "His eyes were drawn to two young men catching pigs in a barley field close to the road..."

"*Sacrebleu*, Gaston!" The Lady snarled. "Do we have to listen to more of this drivel? Now we have pigs!"

"Please, Sergeant," De Vere said calmly, ignoring Rochine's outburst. "Continue with your report."

"Well, Commander...Milady. Pierre also noticed they had a tilt cart with them...and that there was a very faint trackway leading up the hillside, away from the road, to what looked like a small settlement high above them. Since

273

coming back he has asked questions…and there are a whole string of tiny spring-line villages, nestled right up against the base of that huge escarpment, all linked by a single rough track that runs all the way to the castle at Roquefixade…"

"*Nom de Dieu!*" The Lady Rochine cried out, slamming her fist on the table. "That's where those bastards went. No wonder your men could find no trace of them!"

"Well done, Sergeant, well done," de Vere said clapping the man across his shoulder; delighted that the way forward had been found by one of his men…and not pointed out by himself. "And well done to Pierre Rouge. Three bottles of the House's best…on me!" he added tossing the man a coin. But be advised we will be on the move at first light. So…now we know," he said to Rochine as his Sergeant left. "That is good."

"Yes, Gaston. Certainly that is good. But they could not possibly have taken so remote a passage without help. Your men searched all the likely places that a small group might have taken who were ignorant of the countryside. To take such a twisted trackway up into the hills shows greater knowledge than they could possibly have had. So…someone helped them. Either from the Inn…or from elsewhere," she added. "Even from one of us maybe?"

And giving him a penetrating stare, she tossed back her wine, rose from her table and swept out of the room; leaving de Vere very thoughtful, and to organise his troopers for as early a start in the morning as possible, and hoping that the day and night's Grace he had given Alicia before the pursuit really set out would be enough to see her safely to the Baron's arms!

Chapter 41... Last chance inn for the Company of the White Rose.

Chalabre, and the end of their second day on the road.

A small town a good twenty miles further from where they had spent the night at the Castle Inn and another long, hard day's travel albeit on a better road than the poor trackway they had been on that first day. And with their arrival a sign that the weather was changing, the sky filling with more cloud, and the wind that had teased them yesterday picking up weight, channelling its gusts up the valleys with the sound of distant thunder in its wings.

Chalabre, and their last chance of a good night's rest under a solid roof before setting out for Limoux along the steep valley that led to the village of Montjardin...and from there up into the dense forests that covered the Peche Laurague and the Col du Bac, and all the other mountains of that untamed region. With its steep scarps and mist shrouded valleys, twisting roads and sharp bends that doubled back on themselves, serving a handful of tiny hamlets that lay scattered amongst them, it was dangerous country. Each tiny settlement a flickering beacon of Life in a tree shrouded wilderness where fell beasts haunted the mountains and brigands, thieves and murderers lurked in the depths and fastnesses, ready to pounce on any traveller who was not of a strong, well-armed company.

Louis had told them it would be the most frightening part of their journey not just because the road was rough and twisted as it climbed into the mountains, nor because the forests and high hills hid bandits and outlaws, men who had lost their livings as Soraya's father had done...and those who had been cast out of their villages for crime or wickedness...but because they might have to spend a night in them, at Saint-Benoit if they were lucky, or at La Bezol, an even smaller hamlet of not more than half a dozen houses. But if the weather closed in on them, then they might have to bivouac in the open, and even in summer there were wolves in the high mountains and if they had cubs at foot they would fight to the death to protect them.

That night they discussed how best to move on, and quicker though it might have been to leave their pack horses behind in order to push on harder, all agreed that to do so was just too much of a risk for if they did get stranded the following night they would have no way of either feeding or protecting themselves against the changing weather.

"This is hard going, Aquib," Alicia moaned quietly as they waited for the vegetable broth and meat pottage they had asked for. Dipping the bread they'd been given in local olive oil and Italian balsamic vinegar while they waited. "And another early start tomorrow, I suppose. You are a hard overseer, my large Arab friend!"

"We escaped by a whisker yesterday at Saint Cirac, My Lady. I hadn't seen that track when we were riding by. Had he had his wits about him, and not been in such a hurry, that fellow could easily have ridden up it and we'd have been right in his lap. Oh, I'd have killed him...but they would have been on to us the moment he was missed."

"So...it will be another early start tomorrow! Never mind," she sighed with mock resignation. "One day I shall lie and watch the dawn bounce into life without seeing it from the back of a bloody rouncey, and think myself in heaven!"

"God Willing we get that chance, Alicia," Agnes replied in a cheerful voice. "You with your Gui and me with my Allan!" And she blushed.

"*Insh'a Allah!* Mistress Fitzwalter," Aziz said with a wide grin and a shake of his finger. "*Insh'a Allah!*" And they all chuckled at her confusion

"What is your plan, Aquib?" Soraya asked, a moment later. "Where do you want us this time?"

"Tomorrow, My Lady," he said turning to Alicia. "You and Mistress Agnes must wear your armour, helmets and all. And Najid too: I have brought his with me in one of the panniers."

"I didn't think he could fight?" Alicia said, astonished.

276

"*All* those who serve The Prince must fight, My Lady Ali–cia," Aziz said quietly in a very matter-of-fact tone, "no matter what their real job may be. Our Najid may not be a powerful fighter like me," the huge man added with a grin, putting his massive arm across the little cook's shoulders. "But he is a good comrade and a very *Shaitan* with a knife, and in war he is never far from his *Khanjar*. Not as fine as that worn by The Prince of course, the one you saw at Bayonne; but a fine blade nevertheless, and he can move like a cat. He may be soft-hearted in some ways but in others he is ...*Usama*, a Lion!" And he gave the little man a great smile and a friendly shake.

"Why the armour, Aquib?" Soraya asked.

"Because I do not want to let everyone along the way know that we have three women amongst us. I think that would be inviting trouble. And apparently there is a band of naughty outlaws that haunt these mountains sometimes, led by a man called Paul Grillade, the 'Griller', whom no-one can catch.

"'Naughty' outlaws, Aquib?" Alicia asked, astonished. "Naughty?"

"Well, My Lady," he said with a smile in his dark rumbly voice. "It is better to think of them as 'Naughty'...Rather than 'Wicked' or 'Evil': less scary, don't you think? Then while still keeping your eyes and ears open - you..er..won't be so anxious!" And they all laughed.

"Anyway, this way we will be five well armed men escorting one woman; and outlaws do not usually make a nuisance of themselves for the sake of a single chance of plunder. It would not be worth their while to do so! So both Aziz and I will be fully armoured-up. And in truth I have missed my full war harness, so it will be good to wear it all properly. You two ladies will have to lead a pack-horse apiece, but I want you in the middle all the way. Aziz will cover behind us, and Najid will be out up-front, ahead of me. He is an expert tracker and has a 'nose' for things. That's why he is such a good cook!" And as they laughed at his comment, so their food arrived and with much busy chatter they tucked in; no-one knowing when they might get another such occasion again. Nor did any-one linger after their meal, all going up to the two rooms they had hired for the night, intent on what rest they could get before their early start the next day.

277

This could be their last chance of warmth and safety for some days…and no-one wished to waste a moment of it!

★

But in the morning they awoke to a completely grey-white world, for during the night the wind had dropped, and the clouds had come so low that they filled the valley, hiding the slopes and tops of the hills with a wet blanket, the fine mizzle making everything drip water. Everything covered with fine droplets that hung like tiny teardrops from the tips of the horses' manes and even from their long eyelashes, making them shake their heads and hurrumph in the chilly dampness.

Another 'Roman Breakfast', food for later wrapped in the saddle bag each horse carried, along with a flask of watered wine, or watered fruit juice in the case of Aquib and his friends, and before anyone else was stirring they slipped out, all wearing long black cloaks to cover their armour, and all with mail coifs beneath their steel helmets and chain mail mittens with leather palms. Only Soraya was different, wearing a dark leather hat with a wide brim pushed firmly over her long hair, her hands in supple leather gloves lined against the chilly wetness, dark green leather chausses thrust into thigh-high leather boots to protect against chaffing as she rode along, and a dark blue cloak drawn close around her.

In moments they were mounted and with Najid going ahead, they kicked-on into the mist, eyes straining to see their way, their horses' hooves deadened as much by the dripping trackway on which they were clumping as by the thick mist by which they were surrounded.

At first it was easy to keep in close touch with each other, but as they moved further up the valley the mist changed as the wind moved through it, so that sometimes it was almost quite clear while at others it seemed almost impossible to see beyond your horse's head. Sometimes even less, the reins disappearing into a thick opaque, clammy wall. Sounds also came and went in the mist. Hooves clomping right ahead of you on the track one moment and then seeming to be miles away or right beside you the next, and calling out was of little value, the wet, cloying air seeming to swallow all sounds into itself, dampening one's shouts as if you were crying out through a wet flannel pressed close against your face.

And as they went higher the mist grew thicker, and an hour into their journey they found themselves stumbling like blind men into the tiny hamlet of Montjardin, a handful of simple houses clustered around the track that ran through it, before it turned left handed and upwards into a steep valley that was completely blanketed in mist, the trackway running up the left hand side of it, a handful of fields along the bottom from which cattle moaned plaintively from within the white blankness, their voices hollow and echoing as they pushed higher.

*

All around them the great forest leaned and swayed, the trees ethereal in the drifting mist, long dripping fingers, like leaf covered hands, dabbing at their heads and faces as they rode by, sometimes even brushing their shoulders. And all around them an eerie, kind of pattering silence, their horses hooves making little sound as they walked along, any kind of speed being impossible to attempt, and only the sighing wind and dripping leaves and branches any accompaniment to their journey. And now they were climbing higher all the time, both up the valley and also up its steep sides, leaning forward in their saddles to help balance their rounceys as the track wound its way upwards in a series of loops and bends, at one point actually doubling back on itself the way was so steep and they thanked God they did not have the tilt cart with them because they might never have got it up the road. It was when the trackway made a second great twist, deeply right-handed that Aquib finally called a halt, pulling his gelding off the track onto a kind of flattened clearing to one side of the road, so that everyone else could gather safely together.

"By *Allah*, this is miserable stuff," Aziz moaned, wiping the wetness off his face. "What has happened to the weather? This is high summer."

"This is just cloud, Aziz," Agnes Fitzwalter said, laughing. "It can be like this in the high mountains, especially when there is no wind to blow it away. Tomorrow it could all be as clear as a bell, and you'll see for miles. You should live in England…it is often like this at home."

"No Thank you, Mistress Agnes," Aziz replied, his face a picture of misery. "I would rather hunt lions with a kitchen knife than live in your damp island of fogs and rain storms. How about something warm, Najid? If I make a fire with my flint and tinder could you make us some soup, or broth?

"Oh that would be lovely, Najid," Soraya said, wrapping he cloak around her. "Anything to get this wet chill out of my bones. Where is Alicia? I haven't seen her since we stopped."

"I don't know," Agnes replied, sudden concern in her voice. "She was in front of me when Aquib stopped us. Did she go on? She can't be far!" And running a little way up the road she called: "Alicia! *Alicia!*" And was hugely relieved when a moment later Alicia came trotting back down towards them out of the mist.

"Where have you been?" Agnes started to say, when Alicia swung off her horse, held up her hand and stopped her.

"Shh! Be silent…all of you. Not a word, til we are all close together, and gathering her cloak she led her horse swiftly to where Aziz was coaxing a fire to life nestled in a bed of stones on the edge of the trackway where someone else had obviously once had the same idea, Agnes almost running beside her to keep up.

"What is it My Lady?" Aquib said quietly as he moved to join her, the others following except Najid who was rustling about in his food panniers.

"We are being followed!" she said, dropping her voice almost to a whisper. "Someone, or something, out there is tracking us."

"So…My Lady, you noticed too?" Aquib said quietly. "Najid told me an hour back. I wasn't sure myself for a while. But he is right. That is why I have stopped us here to light a fire, and not just for food. Fire is a great protection in the wild; not even a lion will brave fire unless driven to do so."

"A Lion?" Agnes asked, quavering. "Surely, Aquib, there are no lions in France?"

"No, Mistress Agnes, no Lions," he smiled, putting his huge hand comfortingly on her tiny shoulders. "Only Najid! He is *Usama!* Remember?" and he gave his deep rumbling laugh. "Now, My Lady," he said quietly, turning to Alicia. "What was it that alerted you?"

"It was the pattering!" Alicia said, her voice shaking. "At first I thought it was just the wetness from the trees. But when I stopped…it stopped also. It was like this in the great forest at home when I fled from Rochine and her father the last time. Only then it was a stag that was following me. This is very much the same, only now my horse is frightened. I can feel her pulling, and she has been tossing her head and snorting"

"Mine also," Soraya said. "I just thought it was the rain on her eyes."

At that moment, leaving a big pan across the fire, now burning well, Najid came across and joined them and he, Soraya and the other two men exchanged a rapid burst of Arabic while Alicia and Agnes quietly waited. A moment later Najid went back to his cooking and the others came to join them.

"Well?" Alicia asked Aquib. "What did our Number One tracker have to say?"

"He says that there are men out there, he has heard their voices. But he says also that there is also some kind of great beast. He does not know what? He has smelt something harsh and strong on the air, but it is not wolf, that he knows. He says this is different, rank and powerful, and it moves quietly. That is what has frightened the horses…mine too. Few things scare Najid in the wild. But this time he is afraid."

281

The three girls shivered and drew close together, their hands reaching out instinctively for one another, suddenly desperate for human contact in the face of an unknown terror.

"It will be *un sanglier énorme!*" Soraya said boldly, with a sudden high-pitched laugh; clutching Alicia and Agnes' hands. "A wild boar enormous; like the one that killed my mother? Najid will not know *les sangliers*. They have a very strong smell. Very!" And she held her nose and smiled.

"Perhaps it is a dragon!" Agnes said, her voice trembling. "St George slew a terrible dragon that ate girls. It is in all the stories. And dragons are terrible, great beasts. Oh…My lady. Pray God it is not a dragon!"

"Agnes, don't be such a big silly," Alicia said sharply, giving the girl a shake…privately hoping that it really wasn't a dragon! "There are no such things as dragons today. St George killed the last one centuries ago!" Didn't he? Of course you never really knew with dragons - perhaps they were immortal? No, Saints were immortal…dragons got slain! Dear God, she was getting as bad as poor Agnes!

"Come now, girls," she said brightly. "I am sure that Soraya is right - and that what Najid smelt was a great wild boar. They stink to high heaven wherever they are. Even worse in autumn and winter time when they are looking for mates, and this part of France is noted for them! Now…I don't know about you…but I am starving!"

And holding Agnes' hand firmly in her own, Soraya's arm around her shoulder, she walked across to where Najid was stirring a great pan of chicken and vegetable soup, the smell of which was making her mouth water.

Moments later, when she was cupping the wooden beaker in her hands that Najid had given her, Aquib came quietly across to join her by the horses, his huge figure shadowy in the thick mist, more like a wraith than a living man.

"I don't like this, My Lady." He rumbled at her softly, drawing her away from the others. "Men we can deal with…even outlaws. They are always just a rabble. The very debris of society who will flee from true warriors like Aziz and myself, so do not fear them. But if there is a great boar out there we have

282

no spears to hold it at bay, least of all a boar spear; nor hounds to drive it. When we start off again, a short distance up the track, Aziz, Najid and I will slip away from you…"

"*What?*" Alicia exclaimed, horrified. "*Abandon us?* But that will leave us completely unprotected! Nijad said he heard men's voices! What if we are attacked? Or seized on the road? What will happen to us?"

"We are not abandoning you, My Lady," he said urgently. "*No!* You must not think that! Nor will you be unprotected, I promise you, *On The Beard of the Prophet*…as I promised my Prince, remember? Aziz and I *will* be close by. But if we are surprised in this…this *muck!*" He growled forcefully, gesturing around him. "Then it will be very difficult to defend you - especially if the enemy have bows. We need space to move in without…forgive me, Lady Alic-ia," he added sweeping his hand over her and towards Agnes and Soraya…"Without any hindrances. But, if the worse happens and you are taken we will track you, then when they encamp, which they must, then we can attack them - and it will be devastating, I assure you. But you must trust me, My Lady Alic-ia. Please!"

"*Oh, Aquib!*" She exclaimed sounding desperate. "You are asking a great deal of me," she said, looking him full in the face. "And of Soraya, and poor Agnes Fitzwalter who does not have half my courage. But we will do as you suggest. Only Pray God you do not lose us in this mist…nor fall victim to some fell beast from the forest, that you and I both know to be out there!"

"*Insh'a Allah*, My Lady. We will be close." And he seizing both her hands in his enormous grip to re-assure her, he added fiercely as he squeezed her hands: "My Heart and Soul on it!"

"Well, Aquib…just make sure your *Allah, Insh'as* it properly!" And she gave him a smile. Tremulous maybe…but still a smile as she walked back to where Najid was already packing up his things.

Chapter 42... *They seek her here, they seek her there... they seek the White Rose everywhere!*

Away near Gruissan, Baron Roger was already on the move North West towards Carcassonne to catch up with Alicia at last.

With his full Guard Commander, Gaston de Vere, assisting his daughter it was to Sergeant Le Brun, his huge Officer Commanding the Castle Guard, to whom Monsieur Le Baron now turned for the men he needed to mount a rescue of his intended bride.

Two dozen hard faced troopers, well armed and mounted, and only carrying saddlebag supplies for three days had left with him at their head the day de Vere's message had reached the castle pigeon loft. His great house flag of a Boar's Head Erased Sable, armed and langued Gules on a field Vert carried proudly beside him all along the way, the wind of their passage making the green standard with its great black Boar's Head stream behind them, its scarlet tusks and tongue looking as dangerous as ever they could if they were real: every armoured man upright in his saddle, the Baron, on his great black charger, Charlemagne, in the lead.

But despite the news from de Vere, it was a grim look he carried on his face as he cantered along the old Via Aquitania, forcing others off the road as his command forged westwards, for no message had yet come through from either de Courcy or Bertrand de Vernaille, and he now feared the worst. That somehow Gui de Malwood had escaped his trap...and he growled with anger, banging his clenched fist against his thigh.

This time he would make sure that Sir Gui's precious Alicia did not evade his net! And digging in his spurs he picked up the pace, and led his men in a plume of dust towards Carcassonne and the English Lady he had determined would be his bride!

★

Two days behind Alicia, The Lady Rochine had also caught the scent and like a leashed Lymer, or a pack of Rache hounds, was now hot on her trail. And having first arranged for both tilt carts...especially the one carrying the Baron's precious pigeons, to leave with hired drivers, fresh horses and the Cousins as their escort on the Northern road towards Toulouse, and then East past Varilhes to Mirepoix and Carcassonne and so to Narbonne and Gruissan at last...Gaston de Vere, followed by The Lady, led the way out of Foix with his men and gave chase.

By then the sun was rising, and having splashed across the ford they turned south until the guide they had found took them east along a narrow trackway that led towards the base of the huge escarpment that ran right across the countryside to the castle of Roquefixade and beyond. At first The Lady had been doubtful that Pierre Rouge had been right at all, as the further they went along the track, the further away from the escarpment they found themselves. But when they swung back and reached Caraybat, the first village since setting out, she soon got the confirmation she had been seeking.

"This is the right direction, My Lady," de Vere told her after one of his men had questioned two of the local women. "A small group of riders stopped here two days ago to water their horses. Three men and three women, with two pack horses. The men with dark faces...they frightened the children! There can be no doubt. It's them alright!"

And after watering their own beasts, they kicked-on sharply along the narrow trackway. They were two days behind their quarry, and the dust of their passage billowed out behind them.

★

Far to the North, Sir Gui de Malwood and his battered command were still two days from Bordeaux and pushing hard. Their tilt carts rattling and bumping along the road, as fast as the surface and their injured could bear the pace, for they were behind time now from when they had left

Nantes, and every minute counted.

The battle at Saint Jean d'Angeley had cost them time and good men too!

While Allan-i-the Wood and Dickon Fletcher had slaughtered de Courcy's men with their arrow storms, de Vernaille's bowmen had wreaked havoc amongst his command before they had been cut down or forced to surrender, and over a dozen of his Lions had been killed or injured in one way or another. Seven had been buried in the town cemetery, five more were badly wounded, with sword cuts or arrow strikes but would still travel with them, and three more were so badly injured that they might well never fight again and would have to be left behind, with all their equipment and money for their care and their journey home if they could manage it. Father Matthew had done his very best for all of them, but the tilt carts bore witness to the fierceness of the fighting, and the limits of even his surgery: though without him they would all have died.

The two Vernaille brothers might not have been up to much...but some of their men had fought bravely, and did not deserve such poor leadership, and of those whom Gui had spared a dozen had asked to join his command, and after a stiff examination from Fitzurse in weapon craft and obedience to orders, they had been duly sworn in, exchanging the Golden Lion and Stars on Blue of Vernaille for the Rampant Scarlet Lion surcoats of Malwood, stained with blood as they were...and felt privileged to have been allowed to do so.

As Fitzurse had said: "Those lads did well, My Lord. One even managed to take a chunk out of my shield, the cheeky varmint! I'd rather have 'em with us than against us!"

But in the end it had taken two days to get themselves sorted out:...letters to the King on his way to Marseilles on all that had happened, and letters to Sir James Bolderwood in The Forest; the dead stripped and buried; live horses gathered, dead ones burned; spare weapons and good armour saved and the wounded tended. And three left behind in the Abbey Hospitarium as too injured to travel further, with money for their welfare, their horses and their armour left with the Abbot, and orders to follow on if they could...or return to Malwood if the Abbot deemed them beyond further warfare.

286

Then they had left, and as Alicia and her small coterie fled into the mountains pursued by The Lady; and the Baron left Gruissan to capture her...her own leal man was still two days out of Bordeaux, with a week's journeying from there to Narbonne ahead of him, driving himself and his men with unrelenting vigour and determination: Sir Gui de Malwood did not carry the Lion Rampant on his chest and on his flag for nothing!

★

And all were seeking the same goal...the Lady Alicia de Burley!

Chapter 42... The Company of the White Rose are attacked in the forest.

With a shiver the Lady Alicia de Burley re-mounted her horse, shook her shoulders beneath her armoured jacket to settle them more comfortably and eased the sword at her waist, while Agnes Fitzwalter sat there shivering in her armour, and Soraya Fermier fussed with her hat and cloak, making sure her hair was well hidden beneath them both. Then, with Soraya safely between them, Alicia and Agnes both took the long leading rein for a pack-horse each, and with Aquib in front, Aziz at the rear and Nijad ahead of them all, they kicked back onto the road and began to climb the steep right hand bend that had stopped them earlier.

Sixty or seventy yards further up and the roadway began to level out, before dipping away towards a sort of hollow, then rising again...and it was then that Alicia suddenly realised that she could no longer see Aquib ahead of her in the thick mist. The faint blurry outline of horse and rider had simply vanished, yet she had heard nothing. One moment he had been there...the next gone! And although she had been warned of it, she had still hoped that it wouldn't really happen; but now that it had she felt frighteningly vulnerable, not daring to look behind her in case she unnerved the other two, especially Agnes.

She had not realised before just how much she had been relying on their two huge Arab guardians. Facing Rochine knowing they were there was one thing....being suddenly alone in a deeply forested, mist-laden wilderness in a foreign land, where it was known that desperate men were out and about and some great beast might also be stalking them was just terrifying!

Then, just before the roadway dipped down, the whistling started.

First on one side of them and then the other: one moment very faint, and seemingly far away, the next almost right beside them...before dying away to nothing. And there were eyes in the mist. Huge, yellow tigers' eyes, the pupils striped and barred, that moved as she moved; making her heart turn over and her hands flutter with latent terror. Her gelding also tossed his head and snorted with fear, his brown eyes rolling madly as he strove to see what was happening around him, so that he scrabbled his hooves sharply on the track and violently jerked his head up almost tearing the reins out of Alicia's hands as she fought one handed to control him, the other still holding her pack-horse.

"*Alicia!*" Agnes shouted wildly from behind her, her mare also jittering beneath her "What's happening? What's going on? I'm frightened!"

"Close up on me, Agnes. Soraya too," she shouted out behind her. "And keep your nerve. This is just some awful silliness going on around us. Keep your horses well up to the bit and don't let them bolt. We must try and keep together!" And she turned to loosen her sword in its scabbard.

"*Where are the men?*" Agnes screeched at her a moment later. "I can't see them in all this mist. I can't see Aziz behind me...he was there a moment earlier. Now he's gone! And where is Aquib?" she cried out again, panic in every word. "I can't see him either! I can't see anything! *Alicia what is happening?*"

"Calm down, Sweetheart," Soraya called out again, allowing Agnes to come up along her right side her, reaching out to stop her jibbing at the reins by taking the hand still desperately clutching the packhorse rein in an effort to comfort her. But at that moment Agnes screamed out: "The horse has gone! The horse has gone!" And so it had, leaving just a fallen section of leading rein in her hand, cut through as cleanly as if someone had been slicing beans at home for supper. And then she screamed again, piercingly, as a great figure with antlers on its head bounded, roaring out of the mist and disappeared behind her, the stolen pack-horse running by his side, as the whistling reached a sudden piercing crescendo. Then silence!

Hearing Agnes scream, Alicia dropped her leading rein to give her greater freedom, and turned her rouncey hard left to swing back alongside Soraya and sandwich her between herself and Agnes, drawing her sword at the same time, as Gui had taught her long ago. But with Agnes still screeching in terror on the far right side of the track, and Soraya pressed up against her sword arm she was unable to wield her weapon properly. So seizing Soraya's arm she shouted

"*Dismount!* We cannot defend ourselves from the back of these horses...they are not trained destriers. They don't know what to do. Get off! *Get Off!* Agnes...*Get off your horse* and come to me! Leave the bloody thing. God Willing we can catch them up later"

In moments all three girls were huddled together in the middle of the track, now at the very bottom of the slight dip they had been riding down, the ground rising around them, the great trees further apart and the undergrowth not so dense.

"Soraya, can you use a sword?" Alicia called urgently. "Agnes has no skill with weapons."

"A little. The Lady has taught me a few passes."

"Then take Agnes' sword, and her mailed gloves! Quickly, girl. They will be upon us in a moment. And bring her here, now. Good! *Good!* Agnes lie down at our feet sweetheart, we will stand over you. It is what Gui told me I must do if ever he had occasion to defend me. Now, Soraya, brace yourself and sell your life dearly. It will be soon now. I can feel it!"

And then the noises all started again!

All around them in the thick mist, the trees distant dark shrouded pillars, their leaved branches like mighty arms drooping towards the ground; wild figures leapt and shouted their war cries. Sometimes they rushed by them with shrieks and screams, their heads like those of wild beasts: boar and bear and lordly stag; appearing and disappearing like maddened wraiths, almost without human form. While at others they stood still, frozen statues in the dank murk, curled ram's horns to their shapeless faces, groaning like bulling heifers, the noise going on and on and on without remorse, coupled with the thudding beat of great drums hidden in the misted forest.

And then, with a single mighty roar of noise and thunderous drum beats...there was complete silence!

Eerie in its suddenness, terrifying! Making the belly gripe, the heart race and the lungs pant, as the girls stood over Agnes and circled her in the sodden white-out, mouths dry with fear, peering into the billowing mists, their swords

290

twitching. Then more whistling, soft at first and all around them, rising and rising to another wild, insane crescendo…and with that the first attack! Two men rushing in upon them out of the blank wetness, long iron studded clubs in their hands, and screaming their war cry as they came, faces screwed up in murderous rage, one on either side of them.

With no shield on her left arm to ward off a blow, Alicia remembered what both Sir Richard and Father Matthew had said about using the point more than the blade, and as the first man reached her and raised his hands to strike her down, she slipped her right foot forward and drove upwards into his armpit with all the strength she had, her blade piercing his ragged clothes and splitting his shoulder and neck apart so that he fell screaming beyond her, blood pouring from his wound as he thrashed about, his feet scrabbling frantically for several moments before he gave a dreadful groan and died. The other, seeing what had happened to his friend, fled screaming past them into the mist…and all around them the forest howled and hooted.

"*You killed him!*" Soraya cried out, her face white with the shock of it. "You killed him! How did you do that?"

"Gui taught me, Sweetheart," Alicia rasped, straining for breath, her face sweating beneath her helmet, her heart hammering. "He showed me how to defend myself. And I listened to Sir Richard and Father Matthew. You and I do not have a man's strength to wield a blade for long," the words almost falling over themselves to get out, "but you can use the point, as I did. Step forward and thrust, and hope the forward rush will do the rest!"

"*I Cannot!*"

"You *can!* Soraya…you *must* try…*here they come again!*" she shouted at her. "Imagine it is The Lady you strike at and don't hold back."

And with that the next attack came rushing in, and this time Alicia and Soraya met it back to back, their legs straddling Agnes, her small body curled up in a tight ball beneath them, their swords held low as they waited to see which way they should move. One was the clubman whose friend lay dead just beyond them. The other wielded a great curved sickle, and both were wild with rage, advancing slowly, shouting and roaring, flensing their weapons furiously backwards and forwards across their bodies with every step.

"Cock your sword, Soraya!" Alicia called out sharply. "Over your right shoulder, two handed! No thrust will work here, you must try and cut down on their weapon arm. These men are not trained, but they are deadly. This will all be in the timing. I will take the sickle, you take the club. When I say *jump!* Spin round and go for it!"

And all the time she was watching her enemy stride purposely towards her, his wicked curved blade on its thick wooden handle, swishing backwards and forwards, and up and down his front as he moved; determined to slice her as he would a sheaf of wheat, each empty blow enough to cut her head off.

Dancing from side to side on the balls of her feet Alicia watched and waited as the ragged man advanced, feeling Soraya matching her every movement, hoping that somewhere nearby their guardians would be waiting to make their move, but concentrating solely on the two men now intent on killing them. *Left! Right!* Their weapons swayed. *Left! Right! Left!*…**"Jump!"** Alicia shouted and leaping sideways, she brought her sword down two handed in one great swingeing blow that hewed the man's sickle arm off at the shoulder. A massive, single blow that sliced through his bones and sinews as if they were paper, his blood spouting upwards into the wetness that pressed down all around them, covering her face and armour as with a terrible howl of agony he fell writhing at her feet.

And spinning with her momentum, she followed through, sweeping her blade backwards with a vicious reverse cut that almost severed the clubman's head, his left arm already on the ground where Soraya's blade had left it, his horrified shriek of pain immediately stilled as the blood from his neck fountained upwards spraying everything with hot scarlet drops that steamed in the chill damp air. And once more the forest rang with shouts and howls.

"*Well done,* Honeyone!" Alicia gasped, clasping Soraya to her briefly, both with blood on their arms, faces and all over their clothes and armour. "You were brilliant!"

292

"I closed my eyes, Alicia!" She cried out, the tears flooding out. "*I closed my eyes!* And then he screeched and his blood ran hot all over me. It-it was horrible!"

"Yes! It is h-horrible," Alicia stammered, her heart pounding, resting on her sword; her words running together as her chest heaved, the breath almost painful in her throat. "But we..we expect our men t..to do this for us all the time. It is only when..when you've done it yourself...as we have today...that you can understand how a man feels when he kills!"

"And why he needs our loving comfort-and our soft bodies when he-he comes home." Soraya panted over her shoulder

"Is it over now?" A small voice queried from below them. "Have they all gone?"

"No Agnes," Alicia said firmly, reaching down to clasp her hand. "No. Not yet, I fear, Sweetheart. This is only a pause. We have hurt them but not enough to stop them. Stay down where you will be safer. But I will take your helmet for Soraya. She needs it."

"What now, Alicia?" Soraya questioned urgently, as she tore of her leather hat, settling Agnes helmet over her long hair, while Alicia fumbled with the straps, her sword thrust into the ground before her. "And where are the men? Where have they gone to?"

"First we bargain...if we can. And as for Aquib, and the others? I don't know. But I do know that they are not far away. So we must try and buy them some more time! How does that feel?"

"Better," Soraya said strongly, shaking her head to make certain her helmet was secure. "I just wish I had her armoured jacket as well. No matter," she added flexing her arms. "But how do we buy the men more time?"

"Well...suppose we stir this lot up a little?" Alicia said grimly, waving her hand towards the thickly mist-shrouded forest full of calls and whistles and formless capering figures.

"*Are you mad?*" Soraya snarled, horrified. "Listen to them...they are worse than a herd of braying donkeys! What are you going to say?

"This," she said quietly, and then raising her voice she shouted into the opaque mist still swirling around them in the wind: "So...you *Canaille!* You have our horses – and we have killed three of your men. How many more will fall to our blades before you slink back to your caves, or the holes in the ground where you live like the animals around you. Why seek death, when what you have already taken can give you life?"

"Because it pleases us!" An answer came fiercely out of the mists. "Because the real robbers around here are not us, but the heartless bastards who prey on our lives every day. Who keep us sweating and swinking in their fields for no return," the voice continued, making Soraya jump and glare ferociously into the mist. "And they use armed scum like you to carry out their orders!"

"*Excuses! Excuses!*" Alicia bawled into the opaque murk, pulling her blade beneath her arms to clean it, then whirling it around her head, the thick wetness making her voice harsh and hollow. "You prey on others like the reeking filth you pretend not to be!" She shouted towards the distant voice. "You murder whom you please; rape and pillage at will...and then seek to blame others for your wretched plight! You are no better than the ravening wolves that steal your sheep from their folds and tear their shepherds to pieces!" She added, her words deadened by the mist. "You are all just wild beasts!"

But before she could say another word, there was a great shout from somewhere up in the swirling blankness ahead of them, and a wild mob of ill armed ruffians rushed out upon them from the thickly shrouded forest round about, some with great flaring flambeaux, some with thick quarter-staves, others with weapons of iron and bone, some even with just their bare hands: and all baying and rowling, capering like demons from the Pit, in a whirl of rags, tags, leather armour and chained steel.

And Alicia and Soraya fought them as fiercely as they could, while Agnes screamed in fear beneath them, her body drawn into a tight quivering ball.

Twice the girls cleared a space around themselves with their blooded swords. Parrying blows on their blades, as they whirled and flicked them from side to side; now thrusting forward with the point; now cutting sideways at any leg, arm or shoulder they could strike at. Ferociously they defied the mob that leaped and twisted about them like dervishes, all trying to strike down the two fighters who were so famously defying them.

And three more times Alicia and Soraya killed with fierce thrust or cutting edge, while maiming others. The swords they had brought with them from Malwood, edges still like razors, hewing through bones and sinews as if they were mere faggots bound with string: the dead lying in twisted heaps, the maimed dragging their blood boltered bodies from the desperate scene, writhing and crying out with pain and terror.

But it could not last, there were just too many of them, and quite suddenly the strength simply drained out of their arms and wrists, and with the bandit leader roaring for them to be taken alive, their blades were finally knocked from their hands, themselves beaten about their heads and shoulders and hurled to the ground in bitter defeat.

"*Stand them up!*" A harsh voice shouted out from a small mist-shrouded hillock further to the left that dominated the dip in the trackway where they had been attacked. "And let us see what we have caught for our amusement today. What shoats have been sent for us to roast squealing on our spit tonight?"

And stepping forward, dressed wholly in black...padded gambeson studded with iron, black mailed chausses and boiled leather vambraces strengthened with strips of forged steel on each forearm...came a man of medium height, with broad shoulders, strong thighs and a square face across which a terrible scar ran from his left eye right across his nose and face. Both ears had been hacked off, only the black holes they had once shielded showing though the lank hair that trailed around his shoulders, and he carried a sword.

"I am Paul *Grillade!*" he shouted as he strode towards where his men had pinioned Alicia's arms behind her. "I like my meat grilled with the blood running free! I am Paul *Cauchmar!*"...he roared down at poor Agnes, cowering between two of his men, stabbing at her with the point of his sword

295

as she wriggled and whimpered in terror on the bloodied ground. "Your worst living nightmare!"

And whirling his sword he turned and raged at Soraya, where she stood, helmet torn off her, clothes and arms badged with blood all over, head down and utterly dejected: "I am Paul *Le Mort!* The death of all who defy me!"

But suddenly, violently shaking her self free of the two men on either side of her, unprepared for any such action, Soraya stepped forward and looking up she stared at the man with bitter rage, her eyes seeming to stab green fire, and bringing her hand round she slapped him across his face as hard as she could with every remaining bit of her strength.

"NO!" she shouted at the top of her voice as she hit him, the solid **smack!** ringing out across the mist-laden clearing. "*NO!* You are Paul Fermier, *my brother!* Murderer and hunted criminal; driven from our village for your crimes; beggared our father; arrested, slighted and cast out!" And she spat in his face.

White with shock, the mark of Soraya's hand livid across his cheek, the Outlaw leader was struck dumb by what she had said, clutching his scarred face where she had struck him, all around him equally stunned by what had happened. Then, striding up to her he seized her long hair in his hand and twisted her head so he could see her better…and growling with rage he shook her like a tree in a gale.

"By God's Blood, so you are!" He sneered, dragging her round to face his leering followers "My little sister!" He roared out, shaking her at them. "The famous family beauty! So like our dear Infidel Mama," he shouted at her. "That's why Papa loved you so much! Always *you!* You always were his pet, his *petite choux!*" He spat at her. "But I fixed you good and proper, *little sister,*" he snarled, straightening-up. "Good and proper, the Lord Baron and I. *Good and proper* you screeching *bitch!*"

And while Soraya stood there, shocked to the very core of her being by what he had said, bereft of sound or movement, he struck her fiercely across the face, then back-handed her even more so, a vicious blow that raked her face with his knuckles, her teeth tearing them open even as they split her lips and hurled her almost senseless to the ground.

Then swooping down on her he seized her by her long hair and dragging her upright he tore her clothes apart, then hit her again so her head snapped backwards with the force of his attack, hurling her in a crumpled mess almost at

297

Alicia's feet, half naked, her breasts and shoulders spilling out of her ravaged clothing into the damp, chilled air that still swirled around them. Agnes, who had been dropped by the men holding her when their leader had first roared out, scrabbled on her hands and knees across the torn glade to cover Soraya's nakedness with her own body and comfort her in her unspeakable distress.

And leaving Soraya sprawled, sobbing on the ground, he turned to Alicia, still armoured, her helmet still firmly tied beneath her chin with leather straps, her arms pinioned behind her, blood all over her face and hands.

"And who are you, little man?" He sneered at her, his bloodied hands on his hips, his men gathered all around them in a ring of hardened, leering faces. "A stupid soldier boy who carries out the orders of those who drive families out into the wilderness when they cannot pay their rents; take the best of all we have when we die; rob us of our livelihood and burn us out with their wars?" And he smiled at the jeers and howling that his words had delivered for him.

"Let go of his arms!" He ordered her guards with a vicious smirk across his mutilated face. "Let us see what this lump of shite is all about, eh lads? This stupid soldier boy, whom the good Lords of Chalabre and Limoux have sent to us today! Whose twisted guts we will use for bowstrings and whose blood we will drink with the wine we took off the Bishop last month!" He added to rough shouts of brutal humour.

"That'll go nicely with his fucking balls!" Someone shouted with a bark of laughter.

"It did with the Bishop's!" Another crowed. "Shame he didn't like them, and after Raoul had taken such pains to cook them too!" And they all roared with laughter.

"And they'd go well with the goat's cheese we had off those fucking nuns!" Another shouted out.

"Not half as bloody good as those nuns were for fucking though!" Another man bawled out. "They were the tastiest fucking dishes we've had for *months!*" And another gale of raucous laughter swept round the men gathered there, convulsed with the coarse, ribald wit they'd just heard, while Paul

298

Fermier stood in front of Alicia and laughed the most at the wretched look of shock and disgust that ran across her face, ghastly white and blooded from her fight.

Then, tossing off the hands which had held her, Alicia unlaced her helmet straps with studied care, not a single tremble in her fingers, and taking off her casque, and pushing back the steel coif beneath it, she shook out her blond hair to a gasp of surprise, causing all about her to take a sudden step backwards.

"*No!* You scum, *Fermier!*" she spoke out then in words of crystal glass, as he too stepped back amazed. "I am no stupid 'soldier boy'," She sneered. "I am the Lady Alicia de Burley a woman grown, and your sister's friend. And a fighter who can wield a blade with her well enough to slay half a dozen of the disgusting *rabble* you have gathered around you," she mocked, gesturing to the bodies still lying where they had fallen. "And have maimed others who will never fight again!

You piece of choice *filth!*" She snarled, stepping fearlessly towards him...her heart almost leaping out of her chest. "You strike down an unarmed, defenceless woman and boast of your wickedness as if you were a hero. But where were you Paul *Cauchmar*? Paul *Grillade*?...when your men were fighting?" She railed at him. "Hiding in the mists in your fancy clothes and calling out your orders, while two girls, with little skill but great courage, cut your pathetic *mop heads* to pieces! Then, when it is all safely over, here you are," she sniped at him, "O mighty one...a carnival figure in black with a big sword! A mountebank if ever I saw one!" And she laughed in his face.

"You, Paul Fermier, *Le Mort*...The Death !...are no more than a common bully!" She chided him with icy, disdain. "A nasty coward who makes war on priests and women, and then boasts of his brave deeds in the ale house!" She added, her eyes locked on his, moving sideways towards her fallen sword as she spoke, now just a few feet from where it had been thrown down when she had been captured. "You are no better than the beasts amongst whom you live!"

Spell-struck by her words and the sheer forcefulness of her tirade, Alicia, her face and armour still stained with the blood of those she had cut and slain, had forced backwards with every phrase she had spoken, a man known for his

299

wickedness and his brutality. And his whole command of wild killers and gutter fighters, seemingly mesmerised by her words and by her utter contempt for their leader, were unnerved and did nothing.

And it was at just that moment she became intensely alert to wild movement in the murky treeline behind Paul Fermier's shoulders, where the mist seemed thinner, saplings quivering, bushes being thrust aside, everything becoming wilder by the second, and choosing her words carefully she suddenly bawled out in English. "**Come to me quickly!** *Soraya and Agnes are alive. I cannot hold these men much longer.* **Aquib, Aziz, Najid! Come to me! Come to me!**"

Then taking one more sideways step from the big bandit leader, stunned into immobility by the words she had just shouted out in a language he recognised but could not speak; she mocked him mercilessly one more time: "Thank God I am English, *Fermier!* We do not creel like sick babes in England when our lives are tough! Mewling and puking and seeking our mother's paps for comfort! You ignorant peasant! *Vous cochon! Vous maquereau!...*We fight to the death!"

And seeing the fierce flash of wild anger rip through him at being called a '*pig*' and a '*pimp*' Alicia at last dived for her sword as she had so often watched Gui's men practising at home: running, tumbling and sweeping her weapon up into her hands as she moved, to roll up perfectly on to the balls of her feet, crouched down and sword held out...just as a roaring, coughing hell hurtled towards them from the forest edge behind her, hotly pursued by Aziz and Najid both wielding huge flambeaux in one hand and their own chosen weapons in the other.

It was a bear!

Not the massive Kodiak bear of the Alaskan Mountains...but a great Pyrenean she-bear from the High Pyrenees, like a Rocky Mountain Grizzly, galloping as fast as a horse, with a terrifying coughing roar across the glade, eyes red and mouth agape, saliva dripping from her massive jaws, while from right behind Fermier came Aquib, his huge scimitar in one hand, a flambeaux in the other, and driving two cubs before him, creeling in terror as the fled, the stink of them almost enough to make her eyes water.

300

And Pandemonium followed!

Howling Panic! Desperate fear! "*Une Ourse!* ***Une Ourse!***...A She-Bear! *A She-Bear!...Courez!* ***Courez!***...Run! ***RUN!*'** And run they did...in all directions like headless chickens, screaming in fear and terror...but for many not nearly fast enough...and Paul Fermier not at all. Appalled by the sudden dreadful change around him, he stood rooted to the ground for just that moment too long...and when he did turn to run it was too late!

Rearing up on her massive hind legs, enormous forepaws held open in front of her, both armed with great fistfuls of huge black claws, mouth agape and fearful teeth glistening, she came roaring and foaming with rage, towering over the petrified outlaw leader, and with a single ***bat!*** of a mighty forepaw she knocked his sword aside as if it were a harmless pin, and seizing his head in her jaws and his body with her massive fore-claws, she cracked his skull open and ripped him into bloody pieces.

Pausing a moment to savage Fermier's shattered carcase, she hurled it away from her...as desperate to reach her cubs as they were to reach their mother...and rushed on to her next howling victim, and the next, and the next, coughing and roaring as only a wild and angry bear can, her great hind quarters bunched behind he as she strode and rolled from side to side amongst her fleeing enemies, galloping one moment, rearing up on her hind legs the next, her mouth running with blood her ravening claws filled with torn flesh and sinews. Some she swiped with her huge front paws disembowelling them as she passed by, others had their faces ripped apart, or their arms torn off, as she savaged with tooth and claw every terrified fighter she came upon.

And where the bear led, Aziz and Najid followed, both properly armed and armoured, Aziz with his scimitar and Najid with his great curved Khanjar, both with great flaring torches of spitting, snapping pine and resin...and as Aquib had promised they wreaked havoc.

Aziz striking left and right with his huge curved blade, slicing heads, arms and bodies in bloody profusion as they came, some even from crown to navel. Thrusting their great flambeaux in the faces of their enemies, burning out their eyes, setting their hair on fire, making them howl and scream with pain...and while Aziz hacked them down across the neck or shoulder, blood spraying

301

everywhere…Najid thrust and sliced with his wicked curved blade into their hearts and bellies, both shouting and roaring: *"Allah Akbar! Allah Akbar!"*…'God is Great! God is Great!' as they ran, their dark Arab faces and their wild, foreign war cries causing almost as much panic as the bears!

And the noise was appalling! Demonic! Beyond description! Screaming, howling men: crying, bleating cubs: roaring, snarling she-bear…*and* the fierce clash of steel, as fighting men and brawling beasts, reeled backwards and forwards through the swirling mists and battered undergrowth, while Agnes wrapped her arms over Soraya and Alicia, shielding them both with her body, pressing them all into the cold, wet grassy track while she prayed for it to stop.

Aquib, driving the cubs before him with his flambeaux, singed their brown rumps as he bounded forward, making them leap and creel in terror their fur smoking, was just as merciless with his blade as either of his friends. Flensing his enemies with the strength of four, he hewed through bone and steel with the ease of hacking melons, and with the same sound, also roaring out *"Allah Akbar! Allah Akbar!"* at the top of his voice, his armour running with brains and blood til they dripped onto the torn ground with every step he took

Then, in the middle of the small clearing, mother met cubs at last, and with a coughing roar she fell onto her huge forepaws, and with her two cubs close beside her, still crying out in fear, she galloped roaring off with them into the forest, crashing away through the thick bushy undergrowth as desperate to escape the fury of that desperate fight, as the remainder of Fermier's outlaw band…and just as swiftly.

And, suddenly it was all over…and as if at a signal the mist cleared away at last, blown free from the high tops and deep valleys by a warm westerly breeze as the sun broke through at last, great shafts of golden light shimmering amongst the trees, returning colour, warmth and light to all around them.

It fell on Alicia, Soraya and Agnes struggling up onto their knees, gasping for breath and shivering from the aftermath of all they had gone through, tears in all their eyes as reaction set in. It fell on Aquib, Aziz and Najid, chests heaving from exertion, blood from their own wounds and those of their enemies running down their arms and off their armour, dented and torn in places, and on their blades encrusted with blood and hair.

302

And it fell on the ghastly chaos of the dead scattered all around the dipping roadway: heads, arms and torn bodies; brains, entrails and scattered offal... upon the brutally injured, some clutching their bowels in their hands, others their shattered limbs and butchered arms and hands, groaning, whimpering and swearing as their lives ran out in scarlet streams across the glade.

And it fell in glimmering shafts upon Paul Fermier's shattered carcase, ripped and torn by tooth and claw, utterly savaged by the she-bear's violent attack, now lying in a great pool of blood, his skull shattered into broken shards where her great teeth had crushed it and only recognisable by the black clothes and armour he had been wearing.

Then silence!...Both sudden and complete...without the sound of bird or wounded, almost as unnerving as the noise of battle, and at first no-one spoke.

Then, with a grimace, Alicia staggered on to her feet and stumbled, like a drunkard, across to where Aquib was standing looking around him, calm as always, his massive chest still heaving, while Aziz strode off to recover their horses, quietly cropping some distance away along the road, and Najid walked quietly among the injured, his great Khanjar safely in its curved sheath, its fine blade of shimmering blue steel now held sweetly in its place.

"Well,...*Afdal Sadeaky*...my best friend...what kept you?"

"The Bears, My lady!"

"The Bears? What were you trying to do? Eat them?"

"No, My lady. Stop them from eating us first! Then help them to eat your enemies."

"But our enemies almost ate *us*, Aquib! Where were you...oh my Guardian of Guardians?"

"Up a tree!"

"*Up a tree?* Were you mad? Bears climb trees, Aquib! That's one of the things bears can do…they climb trees."

"So I discovered, My Lady," he said with his rumbly laugh. "I have not fought bears before…but we learned, very quickly!"

"So I can see," she replied with a sudden grin. "By the fact that you are here and they are not…and nor are most of this bastard's bloody gang, either," she added going across to where Fermier's mangled body lay already covered with flies. "What do we do about this shambles?" She asked, gesturing around her. "And about the wounded?"

"The dead My Lady? Leave them, as they would have left you; as a terrible warning to others of their kind. The crows, the wolves and foxes, and the rats, flies and beetles will devour them. *Allah Akbar!* As for the wounded? There will be no wounded, My Lady."

"No wounded, Aquib?" Alicia said, raising her eyebrows and waving her arms around her to where there were a slew of men groaning and rolling in agony on the ground, with many others propped up against the trees.

"No, My Lady," he said in his deep, calm, gravelly voice. "Najid is gently seeing to their needs."

"But…" she began to exclaim, shocked by the simple brutality of his solution.

"We cannot take them with us," he said, looking into her deep, blue eyes. "We cannot stop to explain to any authority how all this happened. And we cannot leave them here in their agony untended. Nijad's 'needle' will solve their pain and they will feel nothing.

"'Needle'" She queried, eyebrows up again.

"His next most favourite blade, My Lady," he said in his rich, gravelly voice. "Six inches of finest tapered Toledo steel, with a gold wired ivory hilt and golden quillons…he took it from an angry Spaniard in Algiers."

She opened her mouth to speak, but he simply shook his head: "Don't ask!"

"Very well," she said quietly, looking up at him from the corner of her eyes. "No prisoners!"

"Do not grieve for a single one of them, My Lady Alic-ia. They are all worse than Infidels!" He smiled down at her mischievously, seeing she was one. "*Allah* will deal with them as they deserve, and they will all be free to join their bastard leader in Hell where they all belong."

"*Insh'a Allah!*" They both said together, with sudden wicked grins, Aquib adding in his dry way. "At least we have just saved this area the cost of hanging them all!"

"Aquib is right," Soraya said quietly, coming up beside her, her face horribly swollen, one eye almost closed. "I heard what he said Alicia. He is right in *all* things!'"

"But your brother...?"

"You saw what my brother was like! Saw what he did to me...and what he has done to others, and ordered others to do. He wrecked our family. I knew about the money...I told you on the *Morning Star* that Papa had to find extra. When he went to the Baron for it? But I didn't know til much later why he had needed so much. Poor Papa, no wonder he was broken by all that happened. I shall shed no tears for him, my love," she said, spurning Paul's broken body with her foot. "This is the best way for that...that *bastard* to go...food for the wild things of the wild. Let him rot as he let others. And may God show him some Mercy...for I never shall!" And burying her head in her hands in almost unbearable sorrow, she turned into Alicia's open arms and wept, her whole body shaking.

And putting her arm around her, Alicia led her away to where Agnes Fitzwalter was standing, a rather forlorn little figure surrounded by fly covered corpses, and with soft cloths in her hands with which to bind wounds and wash Soraya's face.

305

Chapter 44...How Alicia and The Lady were divided by a Bunch of Grapes.

They left within the hour beneath a clear sky, the threatened storm from yesterday long blown away with the morning's mists, the forest steaming in the warm sunshine as it dried out, and with the mist melting away they were able to pick-up the pace, Najid riding far along the twisting trackway, all the others following close behind at a fast canter, rounceys and pack-horses all bouncing busily along the forest roadway.

And now at last they were able to make up for time lost during that dreadful morning, and by midday were dropping steeply down into the tiny hamlet of Saint-Benoit, placed at the head of an incredibly sharp bend that doubled right handed completely back on itself, and were astonished by the welcome they received as they arrived there, for the whole village came running out to meet them, men, women and children crowding round them with shouts and smiles and blessèd laughter.

"We have heard you have slain the outlaws! That foul hornet's nest of robbers and murderers led by Fermier *Grillade*. Many called him *Le Mort!* He has been a terrible scourge upon us for years. Yet no-one could finish him, until you!"

And while the children petted the horses, and the men gathered around Aquib and Aziz, fascinated by their dark faces, their outlandish armour and fierce weaponry, they were all offered food and much kindness...especially poor Soraya who was offered soft bandages for her wounded face, with a fresh poultice of Comfrey leaves, and liniment and tinctures of Arnica that she could use afterwards.

But they could not stay long and were soon back on the road, always pushing forward, always worrying how close their pursuers were, knowing that by now The Lady and her soldiers, led by Gaston de Vere, must be hot on their trail; but with no knowledge of how close they might be they felt driven to move onward with all possible dispatch.

With the weather holding, but clouding up again from the North East they passed through La Bezole in the late afternoon, once more enjoying the intense scrutiny and hearty welcome of the tiny community who lived there, delighted to help them water their horses, the children fascinated by the dark skins of their Arab guardians, daring each other to touch their skins to see if the colour would rub off on their fingers! Then with a wave of their hands and shouts of goodwill from that tiny community, they were off again, now riding out of the mountains and forests at last to take to the plains that stretched all the way ahead of them to Carcassonne.

And at the small village of Ajac, surrounded by acres and acres of vineyards, green and fruitful in the evening sunshine, they halted for the night at *Le Grappe du Raisins*... The Bunch of Grapes'...a low slung building of yellow painted plaster beneath red pantiles, and an Aubergist, Monsieur Le Bon, wreathed in smiles for so famous a party of unexpected visitors, and for whom he did his best to make his house welcoming and his village proud.

His wife, Annette, as slender as her husband was large, with liquid brown eyes and a warm heart, clucked over Soraya's injuries with lots of hands thrown up, '*Quelle Horreurs!*' and '*Petite Chouxs*' and bore her off to her kitchen immediately to wash out her eyes and replace her comfrey poultice with something special from her own cupboard.

"This is St John's own plant," she said in a hushed voice, taking out a jar of beautiful, rich red liniment. "St John the Baptist. We call it 'St John's Wort'. It is a plant from the golden cornfields, with beautiful yellow petals that grow like a halo. You pick the flowers on the 24th June...St John's birthday, and when you prick the petals they bleed!" She almost whispered. "Great crimson drops of blood like he did, when that wicked Salome had his poor head chopped off. You put the petals in olive oil and leave them, and this wonderful liniment is borne. Take this, *Petite Lapin*, and Massage it into your poorly face and if you have a goodly heart, *ma chéri*, St John will heal you...and make you *feel* better, too! It is truly wonderful, *ma petite*. It will do you so much good!" And she had given Soraya a great hug and a kiss on her other cheek, and packed her off with the jar in her hands to find Agnes.

307

So, with a bright smile, Soraya had tripped off to find her, and Alicia, and ask them to help her with her face, and see if somehow they could wash off the blood that had sprayed all over her clothes that morning.

But within moments of their arrival it seemed as if the whole village was cramming into the Inn to meet them; to thank them and to gift them with a night of laughter and tales. Everyone wanting to hear how Alicia and Soraya had fought the outlaws in the hollow; how she had dared to defy Fermier *Le Mort* before his own men, and how their huge guardians had rescued them with a sleuth of ferocious mountain bears and great swords of power from distant Arabi, on magic carpets that had flown them all round the world!

And, of course, how the wicked Paul Fermier *Grillade! Cauchmar! Le Mort!*...had come to the dreadful death that so many had longed and prayed for, and been ripped in pieces by the teeth and claws of a ferocious She-Bear sent by God to cleanse their mountains of his Evil!

The wine had flowed, and so had the juice of many fruits for their Arab guests, the first Infidels that most had ever seen. And the food had been wonderful, everyone bringing something to the Inn; Najid using the last of his precious rice to present a fantastic lamb ragout, made with some of his precious spices, such as no-one had ever tasted before. And with shouts and cries of eternal goodwill and best wishes, they had all finally staggered to their rest long after the moon had risen over the silent fields and vineyards all around them, where screech owls on silent wings of white feathers sought field voles among the long rows of vines, from which their grapes hung in huge bunches, swelling beautifully in time for the Autumn harvest.

After such a terrifying start to their day they had all been delighted to find such good comfort and warmth at Ajac, especially Agnes Fitzwalter who had at last begun to recover her spirits after her horrific ordeal in the clearing when she had been unable to do much of anything except scream...a fact of which she was bitterly ashamed.

But as Alicia pointed out to her with much love and kindness: "Not everyone can wield a sword in anger, Sweetheart. I didn't know that I could, really. But I was brought up to it, more than ever you were. But you were always there for me, Agnes, when I was small and needed a caring shoulder, especially when Gui went away to the North and I realised how much I missed him!

Like today, Sweetie. You may not have stood out with a shaft of steel in your hand, and your heart in your mouth...but you were there for Soraya, when she most ever needed you, and you truly hazarded your life for her when you covered her nakedness with your body, and then shielded *both* of us when that bear attacked. It is easy in the rush of fighting to be brave, Honeyone...but to do what you did takes real cold courage...and that is far braver. Oh, Dearest Agnes," she wept then, flinging her arms around her and hugging her fiercely. "I am *so* proud to have you as my friend!"

So that was that, and they all slept that night with warmth in their hearts and a smile on their faces for a night's rest well earned.

One more day's good travelling should see them onto the Via Aquitania at last and well beyond the great walled city itself, then just a half a day's journey to Narbonne with a dozen miles further to Grise, and with Good Fortune smiling on them, they should be beneath the Baron's walls in two day's time...and safety!

★

In La Bezole, just six miles from where they were sleeping, The Lady Rochine and her men were also stopped for the night, having forced the pace all day to catch up with their desperate quarry.

Not stopping as Alicia had done at Roquefixade two nights before...they had pushed further on to Lavalenet, arriving there almost as the moon was rising and managed to force a meal and a bed for the night from the Aubergist of *Le Sanglier Noir*, Monsieur Thomâs: Rochine deciding that as a black boar was her father's blazon it just had to be the best place to stay.

But Monsieur Thomâs had not been too pleased with The Lady's typical high handed demands, nor by her threats and raging…but with a good fistful of silver from de Vere and a quiet word with the Cousins who promised to *'fucking drown him in his own fucking pig shit'* if he didn't find a meal and rooms for the night…he soon did…even though it had meant moving himself and his wife out of their room and into Harry Ostler's simple quarters above the stables.

As for Harry Ostler, he and his doxy had to sleep with the horses in the stables along with de Vere's command, and a very busy night they all made of it too! Harry's doxy, Marie-Anne, particularly so…and while Harry came away with a nasty lump on his head and a surprise headache when he finally awoke…she was left with a good pocket full of silver to show for the stalwart exercises his men had put her through, never really appreciating until that evening quite what 'Good Service' really meant!

Then, up be-times in the morning, they had all left at first light, still following the trail Alicia and her Arabs had left, simply by virtue of their being different, but by the time they reached Chalabre for breakfast the mist that had so bedevilled Alicia earlier was even then clearing from the tops and valleys. And before long the whole tale of how the notorious bandit, Paul Fermier *Le Mort*, had been famously slain, along with almost his whole Outlaw gang that very day, by a small party of armed strangers…now rapidly acquiring both heavenly and heroic status!…was on everyone's lips, only making their chase easier.

By then it seemed as if half the countryside was on the move, all wanting to see the sight of the famous battle…especially as the bodies were still supposed to be there for all to see! So their trail then became more like a procession, with the whole world and his wife busily expressing their opinions as to what had really happened in the thick mountain mists…not least because no-one had been able to deal with this man and his gang of murderous thieves and vagabonds before.

Of course the moment Rochine heard Fermier's name she realised exactly whom the dead murderous outlaw leader might truly be, and was as eager as her

Commander to push on into the mountains and see for herself what had really taken place...and how six people, three of them girls, had actually managed to slaughter so many terrifying fighters, let alone their ferocious leader!

And when they finally got there, impressive it surely was...and very puzzling also as the wounds and torn bodies were more like those made by a tempestuous madman, a completely insane murderer armed with an adze and a sharpened garden rake, so hacked about and mauled some of the bodies were. And there were so many of them...their eyes and tongues already pecked and torn out...and bits of them too had been scattered everywhere. And there were no wounded. Those propped up against trees had all been throat cut; those who had crawled away with frightful wounds had been heart stabbed with a fine blade slipped through the collar bones to pierce the heart as neatly as you please.

Rochine shook her head and snorted with disgust. Not at all surprised that the man whom her father had helped all those years ago, and who had helped him with the Fermier lands, should have come to so vicious and violent an end. He had always been a boastful fool. A pity he hadn't managed to kill his precious sister...and that bitch shielding her. Now that would have been providential! And she kicked her horse on, a grim smile stitched across her lovely face as she did so, still astonished at how much killing had taken place with so few men to carry it out?

★

With the weather now more helpful, and all around them drying out most pleasingly, they had pushed on at a fast canter, passing through Saint Benoit in late afternoon, with more ballyhoo about the deaths of Fermier and his outlaw band from all the villagers. They, only to willing to tell all they could about those who had cleared their mountains of such a frightful scourge, were also full of how smashed up one of the girls with them had been, the one called 'Soraya'...which pleased Rochine mightily!

Here too they learned about the bears that had come down from the high mountains, and how the Arab men had so cleverly used them. And The Lady ordered de Vere onwards again, her anger bubbling, her heart seething with jealousy and spite for what Alicia had achieved. Eaten by it, consumed by it, she urged her men onwards, sparing nothing, despite de Vere's advice to slow the pace.

But with every expectation of catching up with their errant runaways by the end of the day, she refused to listen...until her horse suddenly threw a shoe and de Vere's went lame, and they were forced both by the lateness of the hour and the lameness of their mounts to call a halt to their pursuit at La Bezole.

Here there was no inn, but there was good stabling and a forge, the only one for miles, and the villagers were hospitable enough to offer simple accommodation which Rochine loathed on sight...and de Vere rather enjoyed, along with the comely wife of one of the villagers who was delighted to keep his bed warm for a fair consideration, as her man was away up in the high pastures with the sheep, and she was lonely!

In the morning she and the other hamlet dwellers fed them all well; the blacksmith sorted out The Lady's gelding; de Vere's horse had remarkably recovered from its lameness, and leaving a goodly purse of silver for all their hostess's pains, which she had thoroughly enjoyed being a lively, cheerful girl, de Vere led Rochine and his men back onto the track and down towards the plains that led at last to Carcassonne.

Chapter 46...*How the White Rose was saved by the Wicked Baron.*

The night that Alicia was in Ajac...and Rochine was in la Bezole; The Lord Baron Sir Roger de Brocas was just beyond Carcassonne towards Limoux, in the village of Rouffiac-d'Aude, in *L'Auberge du Reynard et L'Oie*...'The Fox and Goose'...where de Vere had advised him to be when he had sent his last message, knowing where Alicia and her party were aiming for...as of course he had suggested it through Louis at Foix.

But Lord Roger who had set out so precipitously from Grise had already been there a day, and was now getting frustrated, anxious not to miss his quarry...and equally anxious that Alicia should run headlong and panting into his arms...and not into his daughter's, when there was no knowing what the outcome might be, given how deeply jealous Rochine was proving to be and how uncertain her temper was when that happened!

The Inn was both old and well appointed and the Aubergist, Monsieur Hugo Perdrix, was as plump and homely as the game bird whose name he carried, as was Céleste, his equally plump and cheerful wife, and like the French partridges for which his country was famous, and he was named, he too liked to wear red leggings: cotton ones in the summer and woollen ones in the winter. And thanks to his lady, his Inn was famous for both its cuisine and for the comfort of its half-a-dozen rooms upstairs where visiting gentry could always be sure of the warmest welcome. Where the sheets were dry and of good Egyptian cotton, the covers of best English wool and there were no fleas or rats!

In fact it was a far better place to stay than in many of the Auberges in Carcassonne itself, except the castle of course, for the city was always noisy, and pretty noisome as well, with its narrow twisted streets and huddled shops and houses, no proper drainage, the ginnels not paved and even where there were cobbles they were often choked with filth...everyone waiting for a really good storm to wash the city clean. The place was bad enough in winter...in the summer it could be vile beyond description...and from all his contact with Sheik El Nazir and his many Arab traders, Lord Roger had come to value cleanliness most highly. Insisting on regular bathing for all his servants and that all the women working in the castle amongst his guests must be shaved clean to avoid both illness and disease.

So he was more than an occasional visitor, and the Aubergist knew him of old, and when he saw how smartly he had dressed that morning after breaking his fast, and the size of his escort who were putting up with others in the village…even the Officer Commanding his Castle Guard was not staying at the Inn, and his full Guard Commander was not with him either…Hugo smiled to himself and thought…A girl! No, maybe not this time…a Lady!

All knew the Baron needed an heir…and that meant a bride. So perhaps a bridal was in the air for the Lord Baron of Narbonne and Gruissan? And he smiled and louted low, offering Lord Roger his best Burgundy, kept only for the most special occasions, and in the Baron's favourite silver gilt goblet with which he never travelled without, and smirked at the way the man twitched his clothes and stamped around his chamber as he drank it…becoming more restless with every passing moment.

Finally the great Lord of Narbonne and Gruissan, the ally of powerful counts and the friend of Kings and Princes, could stand it no longer and tossing his empty goblet to the Aubergist as he passed him, he stalked outside to find his escort already drawn up ready. Each man had polished his steel helmet till it shone in the fresh sunlight of the new day, a cooler breeze still blowing up from the North East, the sky brocaded with clouds; and each horse beautifully curried till its coat shone and its tail floated in the whiffling air, hooves oiled and gleaming, fetlocks trimmed, manes brushed out…and he growled his thanks briefly to Le Brun, massively waiting at the side of his men.

Then with a short pause, Lord Roger swung up onto Charlemagne's back, his saddle shining, his enormous destrier's coal black coat beautifully smooth to the touch, neck arched proudly, mane clipped, the whole great beast looking magnificent, and with a shout and an imperious wave de Brocas ordered his men to move out, Le Brun beside him, one of his troopers carrying the Boar's Head standard rippling behind them.

★

Meanwhile, though Alicia had risen early as usual, the Company of the White Rose with her, they had all decided on a real breakfast for a change with fresh fruit, hard boiled eggs and new baked rolls, local butter and comb honey, all washed down with hot lemon water from Nijad's hand, his very last lemons from the *Morning Star*.

And so with a proper meal inside them for once, they had set out cheerfully on almost the last leg of their long journey slightly later than expected, but as they had done at the start, with Aquib leading, the three girls next, Soraya still the only one not wearing armour between them, and Najid and Aziz at the rear with a pack-horse each on a long rein.

Overhead the sky was a blue silk patchwork of clouds, the wind light but cool, and with a wistful sigh as she thought of Gui still out there, God Willing...*Insh'a Allah!*... she said to herself with a smile as she looked at Aquib...somewhere to the North. Calling up Najid for a swift leg-up, she dropped herself down into her high saddle once more, and with a brief scrunch of hooves Aquib led them out of the small Inn yard, and with a flick of tails and a toss of heads their rounceys bounced onto the track and they were away.

"How far to Limoux, Alicia?" Soraya asked her, stretching her legs in their long stirrups, the leathers creaking as she put her full weight onto them.

"About an hour...maybe less if we kick-on a bit. It's about twenty two miles altogether to Carc'. We should do that easily today. More I hope. I don't want to get caught in a city I don't know, and where I can't see round corners!"

"Do you know the way through Limoux?" Agnes asked her then, a little anxiously. "It would be awful to get lost now!"

"Don't worry! Louis' little map is quite clear, and Aquib knows where we have to go. There are only three main routes in and out of the place. We are on one, coming in from the West...from the mountains. Of the other two, one turns slightly South of East, to the right of the big river and the other one North, to the left of it. That's the one we want. Stop fussing, Honeyone. We will be alright! Now...lets crack on!"

315

And digging in their heels they cantered gently off, picking up speed as they bounced onto the roadway itself, the horses on long reins lifting their heads as they ran, doing their best to avoid the dust thrown up off the dry road which plumed away from them to the north east, born on the wind that was keeping their faces clear.

Ten, fifteen, twenty minutes good riding followed at a comfortable canter, all desperate not to break into a full gallop with such a long way still to go, the road quite empty ahead of them running all the way to Limoux: rolling miles of vineyards, wide open fields of wheat and barley swaying golden in the wind that blew around them; scattered olive groves with flocks of hardy sheep and goats belling happily amongst them.

And it was exhilarating, the air in their faces cool and fresh as if the world was new, the hammering of iron hooves along the beaten ground, the nodding of their horses heads in tune to their rushing speed, the power of every muscle working beneath them as they pounded along the track…each rider knowing that every horse had more to give if it was asked for, for no-one yet was galloping. Nevertheless it was a beautiful morning in High Summer, they were nearly there, and Alicia felt like shouting!

★

Four miles behind them de Vere saw the distant plume of dust and his heart sank.

That it was them he had no doubt…but just as he was beginning to think Rochine had not seen it too, as it was so like faint smoke from a farmer's cot, she called his attention to it herself.

"What is that, Gaston?" she challenged him as she rode beside him at the head of the column all going at a fast canter. "Is that a fire or riders on the track ahead?" she queried again, pointing over his shoulder.

316

"I don't know, My lady." He replied, and before she could say another word he threw up his hand and brought his command to a panting halt, the dust swirling up from their horse's feet as they bounced to a standstill.

"Just smoke from a cottar's fire, I think!" He said, shielding his eyes with his hand as he searched the distant skyline, twice passing it by in his apparent efforts to see more clearly.

"No, Sir!" one of his men called out, standing up in his saddle shielding his eyes from the glare of the morning sun just then rising up ahead of them. "It is riders, away ahead of us. Look, My Lady, you can just see them as they go, lit by the new sun. See! Their helmets are flashing in the sunlight."

"You have keen eyes, Pierre Rouge!" De Vere growled at him, silently cursing the lad's youthful eagerness.

"How many are there, soldier?" Rochine snapped at him.

"Eight...no! Six...and two horses on long reins. They are a long way off...but the sun lights them well in this clear air."

"By Christos, Gaston! It's them! *It's them*," she shouted out exultantly, standing up in her stirrups. "A golden bezant for each head captured to the first man who can lay hands on the Lady de Burley!" And after swift adjustments to their gear, and with a great shout, de Vere's whole command sat back in their saddles, dug in their spurs and leaped off up the road at the gallop; arms, legs and heels working furiously to bring out the best speed in every horse, some even using their reins to lash their beasts to even greater efforts.

And above them rose a great plume of dust and flying debris off the track that could be seen for miles.

★

317

A

ziz saw it first.

"We have company I think, My lady!" he called out tersely. "There is a sudden great plume of dust behind us. Some miles I think. But coming fast. Do we stand or run?"

"*RUN!*" Alicia called back behind her. "Drop these leading reins and run. Our horses are fresher, and we have not pressed them so hard," she added as they all clustered round in the middle of the track "Now my friends…let's see who best stays the course this day! Aquib, lead off! We will keep pace with you…and we will stay together. And if we have to fight then fight we will together, as we did yesterday, on the ground."

"Ready, My lady?" Aquib asked of her.

"Yes! Ready!"

"Then here we go! Steady at first, than a fast canter. But do not spring your horses until I give you leave." And with those words Aquib led off up the track, looking back to see where their pursuers were, making sure they were not yet gaining on them more than he wished them to. Planning for them to tire before he ordered his small group to clap in their spurs and ride *vent á terre*, 'wind to the ground' away from their pursuers, leaving them to eat their dust with every stride their horses took.

★

A

head of them all, Baron Roger rode at an easy amble, leading his troops to where the Northern road passed closest to the river across from which the town really stood connected by bridges, and riding further they came to the point where the three routes around Limoux all met…and there he waited, looking down the long Western road…up which two palls of dust were already rushing up to meet him, and with a lazy smile on his hard face, he waved his command forward. His great house flag of a Black Boar's head, with scarlet tongue and tushes, on an emerald background, fluttering and flashing in the brisk morning breeze, he kicked Charlemagne into a brisk walk, then a fast loping canter, his body stiff and upright against the tall cantle of his saddle, long legs thrust out before him, hands relaxed, superbly and wholly at one with his enormous coal black charger.

And as the Baron rode out towards them, so Aquib gave the order for his small command to be prepared to ride like they had never ridden before, and as Rochine's men came racing up behind them, hallooing and waving their swords in the air like lunatics, convinced they had them in their bag...so Aquib, Alicia and all her small company sprang their horses at last: dropped their reins, stabbed in their heels, and sat back as their rounceys bunched up their great hindquarter muscles, snorted, tossed their heads, dug their hooves into the ground and took off up the trackway towards Limoux like great lurchers after a hare. Like rache hounds after a deer when the scent is strong, the day is cold and clear and the blood is hot!

"Harrow Away! *Away!*" Alicia shouted out as if she was at the chase, a wild grin on her face as she hurled her gelding up the road, stretching her body down along her rouncey's withers as she had with Sunburst when she had fled away from The Saracen's Head through the King's Forest the night of the fire,

"*Tarooo! Tarooo!*" de Vere's men roared back at her, from the backs of their mounts now visibly tiring as they watched their quarry steadily pull away from them, Alicia's final taunt: "*Gone Awayyy! Gone Awayyy!*" almost lost in their groans of disappointment as they finally pulled up, their horses spent after three days of intensive riding, and a wild final chase, always pushed to the limit and now with nothing further to give, their withers streaked white with foam and sweat, blowing hard and their heads drooping.

Beside herself with frustrated rage, caracoling and titupping her horse all over the track, The Lady berated them all as feckless, hopeless, pathetic cowards, medelessly striking out with her leather quirt at men and horses alike, til de Vere snatched it out of her hand and shouted: "***Look,*** *My Lady!* Your father is out along this track too, and he has her now for certain. Your job is done." And with a final look around him, and a secret smile in his heart, he said tersely: "We can all go home now!"

And captured her the Baron had, for even as Alicia and her household broke away from their furious pursuers, and were just beginning to feel secure in their escape...so she came upon him again at last, much as she had seen him at Malwood that very first time, seated on Charlemagne his great prancing charger, dressed magnificently in black and gold. And with a certain look of hauteur and calm pleasure on his sardonic features, the noble Lord Baron Sir Roger de Brocas, Baron of Narbonne and Gruissan, leaped off Charlemagne's back and opened his arms to his intended bride with a smile, and said with a subtle bow, and a twitch of his black brows:

"Welcome to France, My Lady; I see I am come in good time!"

Glossary

Abigail

An 'abigail' is the generic name for a young female servant, but most 'abigails' often became highly valued close personal servants whose care was given for love not just to order.

Actium

Battle of Actium between Mark Anthony and Octavius...later the Emperor Augustus, first Emperor of Rome...following the murder of Julius Caesar. Major sea battle that Mark Anthony lost because Cleopatra panicked and ordered her fleet to retreat, when it should have attacked!

An 'Alien' House

For monks, not always foreign, and usually a Priory, where the 'Mother House' for those who lived there was overseas. 'Alien' Houses paid no taxes to the Crown and Henry V suppressed them all by Act of Parliament in 1414.

Apollo

The Roman and Olympian God of Light and of the Sun, who drove his flaming chariot across the sky. Synonymous with Helios, an earlier Titan God of the Sun and his brother Hyperion, the Titan God of Light; all worshipped in the same way. The Celtic equivalent was Lugh.

Ashlar

Blocks of smoothly worked stone, every face a flat perpendicular.

Aurora

The Roman Goddess of the Dawn and herald of the Sun.

Bailey (The)

This was the courtyard, sometimes huge and often down to pasture, that lay with in the encircling walls and separated the Gatehouse entrance to a castle from the final defensive fortress itself, at this time often built on a great mound of earth called a 'Motte'! By the time of this story the castle Motte was being replaced by a massive stone Keep...London, Dover, Rochester...sometimes called a Donjon and, because of the Crusades, being built round instead of square...like Windsor, Orford and York. The Bailey contained all the buildings necessary for the castle: stables, forge, dovecote, storage barns etc, and was the final refuge for the local people in the event of an attack.

Bailiff	A man appointed by a Lord to work with the Steward and the Reeve to manage an estate. He comes midway between both, and had wide powers to fine and punish the Manor workers. The Bailiff, with the Steward, determined what work was to be done...the Reeve then managed it, and the workers, supported by the Bailiff.
Baldric	The belt that carries a sword.
Ballista	Roman style stone throwing machine, could also fire a heavy iron-headed bolt, a torsion machine worked by ratcheted arms and twisted animal sinews.
Bears	There were bears in the great forests of England right up to the Conquest and beyond, but not by the time Alicia fled into the Forest! However there *are* wild brown bears still in the Pyrenees, similar to the Grizzly bear from the Rocky Mountains. Now sadly very few in numbers, which the French Government want to increase from a stock of similar bears still wild in Eastern Europe.
Benedictines	Black monks...because of what they wore; and the most influential Monastic Order.
Betrothal.	In the Middle Ages a 'Betrothal'...what today we call an 'Engagement' was like a marriage. Blessed by a priest and accompanied by serious promises, you could not then marry anyone else without first formally being cleansed of your vows. It was because

322

Edward IV married Elizabeth Woodville while still betrothed to Eleanor Butler that his children were later declared illegitimate, and his brother, Richard, took over the throne. Serious stuff, and in Victorian times a broken engagement by a man, without consent, could lead to a suit for Breach of Promise! Very serious stuff!

Bilges	The very bottom of a ship, below the lowest deck cover, where loose water from leaks, rain or sea can collect and then be pumped or bailed out.
Blazon	The heraldic beast, or device, worn by a knight with its heraldic background.
Bliaut	Long over gown, often pleated, worn by both men and women. Very popular for generations and made of every material known in those days.
Borel folk	Illiterate country workers
Brigandine	A tough leather coat studded with metal plates, where the plates are *underneath* the jacket, not on top like a byrnie.
Bulwarks	The sides of a ship above the deck, as opposed to 'Bulkheads' which are dividing partitions below deck.
Byrnie	A tough leather coat to which metal plates, scale armour or chain mail has been fixed. Sometimes just thick boiled leather with loose chain mail on top.
Cable	A 'cable' is taken from the length of an anchor cable in the days of sail, usually 100 fathoms. Six feet to a fathom; so, 600ft in imperial measurement, about 200 yards. Officially one tenth of a nautical mile!
Cabochon	Gemstones were not 'cut' as such in those days, they were shaped and polished. The cutting wheel was not invented until the late 1400's, and true faceted stones, as we know them today, not until after 1914.

Cambric	A light-weight material made from Egyptian cotton and used for making fine shirts, or night gowns.
Candia	Candia, the modern city of Heraklion, on Crete. The whole island was then an outpost of Venice and famed for its slave trade. Candia was seized by the Ottoman Turks in 1669 after a sixteen year siege. The longest siege in History!
Cantle	The high back to a medieval saddle
Casque	The round dome-topped helmet that came in around this time, sometimes with a nasal protector, sometimes with a perforated faceplate when it was known as a 'salt cellar'
Chausses	Trousers, usually leather, like the 'chaps' worn by cowboys, but could be any favoured material. Often overstitched with chain mail, and covered by a long hauberk.
Chemise	An under shirt, or blouse, could be of almost any material to suit the wearer, the occasion and the purse! Worn by both sexes. Sometimes took the place of a girl's shift or nightdress.
Chain Mail	The most usual form of body defence at this time. Best chain mail was a mass of individual iron rings riveted and interlocked one around another, weighed around 80lbs and covered the wearer from head to foot. In these times the hood, and the mittens, were an integral part of the whole suit, and it took two men to help put it on and pull it off.
Christian mail	This was much thicker and heavier than Eastern mail, and Syrian arrows could not pierce it!
Cistercians	White monks, and some of the greatest sheep and cattle breeders in the Middle Ages
'Clack' of wine	A large swallow or good mouthful of wine.

Collops	A cut of meat, usually venison but can be beef or lamb.
Crenellations	The proper name for 'Battlements'. The Crenel is the gap between the Melons...the upright 'teeth' that make up the battlements. Any knight wishing to turn his earth and timber castle into a stone one had first to get a 'Licence to Crenellate' from the King. Any castle built without Royal authority was illegal...Adulterine!...and could be destroyed.
Curtain wall	That stretch of battlemented wall that lies–'hangs'–like a curtain, between one tower and another around a castle.
Cyclas	A knight's long over dress, only ever worn over armour, that carried his blazon, usually of white material...but could be coloured.
Demesne	The home farm
Destrier	A trained war horse, or charger...hugely expensive. Cross between a Shire and a heavy hunter. Now an extinct breed.
Devil Wind	Today this is called 'La Tramontane' and blows violently from the North West down the Pyrenees towards the Mediterranean, sometimes with torrential rain. It howls and rages and can drive people mad, hence its name!
Djinns	Muslim Spirits of fire, we call them Geniis, made famous by Aladdin! Can be really evil, and always tricksy, Can assume human form, often hideous and sometimes found in bottles!
Diana	Roman Goddess of the Moon and Hunting: her twin brother, Apollo, tricked her into shooting her lover Orion in the head while escaping from a giant scorpion. Her father, Zeus/Jupiter, could not make him immortal, but put him in the sky alongside her,

so she could be still be with him every night. Ahhhh! Bless!

Drudges	Menial servants, usually women, who worked in the kitchens or about the castle, doing manual labour.
Doucets	The testicles of a deer: quite a delicacy when cooked in a white wine sauce.
Doxy	A low born mistress, or woman of uncertain morals, often found in ale-houses…what today might be called a 'tart' or a 'slag'. One up from being a whore!
Ermine	The white body and black tail of a stoat in its winter colours; very exclusive and very expensive. Used for the edges of valuable clothes, even a lining, and as a decorative background for a knight's blazon: still worn today in full House of Lords regalia.
Fetlocks	The lovely long hairy bits above and around a horse's hooves
Fewmets	The droppings of any hunted game animal, but especially of deer as in this case.
Fistula	A long, narrow pipe like ulcer that forms in a duct between different organs.
Flambeaux	Flaring beacons in an iron basket on an iron stand, very much like a giant torch.
Friars	Wandering monks, usually in brown habits. The Franciscans wore grey.
Furlong	A measurement of land, still used in horse racing today. One eighth of a mile - 220yards. A cricket pitch is one tenth of a furlong!
Gambeson	Like a thick eiderdown, a tough leather coat, split to the waist between the legs for ease of movement, stuffed with wool and stitched all over in pockets to maintain conformity. Usually worn under a knight's

chainmail armour to protect him from the battering effect of weapons in combat.

Garderobe	A loo.
Gralloch	The gutting of a deer after a kill, usually done immediately; and in past times all the lights and offal were given to the hounds.
Great Helm	A close fitted barrel helmet made of hammered iron, or steel if you could afford it, with slits for the eyes and perforated for breathing. Padded with wool and straw and fitted almost to the shoulders. Secured by a strap under the chin andf sometimes connected to the waist by a chain. Many crusaders had a cross shaped piece of iron/steel across the front and over the back of it for additional strength: could be domed or flat.
Greek Fire	Truly a horrendous weapon, and remains a real mystery even today. Modern chemists believe it was a form of napalm, probably petrol-based based, with pine resin, sulphur and maybe saltpetre added: but no-ones' quite sure! Water spread it and it could only be extinguished with sand, vinegar or old urine! Only the Eastern Emperors had the recipe, and it died with the last of them at the fall of Constantinople in 1453. It could also be pumped out like a flame thrower through a great siphon from the bows of a galley...or used in grenades with a wick of some sort. The Moslems tried to replicate it but were unable to perfect it. Their's was known as 'Arab Fire' and seems not to have been nearly so explosive as true Greek fire.
Guerdon	A reward to a Knight for his courage and his chivalry, usually from a Lady as a symbol of her love, before going into battle or at a Tournament, and signalled by the gift of a piece of silk placed around the end of his lance...to be reclaimed afterwards.

Hauberk	A knight's jacket, or whole coat, of chain-mail or overlapping scale armour, sometimes loose and worn over a gambeson; sometimes stitched or riveted to a tough leather jacket/coat and by our times reaching to the ground if the knight could afford it.
Heater shield	Shaped like the bottom of an iron. Easier to use than the kite shaped shield of earlier years: came into fashion about this time.
Herne the Hunter	Mythical God of the Forests and of the great beasts of the forest also, probably of Celtic origin
Jack	Leather 'Jacks' were the tankards of the Middle Ages, and hugely popular everywhere…they remained in use right up to the 20th Century. Only in England were they made waterproof.
Kist	A large wooden chest, for clothes or armour, often strengthened with iron or brass. In the case of the Royal Treasury…literally filled with gold and silver coins!
Marchpane	What we call Marzipan. Name changed in the 19th century.
Meinie/meisnie	A knight's personal armed followers, his own household troops.
Mie	Your lover: could be used for a much cherished child
Mistral (Le)	Violent cold wind that blows down the Rhône valley from the Alps into the Mediterranean basin, and can cause sudden ferocious storms. Usually blows for about three days. Can combine with La Tramontane to cause even more trouble. Napoleon passed a law that excused 'Crimes of Passion' if committed when the Mistral had blown for more than three days!
Liripipe	A long tail of material attached to a hood, that acted like a scarf in foul weather.

Lure	An essential falconry item for recovering a bird: usually the wings of a wood pigeon, because the grey and white feathers flicker when it is swung, or some other game bird. Sometimes fixed to a small piece of wood and then to a long cord that can be whirled round and round to attract the falcon/hawk, with a tasty lump of meat tied on its back to reward the bird when it has been successfully 'lured'.
Lymer	A scent hound, like a bloodhound, but wholly different in shape from today.
Mangonel	A siege weapon, sometimes like a giant crossbow on wheels, sometimes with an upright bar against which a throwing arm could strike instead of a bow.
Mantling	What a bird of prey does to protect its kill, by drawing its shoulders…its wings right over the prey object. Bats do the same thing.
Medium	Usually a woman through whom Spirits can be heard and even seen when in a trance.
Merlons	The upright 'teeth' that make up the battlements of a castle.
Meurtrières	Murder holes in the roof of a castle gateway passage through which boiling oil or any kind of missile could be poured or hurled upon an enemy below.
Nemesis	Traditionally the daughter of Zeus and the distributer of Fortune and Retribution, neither Good nor Bad necessarily, but each in due proportion to what was deserved. Often seen as the implacable distributer of Divine Retribution against Hubris…human arrogance before the gods!
Orphrey	Beautifully intricate embroidery, often with gold and silver thread, very expensive and very popular at this time.

Ouches	Great broaches of intricately worked gold and precious stones most used to pin a cloak to the shoulders.
Outremer	This word literally means...'Outside the Realm'...and could apply to anywhere beyond the borders of one's own country; but by the time of this story had come to signify the Holy Land!
Palantir	A Seer Stone, a great crystal ball used by anyone of sufficient intellect and mental power to view things from afar, sometimes through a Medium.
Palfrey	A light riding horse, little bigger than a pony and usually ridden by a woman. Infinitely more delicate than a destrier, or even a rouncey.
Paynims	A very medieval word for a heathen, a pagan, or any kind of Moslem infidel.
Pommel	The high front of a medieval saddle, or the weighted handle end of a sword, iron or steel, sometimes with a fancy jewel set into it.
Poniard	A dagger with a fine pointed blade.
Quillons	The cross piece at the top of a sword or dagger: could be chased...incised... with gold or silver.
Rache hound	Like a modern fox hound.
Reeve	A vitally important post held by an important villager who was annually elected by the village/Manor to manage the manpower on the estate. He was given the authority to beat those whose work was poor or slack and he brought wrongdoers before the monthly Manor Court if necessary.
Revetted	Lined with shaped stone
Rouncey	A breed of Spanish horse that was most popular at this time as a 'maid-of-all-work'. About fifteen hands, so not a large animal, but sturdy and strong in work.

Sabatons	Steel boots that could be worn over the foot mail.
Sarcenet	A thick silk material used for lining garments.
Sendal	The finest of silk material used as a lady's light over gown or negligée.
Sconces	Wall fittings for holding a torch, or a big candle. The torches themselves were usually made of long bundles of reeds, or strips of unseasoned soft wood, usually pine, tightly bound together and dipped in pine resin; could come in a portable metal holder.
Scorpion	Similar to a small mangonel sometimes with a sling: a torsion weapon.
Sanglier	The wild boar, big and dangerous, especially around mating in the autumn, or if cornered…or sows with shoats at heel who feel threatened and will defend their young with extreme vigour! A large male can weigh over 600lbs and have five inch tushes that are razor sharp and deadly. Usually nocturnal, but can be seen in early morning or evening.
Seneschal/Steward	A hugely important post on any great estate, or in the Kingdom; usually a member of the Knightly class, like Sir James at Malwood, often a family member on a big estate, who 'ran' everything in the absence of his Lord, or alongside his Lord if he was at home.
Sheets	In sailing, 'sheets' are ropes for handling sails or spars.
Sherbet or Sharbat	A deliciously refreshing drink made with fresh fruit and spices, very popular in the Middle East where alcohol remains forbidden: even better with ice.
Shoats	Young wild boar; prettily striped in ochre, chocolate and cream for the first six months or so.
Sounder	A group of wild boar, usually sows, young males and babies. Adult males are much more solitary except at

mating time in the autumn when, like rutting stags, they are at their most dangerous.

Sumpter	A horse used especially for carrying goods in boxes or whicker panniers carried on either side on a special frame called a 'crook'. Like the rouncey, not a big horse, but strong in work. What today would be called a 'Pack Horse'
Talbot	A very large pure white scenting dog for hunting game, now extinct. The heraldic beast of the Earls of Shrewsbury: like a big Dalmatian…but with a heavier jaw and without the spots. Norman, very popular with the Conqueror.
Thews	The mighty muscles in any fighting man's strong arms and thighs!
Trebuchet	The 18" cannon of the medieval world. A huge stone throwing machine that could hurl a 300lb stone, or even a dead horse, over quarter of a mile! An enormous timber construction worked by a vast counterweight, with a throwing arm the size of a tall pine tree with a sling on the end. Monstrous and accurate. The best example of a full size working trebuchet is at Warwick Castle…and they have never tested theirs to the limit!
Trencher	A large, thick piece of stale bread that served as a plate on which your meaty meal could be served. A good 'trencher man' was one who finished off his meal by also eating his 'plate' having already eaten everything else!
Trumpet sleeves	Long deep sleeves, sometimes almost to the ground and often trimmed with ermine. The sleeve hangs down from the upper arm, which itself is usually tightly sleeved by an undergarment called a chemise…what we call a shirt or blouse.

Tushes	A wild boar's fighting tusks...up to five inches long and deadly!
Vassals	In the Middle Ages a Vassal was anyone holding land from, or owing allegiance to, someone else: peasants were vassals of their Lord, Lords were vassals to Barons and Earls...and all were vassals to the King who, in turn...technically...was a vassal of the Church, which sanctified his Kingship, the Church was a vassal of the Pope and the Pope was a Vassal of God! All of which led to terrible rows between Kings and the Church as to which was the greater, and whom should pay homage to whom! A knotty problem as you can see!
Verderers	Technically they were what today would be called 'Gamekeepers', with all the skills with birds, animals and habitat that that implies, but in the Middle Ages they were also Officers of the Law; and given tough powers of Life or Death over poachers!
Vexin (The)	This was a small buffer 'state' between Normandy and the lands ruled directly by the King of France. Remember, France was not a wholly independent country. Very powerful Barons, like Richard - who 'owned' two thirds of France in 1190! – could do, and did, exactly as they wished. So 'The Vexin' was really hot property, and caused huge problems between the Kings of England and the Kings of France!
Wimple	This was usually a very simply made woman's headdress held in place with a fillet of precious metal, or a different piece of material. Not the hugely elaborate headgear that came into fashion in the fifteenth century!
Withers	A horse's shoulders.
Wolves	Typical European timber wolf...and were a real menace in the Middle Ages, specially if the winter was

cruel, forcing them to seek food from the farms and villages....so very much a part of Gui and Alicia's life in the Forest in 1190. The last British wolf was shot in Scotland in 1680, and extinct throughout the British Isles by the late 1700's

Zeus — The Olympian King of the Gods, whom the Romans called Jupiter or Jove.

Very Simple Heraldry.

Blazon — The whole coat-of-arms, including any heraldic beast on its field.

Colours — Azure: Blue; Gules: Red; Vert: Green; Sable: Black; Purpure: Purple

Fields — Background colours, metals or furs on which the principal device of each family is painted.

Furs — Ermine: White with black tails...the stoat in winter colours.

Metals — Gold: Or; Silver: Argent. These also double as Yellow and White.

Heraldic Beasts: — Too many to mention. I have used several, including dragons: here are the four principals:

Lion Rampant...upright on his back feet, forward facing, paws up...De Malwood

Lion Rampant Gardant...upright on his back feet, paws up but looking at you...Richard L'Eveque

Stag's Head Erased...just the antlered head of a stag looking at you...De Burley

Boar's Head Erased: Just the tushed head of a wild boar looking forward and upwards...De Brocas

Heraldic Beasts Armed:	Claws, teeth and tushes all coloured or metalled differently from the main beast: EG: 'armed gules'…all the 'bits' appropriate to the beast described on the blazon but coloured red. Stags are 'attired' not 'armed'.
Langued :	Tongues coloured or metalled different from the main beast.

The Lion and the White Rose Series

The Lion and the White Rose

The White Rose and The Lady

The White Rose Betrayed (12.11)

The Lion and the White Rose Triumphant. (2012)